LORD EDGINGTON

BOOK I

MURDER IN AN
ITALIAN CASTLE

A 1920s MYSTERY

BENEDICT BROWN

COPYRIGHT

For my father, Kevin,
I hope you would have liked these books an awful lot.

This one is also for my daughter Amelie,
who helped me decide how it should end.

LORD EDGINGTON'S GRAND TOUR

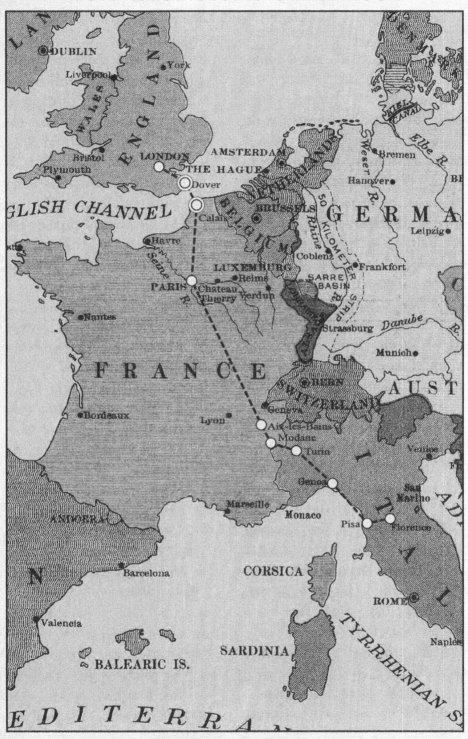

London to Florence

READERS' NOTE

This is the first book in a new series of international mysteries featuring an occasionally cantankerous septuagenarian detective and his ever-improving grandson assistant. You do not need to have read any of the books that were in the first series set in Britain, though I obviously hope you'll love this one so much that you'll race to find the others. This new series will contain no spoilers or require any knowledge of what happened before.

At the end of the novel, you'll find a chapter on why I wrote the book, the amazing things I discovered while researching, a glossary of unusual words and a character list. I hope you absolutely love it.

Happy sleuthing!

CHAPTER ONE

Surrey, England,
1929

In my twenty-first year, I left my home country for the first time.

My grandfather, the Marquess of Edgington, had been promising to take me on a grand tour of Europe for so long that I'd started to doubt we would ever leave. But when the day at last arrived, I realised that I faced it with some trepidation.

I stood in front of the mirror in my bedroom and looked at myself for what felt like the first time in years. I was no longer the young boy I'd been when I'd gone to live on Grandfather's palatial estate. I was very nearly a man, and I finally had some sense of who I might turn out to be.

"Christopher!" someone shouted up to me, and it almost made me jump. I was certain that it was coming from the garden, but my grandfather's voice was such a finely tuned instrument that it was as if he were there in the room with me. "Christopher, have you changed your mind?"

His somewhat sarcastic question was soon echoed by the bark of our golden retriever. I knew that if Delilah were complaining, it really must be time to go. I picked up the longest book I owned to last me the journey, slipped it into a briefcase that was already stuffed full of my most important possessions, and said goodbye to the cold, draughty bedroom that I never imagined I would feel any regret at leaving.

In a sudden rush of comprehension, I realised that I was going to miss every last thing about my ancestral home at Cranley Hall. There was a cracked tile halfway along the upper corridor of the east wing. It made a faint click when I stepped on it, and this very sound made me homesick for a place I was yet to leave.

Even the portraits of my grumpy ancestors, who judged me from their frames as they always had, ignited a flicker of sadness within me. Were the prospect of our voyage not filled with wonder, I might have questioned the whole endeavour.

I took the marble stairs to the ground floor three at a time, then called farewell to the stuffed bear in the entrance hall – which a great uncle had brought back from some far-off jungle, and my brother occasionally used as a hat stand.

I stepped outside into the cool air of the morning, and that was when it hit me. I saw my family and my grandfather's servants waiting to say goodbye, and I knew then that I really was leaving. They were standing in a line beside the most stately of Grandfather's Bentleys, which I thought suited the occasion rather well.

"Oh, Christopher, we'll miss you so much." Mother was already crying.

I was determined not to follow her lead. "I feel just the same."

Albert had made no such plan. "Chrissy! My baby brother." He could barely get his words out. "You're all grown up and heading off into the wide, blue world. What will we do without you?"

He smothered me in a hug, and I could tell he was fighting to maintain even this low level of composure.

"It will be all right, Albert. I'm only crossing the Channel, not heading to the colonies. You can visit if it all gets too much."

He pursed his lips together, but the emotion would not be contained. "Visit you? Yes, that's what I'll do." He had to turn away as he couldn't take the strain any more. "What a fine idea."

"Send us a postcard and that sort of thing." My father was the opposite of poor Albert and would never waste a breath saying such things as *You will be missed,* or *I love you.* He simply nodded, tucked a one-pound note into my pocket, and would have moved to leave if my mother hadn't been there to hold him in place.

I wouldn't let him go anywhere just yet. "It won't be the same without you, Father. I hope you know that."

As we looked at one another, face to face and man to man, I caught a glimmer in his eyes of something approaching sorrow. While he was not the most expressive cove in England, I was glad he was there to say goodbye.

"Of course, Christopher. I hope you have a wonderful time." He put his hand out for me to shake, and I almost told him to steady on. Such an effusive gesture in front of the servants was quite out of character for him.

Mother pulled me over for one last embrace, and I put my cheek to the top of her head as she did so. She was surely the person it would be hardest to leave behind. She was the definition of motherly goodness and, as we pulled apart, she produced a clean handkerchief to push into the breast pocket of my jacket, on the off-chance that I had forgotten to pack one.

"We will see you in Paris before you know it!" she promised, though we hadn't set a date for this reunion. Grandfather had become quite circumspect on the details of our trip. All I knew for certain was that we were heading to a castle in Italy that belonged to an old acquaintance of his. From there, it was hard to imagine what would happen next.

The time had come to say my final farewells to the staff. There was our dear old footman Halfpenny, our maid Alice and her gardener husband, Henrietta the cook, Dorie the reformed thief and little Timothy the page, who actually wasn't so little any more and had now been promoted to hall boy. They all smiled and wished me well, and I felt as if I were bidding adieu to treasured friends, which, of course, was exactly what I was doing.

"Goodbye, all," I said to the whole line of them, and my voice cracked just the tiniest amount. "May you have the most wonderful time without my grandfather here to order you around."

There was some muted laughter, but not from the car behind me, out of which the man in question poked his head. "I heard that, Christopher. Now stop being impertinent or I'll change my mind and take your brother in your place."

I knew this was an idle threat. He would have been tired of Albert's blubbering before they drove off the estate. Nevertheless, I ran around the car sharply and climbed into the back seat beside Delilah.

Grandfather was already smiling to himself, and I noticed that Todd, his right-hand man, wasn't driving. James, the new chauffeur he'd employed to look after his collection of luxurious cars, pulled on his cap, and I realised I hadn't seen our factotum in a couple of days. Still, I was too busy grinning at my family to worry about what secret plans the devious old lord had hatched.

As soon as the car pulled away, Albert came running alongside us, just like when we were children and we saw off our father on his way to work. The car eventually moved too fast for my frankly unathletic brother, and he stood beside the path, waving so fiercely that his arm must have hurt. When he was little more than a blurry dot, I shifted my focus to the towering structure of Cranley Hall. It looked so beautiful in the sunshine, and I found it hard to believe that there could be a more exquisite building in Berlin, Barcelona or Rome – though I couldn't wait to find out for certain.

We reached the country lane that skirted the grounds before disappearing into a tunnel of trees. When I could no longer see the tips of Cranley's towers. I finally felt that our journey had begun.

"I know why you're so pleased with yourself," I told the more cunning of my two travelling companions.

Grandfather was dressed in his usual grey morning suit. His white beard and moustache were particularly well trimmed that day and his shoulder-length silver hair glinted even in the shady automobile.

"I don't know what you could possibly—"

"I can only assume that Todd isn't here to drive us to the railway station because you've sent him ahead to Italy in one of your cars."

"What a preposterous idea," he began, but I wouldn't let him say any more.

"Going by the twitch at the left-hand side of your mouth, it's not preposterous in the least. I might even speculate that several other members of staff will be joining us in there, too."

He had lost his smile by now and was clearly vexed that I had seen through the machinations of the great Lord Edgington – former police superintendent turned world-famous sleuth. He had a strange compulsion for bringing as many servants as possible wherever we went. I'd been wondering for some time how large our travelling party would be, and he'd gone to great lengths to conceal the truth.

Rather than deny my conclusions, he concentrated on a minor point. "My mouth does not twitch on one side."

"Yes, it does." I had a book to read and could already tell I wouldn't get through much of it. "Every time you have a cunning plan, I notice the slightest upturn there, and I know you have a devious scheme in mind."

I stroked Delilah's head as he huffed and fussed.

"Do you know your problem, my dear grandson? I've taught you too well." He laughed then and I couldn't help smiling. "You were right about almost everything you said, which only proves that I have trained you to be an exceptional detective."

I neither confirmed nor denied this but opened *Bleak House* and started on the first chapter as Grandfather read his European railway guidebook.

One thing about which my grandfather *had* told me was our outward journey. We were on our way to Victoria Station where we would catch the newly inaugurated *Golden Arrow*. I'd read of it in *The Bystander,* and so I knew all about the lightning-fast service to Paris. It truly is a wonder that, in just six hours and thirty-five minutes, modern man can travel from the capital of England to the City of Light.

Our own itinerary had us changing at Calais to take the *Rome Express* sleeper service to Italy. The very idea that these trains and ferries were just waiting there for me to discover them, made me feel as if I had an extra pair of legs that I'd never previously used.

We arrived at Victoria Station, and I had another hint that my grandfather was keeping secrets from me when James only took out our hand luggage and two small suitcases from the back of the Bentley.

"I didn't know that you had it in you to travel light, Grandfather," I teased him, and the left-hand side of his mouth curled up once more.

The place was so busy with cabs dropping off passengers that the station guards hurried us along. It was time to say goodbye to our driver – which wasn't too emotional as James had only started working for us the week before – and this undemonstrative parting served as a perfect counterpoint to my brother's teary display.

A porter pushed our bags through the station on a three-wheel cart. There were more than a few turned heads and whispers as the famous Lord Edgington (and his less accomplished assistant) strutted majestically through the ticket hall and on to the platform that was reserved for international departures.

The *Golden Arrow* was every bit as glamorous as the newspaper had made it sound, and I had to wonder whether Grandfather had delayed our trip for so long solely to make use of this luxurious new service. There was only one class on board: first, and we had a compartment to ourselves in a Pullman carriage – complete with waiters serving petits fours, smoked salmon sandwiches and steaming cups of tea. It was like a miniature sitting room, with two grand armchairs on either side of a neat walnut console and a mottled glass lamp on top. If this were the typical standard of international travel, I was certain I could get used to it.

Once the Lord Nelson class engine had built up a substantial head of steam, we positively rocketed to Dover in just over an hour and a half. Fields and buildings whistled past the window at such a speed that it looked as if someone had reached down and stretched them, like a baker preparing dough.

From this luxurious service, we were rapidly transferred to the *TSS Canterbury*. The brand-new steamship glittered in the bright spring sunshine and, as if to welcome me aboard, its immense horn sounded as I walked up the gangplank.

I dared to imagine that Grandfather was just as moved by this experience as I was. He had been quite solemn on the train and had stared at his *Rail Tours of Europe* handbook for at least an hour without turning a single page. He stood beside me on the raised deck at the back of the ship, preparing himself to wave goodbye to the country in which he'd spent all seventy-eight years of his life.

"There's no turning back now," he said, putting one hand on my shoulder and the other on Delilah's head as the Canterbury raised anchor and glided out of port. "The world is ours to explore."

CHAPTER TWO

There was a lump in my throat and another in the pit of my stomach as I stared at the long white wake of the ship. Gulls swooped around us and, to our right, Dover's famous chalk cliffs stood stout and strong as we faded from England's view.

It suddenly occurred to me that we were going about this thing all wrong, so I left Grandfather where he stood to go running to the front of the ship. Delilah was happy to sprint after me and we soon reached the upper prow – if there is such a thing. I held on to the railing as my eyes tried to work out whether the faint black line I could see in the distance was France or just the horizon.

I wasn't the only person who'd had this idea. There was a young lady in a long red mackintosh cloak on the deck below. She looked just as moved by the experience as I was. The only difference was that she was looking forward – to anticipate what lay ahead of us – and I was still saying goodbye to what we'd left behind.

I watched her for a short time and tried to imagine the thoughts going through her head. She had glossy brown hair in ringlets, and I could only see half of her face, but I decided that she was heading back to France or Spain or Italy. The way she gripped the side of the ship suggested that she longed for home, and I wondered whether she were coming to the end of her journey just as we were starting ours.

I must have been staring a little too intently, as when she turned around, her gaze jumped straight up to me. She was enchantingly pretty and so, not knowing what else I could do, I ducked beneath the gunwale.

"My goodness," I muttered despairingly to my dog. "What was I thinking?"

To cover this faux pas, I grabbed the dear creature and lifted her up to suggest that I had not been hiding but merely wished to show my faithful hound the view.

"There you go, Delilah," I said in an unnaturally loud voice. "What do you make of that?"

The young lady had disappeared, but Grandfather had caught up with us and looked really very worried about me.

"I doubt she thinks a great deal of it," he told me. "In case you haven't noticed, Delilah is a dog."

This statement was rich coming from the man who regularly held long, tetchy conversations with the dear creature. For her part, Delilah did not like her master's dismissive comment and grumbled until I put her back down.

I was both relieved and disappointed not to see the girl again. There was something about the half smile on her face that I couldn't forget. The homesick feeling in my stomach had been replaced with a different kind of pain altogether, and I was now worried that I would spend my time in Europe haunted by the memory of a thousand pretty girls whom I would only glimpse in passing.

The grand dining room on board offered an all-around view of the English Channel as we ate our lunch. A musician tinkled on the grand piano in the centre of the room and white-waistcoated waiters zipped about the place serving a wonderful mix of English and continental cuisine. French mussels, Italian ossobuco and Welsh lamb were followed by a delicious spotted dick pudding for dessert. It was the best of all worlds – though I thought the unappetising appetiser of cockles, gravy and brie was the kind of experimental mishmash that our own cook back home would serve.

We shot across the water as I reflected on just how close Europe is to Great Britain. I had always imagined France as some distant land that it would require days of treacherous journeying to reach.

Did the air have a different scent when we arrived at Calais? I really cannot say, but I do know that everything looked a tiny bit removed from the familiar. The buildings around the port were painted in an unfamiliar style – the whitewash was just that little bit whiter. The men unloading our bags were dressed in a manner I had never seen before, too. One fellow even wore a beret, and so I knew we really weren't in England any more.

I don't know whether Grandfather had paid extra for the service, but at every stage of the journey, the assistants took special care of us. We were two of the first people to disembark, and then an eager French porter pointed us onwards. He apparently only spoke three words of English – which is three more than I know in most languages – and sang, "This way, sirs. This way, sirs," until we reached our connecting train. Many of those on board – perhaps including the young lady who, I was now ninety per cent certain, had stolen my heart – would continue on the French leg of the *Flèche d'Or*, but we took the *Rome Express* to Italy.

We were dined and indeed wined on board this second train, and in addition to a small, private lounge, we had a sleeping berth. The service was just as attentive, the furnishings plush and tastefully chosen, and though I nodded off halfway through the afternoon, I found the whole experience quite engaging.

I had planned to read my book, but the scenery outside the window was so fascinating that I couldn't take my eyes off it. Much like in the port, everything was a degree or two different from what I knew back home. It may sound impossible for a wheatfield to look distinct from any other, but I'm sure that, if you'd knocked me out and taken me there, on waking up, I would have known I was not in Blighty.

We got to Paris with the sun low in the sky. I caught a glimpse of the Eiffel Tower, and I had to stand up in amazement. It was like spotting a friendly giant on the horizon. Thanks to several fine books I'd read, that famous city had turned into a place of fairy tale in my mind. To travel through it was like visiting a fantasy world, and I already longed to visit it properly whenever that time would come.

The only disappointment was that much of our journey would take place at night. I tried to stay awake even after the sun had set, but it was no good. I can honestly say that I had a less comfortable bed at home in Cranley Hall than I did on that train – which may have something to do with the spartan room my grandfather had provided. Perhaps my brain was overloaded with the sights, smells and tastes of this new land. I slept through the night and, when I woke up to my grandfather's disapproving look, we were almost at our destination. I'd never been to Scotland or even Wales before, so the idea that we could hop from France to Italy so easily was hard to fathom.

The scenery had changed once more. I saw vineyards and forests; the land was hillier than it had been in the north of France, and the sky was even bluer. It had turned from a pale, rather blinding colour to a rich azure. Once we'd enjoyed a leisurely elevenses (it turned out that I'd slept through breakfast) Grandfather finally told me about the man with whom we'd be staying.

"You will enjoy Renwick's company," he said, apropos of nothing.

"Renwick? Is that your friend?"

"Yes…" He considered this point for a moment before continuing. "Well, he's Lord Monroe to most people, and friend is rather a strong word, but I've certainly known him for decades."

"He's English?" I replied with some surprise. "Ever since you first mentioned him, I've assumed he was Italian."

He ignored my misapprehension and continued with what he was saying. "Renwick is good company, but he is not to be trusted."

This was something of a shock, and I had to confirm that I'd understood him correctly. "I beg your pardon, but why are we going to see a man you don't trust?"

He folded up the newspaper that he'd spent the last hour not reading and looked at me intently. "Well I think it will do you good and, as strange as it might sound, we can't always choose our acquaintances. Sometimes we pick them up by chance. Though we had both attended the same school as children, I got to know Renwick years later. He was the head of a coterie of influential figures and took a shine to me shortly after I became a superintendent in the Metropolitan Police. He threw grand parties where he introduced me to scintillating people from every sphere. I believe I was mainly there to entertain them, but I enjoyed myself, nonetheless."

So many of Grandfather's stories ended with the revelation of an unexpected strain of criminality, and I was immediately curious about Lord Monroe. "Are you saying that he has some dark secret?"

He smiled and leaned back in his chair. "I'm sure he has many, but he's not a killer, if that's what you imagined. I'm merely warning you that he doesn't have the same moral compass as you or I do."

I was tempted to launch another raft of questions across the table at him, but I decided to see what he would reveal without prompting. During my time as Grandfather's apprentice, I've learnt that, sometimes, silence is the key that unlocks doors.

"I never quite understood his perspective on the world." He held one long, fine finger to his cheek as he spoke. "But I do know that he upset a lot of people when he lived in London. He is the kind of person whom, when you first meet him, you think must be the most wonderful human being who ever existed, but it doesn't last long."

"How intriguing," I muttered when he would say no more.

"I'm sorry, Christopher. I'm sure you think I'm being wilfully opaque, but I really don't know how else to explain it."

I had to wonder then whether his detached demeanour had been caused not by what we'd left behind in England, but the person we now planned to visit. My grandfather rarely shows his vulnerabilities, but it was already apparent that Renwick Monroe had made a real impression on him.

"In which case, it will be down to me to make sense of the enigma," I said, by way of reassurance. "I know we're on holiday, but that doesn't mean our trip will be entirely free of mystery."

Before the words were out of my mouth, there was a knock on the door of our compartment, and the neatly attired attendant addressed us in clear, concise French. I could just about understand him… more or less.

"I'm sorry to disturb you, gentlemen," he said, bowing slightly with his hands behind his back. "The American lady in the neighbouring compartment believes that she has lost a small leather box with…" He hesitated then and a look of uncertainty crossed his decidedly grey face. "She says that it contained an expensive diamond necklace. I promised that I would make enquiries on her behalf before we get to the next station."

"Lost, you say?" My companion was ecstatic at the prospect of having a crime to investigate before we'd even reached our destination. Our dog Delilah, meanwhile, went to sleep.

"Mrs Antrobus insists that it was safely beneath her pillow before she went for lunch in the dining carriage. She believes that someone must have stolen it."

Grandfather's brows knitted together, and I could see that he was about to launch into his steely-eyed sleuth persona when he noticed the pleading look on my face.

Can't we please get to our first port of call without having to start a criminal investigation? my expression surely begged and, to my great surprise, he relented.

"What a terrible shame." He cleared his throat, and I could tell just how difficult it was for him not to pull apart the train in search of the missing jewels. "I'm afraid we haven't seen anything. Indeed, we've barely set foot out of this compartment."

The attendant nodded, presumably disappointed not to obtain the assistance of the legendary investigator.

He stressed my grandfather's name pointedly in reply. "Thank you, *Lord Edgington.* I am sorry to have taken up your time."

He bowed once more and backed into the corridor.

"We will certainly inform you if we notice anyone suspicious." I felt a touch guilty not to have been more help.

Grandfather crossed one leg over the other and turned to stare out of the window with an unreadable look on his face that lingered until we arrived in Florence.

Once more, there was a porter on hand to shuttle our bags from the platform, through the ticket hall and out to the street where there was… no one waiting for us.

CHAPTER THREE

"You did tell Lord Monroe what time we'd be arriving?" I asked with perhaps a hint of irritation. For all its numerous comforts, the journey had been a long one, and I was not prepared for the wall of hot air that we hit on stepping from the train.

"Of course I told him, Christopher. I wouldn't expect him to be here if I hadn't."

Delilah let out a disappointed moan, which Grandfather ignored as he made a suggestion.

"Why don't you ask one of the taxi drivers whether he can drive us to il Castello di Montegufoni?"

I tilted my head in bemusement. "Because I don't speak Italian."

This was the first time in years that we'd gone anywhere without servants, assistants or attendants to wait on the spoilt lord.

"Ahh… That is a good reason." He smoothed his black cravat, walked over to the closest taxi at the front of the queue and began to blabber and wave his hands about.

"What did he tell you?" I asked when he returned, looking put out.

"I don't know. I tried my best Latin, but it isn't as close to Italian as I had hoped."

"You mean you don't even…" I sighed and remembered that, despite possessing great expertise in certain key areas, my grandfather isn't always suited to the realities of the modern world. "I suppose I'll have to try."

I walked along the line of black Fiat landaulettes that were all nearly identical.

"Il Castello di Montegufoni?" I asked the second driver, who shook his head and lit a clay pipe to show he wasn't interested. "Il Castello di Montegufoni?" I tried with the next, who pretended not to hear but simply drove out of the rank.

The third shrugged. The fourth laughed, and I was about to turn back when a growler led by a white-booted black stallion, pulled up to the end of the queue. I knew that the castle we wished to reach was some distance from the city, and I didn't like the thought of a bumpy ride out into the countryside, but I saw no other option.

"Il Castello di Montegufoni?" I tried one last time, and the coachman leaned forward in his raised seat to reply.

"Americano?" He had quite the darkest skin of any man I'd ever encountered, which is hardly surprising, as I'd recently travelled a thousand miles closer to the sun.

"Englisho," I replied in my best (and therefore also my worst) Italian.

He made a clucking sound in his cheek as though he understood the problem. "No one take you to Montegufoni."

"Oh, I see," I said as, being a polite Englishman abroad, it was not my place to challenge such a decision but to accept it without complaint.

He rattled off the reasons on his fingers one by one. "Too far. Too steep. No return fare. You take bus."

"Bus," I repeated, in a tone that suggested I'd never heard of such a thing.

As a result, he quite rightly waved his arm in the direction of the bus station at the far end of the concourse. "*Autobus*? *Pullman*? You take to Montegufoni."

I hoped I might learn something more, but he stared back blankly until I thanked him and returned to my grandfather.

Our dog had given up hope by this point and was lying on her side looking hot.

"Any good news?" This was my grandfather talking, not the despondent canine.

"Oh, yes," I replied, then paused for a moment to decide how to reveal what I'd discovered. "The good news is that we only have two cases to carry. The bad news is that you will have to take a bus for the first time in several decades or longer."

I pointed to the vehicles behind him and then watched as his face dropped. First class they were not, and I doubted that they fitted my grandfather's definition of "Pullman" travel. There would be no attendants or even basic refreshments on board, and to call them buses was itself quite generous. They were closer to charabancs, and my first impression was of a long black car that had been stretched to squeeze in ten rows of seats before a leather tarpaulin was suspended over the top.

The first was already packed with people clinging onto their possessions, but we needn't have worried, as that one wasn't going to Montegufoni anyway. A card in the front said Bologna, which I happened to know – thanks to the weeks and months I'd spent studying maps since our trip was announced – was in the opposite direction.

Less happily, the bus to Castelfiorentino via Montegufoni was even busier. Once more making the most of the Latin at which he'd evidently excelled as a schoolboy (but also holding up two fingers and waving a clutch of a hundred lire notes) he secured passage on board the vehicle. I couldn't tell whether everything in Italy was insanely expensive, money worked differently abroad, or the driver had seen the chance to make a profit from a pair of ignorant Englishmen, but Grandfather handed over a surprisingly large number of notes.

We placed our cases in a precarious-looking luggage net that was tied to the rear of the vehicle and then took our seats on the bench behind the driver.

"This will be fine," lied the man who once taught me that eating caviar any more than three times a week was uncouth.

There were already four small boys crammed into the space of one adult beside us. On the other side of them sat an elderly lady who, judging by her tone, was lamenting her lot in life. To make things slightly less terrible for her, I picked up one of the children and put the little fellow on my lap. He peered up sweetly at me, which was his brothers' cue to clamber onto my haughty companion. Grandfather was less than thrilled to be so encumbered, but it did mean that there was space for Delilah to have a seat. She looked most content as she watched the infants wriggle in her master's lap.

And then we sat there for half an hour without moving.

Grandfather attempted to reason with the driver that the bus was full to bursting, and it didn't make sense to wait any longer, but the public servant just pulled his cap down and whistled an operatic melody that I felt I should probably have recognised.

When the clock above the station struck one, it was finally time to go. I had hoped that I would get used to the heat, but the journey was so bumpy, the air beneath that tarpaulin so close, and the children so clammy, that I felt I would expire before I ever got to see Lord Monroe's castle.

What I can say is that it was a very beautiful place to pass out from hyperthermia. We moved away from Maria Antonia station and cut through the centre of the historic city. We passed the polychromatic façade of the church of Santa Maria Novella, and I caught a sliver of a glimpse of the famous Duomo of Florence's cathedral before we crossed over the Alla Carraia bridge. I should probably mention that I didn't know any of these names myself. The little chap who was sitting on me proudly burbled the names of any significant monuments we passed.

My attention was also drawn to the bridges further along the Arno river. The Ponte Santa Trinita and the Ponte Vecchio were perfectly silhouetted in the water, but then we were swallowed up by the neighbourhood on the other bank before leaving the city on the old Roman road.

It didn't take long to reach the countryside. Unlike London, which sprawls across the landscape for miles in every direction, we soon spotted the gently undulating Tuscan hills. We saw forests and poppy-filled meadows before agriculture claimed the land. Endless chains of vines, supported by wooden trellises, ran in rows beside the road, like soldiers awaiting the order to charge. In the distance, lines of lofty cypress trees stood monitoring the nascent battle.

The breeze that rushed into the open bus almost made me feel alive again, and if it hadn't been quite so sweltering, I might even have enjoyed the journey. From what I could tell, there were no formal bus stops. The passengers would occasionally shout or throw something at the driver, and then the shuddering vehicle would come to a jarring halt.

"Montegufoni?" I asked my little friend each time, and he shook his head. There was something very wise about the boy – a certain calm about him that put me in mind of yogis and Buddhist monks of which I'd read in travelogues. I almost wondered whether I should tip him for the wonderful service he was providing, but I felt he might consider it an insult.

To my surprise, the old lady I had taken to be the boys' grandmother got off in a village half an hour from the city. She was still mumbling to herself melancholically, and I realised that, even if I were to devote a decade of my life to studying the language, I would never understand what she was saying.

When we finally reached Montegufoni, it turned out to be a small village high on a hillside. The boy gleefully shouted, "Montegufoni! Montegufoni!" but there were only a few houses and no castle in sight.

Grandfather tapped the driver on the shoulder, and the brakes began to screech. The three smaller boys were quite in love with him by now and each gave him a hug goodbye. I shook my companion's hand, perhaps a little formally, but he was such a sensible type that I thought it fitting. We unloaded our bags, the bus pulled away, and our temporary wards waved farewell.

"Valete!" Despite his initial reservations, Grandfather was clearly sad to say goodbye (in Latin).

"Arrivederci!" they called back, and we watched until the bus had disappeared from view.

"I can't see a castle," I helpfully pointed out.

We stood at a crossroads – literally.

"It can't be far." Grandfather had already chosen the fork that we would take off the main road. "As Hannibal said, *Aut viam inveniam aut faciam.*"

"Well, that's very helpful." I had just about held on to the living foreign language I'd learnt at school. The dead one I'd been forced to study for twelve years had escaped my brain the very same day I was released from that dusty institution.

"It means I shall either find a way or make one. Come along, Delilah!" He increased his pace, and our long-haired friend did the same as I lugged my suitcase behind them. If I'd known that Grandfather was sending his possessions by other means, I would have taken less with me.

With the help of a few locals who pointed us onwards, we did indeed find our way. The castle was at the end of a rough track with olive groves on one side and a vineyard on the other. The sun felt like a clutch of warm hands on my back the whole way there, and I began to question how anyone could live in such a climate come the summer. My friends at school had donned short trousers whenever the clouds parted from March onwards, but I was more of a hide in the shade under a parasol sort of boy.

After what felt like a lifetime, we turned off the path, and I saw the castle's tower over the trees. Two minutes later, having descended a steep hill, we reached a set of stairs leading up through an overgrown path to the grand façade of what looked more like a palace than any castle I knew.

"Here we are!" Grandfather sounded jolly as he mounted the wide staircase. Free from any luggage of her own, Delilah raced ahead of us, and I puffed along behind as best I could.

I hadn't seen so much as a sketch of Montegufoni before, and I was as intrigued by what we would find there as I was by its enigmatic owner. The gigantic wooden doors to the arched entrance stood open, so we walked through them into a large courtyard. I'd had a picture in my mind of what the place would look like, and it bore no resemblance to reality.

While I could have focused on the elegant architecture of the castle – the tower stretching up into the sky in front of us, the matching triple-archway on the opposite side of the courtyard and the yellowish hue to the walls that were so quintessentially *not English* that I immediately admired the building for its novelty – I was distracted by the chickens that were running around everywhere, the piles of automobile parts scattered across the ground and the sound of a loud gramophone blaring in a nearby room.

"Lovely weather we're having," a man came to say, and it was nice to hear English spoken again after so long.

"Isn't it just!" Grandfather's smile confirmed that he felt the same way.

"There's nothing like sunshine to brighten the mood." The fellow spoke with a heavy Italian accent, but he delivered his refrain with such bonhomie that I felt that we had known one another our whole lives.

"I couldn't agree more," I chipped in. "Do you happen to know where we might find Lord Monroe?"

"*Come?*" Switching to Italian, he suddenly looked confused. "*Quello che dici non ha senso.*"

"I said…" I was about to explain when he bustled past us towards the portal through which we'd just entered.

"How curious." Grandfather put his case down and peered around the courtyard.

There was an old lady with a toolbox standing beside one of the stacks of metal and rubber. She wore a black, fringed shawl and a grubby white dress. She couldn't have been much younger than my grandfather, but she had grease on her cheeks and was working away with a spanner, loosening the nut on what I took to be the axle of a motorcycle.

"Excuse me, madam," he began, having abandoned his Latin for now. "Would you happen to know where—"

Before he could finish his sentence, we heard raised voices and turned to look at the tower.

"You swine, who do you think you are?" a recognisably English (and infuriated) voice echoed down to us. "Don't you speak to me like that. I'll have your… No… Wait! Don't you—"

In the next moment, the man who had presumably been shouting fell through a gap at the top of the turreted tower. I saw a shadow moving, and I thought I could make out a dark shape behind him, but it was only a moment, and I was distracted by the doomed figure.

The whole thing happened far more slowly than one might expect. Even his tumble backwards over the low wall was more clumsy than dramatic, but then he was in free fall, his arms reaching towards the top of the tower, as though he thought he could still grip hold of it.

Even the great detective beside me could do nothing to save the poor fellow as his body came crashing down onto the paving stones. There was a terrible, definitive thump and a noticeable crack as his bones bore the force of the impact. We were already running over, but there was little hope he could survive such a fall.

"Is that him?" My words emerged weakly from my throat, and I stood over the bloodied body as Grandfather searched for a pulse.

He looked back up at me and nodded. I thought he might confirm his findings, but there was no need. Renwick Monroe was well and truly dead.

CHAPTER FOUR

I heard the sound of footsteps descending the stairs within the tower, and it instantly spurred me into life. The only problem was that I didn't know how to access the staircase down which the – I doubt I'm getting ahead of myself here – murderer was escaping.

With Delilah at my heel, I navigated a small passageway that brought me to another courtyard, but there was no sign of an entrance to the tower. In fact, I'd already gone the wrong way, so I returned to where Lord Monroe had fallen. Grandfather looked at me as if I was a ha'penny short of a shilling, but there was no time to explain as I ran to the next doorway that led off the courtyard.

This was not a great deal more promising. I found myself in a large room with a glossy wooden floor, a few easy chairs and a phenomenally high ceiling. Turning to my immediate right, I spotted a door and ran through to find a strangely domestic scene. Delilah stayed behind to investigate a bed and yet more pieces of machinery. More importantly, there was another door to try, and so I pressed on.

Sure enough, I came out beside the stairs that led to the top of the tower, but I saw no sign of the culprit. I ascended them in case I was mistaken, but the only things up there were a ladder for accessing the bell above me and a flat metal spike that was lying in the spot from which Grandfather's "acquaintance" had fallen.

Back down I went, this time continuing further through the warren-like building. There were so many small courtyards, joined together by dark, narrow passageways, that it gave the impression of being not so much a castle as a series of buildings that had been joined together over time. I eventually emerged on a long, shady terrace beneath yet more cypress trees at the far side of the building. I was beginning to have an idea of the plan of the castle and realised that I could work my way back to the courtyard if I kept going. This did not change the fact that Grandfather would be disappointed in the half-hearted chase I'd given.

"He got away then?" he asked in a comparatively forgiving tone. "Did you manage to get a look at him?"

"Not even a peep. Whoever it was knew his way around. I didn't stand a chance." I walked over to stand next to him and took in the sight of the dead lord more carefully this time, as Delilah returned from her own exploration.

Monroe was a heavy-set man with bright red cheeks and a single line of thick, dark hair where two eyebrows should have been. It was almost like a visor running across his lower forehead. Considering that the temperature was around eighty degrees that afternoon, the clothes he wore were oddly warm and formal – much like my grandfather's, I suppose. Monroe wore a black waistcoat with shiny golden buttons and a matching black shirt and trousers. They gave him the look of a train conductor, though I very much doubted that most railway workers get their uniforms from a fine Italian tailor.

A little frighteningly, his eyes were wide open, and his large blue irises peered up at me. I don't know why this would be any worse than their being closed – the man was dead after all – but I felt that it underlined the fact he knew what was coming when he was pushed backwards to his death. It was hard to imagine the suffering he went through in his last few seconds as he dropped to the ground, and I eventually had to turn away.

"I'm sorry, Christopher," my grandfather said in a quiet, careful voice, though perhaps I should have been the one to offer my condolences. He didn't explain himself but turned to look around the courtyard to the spot where the old lady had previously stood.

There was no sign of her. Even the chickens had tidied themselves away in one corner, and the gramophone record had reached its conclusion. The stillness of the scene was a little eerie.

"Why are you sorry?" I finally asked, but he had become distracted.

"This doesn't surprise me," he announced, pulling on the cuffs of his jacket as though to ensure that he was presentable. "If I were a superstitious man, I would say that fate has brought us here to witness this very thing."

"You're not, and so you won't," I said to hurry him along. "But why are you unsurprised that we've travelled halfway across the continent to witness Lord Monroe's death?"

For a very short moment, I thought he might say, *Because people are murdered wherever we go.* But that was not his thinking. He walked to the centre of the courtyard, still examining the scattered debris of hollowed out cars and unrecognisable motorbikes before peering up at the many windows on the first floor of the building. Was he looking for someone who was looking at us? Was he already searching for the killer?

"It's not a surprise, because I was always amazed that Renwick lived as long as he did. He had a great talent for making enemies and liked nothing better than to upset, scandalise and stir up trouble."

None of this was delivered in his usual stentorian manner. He was uncertain and restrained, so I walked closer to make sure I caught every word.

"Before he left Britain – this was twenty years ago now – his main pleasure was causing havoc. That's why I warned you about him."

Something about this made my hackles bristle. "If that's the case, then why come here in the first place?"

He was looking at an unglazed window halfway up the tower. I don't know whether he had noticed someone up there, but his eyes became fixed on that one spot, and I knew he wouldn't answer me.

Something felt different about this case. In the time I'd been sticking my oar into murder investigations, we were yet to discover a body without at least having some concept of who might be to blame. There in Montegufoni, the notable absence of suspects was like a school bell ringing in my head, and before I could silence it, Grandfather spoke again.

"What are the chances of our arriving at just the right moment to—"

Before he could finish the sentence, someone emerged from a door in the wing opposite where we stood. A young woman with remarkably curly hair stepped from the building to approach us.

"Are you Lord Edgington?" she asked with a smile. Her accent was ever so English, with the precise, clipped tones common to students of Roedean or Cheltenham's Ladies' College.

When Grandfather didn't reply, she continued. "My name is Eva Mountstephen. I'm Lord Monroe's secretary, but I don't quite understand what you're doing here."

There was a difficulty we had to overcome. It was one thing to break the bad news of a death to someone. It was quite another when the pleasantly oblivious person had such a smile on her face and the body was on the ground nearby.

"Renwick told me that you would be arriving tomorrow." She

looked back and forth between us, and I think she realised something was wrong, as her expression became quite perplexed. "Your rooms are waiting for you if you'd like to—"

"I'm sorry, Miss Mountstephen." It fell to me to interrupt her. "Before we can see to that, we have something to tell you."

This was not the first time I had been called upon to announce a death, but I had never been able to do so just by pointing before. I raised my arm and waited for the strangled noise to leave the young lady's throat.

She stumbled a little, clearly affected by what she was seeing, and Grandfather lunged forward to support her.

"It was just after we arrived," he explained so that I didn't have to, and Delilah pressed her warm flank against him. "There was a commotion and then he fell from the tower."

"The tower?" Her reply came out as a shriek. Her voice still hadn't recovered from the shock. "What on earth was he doing up there?"

"We were hoping that you might know that," I answered, but she was moving towards the body and wouldn't reply.

"He was not alone up there." Grandfather was no doubt already considering what part Miss Mountstephen could have played in the murder. Perhaps she had run around the castle so as to reappear from another direction. It may sound premature to suspect her, but it wasn't as if we were spoilt for potential killers even after her arrival.

She crouched beside the body of her employer, and the tears on her cheeks caught the sun that shone down at just the right angle to bathe Lord Monroe in light.

"What are you suggesting? That someone pushed him?" Her sorrow was now mixed with a streak of anger. "Are you saying he was murdered?"

I looked at my grandfather, unsure how much to disclose, but he put one hand on hers and spoke in a gentle tone. "I can't possibly say that at this early stage. All we know is that we heard Renwick shouting, and then he fell backwards from the second highest level of the tower."

She said nothing for a few moments, but her cries had attracted the attention of an inquisitive cockerel who strutted over, pecking at the ground whenever it took his fancy. Delilah looked at the creature, perhaps considering whether he needed putting in his place, but then she lay down beside Miss Mountstephen to provide something soft to stroke to ease her pain.

"You know, the saddest part of all this…" she finally muttered, still looking down at the lifeless figure as the blood swelled in a pool beneath his head. "The saddest thing is that it feels so inevitable."

CHAPTER FIVE

It was shortly after this that the bell sounded at the top of the tower. Though it was presumably ringing the hour, the clock itself seemed to be a few minutes fast. From every wing of the building, I heard doors opening and footsteps on stairs. Just moments later, seven or eight men appeared from different doors to come together in the centre of the courtyard.

They all wore thick working men's trousers, heavy boots and surprisingly clean white shirts. A few of them had hoes or spades over their shoulders, and I decided that they were the men who worked the neighbouring fields and vineyards. What they were doing inside the castle was harder to fathom.

Running along twenty seconds behind them, two boys of around twelve appeared from different doors. They spotted us there, without noticing the body, and the two of them launched into a routine.

"Lovely weather we're having."

"Oh, indeed!"

"There's nothing like sunshine to brighten the mood."

"I was about to say the very same thing."

With their parts said, they hurried after the group of men. This little display only made me more curious about what sort of place Montegufoni was and how the lord of the castle had run his little kingdom.

Grandfather frowned and I can only assume he was contemplating the same thing.

"I will have to call the police," Miss Mountstephen said long after we should have come to this conclusion. In our defence, we were in a foreign country, and I didn't even know where the telephone was.

"Of course, and we will do whatever we can to help with…" Grandfather resisted describing it as an investigation and instead opted for "…whatever comes next."

She rose and, with her eyes still on the elegantly dressed old man on the ground, she shook her head mournfully before escorting us away. I felt a touch guilty about leaving Lord Monroe like that, even if no one else seemed particularly interested in him. I considered staying behind to guard his body, but Delilah had become quite fascinated by the cockerel and was following him around at a distance. I was fairly confident she would bark if anyone interfered with the scene of the crime. Her master had trained her well, and so I followed the others through the door from which our guide had appeared minutes earlier.

I don't know whether she had been watching us this whole time, but the mechanic who had been there when we arrived now reappeared, crossed herself whilst looking at the body, and returned to her work.

The walls of the castle must have been thick, as it was far cooler inside than out, and many of the tatty wooden shutters were closed. Miss Mountstephen led us through a long, rectangular room which, though relatively simple in decoration when compared to the sparkling gold of that space back home in Cranley Hall, I decided was a ballroom. The floor was finished with the same diamond-shaped wooden tiles as I'd seen in the salon across the courtyard, and there were ornate marble flourishes between the tall windows on either side of the room. They were disembodied corbels shaped like the top of an Ionic column, and each held a bust of a no doubt worthy personage from Italian history. It was hard to know whether they were the likenesses of politicians or the great masters or simply representations of the sculptor's various relatives.

We continued through this space to an office at the end of the castle close to the gatehouse through which we had entered. It was only a small room, but it was far more elaborate than the one we'd just seen. Every surface was covered with scrolling plasterwork. An alcove topped with an ornate moulded conch shell housed shelves displaying a selection of Venetian glasswork, but most importantly for us, there was a candlestick telephone on a neatly organised, marble-topped desk in the centre of the room.

Miss Mountstephen grasped the handset but hesitated for a moment before connecting to the operator. As she began to speak, I noticed that there was another room leading off this one. I had to think that, if she was Lord Monroe's secretary, his office was through that door.

"*Polizia*," she said very clearly, before uttering a complicated sentence of which I didn't catch one syllable. She was silent for a few moments, then launched into a long, passionate monologue in perfect

Italian. Or rather, I assume it was perfect. I would have been none the wiser if her grammar was atrocious and she used all the wrong words, but even I understood the phrase "*uomo morto*".

When she had told them all she had to tell, she hung the receiver once more on its hook and collapsed back into her chair. She stared at the space between my grandfather and me, looking truly spent.

"The police will send someone as soon as they can, but there are no inspectors stationed in the village, so it may be some time."

Grandfather took her continuing passivity as a sign that she wouldn't mind whether we took a seat at the table in front of her, and he motioned for me to do just that.

"I can't believe he's gone." She still didn't look at us but studied the ceiling rose, which was surrounded with plaster cupids at play.

"May I ask, if it isn't too soon for questions, what your relationship to Lord Monroe was?"

This brought her back to the present sharpish. "I beg your pardon, Lord Edgington? If you're wishing to suggest that Renwick and I were in any way—"

Presumably out of discretion, he decided to cut this sentence short. "I do not wish to insinuate anything. But I did know your employer rather well, so you'll forgive me for wondering what duties you performed for him."

I can't honestly say that this made it sound any less salacious, and so I softened my grandfather's approach. "You mentioned that you were Lord Monroe's secretary, isn't that right?"

I hadn't taken the time to view her as anything more than a stock character in the story of a man's death, but I took a good look at her as she considered her answer. I needn't have heard her voice to know that she wasn't Italian. She lacked the famously dark features of that nation's people. In fact, her curls were decidedly fair to match her pale, freckled skin. It was a wonder to me that she had spent long enough in the country to learn the language without becoming bronzed to any degree.

Her mouth was small, her nose straight. When she took her wire-frame glasses off and placed them on the desk in front of her, I noticed that, while some might have unfairly described her as a plain Jane, she had the most captivating blue eyes. The complex pattern within them reminded me of the white breaking waves we had seen while crossing the English Channel.

I believe that my intervention had helped somewhat as, when she finally tried to answer my grandfather's question, she spoke more confidently. "I came to work here over a decade ago. Renwick knew my family when he lived in London."

"Oh! So you're Celia and Anthony Mountstephen's daughter!" Grandfather's whole attitude changed as he made this connection. "They are dear, sweet people. I saw a lot of them at Renwick's parties."

"That's right. Renwick needed help with his work here. He knew that I had completed my studies, and so he sent a telegram to my mother to ask whether I would like to live in an Italian castle."

"That sounds like the kind of sly simplification in which he usually traded."

Her resultant smile did not stay on her lips for long. "You obviously knew him well." Her breathing became more noticeable whenever she paused between words. "And you're right; this was not the luxurious existence that I might have imagined for myself. When I arrived here, there was barely any render on the bricks on the eastern façade. The villagers occupied most of the castle, and a family of wild boar would wander inside from their home in the Cardinal's Garden whenever a door was left open. They did not appreciate having us as neighbours. For all these reasons and more, I like to think that I have had a positive impact on the place."

This raised certain possibilities I had not previously imagined, but Grandfather decided to continue on his existing path.

"Those aren't normally the responsibilities of a secretary. Was this what you had in mind when you trained to be…" He left the sentence open for her to finish it.

"I went to Bedford College for Women. I have a bachelor's degree in arts." She spoke very confidently, and I thought I knew why. I'd met a number of forward-thinking women who were proud to promote the new opportunities available in academia. I had the sense that Eva Mountstephen was of that ilk.

"How interesting." Grandfather could be the kindest man on earth when it came to consoling a bereaved witness, but he was just as likely to terrify a suspect if he thought it would speed up the accumulation of vital evidence. "And how do you like it here?"

She returned his gaze, and I could tell that she would not be intimidated.

"It is my home. The truth is that my fiancé was killed in the war. I decided to leave Britain soon after and have never looked back."

"I'm sure it was a very interesting experience to live here with Renwick." There was an undertone of suspicion to everything Grandfather said. "Did you know him well before you moved out here?"

"As a matter of fact, I did. Renwick used to visit my family when I was a child. He knew my mother in London before I was born, and he and Father became firm friends."

I was struggling to determine her feelings towards the dead man in the courtyard. Despite her initial show of emotion, her answers were now precise and controlled.

Grandfather leaned forwards to pronounce a key question in crisp tones. "Was he still just as much of a monster as he ever was?"

When she'd first introduced herself to us, I'd taken her to be a cautious, mousy individual – a female version of my younger self, perhaps. Over the course of this interview I'd come to see how strong she was, but this question knocked her back some way.

"A monster? I would never call Lord Monroe a monster."

"Five minutes ago, you told us that his death was inevitable." I hadn't meant to say anything, but she did seem to have contradicted herself.

She stared at her fingers that were splayed out on the oaken desk. "That's true." I thought she would need more prompting, but she eventually found her thread. "I'm not denying that he was capable of rubbing people the wrong way. But to call him a monster is to ignore all the fine qualities he had. He could be terribly charming. He also possessed great knowledge of art and literature, and he was an undeniably successful businessman."

Grandfather shook his head, and it was as if something had come into focus for him. I wondered whether it was due to Miss Mountstephen's admiration – and perhaps even adoration – of the dead lord, but he abandoned his needling to concentrate on the facts of the case that we should have established from the outset.

"What of Renwick's children? I heard that they all followed him out here. Are they living nearby?"

"Coralie was due to see her father here this afternoon, and the boys have remained within driving distance, though they no longer come to visit. I will have to ring them to break the news."

Grandfather turned to glance out of the shuttered window. I can't say whether he'd heard something that caught his attention, but there was little to retain his interest, so he returned to the task at hand. "What of the people we've seen since we arrived. Do they live here in the castle?"

"If you mean the locals, then yes. When Renwick bought the property, nearly every room was occupied, and hundreds of people resided here. It was once owned by a rich Florentine family, but over the last century, more and more workers from the local area moved into the various wings."

"Did he realise that his grand estate came with tenants?" I asked, as the very idea was hard to fathom.

Miss Mountstephen smiled sadly. "Not exactly. A local landowner showed him the place in the hope that he would buy and refurbish the castle. Renwick fell in love with it, and there was no turning back. He tried to evict everyone, but it was practically impossible. I think that, over the years, he became used to sharing his home with so many people. This building is like a village in itself. I imagine it would feel very lonely if they left."

Grandfather leaned forward to ask another important question. "And how did the people living here feel about an eccentric foreigner coming to their ancestral home to give them their marching orders?"

"They were not happy, and they made their feelings known. But that was before Renwick spent half his fortune renovating the castle."

"And yet you said there are fewer people living here now. How did that come to pass?"

"That was part of my job. I made sure to find opportunities for anyone who was willing to leave. Bright boys and girls were sent to university. Their families were resettled in new houses in the neighbouring area. Some of the older members of the community sadly died and, each time space was relinquished in the house, Renwick restored the rooms to their former glory."

"So no one minded?" Grandfather crossed his arms over his chest and looked unconvinced.

"I wouldn't say that, but we went about it in the most considerate way possible." Miss Mountstephen tucked a lock of hair behind her ear. "Even if Renwick was never popular around here, we maintained a fragile entente. We all rubbed along together well enough."

"So then who, precisely, did you think would be willing to—" Grandfather didn't finish this question as, just then, a scream cut the air.

CHAPTER SIX

In my life at least, screams often signify an imminent or recent death, but when we raced back through the ballroom, we found that the sound had come from a new arrival.

"Coralie!" Miss Mountstephen called when she saw the expensively attired woman kneeling over the body.

Lord Monroe's daughter was not alone. Standing next to her, with his hand on her shoulder, was a Catholic padre with a wide-brimmed hat and black cassock. Well, he was either a priest or a man with a strange taste in clothes. He removed his cappello romano and knelt to say a prayer. It took me a word or two to realise that it was in English.

"Eternal rest, grant unto him, O Lord,

And let perpetual light shine upon him."

He and Coralie crossed themselves, but the bereaved heir did not cry. If anything, I would say that she looked quite furious, but I couldn't yet imagine whether it was the killer who had provoked this reaction or her own father.

"Who are you, and what are you doing here?" she asked when she noticed us standing at a respectful distance.

Miss Mountstephen introduced us before my grandfather could say anything just a little bit vain. *My name,* he might well have uttered with a slight pause to add to the drama, *is Lord Edgington, former superintendent of Scotland Yard.*

"This is Lord Edgington and his grandson Christopher. They are friends of your father's. I believe I told you there would be visitors here this week."

Coralie waved away the explanation. "Oh, yes. You're old pals of Daddy's." She looked at me then, and there was a predatory glimmer to her glare. "Except that you aren't very old at all. Were you even born when Daddy left England?"

I think the answer might have been *just about,* but my grandfather spoke for the both of us.

"I knew Renwick well when he was the bright light of the Pimlico set. You were often there, tottering around barefoot at parties until the small hours of the morning."

She had no great nostalgic reaction to this. "That sounds like the kind of irresponsible attitude that my father had to parenting. Do you know who killed him?"

"Why do you assume he was murdered?" I had to ask.

Dressed in a modern style, she gripped the black piping on the hem of her white paletôt jacket before replying with just as much bite as I'd come to expect. "Because I knew my father. He spent his life trying to roil and discomfort people. It only stands to reason that he finally got his comeuppance."

"You don't seem particularly sad about his death," Grandfather was quick to remark, but Coralie raised her eyebrows defiantly, and it fell to the tubby priest to step in.

"This is no time to discuss such things," he said without giving any reason for this bizarre comment. From everything I'd learnt, immediately after someone has been murdered is the perfect time to discuss why he was killed.

"And you are?" Grandfather was already staking his claim to the case. He brought his amethyst-topped cane down on the flagstones imperiously as he spoke.

"My name is Father Laurence. I suppose you might say I was Lord Monroe's chaplain, but I serve in the church nearby." He had a thick Black Country accent, much like a games teacher at my school when I was very young. "I followed him over here some years ago."

"He told you about his move to Italy?"

The priest dismissed the question with a batted hand. "Something like that, yes."

Grandfather's downturned gaze suggested that he found this puzzling, and it seemed we had reached an impasse. The dead man was still on the ground where he had fallen. The pool of blood had already taken on an oily sheen, but it was unclear what we should do until the police arrived.

Luckily, it was at that moment that the police arrived. I know nothing of the uniforms or insignia of the Italian *Carabinieri*, but I could assume from the young officer's age that he was of low rank. He strode into the courtyard with no apparent interest in us but walked up to the old lady mechanic, whom he kissed on both cheeks. She must have whispered something in his ear, as he turned to us then and shouted what I took to be a name.

"Guido, vieni!"

Or perhaps it was two names. It was hard to say.

He rushed past us to look at the body and, a moment later, a man emerged from the same door that the old lady had used. He was the very image of the dark-haired policeman but a little older and broader. Dressed in greasy overalls, he was drying his face with a towel and lingered in the shady archway to observe the scene.

The policeman addressed the dead lord's secretary, and she replied in fast Italian of which I could make neither head nor tail. I assumed that they were catching up on the story so far, but it wasn't until the officer changed to English that I could extract anything more.

"Is terrible," he seemed to say, though from the indifferent expressions on the faces of the small crowd, I doubted they all agreed.

Perhaps aware of the contradiction, the priest crossed himself once more. The constable decided that enough was enough and went over to his mechanic grandmother – I could only assume they were related – and seized a tatty old dust sheet which he then used to cover the body.

"I guard it," he said, perhaps thinking that this would reassure the man's loved ones that they no longer needed to remain there.

"Thank you, Agente Lombardo." If anyone looked sad it was Miss Mountstephen. Her face was once more etched with pity. Perhaps she was really only afraid for herself, but I'm fairly certain that the compassion she showed for the man beneath the makeshift shroud was real.

"There was someone with him when he died," I felt I should tell them. "I gave chase, but he got away."

"I'm sorry, but I think this calls for a drink," Coralie said and, as there were no other suggestions, we went along with the idea. She kissed Father Laurence on the forehead and persuaded him to go back to his usual duties, before leading us through the castle and out to the terrace I'd previously discovered.

Coralie stepped outside ahead of us, and Delilah padded along at my side, eager to be part of the action, as I felt a tap on my shoulder.

"Christopher, I'll leave the talking to you," Grandfather whispered. "It's about time you learnt a little more about the man who would have been our host."

Miss Mountstephen needed no instructions; she had tailed off at some point and reappeared a moment later carrying a stack of glasses and a tantalus filled with bottles. There was a white, wrought-iron table beside the stone balustrades, and enough chairs for all of us, but Lord Monroe's secretary would not stay.

"I must telephone your brothers, Coralie," she said with a bow, and I had to wonder just how close the two were. After Coralie arrived in the courtyard, Miss Mountstephen had called out as though they were friends, but I had witnessed no warmth between them and now questioned whether the young employee was anything more than that to the family.

Once she had gone, Coralie lit a cigarette from the small pochette she carried. She took a puff and watched the smoke spiral up into the atmosphere.

I was more interested in what lay before us. The terrace was bordered by two tall trees which grew up from the garden some fifty feet below. They framed a dramatic view of the forests and vineyards on the smooth hills around the property. On top of the one directly in front of the terrace was a rather grand mansion, perhaps a half mile away. Coralie must have noticed me looking at it, as she extended one well-manicured finger and revealed a relevant detail.

"The man who owns that house was an acquaintance of my father's. Daddy sold him that property and they are no longer friends."

I tried to think of a subtler question than, "Why?" and failed.

"I don't know the why. What I can tell you is that, a year after Mr Starkie moved in over there, he threatened to murder my father. He bought a bow and shoots ten arrows in this direction every morning. He has no chance of reaching the castle, but his aim has definitely improved over the years."

I was struggling to push one of the incredibly heavy iron chairs but finally got it close enough to the matching table to sit down. "Are you saying that Mr Starkie killed Lord Monroe?"

"No."

Wouldn't it have been a nice, easy case if she'd simply said yes? Just think how different my life would be if the first suspect anyone identified turned out to be the killer each time. That would be bliss!

"Nor am I saying that he isn't the killer." Although Coralie

Monroe had the clear diction of most well-bred English women her age, I could tell that she had lived abroad long enough to take on a hint of an accent. "I'm merely telling you this to show the sort of feelings that Daddy could arouse in people."

This wasn't news to me. Grandfather had implied as much on the train to Italy. However, I was yet to get to the bottom of why Lord Monroe was such a stirrer.

"And what sort of feelings might they be?" This really wasn't a sophisticated interview. I had yet to extract anything revelatory from the evasive character before me, but then I was only just beginning.

"Father was…" she began before considering the right word to use. "A real greaser. Like some mischievous god of old, he cared only for pleasure and didn't mind who he hurt while pursuing it."

This was still too vague to be of any help, and so I decided to provoke a reaction. "Did you love him all the same?"

She laughed at this. She took a long drag on her cigarette and laughed. The brief sound had a hollow ring to it, and it made me trust her even less. "Did I love my father? What a sublime question. I wish I knew the answer."

It occurred to me then that there'd been no prelude to our discussion. I hadn't had to explain that my grandfather was a master detective or that I was his assistant, which told me that she knew more about us than she had revealed.

"You can at least try. After all, you've already told us just how many people disliked him. Are you one of them?" I sounded more confident than normal. It was almost as if I knew how to conduct such an interview.

She didn't reply at first. She took a sip of whatever cocktail my grandfather had created using whisky, vermouth and bitters. "It might be said that Father was a fraction less objectionable to me than he was to his friends and his two sons. I was his little girl, after all, but the question of whether I loved him is a complicated one. We maintained contact, and I came to visit monthly. Is that any clearer?"

She was dispassionate in the way she spoke, and I still didn't have a clear picture of who she was.

"Did you move to Italy at the same time as your father?"

"Not very long after." She pulled her short, slightly jagged hair from behind the collar of her jacket and looked uncomfortable with what she was about to confess. "He bought me a house twenty minutes' drive from here. I was tired of the English weather, so I jumped at the chance."

"Did he do the same for your brothers? I understand they live in Italy, too."

She bit her lip over and over for a few seconds like a rabbit nibbling a blade of grass. "Father never shared such information. He was notoriously secretive except when it suited him not to be. He might have hinted at certain kindnesses he bestowed upon them, but I could never tell whether he was telling the truth."

"Why not?"

"Because he liked to keep Dashwood, Fletcher and me on our toes. It was one of his little games to sow doubt and suspicion amongst us. I believe he felt that it brought us closer to him. If I was angry at Dashwood, then I was far more likely to come to Daddy to tell him about it." She paused, and I must have reacted in some way as she followed this by saying, "Yes, his morality was most definitely askew. But you must understand that he did everything with such charm that it was hard to think of him as little more than a roguish scamp."

"And yet others wanted him dead." If anything, I was growing in confidence, and I calmly took a sip of the drink, as though imbibing such astringent substances was nothing out of the ordinary. It burnt like rotten on the way down, but I tried my best not to show her.

"Yes." She took a deep breath, and it was apparent that she was already frustrated with me for not understanding her better. She turned to Grandfather, who was stroking the top of Delilah's head and pretending to take no interest in our conversation. "You knew him, Lord Edgington. You must have seen how Daddy could be one thing to your face and ten others behind your back."

Grandfather laughed without making a noise, as though she had told a pleasant anecdote. I could tell that he was putting on an act, I just couldn't be certain why he thought it a good idea.

When this achieved little, she addressed me once more. "You must understand that Daddy had a variety of different schemes on the go at any one time. He would plot to steal a man's wife at the same time as throwing a grand party in his honour. Take Markland Starkie on the hill over there. The two had been friendly rivals in London, and so Daddy rang him with the news that he had found a wonderful property with the most tremendous view of his castle and the incomparable Tuscan countryside. What he didn't reveal was that the foundations were built quite literally on sand and that, as soon as Mr Starkie had sold his home in Britain and moved out to these sunny uplands, the eastern tower of the property sank three feet beneath the level of the rest of the house. It's impossible to sell the place, and Daddy charged the man such an extortionate price that he couldn't afford to move elsewhere."

This was not the kind of thing I would do to a friend, and I was eager to know how it had happened. "Had your father bought the house and tried to cut his losses?"

"You're not listening, boy." She tutted, and her bobbed hair wobbled about her shoulders.

Although she was at least fifteen years older than me, I resented her calling me "boy". "Then please explain yourself." The thought that the Christopher of old would never have replied so bluntly sent a gentle thrill through me.

"Daddy didn't end up with the property by accident. He bought it knowing what a bad state it was in so that he could sell it to Mr Starkie just to vex him."

"The villain!" I said, sounding far more like my easily shocked sixteen-year-old self than I'd intended.

She clapped her hands together and smiled for the first time since we'd sat down. "That's just the word for him. He was a true villain, but when you were with him, it was impossible not to enjoy his machinations."

I really wished that Grandfather would choose this moment to raise some revelatory point that hadn't occurred to me. He wasn't even looking any more. He was making a fuss of Delilah as though nothing else mattered.

"And what do you do with your life when you're not here?" I asked out of frustration as much as anything else.

She had been smoking and drinking alternately but now stubbed out her cigarette in a dirty glass on the table. "I am an artist." She stretched out this last word to show the importance she gave this profession. "When I'm not here, I split my time between Trieste in the north and Salerno on the Amalfi Coast. I've uncovered a community of like-minded creative people in both, and I find the Italian landscape so inspirational as I travel between them."

"That all sounds… expensive." I was hoping that I had used just the right tone to set her nerves rattling. In my mind, she was thinking, *Oh, no! The jig is up! He knows my secret! Within seconds, he'll get the truth out of me. I should never have killed my father for the inheritance.*

What she actually said in reply was, "Gosh, aren't you sweet!"

I cleared my throat and tried to raise the pressure. "I'm suggesting that such a lavish existence must be a drain on you."

"I could just eat you up." She had that same hungry look I'd seen a few minutes earlier.

Despite his very best attempts not to react to the scene before him, Grandfather couldn't stop a brief note of laughter from escaping his lips. He pretended that it was his dog that he found so entertaining, then continued acting as though he wasn't the least interested in our conversation.

Coralie winked, and I suddenly didn't feel like such a capable detective after all. My confidence and competence were sapping away. Even six months earlier, I would have turned to my more experienced colleague for support, but we'd apparently reached the stage of my apprenticeship at which I could no longer rely on his help.

"Expensive…" I repeated pathetically, as she leaned across the table to me and her eyebrows flicked higher.

"You know, you should visit me in my studio. I'd love to show you my *artworks* in greater detail."

It had all been going so well, but she'd shown me up for what I was: an overgrown child with no hope of finding her father's killer and, to be perfectly honest, a genuine fear of worldly women like her. I had no doubt that she was true to her word and would eat me alive.

She stroked the table, much as if she were encouraging a small, fluffy animal to come closer before wringing its neck. I was willing myself to find some authority, just as my mentor tended to do in such a situation, but it wasn't easy.

"Who…" I began again, but my voice sounded gruffer than usual, so I pulled at my collar in the hope that I might be able to fix it. "If you don't think Mr Starkie on the other hill is to blame, who *did* kill your father?"

I had rather hoped that this weighty question might force her to show more restraint, but she pouted her lipsticked mouth at me and didn't seem concerned in the slightest. "Where should I begin? He upset everyone he ever met in one way or another. I'm sure your grandfather could tell you that if he wasn't acting dim for some reason."

Grandfather took exception to this comment and finally broke his silence.

"I wasn't acting dim. I was giving you the rope you need to hang yourself." He was really glaring at her. "And I'll have you know that you still haven't mentioned anyone who could feasibly be responsible for your father's death. Who do you think could have pushed him from that clocktower?"

"Let's see." She paused to think. "Well, any single person who lived in this castle when the wealthy Englishman swooped in to buy it for a pittance could have killed him. Anyone he underpaid, belittled or insulted as he worked on his property. Any of the numerous men in this country, our homeland, and most likely several others in between, whose wives Daddy led astray. How's that for a start?"

She seized hold of her tumbler and tipped her head back to swallow the last drops of drink. I desperately sought something that might scratch the shiny surface of the steely character in front of me before she could stand up and saunter off.

"What about your family?" I demanded. "Could one of your brothers be lurking about the place having exacted his revenge?"

"It's easy enough to find out. If they were at home when Eva called them, that would make it rather difficult for them to have been at the top of the tower."

"Then what about you?" Rising in his seat and straightening his back, Grandfather transformed before our eyes. He had all the strength of purpose and resolve that I lacked.

I believe that despite her previous cynicism, even Coralie was a little impressed. "What about me?"

"Did you come here to kill your father?"

CHAPTER SEVEN

"It was a disaster," I announced as we walked back to the courtyard in search of Miss Mountstephen. "You should have interrupted far earlier. I might have learnt a thing or two from you over the last few years, but I wasn't prepared to deal with a woman like Coralie Monroe."

Grandfather wasn't daunted by what had happened. In fact, he had a smile on his face. "And how exactly would you describe a woman like Coralie Monroe?"

I came to a stop in the salon that gave onto the courtyard. "I would describe her…" I needed a moment to think. "…as a fearsome prospect."

Delilah darted through the doorway ahead of us, and I tried to compose myself, but I knew it would do no good.

"Don't take it so seriously, Christopher," Grandfather told me as we caught sight of the dirty sheet beneath which Renwick Monroe's dead body still lay. "Not every suspect will threaten to eat you. I'm sure this was a one-off."

I was struggling not to shout or cry (or more likely both). I might well have complained further, but I saw that a pair of police detectives – or at least two men in black uniforms and bicorne hats – had arrived.

My grandfather concentrated on the discussion they were having with Agente Lombardo. I can only assume he was trying to make sense of whatever they were saying to one another. I did the same by judging the way they comported themselves, if not the words they spoke, and I felt that the two senior officers were dismissive of whatever the local officer was telling them.

The three men became more animated, and I could tell that the constable was unhappy with his colleagues. This didn't require any great skills of deduction; he was really shouting at them. If that had happened in London, I'm certain he would have been reprimanded for his behaviour, but one of the detectives was still smiling as he walked past us towards the exit. There was something sinister behind the man's expression as he looked me up and down disdainfully.

"What did they say?" Grandfather asked as we reached the constable.

"They say an old man he did climb the tower and fell down. They say they find no signs of violence."

"Did you tell them we heard someone running from the scene?"

Looking quite perturbed by the confrontation, he nodded with his eyes still on the archway through which the men had departed. "I do this. I tell them all, but they don't believe me."

I doubt there was much else to ask him, but this wasn't an option either way. He walked off to talk to his brother, who commiserated with him, or perhaps told him not to be such a lily-livered wimp. Who's to say?

Before we could even consider where to go, what to do or to whom we should now talk, Miss Mountstephen came to solve the dilemma. I'd seen her watching the detectives from a distance, but she clearly didn't want to involve herself in their investigation.

"I spoke to Dashwood Monroe. That's Renwick's elder son. He lives near Arezzo, and it will take him a good few hours to arrive."

"And the younger boy?" Grandfather asked, as though the heirs to the estate were mere children, which, I suppose, to him, they were.

"He was not at his home in Prato, but I left a message with his housekeeper that he is to come here immediately when he returns."

The secretary looked no less nervous than she had when we'd last seen her. She was naturally far paler than the glamorous Coralie, but her face had taken on an even more pallid quality over the course of the last hour. Her fingers were forever moving at her side, too, and I couldn't help but feel sorry for her.

"You've done very well in dealing with everything, Miss Mountstephen," Grandfather spoke softly to reassure her.

"Please, call me Eva. We are not in England; life here is less formal than in your everyday lives."

I doubt she knew just how true this was. As I am the grandson of a marquess who owns one of the finest estates in Surrey and employs a staff of thirty, my family's idea of a simple gathering was a formal dance with twenty servants in attendance. Grandfather's concept of letting one's hair down extended to undoing the top button on his waistcoat.

"I will show you to your rooms. Do you need any help with your luggage?"

I realised two things at this moment. Number one, we'd left our suitcases beside the entrance, and number two, I was yet to see a single member of staff. I dashed off to retrieve our bags and then dashed back again. As Eva turned to lead the way, I had so many questions I could have asked her, but for a reason I can't explain, the one that formed on my tongue was, "Why is there an old lady fixing a motorbike in Lord Monroe's castle?"

I believe that she tried to smile and failed. "Although Renwick owned il Castello di Montegufoni, he did not have the heart to throw out all of its residents. However, to make the most of them, he…" Her really quite attractive features pulled together, and I believe she was trying to think of a discreet way to describe the deceased lord. "Well, he put as many of them as possible to good use. He said that he would make their lives more comfortable as long as they lived by his rules. I'm sure you've already noticed certain ways in which he has influenced them."

"Their greetings!" I said, making sense of the insensible in an unexpected flash. "They've learnt a few English phrases which they exchange whenever there in the courtyard. Was that your employer's doing?"

We had come to the shady passageway through which I'd gone searching for the tower and she looked back at me apologetically. "I'm afraid so. You see, for all that he liked the food and the weather over here, I always had the sense that Renwick wished to be back home. He made the locals speak English within earshot of him. Most of the people who live here don't know much, though he did single a few out to teach in more depth."

"Agente Lombardo for one, I assume," Grandfather said, as though it could prove to be important.

"Yes, he was very fond of Attilio. His brother Guido also lives here, and it is their grandmother whom you have seen tinkering with cars."

So I'd worked out at least one thing correctly, but his still didn't answer my question, so I tried again. "Did Renwick teach her how to use a spanner?"

She managed a real smile this time. I tend to have that effect on people. "No, that was Guido. He's a very capable mechanic and, as I said, Lord Monroe agreed to everyone staying in their existing apartments in the castle on the condition that they made themselves useful."

"So perhaps his altruistic bent wasn't the only reason he kept them around?" Grandfather looked at everything through the dark lenses of a detective. It usually led to some interesting results but could make the world feel like a nasty place.

"I wouldn't say that. He treated the people here quite kindly."

"But poor Nana had to learn a trade," I muttered in a sad voice. I don't know why, of all the things I'd seen and heard since arriving, an old lady with a motorcycle wheel and grease on her cheeks made me feel the saddest. I suppose I'm odd like that.

"Nonna," Eva replied.

"I beg your pardon?" I tried not to sound offended.

"That's the Italian for grandmother. Attilio and Guido call her Nonna."

"I see."

If I hadn't been so confused by the living arrangements in Montegufoni, I would have paid more attention to the architecture. We now reached a second courtyard, which was smaller and more ornate than the main one. There was an arched gallery overhead that put me in mind of Juliet's balcony and, atop the flagstones all around, there were lemon trees in heavy terracotta urns. There was also a door open that led to the far side of the house I was yet to explore, and I realised that, if the killer had found his way here, he could have escaped from the castle entirely. Of course, he could also have run around the building and reappeared through another door, and it wasn't beyond the realm of possibility that one of the Italian brothers or even the workmen we'd seen had pushed Lord Monroe to his death.

"This is known as the Court of the Dukes of Athens," Eva explained when she saw us both admiring the new space. "I don't know all the history, but the Acciaioli family who originally owned the castle were wealthy merchants in Florence. They built it up over many years, dating right back to the fourteenth century, but this stately wing was added more recently by a particularly powerful politician. His brother was the duke after whom this courtyard was named. Follow me."

She led us down some steps, past a stone well, and through one of the many arches, to a door which she unlocked with a key the size of a large cigar. She turned it in the lock, then paused for a second to look back at us. I got a sense of what our arrival would have been like had we not just found a body, and I rather wished we had met this likeable young lady in those more peaceful circumstances.

She threw the door open ahead of her and motioned for us to go through. The sun had been so bright overhead, and the contrasting shadows so dark, that I expected to find myself in a gloomy room. As it turned out, all the shutters in the suite ahead of us had been left open and, along with a great flood of light pouring in from every window, a stirring breeze rushed out to us.

We passed through a small vestibule with a rack of rifles on one wall and a shelf covered in medieval breast plates on the other. This did make it more likely that someone would be shot during our stay in Montegufoni, but I found it oddly reassuring to know that, just like in every British stately home I'd visited, sprawling Italian properties come with far too many dangerous weapons.

We walked around a grand piano – another staple of opulent estates – and into the largest room in the castle. If I had constructed a model of what Italy was like in my dreams before I left Britain, it would have looked just like this. A long gallery with frescoed paintings all over the ceiling depicting any number of angels, gods and heroes was illuminated by the bright sunshine, so that the images seemed to glow from within. There were full-length French windows leading off at regular intervals on all sides of the rectangular room. Between them, I saw gilt-framed mirrors that brightened the space even more, and I felt for a moment as if I were swimming in light. The contrast with the chicken-and-gubbins-infested courtyard was stark.

I peered out through the first door to see what was there and found myself enchanted by the garden beyond. A bushy pink oleander tree, surrounded by neatly laid-out beds with miniature ornamental hedgerows in elegant patterns, stood in the middle of an open courtyard with wide views over the landscape. There was a village on the hilltop in the distance which looked as old as any I'd visited in Britain.

I stepped back inside and had the urge to take my book out and lounge on one of the delicately upholstered divans. If the truth be told, I wanted to spend the rest of my life in those pleasant surrounds, but I just knew Eva would soon explain that this was Grandfather's sitting room and there was a delightful windowless box set aside for me.

"The Gallery dates back to the early eighteenth century and was modelled after an apartment in the Palazzo Medici-Riccardi in Florence. The Acciaioli family, who owned Montegufoni, had many connections to powerful families like the Medicis." It seemed that Eva Mountstephen was not just a secretary, but a historian and tour guide. "Lord Edgington, your bedroom awaits. It's just up the staircase in the far corner."

I couldn't see the stairs to which she referred, but he nodded and, still holding his suitcase, walked off to investigate. Delilah hurried after her master as I prepared myself for disappointment.

"Christopher, I'll accompany you to the Cardinal's apartment." She turned on her heel and led us back to the Hall of Arms.

"How can there be so much space for guests when there are so many people living here?" I asked as she closed the high double doors behind us.

"The castle is quite large, and there are only seven families remaining. At one point in the last century, there were six hundred desperate homeless people crammed within its walls. As I've told you, Renwick was slowly restoring the most important parts of it as they became vacant."

"Was he doing the work himself?" I couldn't hide my surprise, or my naivety, and Eva smiled that sad smile of hers.

"He was very involved in everything that was done here and certainly liked to get his hands dirty. But he employed artisan workers from all over Italy for more technical jobs. The rooms in this wing of the castle needed a lot of attention after two hundred years without care. Everything was in such a state when I first came here that I found a porcupine under my bed."

This resolved my doubt of whether she lived in the castle, though I had assumed that was the case.

Without my incessant questions to distract her, she could focus on finding the next key she needed. We crossed a comparatively featureless corridor and emerged in another elegant salon. I don't know how many areas of the building were decorated with elaborate frescos, but there were far too many to describe. The room was five times the size of my quarters at home, and yet the vast painted ceiling showed a celestial sky with a personification of Aurora, the Greek goddess of the dawn, riding on a cloud in the centre. She was surrounded by birds and more of those blessed cherubs, who were flying about the place dropping petals to the earth below.

I don't know why I'm describing all this, as Eva continued straight through this room into the one next door where I would sleep. I braced myself for the cave-like hole I would now spend weeks of my life detesting.

"Gosh!" I said, taking in the scene before me. "It's certainly unique."

Eva walked over to the window to open the curtains so that I could have a better look at the strange room. "It was built for a member of the family who was a cardinal. That probably explains why, instead of a bathroom in the alcove beside your bed, you have an oratory."

"I'll be sure to make good use of it," I said, still struggling to imagine how a room like this had been conceived.

The dark space in which my bed was located was decorated much like a cave, as I had feared, but the antechamber that it gave onto was painted from floor to ceiling with a mix of Christian and ancient iconography. I had a view of invading soldiers, falling cities, winged men and fantastic creatures. Festooned with abundant boughs and dotted, of course, with cherubs at play, it was a space of dreams and nightmares. I wondered if that was the point; if the frescoes depicted the impossible pathways which our minds wander each night. Or perhaps the artist just wanted to paint something pretty.

"I hope you'll be very comfortable here," Eva told me as she stared out of the window. There was a far-off look in her eyes, and I doubted that she was aware of whatever she saw out there. A gardener was trimming low branches, and I could hear insects singing in the cypress trees, but my guide's mind was on other things.

I put my case down in a corner beside a washstand and spoke my mind. "Miss Mountstephen… Eva, are you quite all right?"

She made that nervous gesture that many people adopt when they wish to pretend everything is fine when it clearly isn't: she shrugged and attempted a half-hearted smile before moving quickly away.

"There's no need to worry about me. This has all come as a shock, but I can't complain."

I wanted to ask whether she believed her employer had been murdered or we'd got the wrong end of the stick somehow, but when she stopped in the doorway, I didn't have it in me to burden her further.

"Signora Acciaioli will serve you and your grandfather lunch in the garden at the end of the corridor we passed through." She bowed submissively, and I wanted to tell her that she didn't have to behave that way around me, but I didn't catch her eye as she turned to scurry off.

I let out a sigh and fell back on the bed. I felt as though I'd been awake for a hundred hours and wanted little more than to sleep. When I looked up at the low ceiling in my pretty cave, I discovered another painting of cherubs. Who could have predicted that?

CHAPTER EIGHT

It didn't feel as if I'd managed to nod off but, when I looked at my watch approximately two minutes later, half an hour had passed.

"Christopher," my grandfather called from… somewhere. I was still coming back to the world and trying to work out where I was. I don't know if you've ever woken up in a Botticelli painting, but it is a confusing experience.

"Christopher, where are you?"

"It's difficult to say," I called back, though I should probably have remembered by this point.

Perhaps fearing that nothing else would work, he clapped his hands loudly and said, "It's lunchtime!" He knew me too well.

I roused myself from my pretty cavern, had a quick peek through the door which contained the gold and white oratory, and then followed the corridor to find Grandfather on the terrace with the blooming pink oleander. Sitting at a small wooden table, he was already serving wine from a carafe in a wicker cradle, and I wondered if it was a good idea to keep drinking.

Delilah was rolling about in the sunshine, apparently having discovered her perfect existence. I half wished that I could join her, as it looked a lot less stressful than chasing a murderer. I had to ask myself whether one of our holidays will ever turn out to be an actual holiday.

I was about to begin the inevitable discussion of my luncheon companion's thoughts on the case when a woman with a great mass of black curls and a simple gingham dress arrived. She held a large wooden board replete with tiny dishes.

"Good afternoon, gentlemen," she began in heavily accented English. "I am exceedingly honoured to make your acquaintance."

Despite the fact that her pronunciation was irregular, to say the least, her phrasing was uncommonly formal. In fact, she put me in mind of a cousin of my grandfather's who sounds as if he has a dictionary stuck in his mouth and wishes to use every word.

"Good afternoon, Signora." Grandfather tilted his head obligingly, but I believe he was more interested in the small plates of fresh vegetables, meats and cheeses than the woman serving them. I, on the other hand, found her quite fascinating. She was around forty years of age, and I was immediately won over by her most cordial manner.

"I took it upon myself to prepare you a simple antipasto for your luncheon today," she explained. "I was of the opinion that, after your lengthy and taxing voyage, you might prefer a lighter culinary offering."

"Your English is excellent, madam," I said not just to compliment her but because it put me in mind of a possibility.

"Thank you kindly, young man." Having deposited her "culinary offering", she performed a curtsey of sorts. "Lord Monroe taught me his very self."

"Well, it is infinitely better than my Italian, and you should be commended."

Blushing and curtseying once more as she backed away, she exited, leaving us to our meal.

I examined what we would be eating, and my eyes were as big as an owl's – whereas I had the stomach of an elephant. For his part, Grandfather took his time dividing the delicious spread before us onto two plates. There were indescribably ripe tomatoes, slices of melon, chunks of moist white cheese dripped with honey, freshly baked bread that still retained its warmth from the oven, and plenty of sliced meats.

"I think it is safe to assume that this is prosciutto Toscano," Grandfather announced rather grandly as he lifted up a piece of ham on his fork. While he does not speak Italian, he is fluent in food.

"There are more important things to discuss than the type of meat we're eating, Grandfather," I told him in as stern a manner as I could muster, but then I tried a bite of the *prosciutto*, and it melted like salty chocolate in my mouth. "Wait. I've changed my mind. Tell me more about this ham."

"The Etruscans introduced pig farming to Italy in the centuries before Christ was born." He'd gone back a little too far and lost my interest.

"Wait, I've un-changed my mind. Tell me about Renwick Monroe."

"I thought I had." He took another sip of deep red wine, whereas I didn't want to have a sleepy head all afternoon and stuck to water.

"No, you hinted at a certain reputation that he had when you knew him. You were typically mysterious and unhelpful."

He did not enjoy this comment and paused his quaffing to look at me over his long-stemmed glass. "That was before he was murdered.

Back when I first mentioned him on our journey here, I merely wished to warn you what a curious character he was. I had no idea he would be killed before I could introduce you."

It was tempting to doubt even this simple claim. My grandfather is such a good judge of the ways of men that he often seems to know things before they happen. There was every chance he had calculated that Lord Monroe would only be able to survive a maximum of two decades in a foreign country without someone trying to kill him. It would not surprise me in the slightest if I'd been brought here as an experiment to train my detective skills.

"Very well, I'm all ears. Tell me of the dastardly things he did when you knew him."

I had prepared a small bite of bread, prosciutto and scrumptious cheese and popped it into my mouth as I awaited his explanation.

"I believe that I've already told you that Renwick took me under his wing after I'd been made a superintendent for the Metropolitan Police." He dabbed at his chin with his napkin before putting it down on the table beside his plate. "Well, that wasn't the whole story."

What a surprise, I thought but didn't say as Delilah looked up at me ever so sweetly with those beautiful black-brown eyes of hers. I resisted for approximately two seconds before tossing her a scrap of meat.

"You see, I was suspicious of his intentions from the very outset, not just because of his reputation, but because I had been sent to find out as much as I could about him."

"By the police?" My voice shot higher over the course of these three short words.

"No, no. A banker by the name of Edward Poole had lost a large sum of money in one of Renwick's ventures. It was an African gold mine or a Burmese ruby importer or some such thing. The point is that he was afraid that the whole affair was a swindle, and rather than go to the police directly, Poole asked me to find out what I could about the supposedly honest lord."

Any story that starts with my grandfather going incognito to look into shady deals in foreign mining concerns was bound to be absorbing. "So was there something worth discovering then?"

He tutted three times. "Patience is a virtue, Christopher. Never jump to the end of the story when the telling is the most entertaining part." To make his point, he slowly cut a plum-shaped tomato into several pieces before continuing. "I engineered a meeting between Lord Monroe and myself at the Reading Room of the British Museum. I made it look like we had crossed paths by happenstance, but I knew exactly where he would be at three in the afternoon on a Friday. I took down from the shelves a book on Lord Byron, making sure that Renwick would notice. I'd heard he had a love of Romantic poetry and that he saw himself as a heroic figure, so I thought this might do the trick."

"And it did," I said, leaping ahead once more.

He didn't seem to mind this time. In fact, he was clearly keen to tell me what came next. His grey eyes sparkled as he led me through the story. "That's right. We fell into conversation – discussing our days at Oakton Academy when we were young – and he soon let slip that he had followed my career closely. Within a quarter of an hour, he had invited me to his club, and by the following weekend, I'd been introduced at the literary and artistic salon he led in his townhouse overlooking the Thames in St George's Square. All the great and really very good artists of the era passed through his living room at one time or another. They treated me as a curiosity – one of the many freakish spectacles Renwick collected. But I can't say that I was immune to the charms of this new world I'd entered. Imagine dining with your favourite writer and not feeling the same way."

"Gosh!" I replied, already aware of how he must have felt. "Was Charles Dickens there?"

Grandfather looked dismayed. "No, Christopher. He'd been dead for decades by then. I was speaking more generally."

"Sorry, I'd forgotten you were already an experienced officer at the time of the story."

I put a piece of bread in my mouth to hide my embarrassment. I was slightly surprised when I found that it had almost no flavour whatsoever.

"It's saltless bread," Grandfather explained, so at least this made him forget my faux pas. "It's a delicacy here, dating back to a time when bakers were taxed depending on how much salt they used. Now, would you like me to continue my tale?"

He would never stop talking to me like a teacher to a pupil, and I couldn't entirely blame him.

"Of course, Grandfather. Please do."

He moved his chair back a few inches to sit in the shade of the creeping vine that grew over our heads. "It took me some time to have any sense of what kind of person Renwick was. He was certainly very popular – his followers worshiped at the altar of the great man even if he was a self-confessed rogue. There were a lot of allusions to his misdeeds – lots of raised eyebrows and titters. But it was hard to know whether they were down to the mythology he had established for himself or deserved notoriety."

I wanted to ask him a question for every new sentence he uttered, but I held my tongue and listened.

"I made it known that I was looking to invest a large sum of money in a business venture – the higher the risk, the better. There were several people in the Pimlico set who would have pocketed the money without a second thought, but Renwick showed no interest. I debated whether this was proof in itself that the man was a criminal. After all, he wouldn't want to take the risk of defrauding a police inspector and drawing attention to his offences."

"And he was!" I couldn't help but feel proud of my grandfather when I heard the tales of his excellence as a detective, and I was grinning from one ear to the other by now.

"No, I was wrong." He folded his napkin so that it made a perfect triangle and then smoothed it flat on the table. "Don't misunderstand me, Renwick Monroe was one of the most incorrigible scoundrels I've ever met, but not for the reasons I was sent there to uncover. It seemed he had slept with at least a fifth of his acquaintances' wives – and one or two of their daughters, as well. He was one of London's finest when it came to hosting an unforgettable party, but he always found someone else to foot the bill. In short, Renwick Monroe was the kind of man who made you feel alive, but not the kind upon whom you could rely in a time of crisis."

I had a piece of really very spicy sausage in my mouth and couldn't ask the question that had just popped into my head. In Britain today, people don't go in for hot foods as they do in the Continent or over in India. Eating horseradish makes me feel as if someone has sprayed petrol on my tongue and thrown in a match. And so, rather than prompting my favourite raconteur for more information, I had a nice soothing drink of water.

"I had a few of my subordinates look into his financial dealings and, while there had been some losses in his past, they all seemed above board. I don't imagine I would have got to the bottom of the matter if things hadn't gone wrong for Renwick. It was some years after we first crossed paths. He turned up at Cranley Hall one night when I wasn't working. Your grandmother had already retired, and my footman came into the library where I was tying flies to go fishing the next day. He was terribly apologetic to disturb me at such a late hour, unlike the man who had just barged through my front door in need of help.

"'Edgington, you must listen to me,' he insisted without a hello or a by your leave. 'I'm in trouble, matey. I don't mind telling you that I am in a sticky spot, and I don't see any way out of it.'

"I calmed him down, sat him down, and then ordered Halfpenny to pour him a measure of brandy. It was the least I could do for a man whom I'd falsely suspected of out-and-out raffishness. Renwick soon recovered his nerve and explained what had sent him haring out of London in search of my counsel after dark. It turned out that he was not so innocent after all. Using the connections he'd made as a denizen of fashionable London, he'd spent the last few years tricking the rich and rotten out of their money. Most surprising, however, was that he did not engage in this behaviour for selfish reasons. Oh, no. From his own slightly perverse perspective, what he was doing was moral."

Grandfather stopped talking for a moment, and the creak and whisper of the towering trees, which jutted up from the gardens below, filled my ears as they swayed in the breeze.

"Are you saying that he saw himself as a modern-day Robin Hood?"

He rubbed his hands together and looked at me appraisingly. "That's rather well put, Christopher, and you certainly got the man's number faster than I did. Just as you said, Lord Renwick Monroe – fourth son of the Duke of Chessington, and heir to no great fortune – thought of himself as a high-class vigilante."

I gave a brief gasp, but Delilah balanced this out with a long, unimpressed yawn. Her master looked down at her, as if to say, *You really are my fiercest critic!*

"He wasn't out robbing stagecoaches or freeing the wronged from castle dungeons. The word altruistic did not apply to him, but he took it upon himself to punish those that he believed most deserved it." He tapped the table softly as he spoke. "It turned out that Edward Poole, the banker who had so discreetly come to me for help, had disowned his son for marrying the wrong woman. Renwick went to great lengths to establish a fictional mining company in which Poole invested before it sadly went into receivership. He passed on the money that he'd fished to the man's rightful heir, and Poole was none the wiser."

I was so consumed by his story, I'd forgotten to eat. I soon put a stop to that, but I continued to listen just as attentively.

"In another instance some months after the first, Baroness Tavistock – a stone-hearted tiger of a pussycat who took great pleasure in berating and even beating her young servants when they didn't meet her impossibly high standards –mislaid a priceless emerald necklace on a weekend jaunt with the Pimlico set. I discovered, in fact, that such carelessness was fairly common at their meetings."

He looked across at the oleander tree, and I could tell that the story was playing in his head like a film in the cinema. "The revenge Renwick exacted wasn't only monetary. He released rumours about those he felt had overstepped the line of common decency, planted stories in the newspapers, bribed journalists to write terrible reviews of books and plays that would all but destroy the authors' careers. He was a secret judge and jury for the entitled and greedy of Great Britain, and he got away with it for a very long time."

"That's quite remarkable." I was trying to form an image of the strange man whose body we'd found just a few short hours earlier. "It's remarkable that no one realised all that he was up to."

"Well, I didn't, and it has been said that I'm a fairly capable detective." My grandfather could be modest and even humble at times, though it didn't happen too often. "It was only that night at Cranley Hall that I got a clear picture of his dubious schemes."

"So what had happened that made him run to you?"

Grandfather took a piece of melon that he had spent the last minute cutting into neat cubes. "Well, he explained that he had tried his best to show me up as a bad egg and failed. He'd been investigating me as I'd been investigating him. And so, instead of swindling or disgracing me, he felt that he could trust me after all."

"Yes, but why did he need your help?"

Grandfather once more sent a look across the table which said, *If you hadn't been skipping ahead in the story, you wouldn't have had to ask that question twice!*

"As it happens, he wouldn't share all the details. He said he wished to protect me, and I didn't force the story from him. The long and the short of it was that he'd practised his tricks on a man whom he should never have crossed. He said there was someone very powerful and potentially violent coming for him, and he was afraid for his life."

I'd learnt my lesson, for the time being at least, and let him finish the story at his own pace.

"You know the incredible thing is, though he thought himself the moral arbiter of high society, Renwick Monroe was no better a man than any of those he sought to punish and correct. He had a high opinion of himself, and I don't believe he ever realised that the wife to whom he was unfaithful or the children he had done little to raise viewed him as just as much of a blighter as those he punished."

By this point, I was silently screaming at him to tell me what he'd done for Lord Monroe all those years ago, but I said nothing.

"Do you know what I told him that night in my library?"

"That he should go to the nearest police station and admit to all the crimes he had committed?"

Grandfather smiled at me again. "No, I could have, but I believed in the danger he faced and felt that, had he been arrested, he would not have been safe."

He paused then and I considered a long list of further suggestions. *You told him that he'd made his bed and had to lie in it,* was one. *You offered to provide him with a new identity as an East End whelk seller,* was a less likely option, but I kept my mouth shut and waited for the answer.

"I told him that people say Italy is a nice place in which to retire, and I didn't see him again from that day until this."

CHAPTER NINE

By the time we'd finished our lunch, the coroner or what have you had removed the body, and there was no longer any sign of Agente Lombardo. His brother and grandmother were still in the courtyard, assembling what looked to me to be a Triumph Model H motorbike. They barely glanced in our direction when we walked over to them, and I couldn't say why my grandfather had led us there.

"Did all the various vehicles upon which you are working belong to your master?" he began, before realising that his terminology was faulty and trying again. "By which I mean Lord Monroe. Did he own that bike there?"

The broad and brooding Guido Lombardo paused with his hands still on the wheel of the half-dismantled machine and looked up at us with those incredibly dark eyes of his. I couldn't say in that moment whether he understood the question or that he even spoke English. Before he could reply in one language or another, we heard a loud hooting from the front of the property. It was not the sound of an owl hidden in the cypress trees, but the unmistakable horn of an automobile.

"Lord Edgington!" a voice just about reached us, and Guido and his grandmother returned to their work.

Grandfather nodded to the pair somewhat furtively, and we followed Delilah – who would automatically run towards any such noise – back to the gatehouse that doubled as the front wall of the castle.

We could see a glimpse of the car through the bushes. Delilah was running the length of it, back and forth with her tail wagging, so I had to assume she knew the person inside. I ran down the steps, between the two long rows of lemon trees in their large clay pots, to see who had come a-calling. Grandfather didn't seem nearly as inquisitive as I was, which suggested that he already knew who was there.

"Todd!" I sang when I saw Grandfather's factotum climb from the driver's seat of the ridiculously large vehicle.

It was immense and immensely shiny, with an abnormally extended black bonnet, white side panels, and a tall chassis with seating for five. I could tell without knowing the make or even from which country it came that it was in a class of its own. The wheel caps were in chrome silver, to match several small details across the car, and the effect was enhanced by the spare tyres, which were stored on the running board on either flank. The ornament on the shiny radiator at the front of the vehicle was in the shape of a silver elephant rising up on its hind legs. I hadn't a clue what type of car it was, but it certainly wasn't British.

"Phenomenal," Grandfather said with awe in his voice. "I truly never thought I would own such a car. How does she drive, Todd?"

"Own?" I asked before my capable young friend could answer. "We've only been in Italy a few hours. How did you come to own a car here?"

Grandfather was circling the automobile in amazement – much like his dog, in fact – and he chose to ignore me. "The Bugatti 41! They call it the *Royale. O*nly twenty-five of them will ever be made, and the company hopes to sell them to monarchs and statesmen around the world. It has whalebone controls and a walnut steering wheel!"

To be perfectly honest, I was happier to see Todd than yet another of Grandfather's fancy toys.

"I'm so glad you'll be joining us on our European adventure," I said as I shook the man's hand most elatedly. "It wouldn't have been the same without you."

"It's nice to see you too, Master Christopher." As Grandfather was still admiring his new baby, Todd answered my earlier question. "I drove to Paris in the first Silver Ghost Lord Edgington ever owned, and sold that to a French duke, who happens to be an admirer of your grandfather. That covered the initial payment on this Bugatti."

The fact that there would be multiple instalments needed to pay off this elaborate limousine made me a little worried that Grandfather had sold the family jewels to cover the rest. I was tempted to tell him that he had twenty similarly impressive cars back home in Surrey, but I decided to let him enjoy himself for a while longer.

"I trust you had a safe journey and there were no bodies to be found in the sleeping compartment of your train." Todd said this with a playful smile on his face, which soon faded. "Oh, my goodness. Please tell me I'm wrong."

Grandfather finally stopped cooing and skipping about and turned to look at his employee at last. "Of course there weren't any murders on the train… Although I must confess that, if you drove here hoping to meet Lord Monroe, you're out of luck."

"I'm sorry to hear that, m'lord." Todd grimaced as he flicked a stray hair into place on his well-coiffed parting. "I have to drive to the airport at Campo di Marte, but I'll be back before very long. I've made all the necessary arrangements as you requested, sir."

"Excellent!" Grandfather was scheming again, and though he was not an unhinged vigilante with only a loose grasp of morality, I could see that he had more in common with the dead man than he would ever admit. "We shall see you shortly."

I believe that a pair of winks were exchanged, and then it was time to return to the castle and our stop-start investigation.

"Now that you've secured the use of an expensive and impractical motorcar for our time here," I teasingly began, "what can we do to discover who killed your former acquaintance?"

"Come, come, Christopher, you surely realise that there are any number of tasks that we must complete. We have barely started."

In anyone else, I would have taken this for bluster while he thought up a better answer. I knew, however, that my grandfather's brain held a constantly evolving casebook of facts, procedures and strategies. Like a good racing driver, he knew not just his next move, but the three after that and was constantly making adjustments in order to predict the unpredictable. Or, in other words, he knew what we needed to do next.

"So, what will it be?" I pushed. "Should we interview Miss Mountstephen a little more insistently? After all, we don't know where she was at the time of the killing. Or perhaps we should talk to some of the bilingual natives about life under Lord Monroe's rule. Young Agente Attilio may prove to be a helpful ally."

"Those are good suggestions, but I have another."

As the dear old fellow lives to be mysterious, he did not simply tell me what this was. He stalked ahead of us dramatically. If Delilah had been capable of doing so, I'm sure she would have rolled her eyes and said, *Gosh, what a ham!* She was in a particularly cynical mood that day.

Back through the gatehouse, under the arches, and to the ballroom we went. Eva's office was empty, and so we nipped through it to reach the room that I had rightly predicted would turn out to be Lord Monroe's study.

"Just what we need!" Grandfather was rubbing his hands together again. He'd been doing that a lot since we left England. Europeans are famous for their gesturing, so perhaps he was getting into the spirit of our new home. Or perhaps there was something in the water that makes one more expressive. Great snakes! Would I turn into such a person myself?

The room looked as though the local population of wild boars had been given free rein to thunder through it. Though it would once have been a fine place to write one's memoirs or perhaps compose a novel or two, the study was covered with loose papers, abandoned books and upturned furniture. The only overture to orderliness was the well-organised desk in the centre of the maelstrom. All it held was a marbled fountain pen, a pot of ink and a stack of clean paper. I had to wonder whether someone had cleared everything else onto the floor.

"Was he a messy sort of person when you knew him, Grandfather?"

"Not at all." He stooped to pick up a document, which he soon dropped back into place. "He was an impeccable dresser, and his house was a thing of beauty, but then he had servants to do everything for him back then. From what we've seen, he didn't employ many staff here at Montegufoni."

I decided to follow his lead and picked my way through the chaos as best I could. "I noticed that myself. What do you think it says about the man he became?"

I heard shuffling and a book thudding down onto the desk before Grandfather replied. "It suggests that either he was poorer than might be expected for a man of his standing, or he was just as miserly as might be expected for a man of his standing."

"You're of a similar standing. Would you describe yourself as a miser?" I turned around to see his reaction. I can't deny that I enjoy piquing him from time to time.

"I believe you know the answer to that question, Christopher. While I am generous to my staff, my family and, admittedly myself, many rich people hold on to their wealth by pinching pennies and begrudging anyone else a share of it. I once knew an earl who did without a head of household to organise the finances of his grand estate, as he insisted on overseeing every shilling and pound."

"Look here! This is interesting," I said, after his lecture had reached its natural conclusion. "It's a demand for payment totalling ten thousand lire from a company in Rome."

I held up the piece of paper I'd found, but he was not convinced. "Remember, Christopher, ten thousand lire is approximately a hundred pounds. That may seem like a lot of money but, as we know, Renwick paid many skilled workmen to renovate this building. It's hardly surprising he would have received such bills."

Tens of thousands of any currency sounded like a lot to me – easily enough to make someone push an old man from a tower – but I accepted that I was mistaken and kept searching through the debris. I came to realise that the papers were not quite so disorganised as I had believed. They were in chronological order, in lines from one frescoed wall to the other. This didn't help me a great deal, as I was uncertain what we needed to find, but it made me appreciate once more just what a complex character the recently deceased owner of Montegufoni had been.

"Have you seen anything from a solicitor, perhaps?" Grandfather put to me. "Based on my knowledge of other romance languages, the Italian word for it will be something along the lines of 'avocat'."

"I can't say I have." I was distracted by a letter that had been scrawled in a messy English hand and couldn't help but laugh at some of the colourful phrases it contained. "What are the chances that Markland Starkie, the man to whom Lord Monroe sold the neighbouring property, is the killer? He really doesn't sound very fond of him."

Grandfather didn't look up this time. "You mean the chap who has spent years firing arrows in this direction, despite the fact that it is scientifically impossible for such a projectile to travel anywhere near that distance?"

"That's the one."

"Does that sound like the act of a killer? To me, it suggests he wishes to express his anger without getting into trouble with the police. We must also consider the fact that, judging by the lack of any serious wounds on Renwick's body aside from the impact of the fall, it is likely that he willingly climbed the tower with his assailant."

I considered this for a moment before disagreeing with him. "That's not true. Lord Monroe might have been up there already when the killer arrived."

"He might have been, but if that is the case, what was he doing?"

I couldn't answer this, but it did remind me of a concern I'd had for some time. "Aren't you at all worried that we're so low on suspects? We have this huge echoing castle and, when the locals are away in the fields, there's hardly anyone here. For the moment, we've really only identified the victim's daughter and secretary as potential killers. I miss the days when suspects would kindly assemble in one location *before* the body was found."

He peered over his shoulder at me. "You are an odd young man, Christopher Prentiss. And besides, we can't rule out the locals just because we don't speak the same language."

"Well I can't say that would be very satisfying." I put the threatening letter back where I'd found it. "Imagine if we went to the trouble of interviewing all the likely culprits only to find out that someone we'd barely considered was to blame. Or imagine it was the postman or the grandmother out in the courtyard. Ooh! Perhaps she and Renwick were lovers, and he broke her heart."

He sighed and straightened up from his search. "If there is one person who I can categorically assure you will not turn out to be the killer, it is Signora Lombardo with the spanner and the greasy overalls."

I was impressed that he could make this statement so confidently. "Gosh, how can you be sure?"

I got four whole tuts this time. Four! "Because she was standing a few yards away from us when we watched him fall."

I admit I had overlooked this small but significant fact in the race to think of someone – anyone – to blame for the killing. "You may have a point. But she could have got one of her grandsons to do it."

"That is true…"

I thought he might continue the speculation, but he returned to his search instead. The silence endured for so long that my ears became attuned to the sound of leaves rubbing against the shuttered windows outside, and the swallows, swifts or house martins (I've never been good at identifying birds) as they went swooping around the building like Allied aeroplanes at the Battle of Istrana.

"Wait one moment!" Grandfather suddenly declared, and I looked over at him with great anticipation. "Actually, no. That wouldn't make a jot of sense."

We kept searching and reading, slowly making our way across the room one page at a time.

"Isn't it possible…" I considered aloud before I too abandoned an unlikely solution. The regular payments Lord Monroe had made to the local police were most likely speeding fines or municipal fees. "Actually, never mind."

Grandfather had reached the desk and pulled the chair back to rifle through the drawers. There were plenty to examine. The rather out-of-place piece of furniture looked as though it had once belonged in a textile factory.

"I refuse to be downhearted prematurely when, as I have already said, there are still many avenues open to us. However, I don't mind admitting that I had expected to find something more substantial in Renwick's personal papers. All I've seen so far are letters from supporters back home in London, receipts for the works on the castle, and a curious chain of correspondence that he maintained for several years with a lady in Nuneaton, who was under the impression that they would one day get married."

I knelt down to read the tightly scrawling handwriting of the next letter. "Then how about a missive from last year in which the elder son, Dashwood, threatens Lord Monroe's life unless he pays off his debts and reverses the changes that were made to his will?"

CHAPTER TEN

To assess the information we'd gained from our trip to the dead man's office, we assembled our small collection of anglophone subjects in Grandfather's long sitting room. Though, now that I think of it, I'm not sure that two people count as a collection.

"I swear that I spoke to Dashwood himself minutes after his father died," Eva promised us and became so nervous in the process that Grandfather had to set her mind at ease.

"I don't doubt you for one moment." He even stopped loitering enigmatically between the two young women who were sitting on the ornate sofas and came to perch next to her. "But please describe exactly what happened so that we have everything clear."

Coralie didn't seem interested in any of this. She was smoking a long cigarette in an even longer cigarette holder and kept blowing the fumes over in my direction and then tittering as if she'd been terribly coquettish. It was marginally better than her trying to eat me.

Avoiding the bitter smoke, Eva took a deep breath and tried to recount the call she had made to Coralie's little brother. "I called the operator, and she connected me to Arezzo 342. I only waited a few moments before Dashwood himself answered the telephone and I told him the bad news."

"How did he bear it?" I asked, though, even if he'd broken down and sobbed, he might well have been acting.

She could look quite avian at times. Her head flicked back and forth quizzically between my grandfather and me before she turned it to one side to consider the question. "He isn't the expressive type, if that's what you mean. He fell quiet for perhaps ten seconds and, when he spoke again, there was a certain hoarseness to his voice. It made me wonder whether he felt the loss more deeply than he would ever admit."

Grandfather stamped his authority on the discussion once more. "And how did he get along with his father in general? We understand that there was some degree of antagonism between them."

Coralie let out a brief laugh before putting a hand to her bright red lips. "Oh, I am sorry. I didn't mean to take the matter lightly. The fact is that Daddy and Dashwood fought like angry puppies. They always had. Even before Mummy died and we left Britain."

"Had they argued recently?" Grandfather asked in reply, but Coralie just shrugged and leant back on the sofa to stare at her nails. This was evidently not the answer he needed, so he turned to Eva instead.

"Not very recently. You see, Dashwood hasn't set foot in Montegufoni for the best part of a year." She hesitated, and I could tell that she was reluctant to speak ill of the family. "And the reason for that was… Well, he had begged his father for money, but Renwick refused. Dashwood said he was in dire straits, and if he couldn't pay his creditors, he didn't know what would happen to him."

Grandfather didn't respond immediately. Personally, I was tempted to say what a beast Lord Monroe was for not helping his son, but my wise mentor kept his opinions to himself. "Do you know why Renwick wouldn't give him the money?"

Eva looked over at her de facto employer, apparently unwilling to answer when there was someone more qualified to do so.

"Don't ask me," Coralie replied. "I stay well clear of my loathsome baby brother. He was born an unfeeling brute, and he has remained one. The last time I saw him, he tried to borrow money from me and called me a very unpleasant name when I declined. Daddy and I rarely talked about him, but I think it's safe to say that he'd grown tired of being Dashwood's piggy bank."

Why this would be the moment she turned to wink at me, I can't say. I may not be the skinniest boy in the world, but I'm no piggy (any more).

"Does either of you know how Dashwood spent his money?" Grandfather persevered. "I thought I'd understood that Renwick provided well for his children when they came to live in Italy."

"He did, but even Daddy couldn't afford to fund Dash's lavish existence. He spends a fortune on wine, women and something you might get arrested for using in public."

I scratched my head trying to work out what she meant, so it was lucky that my grandfather was a little worldlier than I.

"You mean dope? The boy is a drug fiend?"

Coralie wasn't the type to be scandalised, but even she couldn't find anything nice to say about her brother. "I don't know about that, but he's certainly a fiend of some description. He spends all his time with nasty people in nasty places and picks up nasty habits. As you've probably worked out, I'm no great admirer of his."

"And nor was his father by the end." Eva was apparently more comfortable criticising our new suspect now that Coralie had taken a swing at him. "For the last twelve months, Renwick spent much of his time complaining about his son's disloyalty. He really couldn't understand what motivated Dashwood to threaten him. While they might have had their differences, there was no excuse to resort to intimidation."

As interesting as this was, it rather seemed to miss the point, and so I decided to voice the unspoken question. "We've established that he's something of a rotter but, didn't you say his house is three hours away? Regardless of how he felt about his father, if he was at home at the time of the murder, he clearly wasn't responsible."

Coralie had nothing to add and deferred to the capable secretary.

"That's right. Arezzo is the best part of a hundred kilometres from here."

I was tempted to ask how many miles that was, but I decided to hide my ignorance.

"A little over sixty miles then." Good old Grandfather! "And you're certain you spoke to *Dashwood* on the telephone? It couldn't have been someone imitating him?"

We all looked at Eva, who trembled as she considered the question. "I don't see how it could—"

She was interrupted by the sound of laughter from the doorway behind us, and I turned to see… someone I didn't recognise.

"Yes, I was the one Eva telephoned." A dashing man with dark features walked slowly into the room. "And before you ask, I was at home in my villa in Arezzo when she called. I set off soon after and have been driving ever since." The man with dark hair and a prominent brow swept into the room, undoing the cape around his neck as he came closer. "I'm sure you would all love me to be guilty, but I'm afraid there is no way I could have murdered my father."

CHAPTER ELEVEN

Oh, I thought, *so this is Dashwood Monroe.*

"What a pleasure it is to see you, sis," he said with a grimace as he scanned our faces one by one. "And under *such* happy circumstances. Have you read the will yet? How much will I get?"

Previously confident Coralie seemed unsure of herself for the first time. She crossed her hands in her lap and wouldn't look at her brother directly.

"I don't know anything about it," she said in a weak voice, and I wondered just how influential a figure this disruptive new arrival would turn out to be. "But from everything that Daddy told me, as the oldest child, I will be the one to inherit the majority of his wealth."

"Daddy?" he replied in a mocking tone. "Please, Coralie, don't pretend you liked him any more than I did. The man was quite intolerable."

She shot to her feet, her teeth gritted as she offered a retort. "But I did tolerate him, didn't I? While you and Fletcher swanned off to live your lives, I stayed close at hand. I dealt with the old coot and put up with his foibles and fancies whenever he summoned me. I was the one he called for a roast-chicken dinner whenever his lackeys and acolytes grew tired of him."

"Roast chicken?" I asked because, let's be honest, that would be the key to solving the case.

"That was the only thing that Renwick ate." Until now, Eva had been silently observing the scene. She showed no fear of Dashwood, as I would have expected if he really was the debauchee that everyone claimed. "He never explained why, but he lived on a diet of red wine, cups of tea and roast chicken. He made Signora Acciaioli cook him one every morning, and he would eat it, from beak to behind, leaving only the bones and scraps."

"I think we're getting away from the point," Grandfather interposed.

The conceited, agitated attitude that Dashwood had already displayed came to the fore. "That may be true, but who are you to say it?"

"My name…" Inevitably, Grandfather rose from the sofa to deliver this momentous line "… is Lord Edgington, former superintendent of

Scotland Yard. Perhaps you've heard of me?"

The middle child froze for three seconds and then burst out laughing. "Oh, how wonderful! Father's old carousing partner arrived at the perfect time."

"More than you know," I muttered, though if the facts of the case were wrong and he did turn out to be the killer, he knew full well when we had got there.

"I was no one's carousing partner," Grandfather objected, pulling on his grey waistcoat rather primly – he'd loosened his cravat at some point as even he had begun to find the heat oppressive. "When I knew your father, I was already a senior officer in the Metropolitan Police."

"Who used to run around town with him whilst he caroused." Dashwood waved a hand dismissively in his direction. "Now, as you said yourself, we're rather getting away from the point."

"Heaven forbid." His sister injected no small amount of sarcasm in this sentence and fell back onto the sofa, apparently no longer so intimidated by her beastly brother. Delilah was equally unhappy with the argument and went to sit under a chest of drawers, far away from the bickering.

When a modicum of calm had returned, Dashwood spoke again. "Did Father keep a copy of the will here in the castle?"

"It's clear what your priorities are," Coralie sniffed.

"Oh, please, dear sister. I hoped you'd finished your selfless act. I admit that I have not come to offer platitudes. I am driven purely by self-interest, and the only interaction I wish to have with our family from this point forward is to be handed a cheque for my stake in Father's estate so that I can clear off."

"At least you're honest, which is something we haven't always been able to say about you."

It finally looked as though her words had penetrated Dashwood's thick skin. "My question was for the lovely Eva, not you." He turned to look at the secretary. "So, my dear? Did Father keep a copy of his will here at Montegufoni?"

She looked straight at him, and I wondered how well the two knew each other. "I don't believe he did. I'm aware that he had it altered last year, but I know little else about it."

"Uncle Matthew will be able to clear everything up if we visit his office in Florence," Coralie commented in an absent-minded, almost dreamy manner.

As much as I took Eva Mountstephen for a nice sort of person, and my initial impression of Dashwood Monroe was that he was a rat made human, I was yet to decide what I thought of the presumed heir to il Castello di Montegufoni. Coralie appeared to adapt her personality depending on the context in which she found herself.

"Did Renwick have a brother?" Grandfather's right eyebrow rose in surprise. He had impressive dexterity in that part of his face. I'd long attempted to train the muscles in my forehead to convey a wider range of emotions, but to no avail.

"He's not really our uncle," Dashwood clarified. "But Father was always in one form of trouble or another. We saw his solicitor so often he became part of the family."

"Did he move out to Italy at the same time as Lord Monroe?" I asked.

Dashwood let out a weary breath and landed in an armchair with the open door to the garden behind him so that, in an instant, he transformed into a silhouette. "More or less. You may not know this if he was dead when you got here, but Father had a way with people. Several easily led Brits followed him out here over the years. The delightful Markland Starkie, who owns the house on the opposite hill. Father Laurence. A few swiftly disappointed widows who hoped to snag themselves a rich husband. Our dear father was as much of a draw to foreign visitors as Michelangelo's David in the Galleria dell'Accademia."

Grandfather had heard enough and decided to steer the conversation back to the matter we needed to discuss. "While I have the three of you here, I think it would be an appropriate moment to consider the circumstances of your father's death."

I noticed that Dashwood had expressed no interest in who killed Lord Monroe or even the precise details of how he died. Did this mean that Eva had told him on the telephone? Or did he already know somehow? There was nothing to say he wasn't working with an accomplice.

I continued to study his dark outline as the beams of sunlight penetrated the portal behind him. When he didn't respond to Grandfather's carefully phrased comment, his sister took over.

"I have already told you what I know. I didn't kill him, and I can't tell you who did."

"Has nothing occurred to you since this afternoon?" This was a little speculative by Grandfather's standards. I imagine he was testing the waters to see who would react.

When Coralie could only produce a nonchalant shrug, Eva once more gave herself permission to speak. "There is one possibility we haven't considered." She was hesitant again but seemed more afraid of speaking out of turn than igniting the wrath of her dead employer's unstable son. "Renwick didn't always make friends here."

"That's a euphemism if ever I've heard one." Dashwood audibly snorted then. "Which of Father's many enemies do you have in mind?"

Eva's eyes shifted to the shadowy presence for a moment and then back to my grandfather. "Ispettore Stefani."

This merited a sharp draw of breath from Dashwood. "Oh, yes. He's certainly capable of killing a man."

"He was here earlier," Eva continued. "He spent two minutes looking at the body and decided that it was an accident. He didn't even go up the tower to see where Renwick had been when he fell."

Coralie had turned away and wouldn't say anything. In the absence of her response, an uncomfortable silence lingered like mist in the room.

"Who is this Stefani?" Grandfather asked.

"He's a police inspector who took a special interest in our father." Dashwood sounded quite amused.

"I see." Grandfather might have understood this, but I didn't.

With nothing to lose, I revealed a small fact that I hoped would prompt some degree of explanation. "We looked in Lord Monroe's office a short time ago and found evidence of a regular payment he had been making to the local *Carabinieri*."

"Did we?" Grandfather was more surprised than anyone else.

"I didn't mention it because I doubted it would be important."

"That was Stefani," Eva explained. "He was blackmailing Renwick. He accused him of all sorts of things – of being a communist and working against the Italian state. He even attacked him once. He gave him a black eye right on the steps of the castle. I think the main problem he had with us was that we were foreigners living in his country."

I finally cottoned on to what they meant. I followed international events enough to have heard that Italy was run by the *Fascisti*, and though I didn't know a great deal about their politics or governance, they clearly weren't peace-loving, easy-going sorts. I remember reading that many of their political rivals had disappeared or been murdered and that they made use of violent mobs to control and intimidate in the name of their all-powerful leader.

"I can't say whether anything Stefani did was directly sanctioned by his superiors." Eva looked out of the window, her voice cold and cautious. "But Renwick was so outspoken that he made things difficult for himself. Whenever Stefani rolled through the village in his black Alfa Romeo, Renwick would shout and make rude gestures. He despised the changes he saw in his time living in this country and claimed that he would not stand idly by while basic human values were eroded."

"So that was why a police officer punched him," Grandfather muttered, his hands clasped together in his lap. "It is a cautionary tale, but if this started some years ago, is there any reason to believe it would have come to a head now?"

Eva turned back to look at him with a frown. "No, I don't believe so. I hadn't seen Stefani for months until today. And despite his posturing, Renwick came to see that it would do him no good to clash with a man like that. He paid the bribe that was demanded and no longer waved his fists quite so violently as before."

"It's more than a cautionary tale," Dashwood announced, having gone without saying anything for some time. "It's a nightmare come true." He shook his head, and though it was too bright to make out his expression, I had the feeling he was moved by the story of his father's defiance. I had to wonder whether he'd had similar run-ins with men like Inspector Stefani.

Coralie showed no sign of what she was thinking as she watched her morose brother, whereas Eva maintained a sullen expression whenever Dashwood spoke.

"I must apologise, Lord Edgington. I have a tendency to speak without thinking and act on impulse. If there's even a chance that Stefani is to blame for Father's death, then I would like to know. I may not agree with the Italian government for many reasons, but I believe that even they would draw the line at the murder of a British citizen on their soil. I will do whatever I can to help your investigation."

The two women seemed to synchronise their reactions at this

moment. They both pouted, though Eva looked sympathetic to Dashwood's comment, whereas Coralie had turned even more dubious.

"I owe you an apology too, sister." He sat forward so that his face broke through the wall of light, and we could see that he was serious. "You know that I love to shock and offend but today is no easier for me than it is for you. I will try to hold my tongue if you can."

"Well, that's jolly good." Although Grandfather spoke these words, nothing in his voice or demeanour suggested that he was taken in by the hellraiser's speech. "Now, if I only knew what to ask you, I believe we could have a civil discussion."

CHAPTER TWELVE

Therein lay our problem. Before long, all three of Renwick Monroe's children would have assembled, but we were no closer to knowing who had killed their father than we had been when he fell from the tower.

I could reel off the names of the people who might have held a grudge against the eccentric lord (the dead one, not my grandfather) but what evidence had we found to point to one of them over the others? There was a priest hanging about the place somewhere, not to mention the gaggle of locals out in the fields or scattered around the castle of whom we knew little, but beyond the simple blunt question, *Did you murder Lord Monroe?* what could we ask them?

We listened to the conversation between the visibly subdued Dashwood, his sister Coralie and their father's meek secretary, but there was no longer any spark or conflict that might send our investigation off in a new direction. When the presumptive heir but one to Montegufoni finally made his excuses and announced that he would retire to his room, we left too.

"There's one thing I should have already done," Grandfather informed me in the Court of the Duke of Athens outside his suite of rooms. "I know that you examined the tower when the perpetrator escaped, but I would like to take a look myself."

I waved him away to show that I did not object, and he walked ahead of me to the stairs at the rear of the tower. I'd often noticed my grandfather's innate sense of direction. Although he was in what many would describe as his twilight years, his faculties were as strong as I'd ever known them. That being said, neither of us were too fond of stairs.

The stone steps spiralled up past landings with doors leading off, and we met the cook Signora Acciaioli halfway up. She was carrying trays of food, but it was too dark to see much of what they held. I couldn't imagine the main kitchen being up there, so I assumed her own apartment was behind one of the doors. She nodded politely to my grandfather and waved at me, and then we continued our trip to the top.

Even two years earlier – when I had the freedom to spend half my life trapped within a book and was still fighting off puppy fat –

Grandfather would have reached the platform from which Lord Monroe had fallen while I was still huffing and puffing my way up there, but not now. I got there a few steps ahead of him and immediately noticed a difference from what I'd seen that morning.

"This ladder was leaning against the far wall earlier," I told him, pointing at the unsteady wooden steps that were positioned to lean through the hole in the ceiling above us. They now gave access to the very top of the tower, which housed the bell and a lion-shaped weathervane that looked proudly across the Tuscan landscape.

"Are you certain?"

"Quite. But why would anyone have moved it?"

"Perhaps the real question is why wasn't it there in the first place?"

In an attempt to answer this, we walked over to the corner where the ladder had previously stood. The tower was crenellated on two levels, and looking down over the edge gave me a terrible feeling of vertigo. Grandfather must have noticed how dizzy I'd become. He seized my arm and, looking around from the other side of the wall, said, "I think we'll settle for one falling body today. Thank you, Christopher."

I straightened up and pushed my back against the wall, which is when I realised that another change had taken place. "There was a flat piece of metal on the floor here, too. Someone's taken it."

"Perhaps one of the officers removed it," he replied without a great deal of conviction.

"Eva said that the inspector didn't come up here."

"Yes, but two detectives were sent. Perhaps Stefani stayed downstairs while his colleague examined the scene of the crime."

I couldn't see why they would have removed a bit of scrap metal, but I didn't argue.

Grandfather walked to the centre of the concrete square upon which we stood. There was a wooden box there which he lifted up to reveal the workings of what I could only assume was a clock. There were cogs turning merrily and a weight slowly dropping lower to measure the time.

"Or perhaps whoever is in charge of this clock simply came here to wind it and tidied up after the police had finished. Could the piece of metal you saw have been a tool of some description?"

With the end of one gloved index finger, he pointed to a square hole at the top of the mechanism. I imagine he was right in his silent implication that this was where a simple key could be inserted to wind it up, but I couldn't imagine how the metal I had seen would have fitted that task.

"It was flat," I told him and even as I said the words, I began to doubt myself. Memory is so fickle; I think that's why we devote much of our lives defining past experiences so as not to lose them entirely. "I'm sure it was flat and quite thin, with a hole at one end, if I'm not mistaken."

"How curious," Grandfather said, but he had nothing more useful to add than this.

I went back to the spot where Renwick Monroe had presumably taken his penultimate or so breath. I didn't make the mistake of sticking my head over the parapet, but I glanced down at a group of people amassing in the courtyard. There was still a pile of rubble in one corner by the entrance that led down to the road, but the Lombardo family's motor parts had been moved clear, and there was no sign of the chickens just then.

In their place, tables had been laid out in a line and there was a sizeable gathering forming. Children dressed in smart outfits ran around after one another, and a large group holding what looked from up there to be brass instruments talked amongst themselves. They didn't hold my attention long as, off in the distance, winding its way down the road to us, I spied a large black vehicle with two others following just behind.

"Grandfather!" I almost squealed with excitement – though that still doesn't make me a piggy. "Todd is back and, what a surprise, it seems he's brought some friends with him."

He was looking at the bell above his head and didn't respond as I ran back to the open staircase in the floor and shot down it. I swiftly reached the ground floor before getting lost in the maze of passages that led to the courtyard. By the time I was back at the gatehouse, several familiar figures were climbing the stairs to the castle.

That forward-thinking fellow Todd was leading the way and, just behind him, our cook Henrietta was carrying a large hamper. Massive Dorie, the weight-lifting pickpocket turned more-or-less honest maid, had a packing case on either shoulder, and our hall boy Timothy brought up the rear.

"I can't tell you how happy I am to see you," I told them one after the other, so that I sounded like an unimaginative parrot.

"It's lovely to be here," Henrietta replied very formally, and she looked past me at the building beyond.

"Bleedin' 'ot, though," Dorie chimed with some effort before motioning to her load. "Where d'ya want these?"

As strange as he sometimes was, and as much as he was always desperate to bring (for reasons he has never fully clarified) far too many servants with him wherever we go, I could overlook my grandfather's eccentricities because just seeing that wonderful gaggle of people made me feel like I was home again. My only disappointment was that there were only four of them.

"There's no Halfpenny?" I asked, despite the fact that our head footman was a terrible worrier and often a bigger snob than my grandfather.

Todd frowned before explaining. "He says he might join us later in the year if he gets too lonely. He decided that his back wasn't up to the flight here from Croydon."

"It's my back people should worry about," Dorie complained as she plonked the cases on the ground before the archway. "I had to load everything on the plane myself because the porters said our bags were too heavy for them to shift."

"What about Alice and Driscoll? I'm amazed that Grandfather didn't bring his gardener along to help identify all the exotic plants here."

"I heard that, Christopher." Grandfather put his hand on my shoulder and squeezed. "As it happens Alice is expecting their first child, and Driscoll couldn't be happier."

"Then neither could I." I tried not to show the faintest flicker of pain at this revelation as Alice, our lovely Irish maid, was the first woman (close to me in age at least) with whom I'd fallen in love. The fact that she had settled down on her nest showed just how far behind I was. Twenty years old without a hand to hold or pretty cheek to kiss! What a disappointment I must be to my parents.

Todd was already pulling one of the huge cases through to the courtyard, and so I took the hamper from Henrietta and followed along.

"I hope Lord Edgington has been coping in my absence," our

factotum whispered to me with a grin on his bright face. I do believe he'd already caught the sun whereas, however long our voyage around Europe would last, I would do everything in my power to avoid it.

"He's doing very well," I assured him quite honestly. "On balance, I would say that our time here has been less eccentric and largely safer than the life he's used to back home." On at least one score, it turned out I had spoken too soon.

As the others arrived, the group of men standing in formation under the three arches opposite our own raised their instruments to their lips and began to play. To accompany them, a small choir of children sang a song in thickly accented English. I was surprised to discover that I knew it rather well.

> **"God save our gracious King!**
> **Long live our noble King!**
> **God save the King!"**

So that was unexpected.

CHAPTER THIRTEEN

I recognised a few of the faces there. Attilio Lombardo, the young constable or what have you, was puffing away at a French horn. His brother Guido was standing in a line of four hardworking trumpeters and, the only person there who was not dressed in the band's uniform, Father Laurence was banging a military drum that he wore on a strap around his neck.

When the national anthem had finished, a rotund, out-of-breath fellow trapped within a tuba stepped forward to say, "Ladies and gentlemen, the Philharmonic Society of Montegufoni."

There was some polite applause from the people sitting at the tables, and I thought that this would be the beginning of a longer concert. I was wrong.

Guido Lombardo shouted, "*A tavola*!" which I took to mean, *Food's served,* as everyone ran over to the table where Signora Acciaioli had laid out enough food to feed an orchestra, let alone the Philharmonic Society of a small village.

"Was all that for our benefit?" Grandfather asked the constable when he came over to greet us.

"How do you mean?" he replied in a bemused tone, as though he couldn't see what possible connection the song would have to us.

"'God Save the King' timed to coincide with the arrival of a party which has just flown here from England. Are you saying it was a coincidence?" I believe that Grandfather was a little amazed.

"No, no," the constable replied with a chuckle in his throat. "We play this every afternoon at the same time. Now, sorry, but I want cucumber sandwiches. They disappear too fast."

Todd, my grandfather, little Timothy and I stared uncertainly after the officer as he hurried back across the courtyard to find a plate.

I must say that it was a welcoming atmosphere. We left the bags for the time being, as the Lombardo brothers' grandmother beckoned us over to get some food of our own. I can't imagine what she was chattering about as she handed us each a plate, but she had a lot to say for herself.

A small queue had formed ahead of me and, when I got to the front of it, I realised that I would not be treated to a selection of new flavours and dishes. There were piles of cucumber, cheese and ham sandwiches cut into triangles. A little further on, there were buns, scones, a truly gigantic Victoria sponge, Battenburg and strawberry tarts. That's right, the locals of Montegufoni were indulging in a spot of afternoon tea.

It was just then that Guido appeared with a large samovar on a trolley that he pushed out of the ballroom we'd seen earlier. There were cheers at this development and disconnected calls of "One lump or two?" and "A dash of milk for me, please," rang out around the courtyard.

"Weren't you saying this place is less eccentric than our life at home?" Todd whispered so as not to upset anyone.

"Yes, but…" Unable to answer at first, partly because I had a whole sandwich in my mouth, but also because I didn't know how to respond, I looked around the crowd. "The difference here is that the source of all this oddness was pushed from the top of the tower this afternoon. I believe that much of this bizarre behaviour began at Lord Monroe's insistence, and he's gone now."

Now that almost everyone had found a place at a table, I could see them more clearly. I hadn't taken much notice of the two boys I'd seen chasing after the men on their way to the fields at lunchtime, but I realised that both of them had thick black eyebrows that ran almost the whole width of their foreheads. And that wasn't all.

There were three boys sitting next to the maker of this feast. Signora Acciaioli was keeping the children in order and, as they complained or complied with her demands, I noticed their distinctive eyebrows and the formal clothes they wore. With their tiny suits and waistcoats, it looked as though they'd been dressed by a Savile Row tailor.

"My goodness," I said far more loudly than I'd intended, so that my grandfather heard and leaned around Dorie to see what was wrong. "He's left miniature versions of himself behind."

To the irritation of his staff, who assumed that he was jumping the queue, Grandfather stepped out of line and marvelled at the scene before us. I counted at least five children who were the spit and image of Lord Monroe. The oldest was around twelve and the youngest a particularly hairy baby who was being dandled on his mother's knee. Perhaps strangest of all, this brood appeared to belong to at least three different women.

"What a swine!" someone said at an opportune moment, but it wasn't my grandfather.

"I beg to differ! You're a swine," a softer voice declared, and I immediately recalled Lord Monroe's dying words.

"Swine! Swine!" another of the signora's children joyfully shouted. He couldn't have been more than three, and I doubted he knew what he was saying. "Cheery pip! Toodle-oo!"

"Grandfather, what was your old acquaintance trying to do here?"

He had his hand to his mouth and looked just as shocked by what we had discovered as I was. "It's hard to say. Perhaps he felt homesick and wanted to maintain some British traditions."

"It's not just the afternoon tea and the national anthem," I felt I had to remind him, and before I could go any further, Todd worked out what I was thinking.

"Are you saying he's created a colony of children in his mould?"

"That sounds rather too dramatic, yet it's not even the worst part of it." Grandfather put one hand on the table to steady himself as Dorie and Henrietta ignored us to load their plates with food. "I always knew that Renwick was a charmer, but it seems he must have charmed every war widow and eligible lady going. I'm sure you know what that means."

I did, but I didn't have it in me to utter the words. Being a discreet, well-mannered fellow, neither did Todd, and so Grandfather continued.

"It means that every last man and woman here is a suspect. Imagine all the brothers, fathers, jilted boyfriends and perhaps even husbands whom Renwick upset. And then there are the women themselves, not to mention the possibility that a vengeful son or daughter resented being part of this army of replica Renwicks."

"We'll never be able to solve this." These sad words crept limply from my mouth. "We're finally beaten."

It was just then that one of the trombonists finished his cakes and decided to entertain the crowd with a jolly waltz. Other musicians stood up to join him and, by the end of the first measure of music, a few young men had found partners, and they were dancing through the free spaces of the courtyard.

As I watched the children launch themselves away from their parents to go wild together, I had the unsettling feeling that this was not just their everyday, after-work meal; it was a celebration. The blood had dried where Renwick Monroe's head had crashed against the paving stones, but the stain was still there and, all around it, his neighbours were having precisely one whale of a time.

Monroe had bought the homes out from under a whole community of people. Even if he'd been generous about the timing, he'd still expected many of them to up sticks and leave. Any number of locals could have hated him for it, and that was before the honey-mouthed lecher seduced who knows how many of the women.

One person who looked less than thrilled by the party was the priest, Father Laurence, who skulked in one sombrous corner. He wore something of a scowl, and I felt that he was watching us as I was him. Meanwhile, though he was still very much part of the cheerful action as he served cups of tea to our companions, Guido Lombardo could not maintain a smile. His eyes darted about the scene, occasionally landing on Grandfather, or the tower, but always returning to Signora Acciaioli, the fair-faced, middle-aged cook whose children now circled her table in an endless run. His, and then my, vision strayed to the archway that led to the Court of the Duke of Athens, through which Coralie and Dashwood Monroe had just appeared.

As bad as things felt just then, everything was about to get worse. At almost the same moment that a figure I didn't recognise arrived at the castle from the front entrance, Coralie raised her voice to get everyone's attention.

"Ladies and gentlemen." She cleared her throat, and the music swiftly died. "Ladies and gentlemen, if you could look this way… I know that some of you may not understand me, but I'm sure your friends and family will translate. It certainly never stopped Daddy from blathering on at you."

There were a few half-hearted laughs, but she wasn't there to entertain and ploughed straight on with what she wanted to tell them. "I don't wish to interrupt your evening, but I do have an announcement to make. I'm sure you're all terribly sad about the passing of my father, as I certainly am. But there is no going back, and it seems very likely that I will be the new custodian of Montegufoni."

She took a deep breath then, so perhaps she realised the gravity of her announcement. "I promise to be a benevolent and fair mistress of this wonderful old building, and I already have many plans. With that in mind, I will require all remaining tenants to leave the castle by the end of the year. Father was far too lenient, and to be frank, this unfortunate situation has gone on long enough. Thank you for your time."

CHAPTER FOURTEEN

There was a collective groan as she finished speaking, and the same thing happened ten seconds later when the message had been translated for those who didn't understand.

"Coralie, what were you thinking?" a voice cut through the noise and the man I had noticed at the far end of the courtyard strode forward. "No matter what has happened to Father, you can't throw these good people onto the streets."

"Fletcher!" the already slightly despotic ruler replied on seeing the man who it took approximately one per cent of my experience as a detective to work out was her younger brother. "Thank goodness you're here."

He was a less swarthy and devilish version of Dashwood. He did not wear an eighteenth-century highwayman's cloak, for one thing. In fact, he was dressed far more humbly than his brother, in simple slacks and a Bengal stripe shirt. He had the same dark features and blue eyes as his father, but I did have to wonder whether he and Dashwood plucked their brows to reduce the family likeness. Fletcher's face was in general less angular and severe than his siblings'. It was easy to imagine that he was the nice one in the family, even if he hadn't just launched into an impassioned defence of the downtrodden locals.

"It's nice to see you too," I heard him say as he reached his sister.

Grandfather abandoned the buffet table in order to meet the (as far as we were aware) final Monroe boy. The problem that no one talks about when becoming a detective's apprentice is the irregular and frequently curtailed mealtimes. I would not be beaten though and quickly filled my plate before I missed out on the conversation.

"The great trio of Monroes back together, eh?" Dashwood said, and it was hard to know whether he was pleased with this development.

It was at this moment that Eva Mountstephen came running out of the ballroom. She froze a few steps outside it and looked across at us. I could tell that it required great composure to slow herself down as she picked her way around marauding infants and grumbling adults.

"Hello, Eva." Fletcher said nothing more for a short while. He stared at the young woman and clearly found her quite lovely. I'd rarely met a man whose feelings were so transparent – and I know my brother.

"Hello Fletcher. I wasn't sure you'd received my message."

He still didn't say anything, and I wondered how long it had been since they'd last seen one another.

"From what I understand, Eva didn't tell you that your father was dead." Grandfather is not a man to be distracted by something so commonplace as romance. "Why did you drive all this way without returning her call?"

He showed no trepidation but smiled and gave a straight answer. "I tried to telephone, but there was no answer. I decided to come all the same because I knew that Eva would only contact me if something was very wrong."

Fletcher had one of those faces that seems to do nothing but smile. He had presumably just learnt of his father's demise, but the ends of his well-proportioned mouth were pleasantly rounded.

"Perhaps someone should tell me exactly what has happened," he eventually said, but he couldn't take his eyes off Eva for long, and I realised that their reunion was the reason for the happiness he was unable to hide.

For her part, the secretary looked more nervous than ever. She could no longer meet Fletcher's gaze, and I came to wonder whether she had at some point spurned his advances. Something had clearly occurred between them. Perhaps my near-clairvoyant grandfather had spotted a tiny muscle pulsating in a particular area of Eva's neck or around her temples that could only mean one thing but, for the moment at least, I was in the dark.

"I'll tell you what," Dashwood intervened, pointing towards the posher side of the castle - away from where the hoi polloi resided. "We'll meet for dinner and hash everything out like old times. It's been a difficult afternoon, and I'd prefer to have a rest in my old room before anything gets too serious."

I had to question what could be more serious than his father's murder.

"It was nice to see you too, Dash. We'll have to do it again soon." Fletcher gave a cheery bow, and I must say that, despite my unproven assumption that he was a jolly good egg, his apparent lack of emotion at the news of his father's death alarmed me.

"To tell you the truth, Fletch," their sister added in a weary tone,

"I'd like to get changed. We'll meet for a drink in the Hall of the Gonfaloniers in half an hour. I'll tell Signora Acciaioli."

She trailed off to do this, and Fletcher's attention turned to my grandfather. "Hullo there, aren't you Father's old friend? I don't suppose you'd like to explain exactly what happened?"

Eva backed away from the conversation without a word, and I would have lent my grandfather a hand to describe the day's events, but I noticed Father Laurence still skulking about in the shadows. Rather than walking straight across the courtyard, he went all the way around the outside to get to a low arch that I hadn't noticed before. It was far less grand than the other exits: just a dark hole set into the wall really, and I couldn't help finding the old priest's behaviour suspicious.

He peered over his shoulder as he ducked out of sight, and I peeled away from the others to chase after him. I felt that we were remiss not to consider him a suspect. After all, he had appeared at the scene of the murder just minutes after we found the body. Who could say that he hadn't lured the old lord up to the tower to push him down? Perhaps he considered this a punishment from on high. Now that I thought about it, it seemed a little strange that a British priest would have followed Monroe over to Italy. Is that even something within their power to decide?

I paused in the low archway and listened. I could hear the sound of metal clinking against metal as he presumably fiddled with a set of keys. This impression was only enhanced when he dropped them on the floor, cursed himself using some particularly colourful language, and picked them up again. The coordinates in space that these sounds provided gave me the confidence to move further along the passageway. At the end of it, I leaned out a little as I watched him through one eye.

He was muttering the whole time, but I couldn't make out what he said. I got the impression that whatever he was doing was quite exhausting for him as he sighed and complained about every movement he made. He was neither light on his feet nor particularly young, and I suppose such weariness overtakes us all at some point – with the uncanny exception of my grandfather, of course.

With a great deal of huffing, he managed to find the right key and put it into the lock of a grubby black door in the small lightwell where he stood. He looked over his shoulder one last time before opening it, but he didn't see me. The sun couldn't penetrate the narrow shaft, and I was wrapped up in the darkness, but I got a good look at his fleshy face before he disappeared through the door.

Luckily for me, he didn't close it behind him and, once I was certain that he had gone, I hurried forward to spy on him. There was an antechamber through which he had already passed, and he was now busy lighting candles in the further room. The fact he hadn't lit any in the first space gave me the courage to enter and hide once more behind another partially open door.

I must say it was quite exciting. My grandfather's brand of detective work doesn't tend to allow too much in the way of espionage. There's plenty of talking to smart young people and interrogating cunning killers – plenty of luxurious locations, too, but very little in the way of running after dangerous criminals. I suppose that, in the grand scheme of things, this is preferable to being stabbed to death by a light-footed villain, but I did enjoy the thrill of watching Father Laurence through a crack without his knowing anything about it.

Once he'd lit all the candles that were fixed on sconces around the room, he went to the far end of the chapel and knelt down on a bench in front of the small altar. The candles closest to him had taken a few moments to melt the wax on their wicks but they were now blazing quite brightly and, in the light that they poured onto the altarpiece, I saw a series of glass cases with golden edges. At first, I thought my eyes were playing tricks on me, but I was not deceived. Arranged in an elaborate alcove, every last box contained bones, and the one furthest down had a human skull peering out of it. Its teeth were propped up in macabre fashion on a small red pillow, almost like a hunting trophy.

A chill passed through me as I realised that I'd found the inner sanctum of a madman.

CHAPTER FIFTEEN

I don't know whether my hand pressing against the door made it creak, or I breathed too loudly, but Laurence spun around where he was kneeling to call out.

"Who's there? What do you want?"

I tried my very best not to make another sound. I stayed perfectly still, safely out of sight behind the door.

"Is that you Pietro Perugi?" He waited for an answer that wouldn't come. "I will not give you any more books until you return the one I lent you. I may be old, but *The Water Babies* is one of my favourites, and I want it back."

To my surprise, he wasn't acting like a perverse killer who collected the bones of his victims as mementoes of his hellish acts. Indeed, he had a broad smile on his face and, when his first guess proved incorrect, he had a second try.

"Or is that little Serafina? There's really no need to be shy. If you have something you wish to discuss, my door is always open."

I don't know why, but I found myself stepping into the light and shuffling inside. I didn't say anything at first, I just pointed at the terrible display beyond the altar.

Now that I was in there, I could see there were upwards of thirty cases. On the highest shelf, a whole skeleton was at repose, its arms at its side and the head raised slightly on a silver cushion. There were several other skulls looking out at me, their hollow eye sockets strangely mournful.

"What did you…?" I finally managed to utter, but I would say no more.

Father Laurence stood up, unleashing a terrible noise from his throat as he did so. He was laughing at me, and it made me feel quite sick.

"You're not a Catholic, are you, boy?" he said, as if this made what he'd done somehow excusable.

"No, I'm not, but I know that your faith, just like mine, does not permit human sacrifice."

"Human sacrifice!" he bellowed like a bloodthirsty vampire, and that terrible laugh only grew in volume, echoing around the chapel. "These are relics of long dead saints. In my church, such objects are venerated in order to offer thanks to God for the blessings he gave us."

I admit that I felt more than a little silly. I'd obviously heard of relics, but I had no idea that they were quite so... explicit! There was one reliquary with a carved hand on top which, behind a small glass window, held some fellow's radial bone. And now that I knew what they were, I noticed a whole shelf given over to smaller treasures. Lined up in their golden containers, with starbursts, laurel leaves, and crosses on top, they looked like the prizes schoolchildren receive for winning events on sports day. I'm glad to say that my school didn't give out old teeth, finger bones or pieces of desiccated skin.

"I'm so sorry," I felt I had to say before he could think any worse of me. "I saw those—" I didn't quite know how to describe them, so I stopped myself and started again. "I saw the skull on the bottom shelf, and I thought the worst. I promise I'm not as naïve as I've made myself sound, but whenever Grandfather and I investigate a murder, my mind turns to gruesome thoughts."

Despite the profuseness of my apology, his face turned serious, and he backed away to sit down in the nearest pew. There were only three rows of seating, as it really was a small chapel, and, at the back of the room, there was another entrance.

"I'm sorry if I've upset you," I apologised again because, well, what else could I do?

"You thought me a murderer." He dropped his head to his hands, and I wondered whether I should apologise for a third time.

"I wouldn't take it to heart." I adopted a lighter tone in the hope it might reassure him. "Spending so long in the vicinity of killers means that I've been suspected of being one myself a number of times. I can't say that it was very nice at the beginning, but the truth is you soon get used to it."

Even before I'd finished speaking, I could tell that my little speech would not have the desired effect. He simply sat there, his shoulders hunched, his eyes to the floor, and I couldn't decide whether to sidle away as quietly as possible or put a hand out to comfort him. I did briefly consider that he was saying a prayer, but then he looked up at me with an expression of true torment.

"I'm…" I began before having second thoughts. "If you'd like to tell me what the matter is, I'd be happy to listen. You must say that to people a lot, but I wonder how often anyone says it to you."

I felt I'd put my foot in my mouth again. Emotion rushed through the man, and I realised once more that I am a cod's-head-and-shoulders of the worst kind.

Shaking a little, he gritted his teeth to control his feelings and inhaled a quick, crisp breath. "Thank you, young man. That is a truly kind thing to say, and I can see that you have an old head on young shoulders."

Our contrasting judgements of my intelligence couldn't have been more different – though they did rhyme. If anything, his words left me more disconcerted than his unexpectedly generous response.

"Either way, I hope I was not too flippant," I told him.

The chapel was so well tucked away within the castle that none of the noisy gaiety from the courtyard reached us. The only sound was the occasional scampering of a mouse in the room next door.

"No, no…" He had tears in his eyes, which he dried on his sleeve. "It's just that, like you, I have been accused of wishing to murder someone before."

"Oh, I am sorry. That can't have been pleasant."

"You're quite right. It was not a nice experience." He had to pause then and bit his lip as he found the courage to continue. "But as it happens, it was true."

I failed to hide my surprise at this. It's not every day a Catholic priest confesses a desire to kill – well, not to me at least.

"Perhaps we should go for a walk," I said, partly because I felt the fresh air might do us good, but also as I wasn't sure that being alone in a small space with a would-be killer was the best idea.

He nodded to concede my point, then patted his cassock in search of something. I heard his keys jangling there before he rose to lead me to the door which opened onto the eastern façade of the building.

He locked the chapel behind us but said nothing more as we walked down the first few shallow steps of the path that led to the road. I heard quick footsteps and turned to see Delilah sprinting towards us from wherever she'd previously been dozing.

With his bright red cheeks and hair sticking up in clumps around his head, there was something a little parrot-like about Father

Laurence. From a *parrotry* I visited on a previous case, I happen to know that the black palm cockatoo looks really quite similar to the priest of Montegufoni.

We reached the bottom of the slope and turned off into a terraced garden with large stone lions looking down on us. They were covered in the ivy that crept up the castle walls, but their fierce faces poked out, watching for intruders. When we got to the other side of the castle, my companion made me stop to regard the building, which was now high above us.

"Just imagine what it would have been like when the castle was first built." He clearly loved the place in which he lived. "Picture yourself as a peasant descending the opposing hill on foot only to see this magnificent creation with a hundred windows and these great, walled terraces leading up to it. It would have been like stumbling across the Tower of Babel."

I tried to do as he had instructed and found myself travelling back in time several hundred years. From our viewpoint there, I could see that the self-enclosed village really was a castle after all. There were immense, buttressed walls on several levels surrounding it and a grand staircase with what looked like a complex grotto at the top.

Delilah was less interested in the architecture, so she sniffed around between olive trees and large potted cacti. She must have caught the scent of a squirrel or perhaps something more exotic, as she dashed off into the bushes, and I didn't see her again for some time.

"When I heard that we would be staying in a castle, I imagined a huge Norman affair made of grey stone with a keep and a flag flying from the parapet," I told Father Laurence. "It was difficult not to feel that the fairy tale in my head had let me down, but in the short time I've been here, I've come to appreciate this place far more."

"Then you'll know how I felt when I came here all those years ago to kill Renwick Monroe."

CHAPTER SIXTEEN

His words seemed to have knocked all of mine from my brain. It wasn't so much what he'd said as the way he'd said it. He was calm and matter of fact. Even harder to take was the fact that, instead of explaining the circumstances of his first visit to Montegufoni, he asked me my name.

"Perhaps we should know one another a little better before I explain all this. When I first moved here, I went by Mr Brian Laurence, but that was a long time ago now. And you are…?"

"Christopher…" I just about managed to say. "Christopher Prentiss. I'm my grandfather's grandson. Or rather… I'm Lord Edgington's grandson." I tried to inject a touch more confidence in my voice and, rising to my full height – approximately an inch taller than I'd previously been – I told him in a deep voice, "I've been his apprentice on our investigations for almost four years now."

"Yes, yes." He chuckled then, much as he had when he'd thought me one of the local children coming to the chapel to talk to him. "I knew that much, but it's good to put a name to the face. I am pleased to meet you, Christopher."

He held his hand out and I didn't know whether to shake it or run up to the castle screaming, *Grandfather! Grandfather! I've found a real madman, and I can't decide whether he's planning to kill me.* I plumped for the former.

"It's nice to meet you, Father Laurence." I was admittedly worried this would not turn out to be true.

"Thirteen years have passed since I arrived in Italy," he said in a relaxed tone. "I came here because Renwick Monroe had destroyed my life. I'd been looking for him for years, and I finally discovered that he was living his life in luxury out here. He didn't care what he'd done to me."

"What had he done to you?"

"That's not the point of the story," he replied a little sternly. "But he'd destroyed my reputation at home in London. I was a pariah to my friends, and my family wanted nothing to do with me, all because of the stories that Renwick Monroe had spread about me. Back then, he had a wicked tongue and an ever-growing list of enemies."

"And you were one of them?"

"Not always. We had once been friends, but he decided that he no longer approved of me, and that was when my world fell apart."

I'd begun to question why he was talking to me. Was he really so in need of a confessor, or was he just hoping to influence my grandfather's opinion of who killed the dead lord?

"I spent the next years living like a hermit, but I was the opposite of those noble gentlemen of the past who would lock themselves away from the world to reflect on their love of God. I thought only of myself. I was so resentful, so enraged, that I dwelt in a pit of my own making, plotting my revenge without any way to enact it."

"So how did you discover where Lord Monroe had gone?"

"I knew he was in Italy, but I could have driven up and down the Apennine Peninsula my whole life and never found him. I could have walked right past the castle and not known where he was."

I was about to ask the same question again when he answered it. "I eventually received an anonymous letter with Renwick's address. Whoever sent it evidently wished to stir up trouble. That would have given those whisperers and gadabouts back in Pimlico reason to gossip. And you know, it almost worked."

He pursed his lips and looked up at the wide castle, two terraces above the one on which we stood. A bird was singing in the trees near us. I don't know what it was, but it was a sweet sound quite at odds with the bitterness of the priest's tale.

"I returned to London from my exile, obtained a passport, a gun and enough bullets to murder half the population of the village. And I don't mind telling you, Christopher, that at no point in any of this did I question whether I was the one in the wrong. I cared only about the slight against me and how I would return it a thousand-fold."

He looked so melancholy that I felt he must still hold those same tortured thoughts that had brought him to Montegufoni in the first place.

"I barely ate on the journey and didn't stop to sleep. I was totally committed to my task. I arrived here on a Saturday afternoon. I parked my car at the bottom of the hill, then walked up the steps to the castle with the gun in my hand. I walked through the arch and found Renwick conducting his ridiculous orchestra. They were playing 'Land of Hope and Glory' of all things, and I almost shot him right then."

"What stopped you?" My voice sounded more mature than I had expected.

"Propriety, perhaps. A belief in my own righteousness? I wasn't really going to murder the villagers. There were children running around as there still are today. My mind was not so corrupt that I wished to hurt them."

"What happened?"

He paused for five seconds before answering. Even after so long, the story still affected him. "Renwick saw me, and he smiled. He stood there in his bandmaster's uniform, with a baton and a pompous look, and he smiled. I hid the gun in my pocket, and the old devil introduced me to the locals. He said, 'Ladies and gentlemen, my dear friend Brian Laurence has come all the way from London to hear you play.'

"I felt sorry for the people he had forced to dress up and learn their instruments for his pleasure. He was a little Mussolini – a despot who saw his own veneration as more important than the lives of his people. The war was on when I arrived, and fascism was only just emerging as a concept, but I saw a very mild English version of it here. Or perhaps that was just what I told myself to explain why I wanted to kill him."

I could just imagine him standing in the courtyard with a pistol in his trembling hand, preparing to shoot. The mix of fear and excitement, pain and relief must have been overwhelming.

"What did you do when he spoke so calmly?" I finally said to prod him along.

"I listened." He breathed out for far longer than was necessary and then did the same as he inhaled. "I stayed right where I was, and I listened to the next piece of music they played. I'm sure that Renwick chose it to mock me. I'm sure he thought, if that monster has come here to kill me, I'll pick the most inappropriate music possible."

"Was it 'Daddy Wouldn't Buy me a Bow-Wow'?"

"No, although that would have been a good choice." His throaty laugh sounded once more. "Renwick opted for 'Ta-ra-ra Boom-de-ay'."

I had not expected this sombre, emotional man to start singing just then, but that's what happened.

> **"I'm a blushing bud of innocence,**
> **Papa says at big expense,**

Old maids say I have no sense,
Boys declare, I'm just immense.
Before my song, I do conclude,
I want it strictly understood,
Though fond of fun, I'm never rude,
Though not too bad I'm not too good."

He clapped his hands together to show that he had finished. "Renwick joined in with that second verse. He'd always entertained his friends around the piano at parties in St George's Square. I realised halfway through that it wasn't such an arbitrary choice after all. He was telling me that he had no regrets. He thought himself neither 'too good nor too bad', and there was nothing the gun in my pocket could do to change that."

"Did he see the weapon before you hid it?"

"I believe so." He puffed out one cheek then, as though he was still amazed. "But my presence told him exactly why I'd come, and the eccentric fool couldn't have cared less. He made the most of his farewell performance, and when it was over, I just stood there. I'd imagined that scene playing out in so many different ways over the years, but none of them had included a brass band and Lottie Collins's most famous number. The one saving grace was that Renwick did not attempt a can-can."

It was apparently my task to put another coin in the slot whenever he ground to a halt. "What happened after that?"

He'd been staring at precisely nothing, his round face ashen, but he came back to himself and looked at me. "I stood there for so long with my every sense and sensation frozen that he ended up coming over. He put his arm around my shoulder and steered me towards his minions. I suppose it was dreadfully British of me to go along with it all. I nodded to every Benito and Bianca. I might even have feigned a smile, but when the band sat down to have their tea, and I was alone with Renwick, my need for vengeance returned.

"'I came here to kill you, old stick,' I whispered as he played the perfect host, pouring out tea in his Royal Doulton cup and saucers.

"'Now, now. Let's not be hasty, dear boy,' he replied with a diabolical grin. 'There's always time for a cup of char.' I sat at a table with three doting *nonnas* whose English extended to the phrases

110

that Renwick had made them learn about the weather and cricket. I doubt they'd ever seen a cricket match, but they had some interesting perspectives on W.G. Grace's long career."

He stopped talking as Delilah poked her head out of a bush behind us. She was covered in burrs and bits of leaf, and she immediately disappeared back to her previous task as the priest continued his story.

"The occupants of Montegufoni slowly went back to their lives until only Renwick and I remained. We sat opposite one another at a table in the middle of the courtyard and, for a minute or two, I stared at him with my hand on the pistol. I had rehearsed exactly what I wanted to say. There was a short version, which I would have shouted as I shot him, and a longer one that I'd composed for a moment like this. I had a whole list of grievances to disclose, but now that I had the opportunity to do so, I couldn't bring myself to speak."

There were bees buzzing about the rhododendrons behind us. Occasionally, one of them would drunkenly fly off course to lend a calming accompaniment to Father Laurence's stark tale.

"'I came here to kill you,' I managed to repeat, but he wasn't scared. All he said in reply was, 'Why?' and I struggled to produce a reply.

"'You destroyed me,' I finally uttered. 'You ruined my life.'

"Renwick looked quite dignified as he stroked his prodigious moustaches and considered his reply. 'That may be, but what kind of life was it?'

"Whatever furious energy I'd had when I arrived had diminished, and even simple questions floored me. I could do nothing but mumble half-formed thoughts, so Renwick continued. 'I did what I did to teach you a lesson. I certainly didn't besmirch your character because every word I spoke was the truth. You were a corrupt, violent individual who cared nothing for anyone else, but I can see that you have changed.'

"I was quite mystified by this. I didn't believe that I'd changed one bit in the years since the world collapsed around me.

"'What do you mean?' I asked him. 'Am I not the same ruthless, worthless, heartless individual as when you last saw me?' Renwick sipped his tea to make me wait for the answer. His drink was at best cold, but more likely empty.

"'No, of course you're not. You have spent years in the wilderness, and though you came here to seek vengeance, you did not take it when the opportunity arose. You stood in front of a jury of your peers and were found innocent. You could have killed me, but you preferred to talk. This is what you really want – not my blood splashed across the flagstones, or my brains blown to pieces. You came here to share your pain.'

"There were tears in my eyes, but I didn't make a sound. I studied Renwick's face as though it were a great work of art. I tried to make sense of everything he'd said and asked myself whether he was right. My brain was a dark and muddled place just then. It was impossible to come to any conclusion, but the one thing I could say with any certainty was that I was not ready to shoot him.

"He tidied away our crockery and returned to speak to me in a gentle voice. 'Hold on to the gun, Brian, and think about what I've said. If you really want to kill me, I won't take it personally.' He smiled that persuasive smile of his and turned to walk to his apartment in the west wing of the castle."

I had fallen into his story. I was no longer out in the gardens, but up in the courtyard, sitting at the table to watch that strange scene between a would-be killer and his intended victim.

"What did you do after that?" I murmured. "Where did you go?"

"I sat there for a long time and, when the night fell, I wandered from the castle. I thought about returning to Britain, but there was nothing left for me there, so I turned off the path and walked through the garden just as we did. There was a bell ringing. At first, I thought it was in my head, but I followed it nonetheless and found myself right here where we stand. The sound was coming from the church further on the other side of the estate.

"I kept walking and, when I reached the front doors, there were people going in ahead of me. I thought there would be a Mass on, and I could sit at the back and float away with my thoughts. Of course, the men inside weren't parishioners. They were soldiers. Each of them bore an injury and the priest in the narthex was providing them with food. There was a nurse seeing to their dressings, but the queue was long, and they didn't have the resources to go any faster.

"I'd gone in there to be invisible, but the priest called me over. He could see I wasn't injured, and I was too old to have been called up, so he must have known I was fit to help them. He made me take over serving out stew and bread to the soldiers so that he could assist the nurse. There was no discussion about it, which was good because I didn't speak a word of Italian.

"I spent three hours there doing what I could to help. At the end of the evening, Father Posarelli took me to the rectory and gave me a bed in a spare room. He didn't ask me who I was, and I've never understood how he knew what I needed, but he showed great kindness. The next day, I found lodging in a neighbouring village, but I kept going back to help the padre. I spent months here. I began to learn Italian and felt thankful for my lot in life for the first time in years. I bought a simple cottage near the church and made friends with the soldiers whose lives looked so bleak after losing limbs and loved ones.

"But the thing that occupied my time and my thoughts was the conversation I'd had with Renwick. It wasn't just his questions that occupied me, but a particular phrase he'd used. He said that I'd spent years in the wilderness, and I wondered whether that was true. Had my banishment from London been my forty days in the desert?"

I betrayed a touch of scepticism at this, and he was quick with a response.

"Perhaps that sounds self-important or naïve. Perhaps I read far too much into my insignificant existence, but that is how I felt at the time and how I came to convert to Catholicism. I forgot my old life and abandoned all thoughts of revenge. And years later, when Father Posarelli suggested that I become a priest, I didn't have to think twice; I knew it was the path I had to take."

I was sure there was more to the tale than this, but no new questions entered my mind, and so all I could say was, "Thank you, Father Laurence. Thank you for trusting me with your story."

He bowed his head and held it there for a few moments. When he looked back up, he said, "Thank you for listening, Christopher. I believe that it was more for my sake than yours. Now, we should get back to the castle. Your grandfather will be looking for you."

I whistled for Delilah, and we wandered up the steep stone stairs together to work our way through the terraces back to the castle. We passed the seashell-encrusted grotto with its frightening sculptures of demons, monsters and immense beasts. The workmanship was undeniably impressive, but the imagery sent a chill through me, and I didn't stop to look at it for long.

We reached the top of the steps, and he gripped hold of my sleeve to deliver one final revelation. "There was another reason I stayed here for so long. I believe that, deep in my heart, I always hoped to show Renwick the error of his ways as he had done for me. I may never have succeeded in that task, but I tried my very best."

Father Laurence nodded to me and turned to leave. As he walked away, I pondered whether I had just heard the story of a man who learnt to be a beneficent member of society, or he had gone out of his way to convince me that he was no killer.

CHAPTER SEVENTEEN

I heard my grandfather's voice coming from within the castle before I saw him. Father Laurence crossed the top terrace where we'd interviewed Coralie, and I went back into the building and found the others just off the salon.

Little by little, the map of the castle was expanding in my head, and I could see that this impressive space connected to my own rooms in the Cardinal's apartment. It had another unusually high ceiling and, around the top of the walls, there was an elaborate painting of various honourable figures from centuries past. Each man was depicted in noble dress within the frame of a gold medallion. There were sphinxes and other fantastic animals between the different figures, and each man had his name and (a little oddly) job description underneath. I noticed senators, moral philosophers and "gonfaloniers", whatever they might be.

While I admit this looked rather like the board which held the names and positions of the staff in my old school, I decided that each painting was of a member of the original family who had owned the building before Lord Monroe bought it. There was a similar style of fresco around each door and window. Where one might have expected to find plaster moulding, there was trompe l'œil decoration in rich colours that tricked the eye.

Far less charming was the atmosphere in the room. As I looked at the faces of the three siblings, I had the impression that my grandfather was doing his best to unnerve them. Eva Mountstephen was also there, but her expression generally suggested something terrible had just happened, so it was harder to imagine what she was thinking.

"It should come as no surprise to hear me say such a thing," Grandfather announced, and I would have placed a wager that he'd just told them they were the obvious suspects in the murder.

"Very well," Dashwood replied. "It's no surprise, but that doesn't mean it's nice to hear."

"You must have told our father you wanted to murder him fifty times when the two of you were on speaking terms," Coralie reminded him. She was standing on a small balcony with her back to the room, and she peered over her shoulder to make her point.

"It doesn't really change anything." Fletcher was clearly the optimist of the bunch. He ran his fingers through his shiny brown hair and tried to look cheerful. "The fact that something is likely does not mean that it is the only solution. I'm sure that Lord Edgington knows that better than anyone."

Grandfather did not reply aloud but nodded his agreement.

"Think about all the cases you've solved," the youngest sibling continued. "The Nichol brothers, the Dalston Scrobbler, the murders at Mistletoe Hall: in which of them was the likely culprit to blame? When did one of your investigations fail to turn up something out of the ordinary?"

"You're evidently a follower of my work," Grandfather replied, pulling his shoulders back proudly as Todd arrived with a hamper of drinks and a bucket of ice.

"I am indeed." Fletcher had the easy, vivacious charm of many young Englishmen I've known. This attitude was somewhat incongruous considering that his father had just fallen fifty feet to his death. "I've read every article I could find with your name in it since I was a child."

"Then I should probably warn you that the newspapers only ever write about the most interesting crimes. During my time in the police, for every brain-teasing mystery I have tackled, there were five cases which I've forgotten."

Even this didn't put a dent in Fletcher's cheer. His smile shone just as brightly... until Miss Mountstephen spoke, and his eyes fell to the floor. This was markedly different from his reaction when he first saw her.

"Have you considered the fact that Renwick wasn't the most popular man here?" she asked with some hesitation.

"He wasn't the most popular man in our family, let alone the castle." Dashwood was always ready with a pithy reply, and he smoothed his eyebrows with two fingers to underline how happy he was with his quick wit.

"I wish you would stop being so facetious," Coralie snapped. "Even if you don't care about who was up on that tower with Father, it could have a significant impact on the rest of us."

Dashwood apparently decided to placate his sister, as he turned to the detective to mount a defence. "Let me make things simple for you, Lord Edgington. Fletcher is too nice to have murdered our father, Coralie too self-interested, and I would love to have done the job, but I was sadly detained elsewhere."

His attitude was forever changing, and it was hard to know who he really was. He had exploded into the castle that afternoon and marked himself out as a brooding hellraiser before undergoing a Damascene conversion and trying to be everyone's friend. Perhaps it was the knowledge that the murder could not be pinned on him, but he was unfathomably blithe.

If I were suspicious of his behaviour, then Grandfather was doubly so. "And why should I take your word for it?"

Before Dashwood could fashion a retort, Todd decided to announce that the first of the evening's cocktails was almost ready. I'm sure he had picked his moment in order to defuse the tension in the room.

"Ladies and gentlemen, I've taken it upon myself to prepare a libation that I believe is well-known in this part of the world." He was finishing the final drink as he spoke and poured a brown liquid and a red liquid (I'm sorry I can't be more specific) into a chilled glass with the ice still inside it. He topped this off with soda water and a slice of orange, and I had to wonder whether the reason he'd come to the castle before collecting the others from the airport was to deliver these supplies. "It's known as an Americano. It is originally from the north of Italy, but I hope that's close enough to appeal."

"If it contains alcohol, it will do the job." Perhaps surprisingly, this was Fletcher speaking, not his brother. He smiled gratefully as he took a glass from the tray Todd now brought around.

On cue, our maid Dorie appeared with a selection of hors d'oeuvres. It seemed that il Castello di Montegufoni had been well and truly overtaken by the English contingent, and no one was complaining. We'd have to see how they felt after they'd tried our cook's idiosyncratic dishes.

"You can't beat an Americano." Dashwood drank half of his cocktail, before most of us had taken a sip.

I'll admit that it was a refreshing beverage. It was not too strong, and the bubbles were pleasant as they worked their way down my throat.

"Perhaps we should make a toast to Father," Fletcher said about ten seconds too late, but we pulled our glasses back from our lips as he raised his. "The truth is that, while he might have been the most infuriating person I've ever known, I've always accepted that I loved him."

"Come along, Fletch." His brother tutted and looked away. "I've had enough of Coralie pretending that we all got along. Don't you start."

Fletcher got up from his seat and, for a moment, it seemed he might challenge his brother, but he walked right past him to stand with Coralie on the balcony. Eva, who had barely touched a drop of her cocktail, watched him throughout with such affection. And yet, in her gaze there was the same sorrow I'd noticed there since her employer had died.

"I'm not lying." Fletcher spoke in his typically sincere voice. "I really believe that our father had a good heart. He just went about life in the most complicated and infuriating way imaginable. Of course, if he hadn't, we wouldn't be inheriting this wonderful old curiosity." Standing side-on to us, he cast his gaze across the landscape. "Father had his own peculiar sense of justice. He believed he could make the world a better place by infuriating everyone around him. The truth is that he caused himself more problems than anyone else."

"He was kind to me," his secretary responded in a low voice, and I doubted she would have interrupted Dashwood or Coralie like that.

"Yes." Fletcher's enthusiasm immediately dropped. "Yes, we know how good he was to you, Eva, but you were a special exception."

My grandfather's right eyebrow moved an almost infinitesimal fraction – a twelfth of a twelfth of an inch, perhaps. If I hadn't known him so well, it would have been quite easy to miss, but I was certain he took something significant from Fletcher's comment.

"To the rest of us," the younger son continued, "he was more like an eccentric headmaster than a father. Even with the locals, he was forever shaping and correcting them. I don't know why he felt that he should be the one to decide how we acted, but he was not the sort to question himself."

"That is very much the person I knew when he lived in London," Grandfather agreed, raising one hand as if to assert his authority over the matter. "He used to say that your mother left him for that very failing, though as I only heard the story from his perspective – and it was widely known that he was something of a womaniser – I could never be certain."

I thought they might tell us something of their deceased mother, who had barely been mentioned until now, but Coralie shook her head and looked over the balcony as she responded to the main discussion. "He once told me that the world would be a worse place if no one tried to make it better. He said that every country would slide into despotism and degeneracy if good people turned aside whenever they sensed injustice."

This comment even seemed to deter Dashwood's inevitable rebuttal. "Very well. I'll raise a toast to the old bleeder." He paused to consider what he wanted to say before taking his glass from the table beside the sofa. "To Father, he certainly meant well, even if the result of his actions rarely matched their good intentions."

One by one, we raised our glasses in turn, and when all were aloft, we drank. This was possibly the first consensus the siblings had been able to find that day. It was a small, precious moment of cordiality in the middle of a tempest. I didn't dare hazard a guess as to how long it would last.

CHAPTER EIGHTEEN

I'm happy to say— and, no, I'm not about to tell you that the three siblings got on marvellously from that moment onwards. I'm happy to tell you that Signora Acciaioli prepared dinner for us that night and, though our cook Henrietta definitely had a hand in things, it was largely an Italian affair (with the exception of a side dish of stewed radish).

We ate on the long, shaded walkway at the side of the castle, known as the Avenue of the Spalliere for a reason that no one explained. There was a pergola overhead with wisteria growing all the way along the wall of the building. The spring's final purple blossoms – like bunches of grapes hanging down to us – filled the air with their sweet nectar, and a warm breeze tickled my skin as we ate.

Everything I tried was mouth-wateringly tasty and, best of all, Todd convinced the chef to come down to us to explain what we were eating. I imagine that the Monroe siblings could have done this, too, but it wouldn't have had the same flair.

"The dish to which I now present you," she said in her excessively formal English that I was increasingly confident had been taught by Lord Monroe, "is a type of pasta called *pici Sienese*."

"I've never heard of it," I admitted as Todd served wine, and I realised that I had to stop drinking or I wouldn't be able to solve the case for several days.

"You've never heard of *pici*?" She laughed at me rather musically, but I didn't mind.

"I've never heard of pasta."

This led to more laughter at my expense, but Grandfather kindly leaned in to explain. "Yes, you have, Christopher. We commonly refer to it in England as vermicelli or Italian paste. You've had macaroni before, and I imagine you've come across spaghetti at some time or another."

This was true, but I'd never realised they were in any way linked.

"They're simple, peasanty dishes made of durum wheat," Dashwood both helpfully and rudely summarised, and then the cook was free to continue her explanation.

"The dish I have chosen to prepare for you this evening is served in a ragu known *as Pici con la Nana*. It contains duck, tomato, onion and there is *pecorino Toscano* on the table for you to add to your liking."

She bowed out of the scene leaving an odd atmosphere behind. On the one hand, a man was dead before his time. On the other, no one could say with any certainty whether they'd liked him. Furthermore, the food was so palate-pleasing that it was hard to be sad. The duck was rich and moreish, and I doubt I'd ever had that particular bird cooked with such a tender result. The only problem was that I'd already had a selection of sandwiches and cakes followed by a not so tiny appetiser. By the time the main course arrived, I was almost bursting.

"What is it, Christopher?" Grandfather sounded alarmed. "Is there something wrong? I've never seen you look so uncomfortable before."

"I'm fine," I lied as I laid eyes on what Signora Acciaioli was about to serve.

"It's as if someone has put poison in your drink," he persisted, turning my chair around so that he could check my eyes for signs of intoxication. Inevitably, this caused some consternation around the table.

"You do look quite sick." Coralie observed, though this was presumably down to my normal complexion.

"Quick, man," Fletcher said, jumping up from his seat to dash across to me with a carafe. "Have some water." He clearly didn't know a lot about poison if he thought a swift drink could save me.

"I haven't been poisoned," I said to reassure my fellow diners. "I don't know how to say this, but I'm… full."

Concern transformed into confusion, whereas Grandfather let out a laugh. "I never thought I'd see the day."

"Very funny, but it's not my fault that we've spent the afternoon eating. And now we have—"

"*Bistecca alla Fiorentina*," the nice Italian lady (who was clearly trying to make me explode) interrupted before I could bemoan the amount of meat she had just brought. "That is to say, beef cooked for an exceedingly short time over white-hot coals and brushed with rosemary and sage. I now go to retrieve the other pieces."

As soon as she said it, I realised that the smoky odour that had been wafting over to us for some time was from an outside grill somewhere nearby. It was an enormous sirloin with a bone in the middle. Todd was already cutting off huge chunks ready for our consumption, and our cook reappeared with two more pieces that were even larger. As there were only six of us dining, it appeared that each cut was to be shared between two people. Well, I had to hope this was true, as if that was one portion, I'd need several days to finish it.

She placed the last piece on its end like an upside-down T. "The bone in the centre divides the fillet from the richer sirloin. *Buon appetito!*" Her pretty black curls seemed to compress and expand like springs as she moved to leave.

"Signora Acciaioli, it looks truly extraordinary," my grandfather said to halt her retreat. "I very much look forward to it, but I do have one question before you go."

"Of course, Lord Edgington."

"Your surname: Acciaioli – may I enquire whether it is your husband's?"

She hesitated but soon answered the question. "No, it is mine. My husband died in the war and, as we had no children, and no one ever got used to calling me Severini, I returned to the name of my birth."

"So you hail from the same family who built and previously owned this castle?" There was no suggestion of a hidden motive in his manner, but the question immediately filled my head with possibilities.

"That is correct, My Lord Marquess." As accurate as her English was for the most part, I had learnt at school that you should only ever refer to someone as My Lord Marquess in writing and never in speech. I doubt anyone noticed except for my grandfather and me, but it is the kind of thing about which people with nothing better to do with their time like to complain.

"How interesting." His cunning was clear in the twinkle in those magical grey eyes, and he finished the conversation with a smile. "I hope we can discuss the history of this remarkable place at some point while I am here."

She sounded less assured now. "Yes, of course, Lord Edgington." She bowed and hurried away. As she went, I felt she was approximately as excited about the prospect of a friendly confab with my grandfather as I was of being forced to eat all that beef.

"Hussy," Dashwood pronounced under his breath once she was well out of earshot.

"Dashwood!" Eva admonished him.

"Oh, I'm terribly sorry." The way he said this told me that he would soon undermine the apology. "I suppose I should also mention that she's a wonderful chef, but she's still a hussy."

"You make my skin crawl." Coralie was typically unimpressed by his humour.

"Come along, sis. She put up with our father for more than a decade, and I very much doubt it was for the sparkling conversation he provided. She wanted her sons to inherit this place. Assuming that he didn't change his will without telling us, she will be out of luck."

"You really do have a negative view of the world, don't you?" It was Eva saying this, not his sister.

"Signora Acciaioli's sons were your father's, then?" Grandfather asked to reduce the tension and force the group to focus on something equally contentious. "Which would make them your half-brothers."

Fletcher had not contributed to the conversation until now but glared at his brother and answered the question. "Father did nothing to hide his affairs from us."

"Or the rest of Italy," Coralie added. "Which is probably why he was killed."

"I don't agree." Grandfather had clearly decided that the troublesome siblings needed a firm hand. "We have already established that Renwick was not afraid of breaking eggs or stepping on toes."

He was a master at delivering such proclamations to unnerve our suspects. If I'd tried something like that, I would have got muddled and suggested that Lord Monroe enjoyed breaking toes stepping on eggs.

"More to the point," Eva added, "why would she have killed Renwick unless she could be sure that her sons would benefit?"

Why this was the thing to upset the usually jovial Fletcher, I couldn't imagine, but he stared across at Eva as though she had slashed his throat with one of the ever so pointy knives with which I wasn't eating my steak.

"Either way, she certainly doesn't seem too disconsolate that Father is dead," Dashwood declared when no one had an answer.

"Which of you is?" I replied, as someone had to say it.

"Oh, come along, Christopher," he said in a teasing voice. "Eva has managed to look maudlin about it ever since I've been here. I'd say that was bally good going on her part. She deserves a round of applause for effort."

Perhaps this was his revenge for the criticism she'd directed at him, but there was clearly little affection between them – though that didn't mean there was no respect. Dashwood's barbs were unusually tame when it came to Miss Mountstephen, and it put me in mind of the way that my brother and I used to squabble when we were living under the same roof.

"Stop it, Dash." Fletcher gave his brother a furious look that made his normally handsome features crumple. "Can we not eat a pleasant dinner together without throwing around accusations?"

It fell silent for a moment, and I took in the reactions to his unexpected outburst. Grandfather looked quietly pleased that he'd instigated a touch of drama. Eva had that compassionate glean in her eyes that she apparently reserved for Fletcher alone, whereas Coralie stared at Dashwood with pure loathing written all over her face.

In return, he simply couldn't stay quiet. "I'm sorry Fletcher, but Father's body being scraped from the courtyard paving stones by the police is less than conducive to a 'pleasant' family dinner."

"That's enough!" Fletcher brought the end of his knife down on the table, and his plate rattled against the other cutlery.

I thought this would be the catalyst for more raised voices, but a strange thing occurred. Somewhere above us, beyond the leafy pergola and my own suite, a man had stepped onto his balcony and was singing lines from a no doubt famous opera as the sun set over the Tuscan landscape.

> **"Riddiamo! Riddiamo! che il mondo è caduto!**
> **Riddiamo! Riddiamo! che il mondo è perduto!"**
> he began, and there was something unnerving about
> the intensity of his delivery. Though he had an almost
> inconceivably perfect voice and could have been on the
> stage at Covent Garden or La Scala, each word he sang
> filled me with dread.
>
> **"Sui morti frantumi del globo fatal**
> **s'accenda, s'intrecci la ridda infernal.**
> **Riddiamo per lungo! riddiamo per tondo!**
> **Riddiam! Ch'è venuta la fine del mondo!"**

Those last four words stood out to me. Until now, I had very much doubted that my knowledge of French would help me to work out more than the odd word of Italian, but this was clear. He was singing about the end of the world.

I don't know if it was the bitter conversation we'd just endured or because the others were as unsettled by the song as I was but, for the rest of the dinner, no one spoke another word.

CHAPTER NINETEEN

"Do you think that Signora Acciaioli could be to blame?" I asked my grandfather on our way back to our rooms that night.

"I think she is a possible suspect."

"Might it not be that she had a lover's quarrel with Lord Monroe, lured him to the top of the tower and pushed him to his doom."

"You're quite right, Christopher. It might not."

I really didn't know what to make of his sharp replies, but I asked another question, nonetheless. "And what about Dashwood?"

He was not in a forthcoming mood. "What about him?"

I came to a stop in the courtyard in the hope it would jolt him into being a touch more reasonable. "Do you think perhaps he's almost too obvious a killer to have done it?"

He eventually realised that I was not walking alongside him and turned to see what the delay was. "I would say quite the opposite is true."

"What does that mean!?"

"It means that he has an alibi that places him three hours' drive from the place in which his father was murdered."

"Yes, but what if it *was* him?"

"Christopher, you're not listening. If Miss Mountstephen really did speak to him on the telephone, and she was connected correctly to his home in Arezzo, then he cannot have killed Renwick Monroe."

"Yes, but isn't it worth considering the possibility that, through some clever trick, he wasn't at home at all?" I searched my brain for a way to resolve this impossible crime. "Perhaps the smooth-tongued devil charmed the operator who connected the call. Perhaps he was in a pub around the corner from here."

"I admit that is one solution, but a simple conversation with the lady in question would instantly uncover the plot."

"I still think he must be the killer."

He seemed to relent then and looked at me a little more forgivingly. "I assume you're swayed by the fact that, in cases such as this one, it often turns out to be the least likely suspect who committed the crime. However, I do not think that will prove to be the case this time around.

For one thing, this plan would have come to nothing if any of the people who live here had spotted Dashwood running about the place. It simply foolish to think that he would have taken that risk."

I thought for a moment, weighed up his words and finally replied, "Yes, but what if it is?"

He no longer looked so forgiving. "I can see that you will take some convincing."

This give-and-take would have continued had I not noticed something curious on the tower which cast its shadow over the otherwise moonlit courtyard. "Grandfather, the clock has stopped."

He turned to see what I meant. "How do you know that it's stopped and not just wrong?"

"Because it showed the same time when Lord Monroe fell from the tower." It was at this very moment that the bell rang for eleven o'clock. "I don't think I've looked at it since, but it's showing three minutes past two now, just as it did then."

"How curious. Perhaps he knocked it as he passed." Grandfather stroked the short white hairs on one cheek as he considered the possibility. "I suppose that it at least helps us to remember the time at which he died, should that prove significant."

"I suppose so." I still thought that there was something more to take from this but couldn't decide what it was.

"You know, Christopher. You and that clock have a lot in common." I waited for him to finish the inevitable joke and, when he didn't, I foolishly helped him along.

"Oh, yes. And why's that?"

"You're both right twice a day." I'm surprised he didn't stretch his arms out or bow to elicit applause.

I replied with a perfectly straight face. "And you're funny once a year."

He started to laugh, whereas I had not. So I think I won that little battle.

"Christopher, my boy, that's too witty. It really is. And you know I'm only teasing you." He was already walking off towards his apartment. "Come along. We haven't found the killer yet, but we can get a full night's sleep and rise all the earlier in the morning."

This did not sound like him. He normally kept me up until the small hours to wring every possible second out of the investigation. It was hard to say whether his attitude to the events of the day was down to his feelings for the man who had died, or the fact we had been travelling for an awfully long time and we were both dead on our feet.

I trailed after him, longing to reach my own private cave where I would collapse on the bed. We said goodnight in the Gallery and, as I crossed the corridor to my dream, I daydreamed of dreaming. I couldn't wait to pull on my pyjamas and close my eyes, which was not going to happen just yet.

"I've been waiting for you," Coralie Monroe whispered from an armchair in the long-dead Cardinal's bedroom. To be honest, no matter how dead he was, I think even he would have been roused by her sultry voice cutting through the darkness.

She was smoking again. She did that a lot.

"Good evening." It's not every night that a beautiful, sophisticated woman appears in my bedroom. I hadn't a clue what one should say in such a situation.

"I must admit, I've been awfully impressed by you today." She stood up to walk seductively across to me. Now that I think about it, I'm not sure how a walk can be seductive – any more than say knitting or mowing a lawn can be – but that's how it seemed at the time.

"You have?"

She released a cloud of smoke straight into my face. I tried not to cough and failed.

"I could go further." Her voice was deeper than I remembered it being. "I might even say that you outsmarted Lord Edgington himself. I can see that if anyone is going to find my father's killer, it will surely be you."

She laid her hand flat against my chest, and I stayed as still as a stone. After a few moments, I realised that I should probably respond.

I tried to make my voice deeper but ended up sounding as if I were doing an impression of her. "Oh… thank you. That's very kind of you to say so."

She stepped around me as though she were looking at a new jumper she was interested in buying. "It's not every day that I meet someone so wise beyond his years. Not to mention brave. I heard about how you ran after the killer without caring one stitch for your own safety." She over pronounced this word as if it were hot in her mouth and she needed to get rid of it. "You're really quite special, Christopher Prentiss."

If I'd managed to say, "Ta very much," at this point it would have been a lot more eloquent than my actual response, which sounded like a cat learning to oink. It was halfway between a purr and a grunt, and I immediately regretted opening my mouth.

Her face was inches away from mine now, and she was leaning in ever closer. "What do you really think of me, Chrissy?" Her voice was a whisper, but it rattled around my brain.

"I think you're," I began, but there was no time to say anything more as she moved forward to kiss me.

I'm not a total novice when it comes to the ways of love. I had kissed (and almost kissed) two different women prior to that moment, and I'm happy to say that on neither occasion did I accidentally poke my nose into their eyes. That winning streak was always going to come to an end one day.

"Ow! What's got into you?" Coralie complained.

"I'm so sorry. I thought that— I am genuinely honestly so sorry."

"You foolish boy, I knew you were wet around the edges, but I'm surprised that even a tadpole like you could get things so wrong." She held her hand to her face and tested the impaired organ with a blink.

"I hadn't expected you to do anything like that." I was about to apologise again when something occurred to me. "Wait a moment. Why are you in my room?"

She clapped her hands against her hips, and the glittering beaded dress she had worn since dinner made a shimmying noise. "Do you really need me to explain everything? I was trying to kiss you."

"Nice try, but I don't believe it." I had my detective's head screwed back on now and wouldn't be taken in by her. "You only came here to find out what I'd discovered about the killer."

"Don't sell yourself short. You're not that bad."

This was almost a compliment, but still not the kind of thing she would say to a young man she found so irresistible that she would risk scandal by invading his bedroom.

"And you're a decent liar, but I'm not fooled." I took a few steps away from her and looked for a light switch to dowse the previously sultry atmosphere. After a minute, I realised that I hadn't seen any electric lights in the whole castle.

"Why are you stroking the walls?" she asked, quite bemused.

"I'm looking for… Why is there no electricity here?"

"Because Daddy didn't trust it. He said he'd rather live in darkness than die in light."

"He was a strange man."

"Says the boy who runs around looking for dead bodies to rifle."

I considered pointing out that it was my grandfather who usually did the rifling and that, actually, rifling did not take up a large part of our time.

Even in my head, none of that sounded good, so I changed the topic. "Why did you come here?"

"Because I wanted to spend time with you." She became more offended the longer we talked, though something in her manner didn't ring true. "If you're going to act like this, I'll have to look for company elsewhere."

In the moonlight that flooded through the curtains, she did look rather gorgeous with her glossy bobbed hair and lithe figure, and I regretted being so suspicious. Perhaps she really did like me, and I'd ruined my chances, or perhaps she'd got me alone there to stab me to death. I suppose there are worse ways to go than looking into the eyes of a beautiful young woman.

"Did you murder your father?" I demanded, to kill off the faint possibility that she might try to kiss me again.

I couldn't think of an adjective that means really, really offended, but that's what she was. "How dare you?" Outraged: that does the trick! "You arrogant, short-sighted, pig-headed wantwit!"

She turned to leave, and I *almost* almost apologised again. Instead, I watched her strut towards the door. The movement was much the same as when she had approached me for the ill-fated kiss, but it no longer looked seductive. If anything, I would say that her walk was rather furious.

To confirm this theory, she had a parting message for me.

"Good night, Christopher Prentiss. And good riddance!"

CHAPTER TWENTY

I can't have been too disappointed about what happened with Coralie as, when I woke up the next morning, it was not her pretty face I remembered, but the steak I barely nibbled and the Tuscan apple cake that I didn't have room to even try. The image of the apple slices arranged like a flower's petals atop the cake would not leave me for some time. I'd never known true heartache before, but the feeling when I opened my eyes and remembered those forsaken delights was surely similar.

I lay in bed, looking up at the fresco on the ceiling of a lady perched on a cloud with two winged cherubs holding a sheet of gossamer fabric over her face. I hadn't a clue what it was supposed to mean, but whoever decorated the castle clearly loved heavenly scenes. Perhaps the best artists stick to a limited range of subjects so as to get really good at painting them. Perhaps if you'd asked Michelangelo to paint a dog, it would have looked like a child had done it.

As I lay there musing over this important topic, I heard movement in the corridor directly behind my chamber. As this led to my grandfather's apartment, I decided it was time to rise.

I had a quick wash, selected some new clothes to wear – so often on our investigations, I dress in a hurry and end up in the same suit for the duration – and then sailed from the chamber feeling refreshed by my repose and ready to face the world.

When I peeked into Grandfather's apartment, there was no sign of him in the Gallery. I shouted up the spiralling stone staircase which led to his room, but there was no reply. Nor was he in the Cardinal's Garden where we had eaten lunch the day before. Out in the main part of the courtyard, I found Fletcher already awake. He was one of those clean-limbed types who no doubt gets up with the dawn to run to Florence and back before doing a hundred star jumps and fifty lunges.

"Christopher, have you seen my sister?" I noted the apprehension in his voice, but I was more concerned with why he would ask me this question.

"Me?" This word squeaked out of me like a frightened mouse. "Why would *I* know where she was?"

His brows tilted somewhat. "I just mean that I've been looking for ten minutes already and can't find her. She's not in her room upstairs."

"Might she have gone out somewhere? To the city, perhaps?"

He shook his head and looked at the various doors as if calculating the possibilities of Coralie being behind each one. "I've never known her to be an early riser. She tends to lounge around in her room for hours doing approximately nothing, which is why it's so surprising that she isn't there."

The almost offensively handsome mechanic, Guido Lombardo, was already working away at a machine of some sort, and Fletcher called across to him in Italian.

"*Hai visto Coralie stamattina?*"

I think it's safe to assume this meant, *Have you seen Coralie this morning?*

The swarthy fellow took a few moments to answer and rubbed his hands on a cloth as he did so. "*Non. Non la vedo da ieri sera.*" Sorry, I've no idea what that meant, but he put the cloth down, dropped his tools on the ground and walked over to us.

I found it strange that he never looked at me. I mean, not once had I noticed his eyes turned in my direction. It was as if he wanted to pretend I wasn't there. I offered a no doubt abysmally pronounced "*Arrivederci!*" but he just nodded and walked closer.

"We should try the gardens," Fletcher decided, and we passed through the open salon and out to the terrace with a view over the hills. I half expected to see Coralie puffing away at her cigarette, as she had when we'd interviewed her there after her father died, but there wasn't a soul to be found.

Guido went to look along the Avenue of the Spalliere, and we descended the first staircase towards the gardens. I stopped at the bottom and was once more haunted by the grotto there. The arched entranceway made me think of a portal to the underworld in the tales of Orpheus and Heracles. Jets of water obscured my view, but I could make out the stone figure of a woman in the centre of the niche beneath the terrace. At her side were two tiny children and what looked like a man with a frog's head.

That's exactly what it was, and now that the water receded and I moved up a step, I could see that there were other half-human characters along with giant frogs around the bottom of the tableau. I remembered the story of the goddess Leto who cursed the Lycian peasants after they failed to show her due hospitality. Her arms reached up to the sky in suppliance, and I was glad that I'd never come across such a vengeful character myself.

Even more frightening was a long strip above her head. There were demons studded with seashells, which gave the effect of scaly skin. Their hungry mouths were open to display jagged teeth and, in between these monstrous pairs, there were plaster reliefs of famous scenes. Apollo chased the object of his affection. Dryads danced, and the Greek god of metallurgy (I don't remember his name, though I had been re-reading my copy of *Bulfinch's Mythology* recently) was working away in his forge.

No space in Montegufoni would be complete without a fresco of mythological figures in the sky, and the grotto didn't let me down on that score. As Fletcher went to stand in the adjacent archway, I noticed Artemis on a chariot pulled by golden stags, her brother flying through the air opposite and, in the centre, Zeus, the king of the gods, looking down on the terrible scene. I knew it was Zeus because he was seated on a rocky throne with a thunderbolt at his feet.

You might wonder why I would focus on this when we were supposed to be looking for the missing sister, but it was either that or force myself to look down at Coralie's lifeless body. The jets of water rained upon her as though she were part of the grotto. Her arms lay limply in front of her and, dressed in a flimsy silk negligée, she looked as if she had been placed there as an offering to the gods.

CHAPTER TWENTY-ONE

"No!" Fletcher intoned before seemingly losing control altogether. "Not Coralie. Please not her!"

He fell forward through the fountains that, shooting from the mouths of the various stone figures, crisscrossed from one side of the grotto to the other. His eyes already welling up, he dropped to his knees beside her and put his face against the flat of her back to lie there sobbing. The water was really coming down on the pair of them. Coralie's hair was soaking wet. She had clearly been there for some time, and I had to move around to the far side of the entrance to get a better look at her.

That was when the sadness hit me. It would be easy for my job to leave me cold and callous, but I'm glad to say that hasn't happened yet. I felt for Fletcher, and I felt for the woman who had died. I could see scratches on her arm and bruises on her wrist, and I knew that she had suffered before she was killed. There were marks on her neck too and, without turning her body over, I could only assume she'd been strangled.

"It must have been someone from the castle," Fletcher said in a small, hollow voice. "After what she said last night in the courtyard, the people here must have been angry."

I would have told him that things weren't always so simple, but I heard a bark behind me and turned to see Delilah running up the stairs from the garden. I grabbed her around the flank to make sure she wouldn't disturb the body, though the fountains and Fletcher were doing a good enough job of that.

My grandfather arrived a few moments later, but he didn't say anything. He just stepped through the web of water and helped the mourning brother to his feet. That was as far as Fletcher got before his strength deserted him and he had to put his head on Grandfather's shoulder. The great detective showed no discomfort at this outpouring of emotion but was less keen on drenching his suit, so he steered Fletcher back to the steps outside.

He asked him the question that I hadn't had the heart to utter. "Do you know how this happened?"

"Of course I don't!" The younger brother sounded insulted by the aspersion. "I love Coralie. I would never hurt her." He was breathing heavily, as though he'd just sprinted up the stairs. "I know she wasn't the easiest person, but she was my sister." Saying these words aloud must have felt like a fist to the face. "She *is* my sister!"

Stillness took hold of the scene. The water in the grotto still trickled and splashed. The breeze still bothered the tall trees that towered over the terraces from the garden below, but no one spoke for a whole minute as we assessed the sad new discovery.

Personally, I didn't know how to feel. In so many of our cases, the suspects can be divided by a clear dichotomy. They are either good or bad, loathsome or likeable. Coralie was one of those unusual exceptions, in that she fell perfectly in the middle. She was no saint, and I think we could now rule her out as her father's killer, but she'd had little warmth in her. If Lord Monroe had been an unpopular custodian of the castle, she marked herself out as potentially far worse.

I thought back to the scene in my room the night before and hoped that I hadn't misinterpreted her intentions. For a moment, it struck me that she might simply have been poor at expressing herself. Perhaps she really had wanted my company, and I'd insulted her. Or maybe she knew the danger she was in and, thanks to my suspicious mind and clumsy tongue, I'd thrown her out to fend for herself.

No matter how much I'd grown up recently, I still had to question whether I really knew anything at all. I took another look at Coralie – at the channel of water running down her bruised neck and her previously straight fringe now hanging sodden – and I was filled with guilt.

Guido had evidently completed a circuit of the property as he appeared from the garden and came to stand looking mournful next to my grandfather. I didn't want to go through the rigmarole of asking the same people the same questions we'd already put to them. I didn't want to continue with the slow and steady approach that Grandfather insisted was a detective's best strategy.

There was an obvious culprit: a selfish, drug-taking, trouble-making jackstraw. In my head at that moment, the solution to the mystery seemed inevitable, so I left the others behind and ran up to the castle.

"Christopher, come back!" my grandfather called after me. "What the devil's got into you?"

I crossed the terrace and passed through the large salon to a set of stairs I hadn't taken before. For various reasons, I was fairly certain that this was where the siblings had their rooms.

I arrived at the floor above the Hall of Gonfaloniers and my own apartment to find a long corridor much like the one behind the Gallery. It was decorated with simple painted patterns on either wall. Garlands of fruits and foliage ran alongside me as I tried the first door I reached.

The room beyond it was largely empty. There was a man's Norfolk jacket hanging over the back of one chair, a small pile of papers on a table in the centre of the room and a large bed with an iron canopy and red damask curtains. Even the bed was tidy, the sheets tucked in, and the only personal touch was a framed photograph next to the washstand which showed the three Monroe siblings together as children. Next to them, their slight, cautious mother peered out of the frame, as though afraid of whatever she could see there.

I decided this was Fletcher's room. I knew he didn't live close by and there was no reason to think he maintained a presence at the castle. I moved towards the second door and, based on the wisdom that the third time is generally the charm (and my own poor luck), I did not expect to find what I was looking for.

"What do you think you're doing, coming in here at this time of the morning?" Dashwood demanded when I pushed open his door.

I would not be put off my task. "It's half-past nine!"

"Precisely!" Sitting up in bed, he put his hands to his eyes, as even the weak light that came in from the hallway was too much for him.

I looked about the room before he could say anything to defend himself. It was a mess, and I found it hard to imagine how one man could have so much of an impact on a place in such a short time. There were empty bottles on the floor, a suitcase had been emptied on top of a chest of drawers, and a few books had found a resting place on the shuttered balcony. Most noticeable, however, was an occasional table in the centre of the room with a small pile of white powder, some dirty glasses and, just for contrast, a lovely posy of pink flowers in a tumbler of water.

When I didn't speak again, he really shouted at me. "Christopher! What do you want?"

"I want you to admit that you're the killer, because it's the only thing that makes one iota of sense." I knew that my grandfather would be upset when he caught up with me, but I didn't care.

He threw back his bedcovers and fumbled on his nightstand for a black silk dressing gown. If I'd had any doubts before, they were now resolved. What sort of person wears a black silk dressing gown?

He put on a pair of glasses, which, I must admit, made him look a little more sympathetic for some reason. When he spoke, he did so in a weary, yet stoic manner. "We've already discussed this. You know that I was nowhere near here when Father was killed. As you've only just arrived in Italy, I don't suppose you're familiar with the geography, but it's not easy to get from Montegufoni to Arezzo in the time it takes for a telephone call to be connected."

"I still believe you found a way around that," I said, refusing to grant him even this simple concession. "But I'm not talking about Lord Monroe. I'm talking about your sister."

"My sister?" HIs tiredness was immediately forgotten. "You mean…" He didn't finish the sentence but clamped his mouth shut, and I could see the tension in his jaw from the way his cheeks tightened.

Grandfather had taught me that the culprit and the likely suspect are not always the same person. I knew not to equate the grumpiest, angriest or even the cruellest person around with the killer. And yet I couldn't shake the idea – even as he looked at me with such shock in his eyes – that Dashwood Monroe was to blame.

"You strangled Coralie and left her body in the grotto." My bitter proclamation surely betrayed more emotion than he was capable of showing for his sister.

He stood up from the side of the bed and turned around to face me, pointing behind him as he mounted his defence. "I've been right here since I bid you goodnight after dinner. I got blind drunk and would still be asleep if you hadn't forced your way in here."

I pressed forward to deliver my accusations a fraction more forcefully – but made sure to keep some distance between us just in case. "That's not proof. And even if you told me that you were in here with fifty other people, and they could all vouch for your whereabouts, I would still think you'd conspired to kill her."

He put his hand out to steady himself. I don't know whether it was all an act, or perhaps the alcohol and whatever else he'd consumed suddenly hit him, but he stumbled a few steps forward and seized hold of a twisted golden column on the four-poster.

"Listen to me, Christopher." He rubbed his head with his free hand, either to soothe the pain or wake himself up. "I'm no killer. I didn't know anything about Coralie until now. Why would I do that to her?"

"Why?" I might just as well have emitted a yelp of disbelief as this word came out so mangled it was barely decipherable. "Why would you kill the woman standing between you and a fortune?"

I thought he'd deny everything again, but it was all too much, and he wrapped his arm around the barley-twist post, much like a tiny child clinging to his father's leg for comfort.

"Coralie…" he managed to whisper before a cymbal crash of sorrow hit him, and his lower lip began to tremble.

"You and Fletcher are the ones who will gain most from your sister's death. Your only alibi is that you were too stupefied to leave your room." I pointed to the heap of what I took to be narcotic powder on the table. "Considering the state you were in, how can you be sure you didn't do it?"

"I wouldn't… I…."

His head dropped. His eyes fell to the floor, and I still wanted to hurt him. I was not in love with Coralie Monroe. I had not particularly appreciated her presence in my room the night before, and I really didn't like her cigarettes, but that did not lessen my anger. I wanted Dashwood to be punished because I was certain he was the only person there with the savagery, desperation and ruthlessness to kill off his family in order to escape from the squalid existence he'd forged.

"Go out to the garden and see how she died. Look at her lifeless body and tell me you didn't kill her."

Sometimes murder can be a surprisingly genteel affair. We'd investigated truly subtle killers who did everything they could to hide their involvement. We'd even looked into a few deaths that barely seemed like crimes. But this one was quite different. Coralie's windpipe had been crushed by a strong pair of hands. The killer most likely looked into her eyes as it happened. Maybe it was the guilt I felt over her death or the simple fact that I was not in my home country, and everything looked just that little bit askew, but I felt a deep yearning for justice.

"Answer, you coward!" These words came screaming out of me.

I was about to move closer when I felt a hand on my shoulder, and I couldn't move. It was Guido the mechanic. He didn't say anything. He apparently wasn't the type for conversation – but he nodded solemnly and gestured for me to accompany him from the room.

I looked at Dashwood one last time. All the cocksureness that he'd shown when he first arrived the previous afternoon had drained away. He couldn't even stand any more but collapsed back onto his bed. Perhaps he'd killed her in an impaired state and forgotten but, however it had happened, he would have to face the consequences.

I walked away with Guido at my side. It was the first time I was glad that he couldn't speak English, as I really didn't want to have to explain myself. Sadly for me, I knew that my grandfather wouldn't be so forgiving.

CHAPTER TWENTY-TWO

"I don't understand what you were thinking, Christopher."

I said nothing.

My mentor, forebear and, though I might not usually admit it, closest confidante watched me attentively. His calm grey eyes studied every inch of my face. "I'm not upset. I just need to understand what you thought you could achieve with your rash actions."

I was sitting on the floor in the hallway with my head resting against the wall. "I was trying to catch that snipe with his guard down."

"Very well." Grandfather tapped his opulent cane on the tiles a few times before saying anything more. He was just as upright and vertical as the silver shaft in his hands. "And what did you discover on your morning raid?"

I kept my mouth firmly shut once more. I couldn't admit that I hadn't discovered anything significant, as I would have felt like I was letting Dashwood Monroe off the hook.

"I see." To be honest, he was a lot more civil than I'd been expecting. "I must say this isn't like you, my boy. I'm not criticising your passion or initiative, but we must rely on the evidence as it currently stands. We've found little to suggest that Dashwood killed his sister, or his father for that matter. Is there anything that you haven't told me?"

Guido had walked along the corridor to the end of the hall but lingered in the shadows – perhaps to check that I would be all right before slinking off to the ground floor. He was an odd character and, had he not been the very picture of a Latin leading man, I might have compared him to Quasimodo, skulking through the darkness in a grand old pile.

"Well?" Grandfather prompted me when I offered nothing in response.

"She came to my room last night." This was the very last thing I wanted to tell him, but he instantly got it out of me. Now that I think about it, I'm not so sure that "confidante" is the right term for him. Perhaps *manipulative old terror* would be more accurate. "Coralie came to my room, and I should have been nice to her. I should have kept her up talking about her favourite books or her art. She could have bored me all night describing every last detail of the type of brushes she used on her paintings if she so desired. But instead, I was rude and suspicious, and she wandered off to die."

He remained silent for a moment and, when he spoke, his voice was unexpectedly compassionate. "Oh dear. It's really no wonder you're feeling so blue if that's the case. I have been in your position several times myself; the feeling that one is indirectly responsible for another person's death is difficult to overcome."

From the way he had phrased this, it rather suggested it was my fault after all.

He raced to correct himself. "Not that I believe for one moment that your actions led to her murder. You had no way of knowing that she would be killed. If anything, I, as the more experienced detective, should have been alive to the possibility."

"Thank you." I didn't feel much better, but I had to say something.

"If it's not too indiscreet to enquire, may I ask why she came to your room?"

I really didn't want to answer this question. If I'd told him the reason Coralie gave, my whole face would have turned red, and he would have thought I was having an attack of some kind.

"I've considered this at length," I began, choosing my words ever so carefully, "and I believe that she wanted to discover whether we suspected her. I think she was afraid that we would blame her for what happened to her father. She was close to the castle when he died, and she gave us no alibi. With Dashwood theoretically ruled out as a suspect, she might have thought herself the obvious choice."

He wasn't the type to sit down on the floor next to me, but he moved to the wall opposite and leaned against it, which was a phenomenally casual act by his standards.

"That does match my impression of her. She was less certain of her feelings towards her father than her brothers are. She made no pretence of having any great allegiance to him, and yet I believe she did love him in her way. Her reticence when we spoke to her each time most likely came from her fear of arrest, but I doubt she had anything to do with the murder. For one thing, she struck me as a self-satisfied person; she was too contented in her own life to think about ending someone else's."

144

I thought this both a sad and accurate description of the dead woman, but my guilty conscience still made me wish there was something nicer I could say about her.

"It's a terrible affair," I uttered half-heartedly. "I can't help thinking that, whatever Lord Monroe's intentions, all his scheming taught his children to be duplicitous. Which only makes it more likely that Dashwood is the killer."

As his brow creased, his cheeks puffed up somewhat, and I could tell how sympathetic he really was.

Rather than contradict this idea outright, he tried to reason with me. "Christopher, I can't deny that Dashwood Monroe is a complicated man, but we must not jump to conclusions. How many times have we met a roguish figure whose every word and act screams that he must be the miscreant for whom we are searching?"

I didn't think this required a response, but when he said nothing more, I realised I had no choice. "Many times."

"And how often has the killer turned out to be that very first person we suspected?"

"Quite a few," I replied without thinking before adjusting my answer. "However, in each of those instances, the killer had worked out some special strategy for distancing himself from his crimes. Overall, I admit that there have been far more examples in which an initially innocent-seeming suspect did a good job of hiding his true intentions."

"Exactly. So why would this case be any different?"

There really was no real answer to this. All I could say was, "Because there's something about Dashwood I don't trust."

He laughed then. He let out a hearty chuckle that echoed down the corridor and most likely around the castle. "But Christopher, there are things I don't like about every single suspect here. Fletcher's just a bit too easy-going to be trusted in the light of his father's death. The clutch of locals we keep seeing in the courtyard must have seen something incriminating by now, and yet they haven't said a word. There is a corrupt and violent police inspector strolling about the place. And Signora Acciaioli may have her own reasons for wanting the father of her children dead."

"And the priest told me he'd plotted to kill Lord Monroe in the past," I chipped in, as I should probably have told him this before.

"There you go! And that's without mentioning the demand Coralie made last night for practically everyone to get out of the castle as soon as possible. All in all, I would say we have gone from having not nearly enough suspects, as you complained just after Renwick was killed, to having far too many to know where to begin."

For some reason, this made me feel a lot better. "You're only half right. We do have a lot of suspects, but there is an obvious place to go next."

"Oh, yes?"

I pushed myself up to standing and walked past Dashwood's room to a final door that I hadn't previously approached.

"I am quite sure that this is where Coralie slept when she stayed at Montegufoni." I placed my hand on the door and waited for Grandfather to join me before pushing it open.

Inside was an opulent, frescoed room like so many we'd seen in the castle. Seeing as I'd been born in a manor house, lived in a boarding school, and resided in an immense stately home, houses with many rooms are nothing new to me, but I'm still regularly amazed that anyone could consider such ridiculously large dwellings to be a necessity.

I rather liked Montegufoni because, at one point or another, the rooms had all been occupied. As far as I could tell, there was no guest wing, where the rooms sat gathering dust on the off-chance the owners decided to throw a party. I doubt I'm exaggerating when I say that I've entered less than half of the many salons, parlours and sitting rooms back home in Cranley Hall. And when you bear in mind that I've turned the place upside down looking for murderers on two different occasions (and often played hide and seek there), that's a rather damning statistic.

"It's surprisingly impersonal," Grandfather declared as we walked about the dead woman's room with inquisitive looks on our faces. "I know that she and her brothers lived in Britain until they were adults and may not have spent much time living here, but I expected some sense of who she was."

"If you think this is bad, you should see Fletcher's room. It looks as though he's never set foot in it."

Grandfather was right that there was little evidence it was Coralie's bedroom we had entered. The wardrobe was full of her luxurious clothes, no doubt bought from some expensive Italian fashion house, but in terms of personal effects, there was nothing to find.

My companion must have noticed this too, as he said, "There's not even a handbag, and I know she had one with her yesterday when she arrived."

"Might it not be a robbery then?" I knew there was a more likely explanation, but I thought I'd let him draw that conclusion for himself.

"Or perhaps that's what the killer wanted us to think. Either way, this was instantly undermined by the fact he took her body downstairs."

I tried to solve this apparent contradiction. "Perhaps she was killed down in the grotto after all?"

"No, no. It was here."

He did not offer any evidence of this assertion and so I looked at the one place I was yet to explore. There was a door ajar in the corner of the room and, beyond it, a small water closet held a sink, a toilet and a towel ring. There was also a mirror fixed to the wall that was cracked from the centre outwards. Pieces of glass were still in the basin underneath it, so it had clearly happened recently.

When I returned to the bedroom, Grandfather was crouched on his haunches inspecting the carpet around a low table with two upholstered chairs.

"As I see it, the killer had no trouble coming in here. He was known to Coralie, and she was about to pour the drinks when he attacked her."

I couldn't see at first how he'd come to this conclusion, but something must have caught his attention. There was a bottle of Chianti wine and a single glass on the table. The cork had been removed, but it was still full, and now that I looked, a corkscrew lay on the floor nearby.

Grandfather revealed the missing element that I'd overlooked. "There are signs of a struggle. I propose that Coralie brought out two glasses from the chiffonier in the corner, and she was preparing to pour when the killer smashed his glass over her head."

I moved around the table to see what he'd found, and sure enough, there were shards scattered over the carpet, but the stem of the glass was missing.

"How fascinating," I whispered, still impressed by the magic of Grandfather's mind whenever he entered this mode of detective work.

"The killer held the makeshift weapon in his hand and brought it down on her head, which meant that the bulb of the glass smashed to pieces, but the stem remained intact. He must have pocketed that, as it surely had his fingerprints on it."

"That's exactly what I was thinking." He actually looked rather pleased with me then. "If the glass had merely fallen from the table onto the thick carpet, it would not have broken so violently, and the stem would be somewhere nearby."

"But a wine glass wouldn't be strong enough to knock someone out, so after that, what happened?"

He cast his expert gaze around the elaborate room. It was not the medieval-looking bed that interested him, or the wardrobe full of clothes. It was not even the frescoes on the ceiling of – you guessed it – mythological figures on a cloud. He pointed back to the W.C. I'd just examined.

"She ran to the lavabo for safety, but he was too fast." Grandfather walked over to look inside. "I believe he caught her as she was trying to lock the door and forced her head back against the mirror. Remember, there were no cuts on her face when we found her body, so that would seem to be the way it occurred. The police will be able to confirm this, assuming that the fountains haven't washed away the evidence."

He paused and considered the final moments of Coralie's time on earth. "From there, the murder itself would have been fairly simple – in terms of its execution, at least – though even the most unfeeling and misanthropic brutes lose something of themselves when they take another's life."

"Does any of this help to determine who killed her?" The precision with which he had outlined the appalling series of events sent a shudder through me.

He rubbed his lips together as though they were dry. "I can't possibly say yet, but it is important that we understand as much as we can if we wish to solve this case."

A thought occurred to me then. "Perhaps the culprit took the body to the grotto to wash away any evidence that might connect him to the killing."

"It's one explanation. Although I think it more likely that he has a theatrical bent. There are few more dramatic locations in which to leave a victim than that grotesque shrine."

There was something else that was niggling at me. "Coralie's face was very pale when I found her. I wondered if it was due to the cool water or she had been there for some time. The fact her bed is still made suggests she never went to sleep. She was wearing a negligée, however, so perhaps she was killed as she was about to retire."

He nodded and, instead of responding to my point directly, he reeled off a series of names under his breath. "Miss Mountstephen, one of the Lombardo brothers, one of the Munroe brothers, Father Laurence, perhaps even the old lady who spends her days fixing vehicles or a member of the band: there's really no one we've met to whom Coralie would have automatically refused entry, so we cannot narrow down our suspects for the moment."

"Fabulous!" I said in a disconsolate tone as I clapped my hands together. "Which gets us precisely nowhere."

He moved across to the main door and then looked back at me with a suitably mysterious visage. "In a murder investigation, there is no such thing as a backwards step."

With that, he disappeared out to the hall, and all I could think was, *Well, bully for us!*

CHAPTER TWENTY-THREE

Dashwood was standing in his doorway as we passed. He'd put on some clothes and presumably splashed water on his face, but he still had an unhuman look about him. Drink and dope and waking up to a dead sister is not a good combination for anyone.

"Do you have anything to tell us?" Grandfather stopped to ask a little vaguely.

"I didn't know a thing about it until this rude boy burst into my room."

I took exception to the boy part, though I fully admit that I'd set out to be rude.

Grandfather ignored his petulance and asked something more important. "What time did you go to bed last night?"

Leaning against the doorframe, he bothered the thick black hair at the back of his head. "After dinner, I left the table before the rest of you and came straight to my room. I fell asleep in my armchair, having consumed the remainder of a bottle of gin that I hid the last time I was staying here. I must have popped downstairs to get some wine, too, though I have no memory of doing so."

"The time you fell asleep would have sufficed." Over his decades as a police officer, Grandfather had developed the perfect blunt tone to hurry along suspects.

"It must have been the middle of the night, but as I've already implied, I was not exactly *compos mentis* for some time before that."

"And you didn't hear your sister being strangled to death in the room next door?"

"Next door?" he looked at me then. "I thought you said that she died in the grotto."

He really was a very good actor… or innocent. I could no longer say which it was with any confidence.

"She was found in the grotto," Grandfather explained. "But we believe she was killed in her room."

Dashwood's face clouded over like an English summer's day. Something about his reaction didn't sit well with Grandfather and he immediately barked an order.

"Show me your hands!"

The suspect looked even more confused but did as instructed. "Why do you…?"

Lord Edgington took them one by one and inspected either side and between the fingers. I saw no cuts or wounds, and he released Dashwood with an unsatisfied *hmmm*.

"We will talk to you again before long." With this said, he marched off ahead of me, his cane clicking on the polished wooden floor as he went.

"Wait one moment," the supposedly grieving sibling called after us. "I can't say I don't have a reason to kill my way to a fortune. I'm in more debt than the Duke of the Marshalsea, and even my inheritance may not cover it. But if there is one thing at which I would draw the line, it's hurting a member of my own family."

I stopped walking, and I was tempted to utter a curt barb, but I felt that simply ignoring him was the biggest insult in my arsenal.

"I mean it!" he shouted as we continued on our way. "I had nothing to do with my sister's death."

When we found Delilah on the ground floor, Grandfather patted her on the head. "Good girl. You've done an excellent job."

"Did you set her to guard the stairs behind you?" I asked when she'd happily wagged her way through the salon.

"She likes to feel useful."

At first, I accepted this reply at face value, but then I began to wonder how he could possibly know such a thing.

Out in the courtyard, Fletcher was being comforted by Eva Mountstephen. He must have just told her what had happened, as she put her arm around him and they stayed linked together for a few seconds before Fletcher jerked away. Eva looked understandably hurt but continued to pat his shoulder.

"You'll survive this," I heard her reassure him as we approached.

Before we could speak to them, the young officer, Attilio Lombardo, led his superior through the castle towards the spot where we'd found Coralie. It was the same black-uniformed inspector we'd seen the day before. He was the one who'd threatened Lord Monroe and subsequently dismissed his death as nothing more than an accident. I didn't hold out much hope of his finding the real killer. He was the type to arrest the first person he encountered and make the evidence fit his theory.

He wore a smug look as he passed us, so he obviously knew who we were. My grandfather has always impressed upon me his respect for good police officers and his outright contempt for corrupt ones. He remained dour as the inspector offered a wave before sweeping through the door to the salon.

I don't know whether Fletcher observed any of this, but he went to sit down on a bench which held a number of Guido's tools. The Italian was sitting on the ground, working on an upturned two-seater sports car of some description. His grandmother apparently hadn't started work yet, and, realising that he was called upon to offer his condolences, Guido spoke to the grieving man in hushed tones.

"Lord Edgington," Eva said when she'd finished watching the sorry scene. "There's something I must tell you."

Even then, she gave one last look at Fletcher, and I really wished I knew what had passed between them. They behaved oddly around one another, to say the least. Were they former sweethearts? Had she done something terrible to him (or vice versa) which meant they could never be together? He certainly seemed to have eyes for her alone, and I'd felt the tension that existed between them on a number of occasions.

"What is it, my dear?" Grandfather adopted his sweet, accepting persona, which it would be nice to see more often.

She walked a few steps away from the two men and we followed. "I went into Renwick's office just now. Even though he is dead, I still have work to do to manage the estate." She paused as if struggling to put into words what she wanted to say. "The whole room is a mess."

I was tempted to tell her that it was like that the day before and was glad when Grandfather spoke instead of me. "Perhaps you should show us what you've found."

She nodded, just as nervously as ever, and the three of us headed to the ballroom. It still looked lonely and a little neglected, and Eva continued straight on to the door in the left-hand corner behind which stood Lord Monroe's office.

"It's exactly as it was yesterday," I said aloud this time as I took in the piles of papers all over the floor.

"No, it's not," Eva insisted. "It might have looked chaotic to you, but there was an order to everything in here. Renwick was never a tidy man in a conventional sense – I'm aware how this room must appear – but the truth is that I always knew where to find what I needed. Now look at it."

She held her hands out as though it were simple to understand what had happened. In response, Grandfather peered down at the nearest pile of papers before moving along the line as we had the day before.

"The dates are all muddled," he concluded. "They were in chronological order yesterday."

"Yes, and that's not all. They were arranged thematically, too. Agricultural matters were with agricultural matters. Papers concerning the upkeep of the castle were all together near the window, and general bills and expenses were in the centre of the room. To me, it looks as if someone has ploughed through the place, reading pages from here and there and not putting them back where they should be."

As Grandfather presumably considered what could have led to this even more chaotic situation, I searched once more for the paper I'd found detailing Lord Monroe's payments to the *Carabinieri*. It took me a little while but, sure enough, it was not far from the spot where I'd first seen it.

"If Ispettore Stefani was blackmailing Lord Monroe, why did he have a receipt?" I held up the paper in question, but Eva showed no particular surprise.

"That's what the inspector is like. He wanted to prove just how much power he had. The money itself wasn't what interested him, though I'm sure he spent it well. By making Renwick travel to the police station twenty kilometres away in Castelfiorentino, he was showing that he had the force of the Italian state at his back."

I had to wonder whether the money even ended up with Stefani if this was the case. For the second time that day, I was glad not to speak Italian, as it meant I was less likely to come into contact with that thug of an inspector. I felt sorry for any suspects he chose to investigate. He could surely no longer deny that there was a murderer at work in Montegufoni now that Coralie was dead.

"Perhaps it was the will," Grandfather finally declared when he'd completed a circle of the room. "From what I can observe, the piles that were most disturbed are the ones in the south-eastern corner, most of which relate to legal matters. It's more than possible that whoever came in here wished to know what they would inherit."

I was about to mention something I'd seen upstairs a half hour or so earlier, but he was suddenly full of excitement. "Christopher!" He took me by the arm and pulled me through to the neighbouring office where we'd seen the telephone the day before. "You will go into Florence to speak to Renwick's solicitor. He will be able to clear up any doubts."

Eva had followed us and, like the good secretary that she was, noted down what Grandfather said on a pad of paper. "I'll make the appointment with Andrew Longfield. When would you like to see him?"

Grandfather picked a thread of cotton from his immaculate grey coat. "As soon as possible, my dear. There is no time to lose."

She set to work, and Grandfather and I hurried back through the ballroom to see what new developments had occurred since we'd been outside a few short minutes earlier.

"Breakfast has been prepared on the terrace of the salon, sir," Todd informed us – which was surely the most important news we would hear all day.

"I'm afraid that will have to wait." Have I ever mentioned what a terrible person my grandfather is? "Christopher has an appointment in Florence this morning, and I'll need you to drive him."

"Very good, sir."

Grandfather put a finger to his lips as though he were considering something of great moment. "Actually, Todd, you had better take a package of food for Christopher. He'll just get grumpy otherwise, and then he won't concentrate on the task I've set him." As I was saying, Grandfather is a kind and considerate person, and I love him very much. "Of course, if he gets the seats in the Bugatti dirty before I've even travelled in it, feel free to leave him at the side of the road somewhere."

Well, perhaps he's somewhere between the terrible and considerate. I believe the phrase *benevolent dictator* suits him well.

Todd walked off to see to his work, and I had an important question for my brilliantly awful and awfully brilliant mentor. "Why am I going to interview the solicitor on my own?"

"Because there are things here at Montegufoni to which I must see. I'm sure you'll be fine without me."

"I'm sure I will," I lied. "However, I'd still prefer to have you there.

What if he turns out to be a mendacious trickster, and I fail to see it?"

He moved his hand up to his forehead then, and I wondered whether I had given him an instant headache. Before I could check, Father Laurence appeared from the salon, and I had to conclude that he had been informed of that morning's crime.

"Was it one of you?" he shouted across to Fletcher and the mechanic.

The grandmother was back at her post now and yelled something at the priest in loud Italian. I have no idea what she said, but the response was accompanied by a number of hand gestures, and not all of them seemed very polite.

Guido left Fletcher to calm her down before responding.

"Why you ask this, Padre?" I was a little stunned that he spoke English after all.

"Because you, more than anyone else here, have been critical of the Monroes."

Grandfather and I looked at one another, and I imagine we were both thinking the same thing: *Has he?*

"Lord Monroe gave you a good job and allowed you and your family to stay here, and yet it was never enough for you. You couldn't see what a comfortable situation it was. And now look where we all are!"

Guido held his gaze on the furious priest, and I thought he would launch a response across the courtyard, but nothing more came, so Father Laurence turned his attention to the second suspect.

"And what about you, Fletcher? Did you kill your poor sister? You know that I loved that young woman. I thought of her as my own daughter and treated her more like one than your father ever did!"

Fletcher still looked distraught, and these questions took some time to knock about in his brain before he could reply. "What do you want me to say to you, Father? Do you want me to disagree? Because I really can't. All I can tell you is that I loved Coralie just as much as you did, and I don't know who would have done this to her."

"There is no justice…" Father Laurence pulled his hat from his head and threw it to the ground. "No justice in this…" He couldn't finish this thought; it was all too much to bear. He turned away, and I was once more forced to question if everything he said was for our benefit, or he really did feel the emotions on display.

"And that," my grandfather said when the priest had shuffled off

156

despondently towards the chapel, "is why I want to stay here while you go to Florence."

"Lord Edgington," Eva called from the window of her office. There really was a lot happening in the courtyard, though I hadn't seen the chickens about for some time. "I've just spoken to Andrew, and he says he will meet Christopher at the Helvetia and Bristol Hotel in an hour."

"Perfect." Grandfather raised his eyebrows a few times. It was the happiest I'd seen him that day, and seemed to say, *Things are finally coming together.* Personally, I thought everything was an incomprehensible mess, and it was only about to get worse.

"Where are you taking that man?" Grandfather practically shouted, and any enthusiasm that I'd spied in him instantly vanished.

He pointed past me towards the door to the salon through which Ispettore Stefani had just pushed Dashwood ahead of him. The way in which the inspector held on to the man's shoulder told us that he had claimed his prisoner.

The policeman was not afraid of a retired English officer with no jurisdiction and told him just this. Well, I assume that's what he said. To be honest, there was a lot of shouting in Italian and then Stefani laughed the big booming laugh of a villainous Moriarty figure. He waved farewell with mock civility, and this final burst of action in an already very busy period sparked Fletcher into life.

"My goodness, Dash." He looked truly shocked that his brother would be suspected of their sister's murder and ran after him. "Don't worry, brother. I'll make sure that they don't punish an innocent man."

Eva was still watching from the window and clearly suffered Dashwood's arrest almost as much as his brother did. Guido the mechanic appeared to have no more love for the inspector than anyone else. He spat on the floor and mumbled as Stefani proudly paraded his prisoner through the courtyard.

Grandfather, meanwhile, was doing his best to concentrate on our already established priorities. "Don't worry about that, Christopher. Fletcher will do what he can to look after his brother. You go to Florence with Todd."

Everything was happening at the same time and, if I'm perfectly honest, I was glad that someone had made this decision for me.

CHAPTER TWENTY-FOUR

Delilah chased after me to the car, and I was loath to tell her to return to the house, but I knew she would be happier with all the space of the castle and its vast gardens to explore than in an almost as spacious but man-made car.

"I'll be back before you know it," I called to her as Todd started the engine.

She looked at me with an expression which surely meant, *Well you would say that.* She was incredibly talented at making me feel guilty, though now that I thought about it, this expression was really very similar to the look she gave me when she wanted food.

I sat in the front of the Bugatti with Todd. Having been waited on far too often in my life, I have no truck with standing on ceremony, especially when I consider the person who is supposed to be my servant a personal friend.

"Would you like to talk about the events of the last day?" he asked most considerately, as he is simply that kind of person.

"I would very much *not* like to talk about the events of the last day," I replied without hesitation.

We drove in silence for a minute along the Via Volterrana to Florence. I'd read in Grandfather's guidebook that it was an important thoroughfare dating back to Roman times. It was this kind of completely irrelevant information that I needed to distract myself for a little while. Well, that and the wrapped breakfast I'd been given.

"I'm sorry," I eventually told Todd. "I didn't mean to sound rude. I just…" It was hard to put into words how I was feeling, so I didn't try.

"There's no need to apologise, Christopher." He tended to be less formal when Grandfather wasn't around, and I appreciated it. "I'm sure it has been a trying time, what with the luxurious travel you experienced all the way from London, including the sleeper carriage from Calais. I'm sure it didn't compare to spending two nights parked in a field, kipping on the back seat."

Whenever he teased me, he had a cheeky smile that I doubt his employer had ever seen.

"I'm sure you had the most tremendous adventure," I responded, perhaps optimistically. "I love the idea of getting in a car and driving as far as it will take me."

I looked at the ridiculously ostentatious vehicle. Were the knobs on the levers and thingamajigs really made of whalebone? Or had Grandfather been pulling my leg? There was certainly a lot of brass and walnut. The seats in the driver's compartment were in the softest hand-stitched leather, and almost everything in the cabin behind us was upholstered in what looked like a velvet carpet. This was the kind of car that you bought if you wanted people to know how much you'd paid for it, though I would give my grandfather the benefit of the doubt and accept that he simply loves automobiles and wished to own the best.

"I had a very nice time on my travels," Todd said somewhat diplomatically, before adding a caveat. "That being said, crossing the border without being able to speak a word of any other language when the Italian police were shouting at me and rifling through the car was not my favourite moment. I'm sure they suspected me of stealing it."

"Ah, that doesn't sound so pleasant."

I was worried about a lot of things just then. At the top of my mind was poor Coralie, of course. It may sound terrible to admit it, but as I'd never known her father, his death had seemed rather routine to me. It's standard practice when travelling with the great Lord Edgington for someone to be murdered soon after we reach our destination. The fact that it happened so quickly this time made it feel even more inevitable.

Finding Lord Monroe's daughter that morning was a very different experience, however. With all due respect to my slain aunt and uncle, to whom I'd never felt particularly close, I could only think of one murder I'd investigated that had disturbed me quite so much. If Coralie hadn't come to my room, then I'm sure I wouldn't have felt so responsible, but that's what happened, and there was no escaping it.

"The thing is…" I said when a comfortable hush had settled between us. "The thing is, I blame myself for the murder that occurred during the night. I feel I could have stopped it from happening. I have become so inured to investigating murders that I didn't take the first death seriously enough. I thought he was a rich, powerful old man, and people were tired of having to put up with his despotic ways. I didn't imagine it would go any further."

"If you don't mind my saying, Christopher." He paused to look at me through the side of one eye. I couldn't stand it when Grandfather did this while driving, but Todd was such a capable, steady sort of person that he always filled me with confidence. He was the kind of humble, brave young man that a good author would make the hero of a thrilling book – no, a whole series of the things. I'd certainly read them.

Anyway, Todd was in the middle of explaining something helpful. "If you don't mind my saying, Christopher, it seems that, deep down, you *would* like to talk about everything that has happened since you arrived here."

"I think you're probably right."

So that's what we did. We spent the drive to the city talking, and with each mile we travelled and each new confession I made, I felt just a little bit better – the marmalade-covered muffins also helped. And so, when we rolled down the hill towards the Roman walls on the outskirts of Florence, I wasn't nervous about my appointment with Lord Monroe's solicitor, and I didn't return to my old fears of not being up to the task my grandfather had set. Perhaps it was the simple, encouraging advice that Todd gave me, but I actually felt quite confident.

We drove through the city, over the Santa Trinita bridge and right up to the Piazza Vittorio Emanuele II, where Todd parked the car so that I could pop along to the Hotel Helvetia and Bristol. I had to think that they'd added the second part of the name so that British people didn't worry about pronouncing the first bit.

I don't know how Todd knew exactly where I had to go, but he pointed me away from the square, with its long gallery of porches and its statue of a man on a horse. I walked through the grandest arch and along a quiet street. When I found the address I needed, it belonged to a perfectly normal housing block. It would have looked terribly opulent in the East End of London, but I can't say it caught the eye in the Tuscan capital. Every other building I had seen took my breath away, and the brief flashes I'd caught of the colourful cathedral a few blocks from the hotel tempted me to explore further.

There was a shop on the ground floor selling religious art and, just across the road, offering a glimpse of what was to come, a barely lit jeweller's window advertised Cartier watches, De Beers diamonds and Bulgari silver.

The inside of the hotel was suitably luxurious for its refined location. A commissionaire dressed in a long black woollen coat and top hat (that must have been sweltering) immediately approached and directed me through the main foyer to the conservatory. He apparently knew just who I was and why I'd come there. Perhaps he'd been told to look out for an out-of-place English boy whose suit was a little too big for him after he'd recently lost a few pounds.

I took a seat in a room with ten different palm trees in pots and a glass and metal ceiling that must have been in the absolute centre of the building and acted as a skylight. Bright sunshine flooded down to me, and I felt quite comfortable at my wicker table, imagining that I had taken a flight to some far-off British colony. I'm uncertain why I was put in mind of India or Malaya, but it was just a daydream, and I think I can be forgiven if I'm wrong.

A waiter brought me a glass of water with lemon and lime and offered me something stronger, which I politely declined. As I waited for Mr Longfield to appear, I would like to tell you how peaceful I felt, but sadly there was a supercilious British woman complaining loudly in reception.

"Are you running a hotel or a doss house?" she demanded and, though the receptionist's English was really very good, the meaning of this term was presumably lost on him.

"Madam, I assure you, we are doing all that we can."

"That's what they said on the train when that nice American lady had the same problem. I really wonder what the world is coming to when one pays all this money, and it still isn't safe to travel."

"Really, madam." I couldn't see the man, but I imagined him closing his eyes and bowing a little as he spoke. "You are perfectly safe here. There is nothing to worry about. Nothing like this has ever happened before."

As I was listening, a young woman had taken a seat on the other side of the room. She had wavy brown hair, but I couldn't see her face because there was a large plant in the way. I could just make out the book she was reading, or rather, I could just about tell who wrote it.

"Charles Dickens!" Quite against my better judgement, I said this out loud and then immediately pretended that I hadn't. "I mean… what the dickens?"

She briefly looked in my direction before turning back to her book.

When I was sure she had forgotten about me, I shuffled my chair a few inches to the side and was about to get a glimpse of her when a rotund gentleman with a huge bushy beard, a cream suit and a pocket watch in hand rushed forward to block my view.

CHAPTER TWENTY-FIVE

For a moment, he looked just like the White Rabbit from *Alice's Adventures in Wonderland*.

"Mr Prentiss, I presume?" he asked. "May I sit?"

He did sit, and though he was serious in his manner, he had a great warmth to him. His perfectly round cheeks gave him the look of a man who didn't know how to frown.

"Mr Longfield, I presume?" I replied without meaning to echo him, but then, as we've long since established, I'm not the best when it comes to controlling my own tongue.

"That's right."

The girl with the lovely hair and fine taste in books was looking over again, but I still couldn't see her face.

"Terrible business about poor Renwick. Terrible business. It makes you wonder what the world is coming to. It really does." He sighed, and it seemed that he'd used up all his good humour. "I've brought the papers that your grandfather requested. In normal circumstances, I would not disclose such information, but as your reputation precedes you, I have decided to make an exception. I would, of course, ask for your discretion in sharing the contents of the will before it is read to the family."

He watched me for a few seconds, as though to ensure he had made the right choice, then reached into his shiny brown leather briefcase to extract a slim paper envelope. It was sewn shut with a red thread, but this was easily undone, and then he was free to place the file in front of me.

"This is not the will itself but the English document that I composed with Renwick to understand exactly what he wished to do with his estate after he died. The actual will is in Italian, and it is locked away securely in my office."

I looked at the date at the top of the front page. "This was written last year. Is that correct?" He nodded, and so I asked a further question. "Can I ask why he decided to amend his will?"

Longfield once more contemplated his answer. I imagine that cautiousness is an important tool for men in his profession. "Perhaps you should read what it says there first."

I skimmed my eyes across the paper in the hope I might find a quick summary of who would get what from the Montegufoni estate, but it was all too complicated for that, and so I gave it a thorough read.

The most important thing that I took from it was quite clear. "All three of Lord Monroe's children would inherit a portion of his worldly wealth, with Coralie receiving the castle and five-ninths of any money and investments. Fletcher, meanwhile, would receive a third and Dashwood just one ninth, unless the others were deceased, in which case the inheritance would pass between them in order of preference, not birth."

"Yes, that is the most significant part of the will, but other factors have been taken into account."

I wasn't ready for that yet and returned to my earlier question. "From the look of things, Lord Monroe made changes to reduce the amount that Dashwood would inherit. Am I right in thinking that, previously, the siblings received a proportion of the estate depending on birth order?"

"You are. Renwick wished to ensure that Coralie, as his first-born child, would have the Castle of Montegufoni and the resources to maintain it, but he was previously more generous to Dashwood. It was a near even split between the three heirs. Coralie was only given more money to help with continuing refurbishments."

"So he changed his will to punish Dashwood?" This certainly fitted with the letter we'd found in Lord Monroe's office.

"Among other things. If you keep reading, you'll see what I mean."

I turned over the paper and did as instructed. There was rather a lot of confusing legalese in the next paragraph, but as there was no mention of anyone by name, I felt confident in skipping it and reading the list beneath.

Fr. Brian Laurence – £10,000
Domenico Augello – £10,000
Giuseppe Fazio – £10,000
Agatino Catarella – £10,000
Angelo Acciaioli – £10,000
Cesare Acciaioli – £10,000
Peppino Acciaioli – £10,000
Annina Acciaioli - £10,0000

"My goodness," I was quite taken aback, as I had no idea that Lord Monroe was so rich that he could afford to make such grand bequests in addition to the fortune he was leaving his three first-born children.

"I should point out that those sums are in lire, not pounds. The symbols for the two currencies are infuriatingly similar."

This did change things somewhat – approximately one hundred times in fact – and so I focused on the names of the people rather than the amount of money they had been left.

"With the exception of Father Laurence, is this a list of Lord Monroe's illegitimate offspring?"

Longfield leaned over the table to answer. "Yes – except for the very last name."

I inspected the list again and realised that the final person received ten times the amount of the others. "So Signora Acciaioli will inherit more than her children and the other children from Montegufoni. I assume that Annina is the cook there?"

"Correct once again, Mr Prentiss." He sounded rather pleased with me. "It is clear that everything I have read in the paper about your skills of deduction was accurate."

He was not the first Christopher admirer I had met, but such compliments still made me feel self-conscious. I tried not to blush and focused on the document once more. "Am I right in understanding that all these amounts are taken out of the Monroe siblings' portion of the estate?"

"In a manner of speaking, yes. But those are relatively small sums when compared with what Coralie, Dashwood and Fletcher have been left."

"And how will everything be divided now that Coralie is dead?"

"I beg your pardon?" His face turned grave. "What do you mean?"

I was not prepared to break this bad news to him and had to take a deep breath. "I'm so sorry, Mr Longfield. I assumed Eva had told you. We found Coralie strangled at the castle this morning. That was one of the reasons that I had to come here so urgently."

He did not respond. He could not respond. He sat staring into space and I didn't know what to do as, though I desperately needed to ask him more questions, I couldn't intrude on his suffering.

"That poor girl," he eventually muttered. "She was like a niece to me. I suppose they told you that." He shook his head and exhaled ever so slowly. "She was a truly decent person and didn't deserve such a fate."

Another whole minute passed when the only sound was the girl on the other side of the room turning the page of her book and a telephone ringing in an office beyond the reception. I sipped my water and waited with a sympathetic expression in case he were to look back at me.

"This is tragic news, but I will do everything I can to help. You and your grandfather must find the savage responsible." He steeled himself for the conversation and pointed to the bottom paragraph of the page that I hadn't yet read. "In the event of one of the siblings predeceasing Dashwood, his father stipulated that he would only get one third of the estate. Renwick told me that, while he loved all his children equally, he was unwilling to spoil his errant son, who was already doing such a good job of spoiling himself."

"And if there were only one child left?" I asked, my voice wavering a touch.

"Then the whole estate, minus the specified bequests we have discussed, would go to the remaining heir." He pursed his lips and looked uncertain how to proceed. "I believe that Renwick wanted, above all, to continue his family name and so, while he was upset with his elder son when he changed the will, he would not have wished one of his illegitimate children to inherit Montegufoni. You know, he originally bought the castle for his three children and hoped that they would establish their homes there."

Longfield's tone was so warm and enthusiastic whenever he spoke about his client that it was clear they shared a bond. "You knew Lord Monroe very well, didn't you?"

He closed his eyes as he nodded. "All my life, in fact."

"And you followed him out here to Italy?"

Another silent confirmation followed.

"So which are you?" I asked quite opaquely.

"I beg your pardon?"

I was thinking out loud and should have paused to reflect first. "It seems to me that there are two kinds of people who trod the same path as Renwick Monroe. There are those whom he loved and wished to bring with him to his exciting new life out here, and those to whom he

168

dealt out his own brand of revenge."

He blinked a few times before replying. "I see. You're referring to the various neighbours and ne'er-do-wells Renwick crossed over the years."

"There's a man who owns a property near Montegufoni who apparently hated him. I've also spoken to Father Laurence, who admitted outright to wanting Lord Monroe dead, and I can only assume from your comment that there are plenty of others. Do you think any of those people could be behind the deaths?"

He reflected for a moment and looked up at the glass ceiling. "Of Renwick, perhaps. He had a singular way of rankling his chosen foes, but I doubt any of them would have killed his daughter. What would they gain from it?"

"Indeed," I politely replied before changing to something far ruder. "However, you didn't answer my question. Were you one of the lucky ones whom Renwick treasured and wished to keep close at hand? Or was your relocation to the Continent a punishment of some variety?"

"Renwick Monroe was a very moral person," he insisted and, for a moment, I thought he would avoid answering again. "It is true that his concept of morality was quite different from most people's, but I always believed him to have good intentions. He suggested that I might move to Florence as he, like many British expatriates here, could use the services of an Anglophone solicitor. I already spoke Italian, as my wife is from Rome. Bringing my family was one of the best decisions I have ever made, and I am truly thankful for the part Renwick played in it."

So that told me! I was about to ask him whether he knew anything else that might affect the investigation when he spoke a little less defensively.

"I'm not going to deny that my friend was an eccentric individual, especially in the latter years of his life, but I can't honestly say that I disagreed with the actions he took. He might have considered himself a judge of his peers' behaviour, but the punishments he meted out were, for the most part, proportionate to their crimes. That fellow to whom he sold a house with no foundations had fleeced his way to a fortune. Father Laurence was known as a violent sort back in Britain, and it's a good thing for everyone that Renwick showed him the error of his ways."

"I'm sure you're right," I was quick to agree. "I'm merely trying to understand what could have brought this curse upon Montegufoni. While you may think fondly of Lord Monroe, there are evidently plenty of other people who do not share your perspective."

He looked so intensely sad then that it was hard to believe this was the same light-spirited man who had arrived a short time earlier. "I will miss Renwick and Coralie immensely. I wish I could tell you why they were killed, but I simply don't know."

He was already packing away the papers into their envelope, which he then put in his bag. "If there's nothing more you need to know, I'm afraid I have another appointment."

"Thank you for your time, Mr Longfield."

He stood up from the table and came to stand next to me, as though I were the one who needed comforting. "I hope that you can find out the truth of what happened." He shook my hand with great vigour. "Godspeed, Christopher Prentiss. Godspeed."

As he walked away, I was left wondering whether I'd just received the information I required to solve the case, or nothing I had learnt that morning would prove the tiniest bit relevant.

CHAPTER TWENTY-SIX

I must have overstayed my welcome somewhat as the same waiter came to offer me the same selection of drinks, and I once more had to refuse. I was so distracted by the details of Lord Monroe's will that I almost forgot about my fellow fan of Dickens, who was still at her table reading.

I sneaked a look at her as I walked past and immediately became flustered. She had lovely hair and apparently liked the same sort of books as me, so any kind of face would have been just fine. Two eyes, preferably a nose, and most definitely a mouth would have suited me to the ground. As it turned out, she was exquisite to boot. Just seeing her from that awkward angle was enough to make my knees buckle, and I'm sure that I did a very silly walk indeed as I hurried over to the reception, relieved that she hadn't noticed my gawping.

I stood with my back to the conservatory, trying to find the courage to sneak one last look at her.

"Can I help you, sir?" the receptionist asked in English, as I clearly wasn't Italian.

"Well…" came my eloquent reply. "No, not really. I thought I'd have a bit of a stand over here for a moment. When I've finished, I'll probably turn around and, shortly after that, I might well leave."

The small man with a pince-nez and no hair smiled kindly. "Very good, sir." I got the impression that he frequently had to put up with mad Brits and knew how to deal with us.

I did as I'd planned, and when I turned around, the girl was staring straight back at me. Her eyes met mine, and it made my muscles seize up so that I could no longer move a single one of them. It wasn't just because she was literally and without doubt the most delightful human being on the face of planet earth. I recognised her.

She smiled then, and I thought I might faint. When she proceeded to wave at me, I thought I might explode. I was tempted to drop to my knees in search of cover, but there was nothing to hide behind. It took all my effort to wave back coolly and walk at a normal speed from the hotel, but as soon as I was outside, I ran as fast as my stupid legs could carry my stupid body, and I didn't look back until I reached the square where Todd was standing in the sun reading the newspaper.

"The girl!" I said, but I was barely able to talk because it felt like I'd just been hit by ten lorries which had then each taken the time to reverse over me.

"I beg your pardon, sir?"

I didn't blame him for not understanding me. I was squeaking in a language that only mice could understand.

"The girl," I tried again, a little more clearly. "The girl from the boat."

"Which boat, sir?"

"The big one!" I said, as if this clarified anything. "The one we took from England."

"I see, sir." Todd is three times smarter than me and almost as bright as the old mastermind who employs him. He did his best to reconstruct the nonsensical fragments I'd provided into something approaching a whole. "So you saw a girl on the big boat from England and she's here now?"

"You're a genius, Todd. A verified genius."

He bit his lip, as there was no obvious response to this. "May I ask why this girl made you do something that you generally can't stand?"

He was referring to the forty-five-second run I'd just endured to reach him. I've never been one for exercise.

"It wasn't her fault." I probably sounded a little offended on her behalf. "She may well be perfect, Todd. I doubt she is capable of fault."

"And you know this because...?" The dear fellow spent far too long with my grandfather and had turned into a cynic.

It was a difficult question to answer, but I did my best. "Well... because of her eyes, and her smile, and also her hair, but mainly her eyes." I was still, evidently, flustered. "She may well be perfect."

"Yes, sir. You've already explained that. Did you happen to learn her name?"

"Of course not."

"Her nationality then?"

"Not even that." Now that I'd recovered from my exertions, I had the energy to walk nervously back and forth along the pavement.

"Did you at least talk to her?"

"No, that neither. But you're overthinking the situation, man. It's as simple as this: she was reading a Charles Dickens novel. She had pretty hair, and now I know who I am destined to marry."

In general, Todd had the discretion and resilience of a Beefeater guard, but he couldn't help laughing at me. "Congratulations, sir. I'm very pleased to hear it. Don't you think it might be a good idea to introduce yourself and tell her the plan for your shared future?"

Now I was the one laughing. "Don't talk rot, man. How could I, a mortal, talk to her, some form of heavenly European cherubim sent to earth to help me realise just how low and base a creature I am?"

He folded his newspaper and threw it onto the driver's seat. "Please correct me if I'm mistaken, but won't it be difficult to marry a woman if you never actually speak to her? At the very least, you must consent to the union at the altar."

I was trying to make sense of the sensations that were passing through my body and brain. It was not an easy thing to do. "You may have a point, but I have a better idea."

I walked to the centre of the square and stood watching the passing shoppers and tourists.

"Christopher," Todd began, dropping the formality once more, "what are you doing?"

"Based on the undeniable conclusion that I'm acting like lunatic, I'm trying to prove myself wrong," I muttered without looking back at him. Just then, a young lady with the loveliest dimples wandered past. She smiled at me, and I nodded cordially and pretended to tip the hat I wasn't wearing.

"How is it going so far?"

"Not very well, but give me ten minutes and perhaps things will improve."

Todd knew when to share his opinion and when to stay quiet. The aforementioned ten minutes passed at their usual rate, and he didn't say a word. When the time was up, he walked over to the bronze equestrian where I stood in the hope I might provide an explanation.

Rather than make the poor man guess, I revealed my thinking. "I thought that if I stood here long enough, I would see any number of beautiful young ladies, several of them would be enchanting, and I could knock the idea from my head that I had met the only woman in the world for me."

"Did it work?"

"Not in the slightest. It's not that there aren't any breathtakingly beautiful women – with hair and eyes – and I'm sure that they all have winning personalities, great intellect, diverse interests and that each is lovely in her own right, but none of them can compare to the girl on the boat."

"Does that mean you're ready to go back to the hotel to talk to her?"

I considered the possibility for approximately four seconds. "No, that would be even worse. The chance of her wanting anything to do with me after I open my mouth would instantly plunge. At least if we leave the city now, I won't have to face up to the fact I am unworthy of her."

I thought he would do his duty by bowing his head and saying, *As you wish, sir,* so that we could drive back to Montegufoni with me looking sullen all the way. He really let me down in that respect.

"Christopher, my friend whom I've known since you were a tiny lad, I don't like to speak out of turn, but I very much doubt that what you just said is true," he dared to contradict me, and I had to appreciate his honesty. "The fact is that you are quite the catch, and I can't believe that the young lady in question would be anything but charmed by you."

I knew I was acting like a prize fool. I'd spent the last few years trying to become the mature, capable person my grandfather believed I could be. The very sight of a pretty girl had turned me into a drivelling juvenile once more, yet none of that meant I could do anything about it.

We walked in the direction of the Bugatti, and I did my best to adopt Todd's perspective. "You speak a lot of sense, Todd, but you're judging the person standing before you, not the mumbling nincompoop I'd be if I were to engage the woman of my dreams in conversation." I stopped at the passenger door but didn't open it. "We have a murder to solve. By the time I get back to the castle, I will hopefully have accepted my lot in life."

"Very well, sir. I personally think you're making a mistake, but it is not my place to argue with you." And so he didn't.

I whistled for Delilah before remembering she wasn't with us. I longed to explore Florence – to stroll down its paved streets and through famous galleries. I wanted to see Michelangelo's David and the Titians in the Uffizi. I wanted to climb to the top of the famous bell tower, but now that city would forever be connected with the day my heart was shattered without a word being spoken.

Presumably because he was aware of my suffering, Todd did not drive directly to Montegufoni. In fact, he drove out of the square in the opposite direction and along Via Roma to the Baptistery of St John and the cathedral in the Piazza del Duomo. It was quite unlike any such building I'd seen before. With its lines of red, green and white, it looked as if a child had very carefully coloured it in with the few crayons he had to hand. It was deceptive in its simplicity but remarkable nonetheless, not least for its sheer size. The bell tower positively towered over us, and as for the red-tiled dome which protruded from the roof of the long, cross-shaped building, it made my heart skip a beat to imagine that humans with simple tools had created such a work of art and engineering.

As we rolled around the square in Grandfather's luxurious automobile, I believe we got as much attention as the church itself. There were hundreds of people out in the sunshine, and I even noticed the angry British lady I'd seen in the hotel, though there was no sign of my nameless love.

When our brief drive around the centre was complete, Todd drove us back to the river and over the Ponte Vecchio – which was so busy with pedestrians, merchants' carts and a particularly slow donkey, laden with produce, that we would have been quicker walking. This leisurely pace did give me the chance to look inside the shops that lined either side of the bridge. Jewellers of all stripes sold their wares, and every window sparkled with a hundred different gold bracelets, bangles, brooches and *bagues* (which is the French word for ring, but I couldn't think of an English equivalent beginning with B to complete the set).

And when we crossed to the other side of the river and drove along its banks, I was afforded a sumptuous view of the city and its buildings which dated back hundreds of years, to a time when the Medicis owned half of Italy. Such elegance and grace was hard to ignore. I'm not suggesting that the pain in my heart had lessened, but I did come to remember that, just as cities like Florence take millennia to build, finding one's path through life can be an arduous process.

In the end, we would not go home directly, as, while I was in the hotel, Todd had befriended one of the newspaper sellers in the piazza and obtained the recommendation of an *Osteria* on the banks of the Arno. We sat at an outdoor terrace eating more delicious pasta dishes, more disappointingly saltless bread and a huge selection of seafood.

I also enjoyed sampling local desserts and, as my grandfather wasn't there to look down his nose at me, I ordered two. I initially enquired about a Florentine biscuit, to which I'm rather partial, but the waiter informed me that, despite the name, they are actually from France. Instead, I opted for chestnut flour pancakes stuffed with soft cream cheese and pieces of dark chocolate. This was followed by a tart filled with lemon custard and pine nuts. All I can say is that I left the restaurant full, satisfied, and perhaps a few degrees sunnier than when I had entered.

I said very little on the journey back. The image of the girl was lodged in my mind. Her smile as she waved at me was like a flare bursting in the night's sky and her eyes were… well, I was actually too far away to see what colour they were, but they captured me, nonetheless. It was while I was thinking about her that the image of another woman entered my mind. Not a noted beauty or a heart-stealing *femme fatale* – the woman who suddenly took possession of my thoughts was Lord Monroe's secretary, Eva Mountstephen.

As we pulled up to the steps in front of the castle, I realised that she was the only one of our suspects who was not mentioned in Lord Monroe's will.

CHAPTER TWENTY-SEVEN

"Christopher, did you stop somewhere on your journey to repaint the *Mona Lisa*?" Grandfather griped with a playful smile when we found him in the Cardinal's Garden. He looked as if he had enjoyed another of Signora Acciaioli's feasts, so he could hardly complain we'd stopped somewhere to eat. What am I saying? Of course he could!

"I'm afraid it's my fault we took so long, Lord Edgington," Todd kindly intervened. "I insisted that Christopher take lunch in Florence as he looked a little pale after all that running."

"I see." Although Grandfather could (and did) complain at me for almost anything, he was more forgiving when it came to his hardworking factotum. "Actually, no I don't. Why were you running, Christopher?"

I considered lying to him but felt that anything I might invent would only lead to more questions. "I saw the most enchanting human being with whom I have ever crossed paths. She looked in my direction, and so I decided that the only sensible action was to get away as fast as I could."

"Well, yes. That does sound like something you would do." You see, he instantly lost interest in my story and brought us back to the more important matter of murder. "Now, what have you discovered?"

"Eva Mountstephen is not mentioned in the will," I said rather proudly, and he once more looked at me with an expression which seemed to ask, *Why would you have expected any such thing?*

"No, listen, Grandfather. Every other significant person we have met here – from the woman who just made your lunch to the priest you have presumably spent the last few hours interviewing and Lord Monroe's…" I had to count them in my head "… six illegitimate children all get something. Signora Acciaioli inherits quite a lot, in fact, but there is no mention of Eva."

I was so convinced that this would be of great importance to the case that I crossed my arms and looked rather pleased with myself. I did not go quite so far as to blow on my fist and rub it on my jumper, but that's more or less what I was doing in my head.

Grandfather changed the topic. "But what of his own children?"

Todd took this as his cue to check on Delilah, who was engaged in one of her three favourite pastimes: rolling on her back in the sunshine.

"Well, that's also interesting," I replied. "To put it in a sentence or two, Coralie would have inherited the most, then Fletcher, with Dashwood receiving just one ninth of the total estate. Lord Monroc changed his will from a more equitable arrangement just a year ago, much as we discovered in the threatening letter that Dashwood sent."

To me, this was yet more proof that the elder son was our likely killer and – had it not been for the fact he was sixty miles away at the time of the first murder, I would have reminded the real detective of my excellent theory.

"No, Christopher." He wiped his lips with a chequered linen napkin and read my mind. "There's still not enough evidence to prove he did it. A motive for murder is not proof that someone is a killer. Let us not forget that you would greatly benefit from getting rid of me."

"That is true, and as I consider doing it approximately three times a week, you might just as well arrest me now."

"How very droll." If he found this funny, he didn't show it. Instead, he rose from the table and set off towards his apartment. "Whether you would like to believe that Dashwood somehow tricked us and was actually here when his father was killed—"

"He could have had an accomplice," I interrupted.

"Oh, could he? And is it easy to find such a person? If, for example, you were hoping to recruit a co-conspirator in your long-established plot to *do me in*…" He bent two pairs of fingers in the air at this point to show that he would normally never use such a modern and colloquial phrase himself. "…who would you ask?"

The dear fellow was smart, but I was impudent, and I had an answer already in mind. "That's easy: my brother Albert. While on the one hand he would make a terrible murderer, we could split any inheritance we got and, if things went badly, the police would be sure to blame him."

"So then you must think that the two Monroe brothers are working together. After all, Fletcher has not provided an alibi for the time of his father's death. The fact he lives some distance away does not mean that he was there when the killing occurred."

"Fletcher?" Bother! Grandfather was a step ahead of me as ever, and he'd backed me into a corner. "No, I wasn't suggesting that *he* was involved."

He stopped in one of the open doors to the Gallery and was very happy to point out my double standards. "So what you're saying is that Fletcher can't be the killer because he's a smiley, jolly sort, and his brother must be because he's a wild, reckless devil with a tendency to wreak havoc."

"Something like that," I replied unapologetically. "Yes!"

"Tsk tsk," he tsked. "When will you give up on these rigid ideas of yours? Surely we've investigated enough murders now – the perpetrators of which have surprised even me – for you to see how difficult it is to rely on our general impressions. The way I see it, Dashwood is less likely to be involved in the crimes as he knows that, as the black sheep of the family, he is the one who will be blamed for all that goes wrong."

"Whereas Fletcher could get away with anything and, as he's the youngest and he may be unaware of the changes to his father's will, he would have gained most from the two deaths."

"Precisely." He stepped inside and into the shade, and I must say it was refreshing to follow him. The midday Tuscan sun can be rather torturous, even in spring. "You are coming around to my way of thinking."

"But you yourself are guilty of lazy thinking. What if Dashwood realised that any detective would think him the least likely culprit because he is so likely a culprit?"

"You clever little…" I don't know how rude a word would have concluded this sentence, but the fact that he'd almost uttered it suggested I'd roiled him. "I believe we have arrived at what might best be described as a stalemate."

"Then we'll call it a draw." I was rather happy with the result. Anything more than a loss was good by my standards. "Do you have any idea how we can solve the puzzle that still remains?"

"For one thing, I've asked Agente Lombardo to travel to Dashwood's home in Arezzo and Fletcher's on the other side of Florence to see whether he can establish an alibi for either of them."

"That's excellent work," I replied a touch glibly.

"I thought so." He apparently didn't realise I was being facetious.

"Obviously we must wait to see what the police make of Dashwood. From what we know of Ispettore Stefani, it's possible he'll charge whoever takes his fancy and not worry about anything so vexatious as proof."

"And in the meantime? What should we do now?"

He had led me across to another of the French windows that had its shutters closed to keep the sun out. I realised as he stood there just how often he pauses for effect before leaving a room.

"In the meantime, we have another suspect to interview."

He finally pushed the door open, and looking through it, I thought, *Oh, of course. I forgot about him.*

CHAPTER TWENTY-EIGHT

Guido Lombardo was a muscle-bound mechanic with thick black hair speckled with silver. He was probably just entering his forties but could have been mistaken for a man years younger. As I watched him testing an engine in the sunshine, surrounded by cars, I was once more reminded how difficult I find it to talk to practical, he-mannish men like him. They're almost as frightening as beautiful women.

"Signor Lombardo," Grandfather began, stepping from his apartment onto a stone double staircase that led to the gardens on one side and the side of the castle on the other, "would you mind if we had a word?"

"Do I have choice?" Guido replied without looking up from his work.

"No, I don't suppose you do."

To the north-western side of the property, backing onto the road, there was an avenue of tall trees which I could not identify. Underneath them there was a selection of perhaps fifteen cars, which I also couldn't identify, and, in front of them on the dusty ground, were countless pieces of engines and the like, which, you will be shocked to discover, I could not identify.

As our suspect was in no hurry to start the interview, Grandfather went for a short walk to look at the vehicles in the shade. I could see from the look in his eyes just then how excited he was to see so many foreign cars. Some were little more than old crocks, but there were a few real beauties, too, and he helpfully pointed out his favourites.

"You'll recognise the Alfa Romeo, of course," he said, pointing to a chassis with no wheels that was rusting away into the earth.

"Yes, of course," I lied.

"We can also see a few Nazzaros. And if I'm not mistaken, that beautiful beast over there is a SPA 30/40. Signor Lombardo, did you do the work on these yourself?"

"No." He stopped what he was doing, presumably because it was so hot and he needed a moment to breathe. "My grandmother, she help me."

"Well, it's fine work." Grandfather's eyes were the size of the cars he was ogling. "I have a small collection of automobiles back home in England. You know the sort of thing: a few Daimlers, some Rolls Royces. I even have an Alfa Romeo Targa Florio."

"Yes, I know that sort of thing," the surly mechanic said rather dismissively. It was going to be difficult to get anything useful out of him.

"Have you always liked… cars?" Grandfather sounded like me trying to make conversation when I don't know what to say.

"I work on the cars because, after he buyed my home and forced my friends to leave it, Renwick Monroe tells me it was good idea to work on them." He had a rather interesting way of speaking. His small grammatical errors made everything he said sound philosophical. "Cars themself, I have no opinion. They are objects with one function. No one man, he need so many."

I could see just how uncomfortable this made my grandfather and so, being a loyal and loving grandson, I had a good laugh at his expense.

To try to cover my amusement, I put a question of my own to Guido. "Did you like your employer?"

"No."

"Then perhaps I should ask, did you hate your employer?"

He had a very large spanner and was straining to undo a bolt as sweat glistened on his dark forehead. The question seemed to tax him just as much as his task. "All I say is I don't like the way he is." He could see that this was not clear and eventually explained. "He order people to do this and to do that. To speak his way and eat his food. If he wants England, why he doesn't stay there?"

This was a fair enough question. I also found it alarming that Lord Monroe had interfered in the lives of those around him to the extent that he had.

"That's an interesting point." Grandfather was trying to win him around, but I doubted it would work. "Except for fixing his cars, what else did you do for him?"

"I do everything. I am his donkey – I was his donkey." He nodded at this, but I couldn't tell whether he was pleased with his metaphor, his grammar, or Monroe's death. "The toilet breaks: I fix it. Pipes block: I unblock. Isn't electricity? No problem cos he never allowed it anyway."

"So you were an odd man?" I put in to try to bridge the gap between them. Guido turned to look at me and I could tell that he didn't like this description, so I raced to explain. "I mean, an odd job man – that's what we call them in Britain."

"Nothing odd about Guido Lombardo," he replied, and I think he might have been teasing me. It was hard to tell, as he didn't appear to possess the requisite muscles to smile. "I also look after artisans when they come to fix castle. I make sure no one makes everything worse."

I had to wonder why he would work out there in the sunshine when there was plenty of space in the shade of the trees.

"Was there anything else that Renwick stole from you?" Grandfather asked a little more pressingly. "Aside from your home, I mean."

Guido walked across the dusty space to pick up a large piece of shiny metal, the function of which I could not imagine until it was secured to the other elements he'd already been fixing.

"Renwick Monroe, he don't understand that word. He think that possession is the only thing that matters. 'Ten tenths of law' he used to say. He treat us all like we are his pieces of chess."

It was clear that, though the two men had lived and worked alongside one another, Guido had little respect for him. I also noticed that he hadn't answered the question. But there was something that Grandfather had inferred that I was yet to see.

On the second floor of the castle, high above Grandfather's apartment, a door on a balcony creaked open. A woman came out whistling a melody that was as sweet as the smell of oleander in the neighbouring garden. Signora Acciaioli placed an old carpet on the metal railing without noticing us.

We all three looked up at her. One had curiosity, one had surprise and one of us had nothing but desire in his eyes. In a flash, we'd discovered surely the most important reason for Guido's dislike of his dead landlord. It seemed he was in love with the Montegufoni cook, and Lord Monroe had stolen her from him. I knew that to be the case as he was looking at her much as I had gazed at *unnamed girl with book*.

Grandfather suddenly changed his point of focus. "Did you serve in the war?"

"Of course." He kept working for a minute or so without saying anything, but we were happy to wait. "I fight at the Battle of Monte Grappa and six months later at the Piave. Italy fight for Britain and

183

France and all of Europe, but what do we get in return?"

Guido was disgruntled about more than a few things. I was no longer sure why I'd set aside the possibility that he or one of the other locals was the killer.

Somewhat optimistically, Grandfather decided to answer the question. "I believe that Italy was granted certain northern borderlands. Trieste amongst them."

The mechanic gave him a withering look, which said more than a hundred of my grandfather's well-informed speeches.

I had to wonder why he they were discussing the Great War and considered how it was connected to Guido's feelings for Signora Acciaioli. For a moment, I wondered whether they had been a couple until war broke out, and then that mouse Lord Monroe had swept her off her feet while the big, burly cat was away.

"I take your point," the normally savvy sleuth replied, having realised that it was not worth exploring the topic further. "Now perhaps you can tell us where you were at the time your employer was pushed from the tower?"

The Italian hardly gave him time to finish this sentence before firing off his answer. "I was right here trying to bring Isotta Fraschini back from the dead."

I must have shown my surprise, as Grandfather turned to me to whisper, "That's a type of car, Christopher." He sighed; it must cause him great pain that the youth of today know so little about obscure foreign automobile marques.

"I was hammering on brake lining when he die," Guido continued, and I understood what he meant this time. "I didn't hear about it until I return to the courtyard."

Grandfather cleared his throat and tried again. "And what about your grandmother? Was she with you?" This was a trick question. She was in the courtyard with us when Lord Monroe fell from the tower.

Guido considered his answer for a few seconds before admitting, "No, she was not. I was alone."

Over the years, my grandfather has done his very best to teach me, as he puts it, to "read the faces of the people we interview for signs of disingenuity." I tried to do this with Guido Lombardo with no clear result. There was a certain straightforwardness to him which made me think he was telling the truth. But he also had a clear distaste for those in power – which not only manifested itself in his attitude to my grandfather, but the nasty looks he had given the inspector earlier that day and his feelings toward Lord Monroe.

Still at a loss, I decided to read my grandfather's reading of Guido instead. Despite one newspaper article describing him as "the enigmatic and unfathomable Lord Edgington", if you spent the amount of time with him that I have, you would start to identify certain clues as to what he is thinking. The fact that he stood in front of the mechanic, looking as though he'd just identified our culprit, could be for one of two contradictory reasons: either he really felt this way, or he wanted Guido to believe that was the case.

"How exactly did you feel when a foreigner came here to Montegufoni and evicted your countrymen from their homes?"

"I hate it." The Italian looked a little proud and threw down a bolt so that it went skidding across the dusty ground.

"And what about Coralie when she spoke in the courtyard last night? How did you feel then?"

He clamped his mouth shut, his lips pushed out, and a snort of laughter escaped through his nose. "She was the same as him. *Avidi! Egoisti!*" The emotion was too much, and he had to slow himself down so that we'd understand. "Both of them greedy and selfish."

This was just the kind of reaction that Grandfather had hoped to inspire and now that he'd got a rise from our suspect, he returned to the most important point of all.

"I need you to think very carefully, because I'm going to ask you the same question again, and this will be your last chance to tell the truth." He paused, his shoulders pushed back, and his neck bent at such an angle as to direct the full force of his stare down on his victim. "Tell me, Guido, where were you when Renwick fell to his death?"

I saw the very first flicker of fear from the man dressed in the grease-stained white shirt and braces. His muscles flexed as he once more did battle with a spanner, but I doubt that the sweat that bothered his brow was from the sun alone.

"I was here," he muttered, but he couldn't look at his inquisitor. "I was here just like I say."

"Did you kill Lord Monroe and his daughter?"

There were three seconds of silence before Guido Lombardo shot to his feet to stare straight into the fearless detective's eyes. I held my breath to await the answer, but it never came. Our suspect seized a rag to wipe the grease from his hands and strode away without a word.

CHAPTER TWENTY-NINE

I waited until he was out of earshot to trumpet this small success. "He was lying, wasn't he, Grandfather?"

"I believe he was."

We entered his apartment, but Grandfather didn't stop there. He walked the length of the Gallery and back again. I took this to mean he was as energised as I was by what we had just seen.

I felt like cheering in celebration, but I'm sure my colleague would have disapproved of such an excessive display of emotion, so I indulged in a brief smile instead.

"That doesn't mean we've found our killer."

As disappointing as this was, I thought he might at least explain his thinking.

"Would you care to say why not? Guido was clearly hiding something, and there was no ambiguity to the question you asked him."

He sat down on one of the divans but was so restless that he stood straight back up again. "I will happily reveal the missing element, Christopher. While the man may not have been where he claims at the moment his employer drew his last breath, that does not mean he was at the top of that tower. Surely you know by now that people lie for many reasons."

I did know this and was open to the possibility that the new hot favourite was concealing something other than the part he'd played in the murders. "Yes, but—"

Grandfather presented more possibilities of his own. "He might have been engaged in some illicit act. Don't forget that his younger brother is a police officer and, were it to come out that Guido had been up to no good, it would put Attilio in a difficult situation. And we must consider that he won't tell us where he was because he witnessed the true killer escaping. After you pursued the culprit, he could have passed Guido where he was working."

"Or?" I asked.

"I beg your pardon?"

"Oh, sorry. I just expected you to have a third option that would explain his furtive manner. You normally have three."

He looked a touch aggrieved. "Then I am sorry to disappoint you. I had hoped that two would be—" He interrupted himself this time. "He might have been with someone with whom he shouldn't have been!"

"There you go!" I was quite animated once more, and now it was my turn to bc patronising. "I knew you had it in you."

I was sure that this would get his goat, but he didn't react. In fact, he ground to a complete halt as though he were out of petrol. He stood in the middle of that long, light room, held one finger up, but made not a sound.

"Grandfather, are you feeling quite yourself?"

He soon came back to life, like the car Guido had fixed. "You clever boy!"

I'd heard such compliments too often to get excited. They were often followed by veiled criticism.

"Did my simple-minded thinking push the great Lord Edgington on to some higher level of understanding?"

"Well, yes, I suppose you could put it like that." Point proven! "If it hadn't been for you, I would not have considered the essential question: what if Guido Lombardo isn't lying to save himself but because he was with someone whom he wishes to protect?"

I didn't think this was so very different from a point he'd already made, but I didn't tell him, as I was too busy considering who this unnamed person could be.

"Signora Acciaioli!" we both said at the same time, and Grandfather enjoyed a good old click of the fingers.

We sailed up the stairs to the second floor, down another long corridor with various rooms in disrepair leading off it, and all the way to the Acciaioli family's apartment. There was one other closed door, but it was easy enough to work out which was hers.

"Will you do the honours?" Grandfather asked, and I must admit that I felt rather proud as I raised my fist to knock.

Ten seconds later, one of the single-browed boys we'd seen at afternoon tea opened the door to us with a cheery greeting. "Hello, you pig's dinner!"

Grandfather looked suitably disturbed by this insult coming from such an innocent-looking little chap. "Hello... young man. Is your mother at home?"

"Son of a donkey!" the dear creature responded, and a moment later, his older brother came to grab him by the ear.

"I'm sorry about Cesare," he said in a far kinder tone. "He doesn't know what any of those things mean, but he likes to copy Renwick's funny words." I think it's fair to say that this eight-year-old boy spoke better English than any of his compatriots we'd met in the castle. "Can I help you?"

"We're looking for your mother," I said, as Grandfather wasn't used to being insulted and had apparently gone into shock. "We saw her on the balcony a few minutes ago."

I heard a call of "You mumbling blowsabella, everything is in a parlous state of decay!" from deeper within the flat, but the big brother just ignored it.

"I'm afraid she has just gone out. Perhaps she is making the food for your dinner."

"Ah, I see." I didn't know what to say after that, and the helpful boy smiled and closed the door on us.

"Thank you!" I called through the keyhole, but all I heard back was the cheeky urchin singing another insult of "You're a death's head upon a mop stick if ever I saw one!" before his brother presumably put a full Nelson on him to calm things down.

It was only as Grandfather and I were walking back towards the tower that he broke his silence. "Christopher, I don't suppose you know where the kitchen is?"

"I was wondering the very same thing."

CHAPTER THIRTY

We went down to the courtyard where Nonna Lombardo (I'm afraid I never learnt the old lady's name) waved us towards the ballroom and, rather than turning right to Lord Monroe's and Eva Mountstephen's offices, we headed towards another set of doors I had previously ignored.

I don't know why it surprised me to find a large kitchen there, or why I was startled by the presence of our staff from Cranley Hall, who were presumably settling into their new lives abroad, but that's what happened.

"Lord Edgington, your highness," our large and poorly educated maid said with a curtsey when she saw her employer. It wasn't her fault that she didn't learn how to address a marquess when she was a child, though I suppose she might be at fault for not remembering when her colleagues remind her once a week. "Lovely to see you, your excellency."

"Lord Edgington, we're learning to make Italian food," our cook Henrietta revealed with great excitement before turning back to the large wooden worktable in the centre of the room where Signora Acciaioli was rolling out a very fine dough.

It wasn't just Henrietta who was mesmerised by the process; Delilah watched her every move – though perhaps this was in the hope of obtaining scraps of food. Todd was there, too and looked just as in love with the Italian chef as I was with the girl I would never see again. To be honest, I was terribly grateful for the investigation as I would have been locked away in my bedroom otherwise, hugging my copy of *Bleak House* and reliving the moment Jane Doe had waved at me.

"Do you see how I am going about the process of making the pasta, Henrietta?" the signora asked in that strangely formal English of hers.

"I do, my dear. I can't wait to try it myself."

I must confess that I was now tempted to give up my life as a detective and learn to be a chef. The work looked so appealing, and the way in which she manipulated the sheet of unleavened dough was just a few steps away from true magic.

"Should I get a knife to cut it?" Henrietta was normally such a bold and blunt person that it was curious to see her in a new role as a cautious apprentice. Her Italian counterpart nodded encouragingly, and she scampered over to a pot of cutlery beside the sink.

I kept expecting Grandfather to interrupt in order to take the chef away from her admirers, but he was apparently just as enchanted by the display.

"I brought another bag of flour, Annina." Timothy, our youngest employee, walked (or rather wobbled) into the room with a large hessian sack.

"That's wonderful, Timmy." Signora Acciaioli beamed at him, and he looked most pleased with the response.

I hadn't considered until now what his job might be on our travels. It would be hard to continue his previous job as a hall boy, seeing as we no longer had a hall for him to call his own. I had a feeling that Grandfather had brought him along as a general dogsbody, running around doing whatever was needed. Or perhaps he intended to train him for a higher level. Personally, I saw Timothy as an under-under footman but, in time and with a little hard work, the enterprising youngster would surely make it to under-footman.

"Now we cut the pasta into strips for the dish we are intending to produce." The curly-haired cook was adept with a knife and made the most exquisitely even cuts all along the large square of dough. In thirty seconds, she had twenty or so thin, flat ribbons that would be boiled up for dinner. "The name for this type of pasta is *pappardelle*, though if you cut it too thin, you will have a case of *tagliatelle* on your hands." She found this very funny and, though I doubt any of us got the joke, we laughed all the same because she was such a friendly presence there in the kitchen.

"It's fabulous." Todd shook his head as though she had just performed a trick he couldn't comprehend.

"After everything is cooked, it's a really quite simple matter of combining the pasta with the ragu sauce we will now make."

"Right you are." Henrietta eagerly rubbed her hands together. "I'll see to that. Although I do have a small suggestion to make regarding the recipe you gave me. Have you ever considered adding swede? Herbs and spices and garlic are all well and good but name me one dish that doesn't improve with a chunk or three of swede."

The contrast between these two queens of the kitchen was entertaining to see. Our cook from Cranley Hall was a plain-speaking woman with a penchant for culinary experimentation, whereas Annina seemed, to this unworldly Britisher at least, to be all charm and sophistication, and she relied on local recipes that had been handed down to her through the generations. It was a shame that I had to bother her.

"Before you start the next delicious element of this evening's dinner, may we have a few minutes of your time, signora?"

She had been so calm and composed until now, but this seemed to perturb her. "I?" She pointed to herself to check that she'd understood. "I am the one to whom you wish to speak?"

"That's right," I replied, hoping that it might sound less daunting coming from me. "I'm sure it won't take too long."

She nodded and wiped her hands on her pinafore, though they did not appear to be dirty. In the corner of the spacious, white-tiled kitchen, there was a small table where, in a well-staffed house, a maid could sit chopping potatoes, or a scullery boy would dry crockery. There were only two chairs, but I was more than used to hovering in the background whilst my grandfather did the important work.

The Cranley Hall staff gathered together at the sideboard to watch Cook's preparations as we talked to the charming Italian lady in the opposite corner of the room.

"May I start by asking whether you are, or rather were, employed by Lord Monroe?" Grandfather began the questioning in a clear, confident tone.

Even this simple enquiry seemed to disquiet her. "That is right. I am the cook of the castle. I prepared all his meals and also for some of the families who worked on Renwick's land."

"Very good." He spoke more slowly than normal, though it was clear she understood us perfectly well. I suppose this was a technique to put her at ease before he said the words "And yet you were also his paramour. Isn't that right?"

Far from upsetting her, this just made her laugh. "Paramour is rather a romantic word for it. We shared a bed and the responsibility for my three boys."

Grandfather was determined to unnerve her and pressed on. "He had children with other women, too. Isn't that correct?"

"Oh, yes." Her smile grew. "He was quite the rogue, and that is why I would never describe him as my paramour, my sweetheart, or my love, and why my children never called him father."

It was Lord Edgington who now looked uncertain, and he could only reply with a slightly scandalised, "You are a Catholic, are you not?"

Perhaps the ridiculousness of his questions helped her, as she now sought to calm his fears. "Yes, but I am also a widow. My husband, may God have mercy upon him, was killed in the war, and we were not blessed with babies before he went away. I had no need to marry again, but I did want children of my own. Renwick was kind to several women here and no one, to my knowledge, has ever looked down on me for making the best of a bad situation."

I enjoyed hearing all her little phrases pronounced in that wonderfully Italian manner. She seemed to take as much care over them as she did her cooking.

"So it was an affair of convenience?" Grandfather seemed desperate to make sense of the liaison between them and was clearly trying to fit it into the frame of his own experience.

"If it makes you happy to look at it like that, then yes. But I also respected him and shared my apartment with him… most of the time."

It occurred to me that we still hadn't found Lord Monroe's private quarters, but perhaps he didn't have any. Perhaps, being the libertine that he was, he split his time between the bedrooms of whoever would have him. This would have sounded genuinely seedy if Signora Acciaioli hadn't presented it in such a cheery manner.

Getting nowhere, Grandfather moved on to another point of attack.

"Your surname," was all he would say at first, and our suspect waited patiently for more. "We have seen it all over the castle. In the stone shield on the wall of the Cardinal's Garden. In the inscription in a large plaque in the bell tower, and under so many paintings in the Hall of the Gonfaloniers."

He hadn't posed a question, and so she continued to wait.

"Was the castle stolen from your family by Renwick Monroe's invasion?"

"Oh, Lord Edgington," she said his name rather affectionately, and her smile made her cheeks all the rounder, "you really do think the worst of everybody. If you're wishing to suggest that I strove to plot against my children's father because my ancestors happened to have built this castle, then you have been reading too many fantastical novels. I am a cook. I was never an aristocrat like you or him. What influence my long-dead predecessors may or may not have wielded makes no difference to me."

I decided that Grandfather was having the same conversation with himself that he so often criticised me for having. *Could this woman really be as nice as she seems?* I imagined he was thinking. *Or is she putting on an act to fool us?* He'd detailed several excellent motives for why she might bear a grudge against her murdered… What word could I use for him? Roommate?

"Very well." He wasn't giving up. "Then what about Guido Lombardo?" He spoke in the manner of a man who was about to lay down his trump card. "What exactly is your relationship to Lord Monroe's mechanic?"

"I believe we are third cousins. I'm not sure of the precise details, but my great- great-grandmother was—"

Grandfather's vexation was beginning to show. "Your romantic relationship, madam! I'm asking as to your feelings for the man."

"Guido?" Her confusion was replaced with amazement. "For one thing, I could never love a man named Guido, but the Guido in question is like a little boy who has never matured to adulthood." Her phrasing really was remarkably close to how I imagined her murdered roommate speaking.

"So you're saying that you were not together when your…" I can only think he searched for an Italian expression for boyfriend at this point and had to settle for a French one. "…*petit ami* was killed?"

For the first time in some minutes, she looked a little nervous. I couldn't really blame her. If she had nothing to do with our current pick for killer of the week, she was right to fear that we would unfairly connect her to him.

"Of course I wasn't. I was alone in my apartment. The boys were away at school, and I remember finishing my tasks for the morning and sitting down to enjoy the peace and quiet as a warm breeze blew about the place. For someone like me, those moments are worth their weight in diamonds, and part of me knew that it wouldn't last long. I heard the scream and went to the tower to see what had happened. I looked out of the window and saw Renwick dead on the ground with the two of you standing over him."

This excited me for a moment, but I realised I already knew the answers to the questions I was about to ask. "You were in the tower just after he died? Does that mean you saw someone coming down from the top level?"

She shook her head and frowned as though she felt she had to apologise. "No, I'm afraid not. I heard someone running down the steps before I arrived, but that was as I left my apartment at the end of the corridor. He was long gone by the time I reached the tower."

Grandfather had a certain look about him when he thought he knew the exact question that needed asking. It wasn't anything so simple as a raised eyebrow or a puffed-out cheek. His supreme confidence practically radiated from him.

"So you stood looking out of the window, saw that your lover was dead and then simply returned to your flat. Is that right?" This required no answer and didn't get one. "I put it to you, madam, that you have shown no sorrow over Renwick's passing because you were the one who accompanied him to the top of the tower and pushed him to his death. I believe that he told you that he had changed his will in your favour, and you wished to inherit the money sooner rather than later."

"Oh, no," she replied in a perfectly relaxed tone, much as if she were discussing what she was planning to make for the next morning's breakfast. "That wasn't me. I've already told you that I was in my little flat at the time. And as for showing sorrow, I'm afraid I cried all my tears many years ago."

"Then what about Coralie?" I jumped in to maintain the pressure on her. "Perhaps you were upset by her authoritarian behaviour in expecting everyone to leave the castle, so you decided to protect your loved ones by killing her."

She looked a touch nonplussed by my accusatory tone but was less than alarmed. "No, no. Nothing like that."

"She would have thrown you out of the castle," I tried again.

"Yes, but it's only a building. We could have found a place to live elsewhere."

We've come across some unbelievably skilful liars over the years, but Annina spoke with such clarity and openness that it was impossible to imagine that she was anything of the sort.

Grandfather gave her one last push. "To be clear, you weren't jealous of Renwick's infidelity. You didn't feel any great sadness when he died, and you took no umbrage at his daughter's decision to force everyone from the castle. Is that a fair summary?"

She at least hesitated for a moment before answering. "I probably sound quite heartless, but it's the truth. I didn't own Renwick, and he didn't own me. He was fabulous company, kind to our boys, and we enjoyed our time together, but I never loved him. And perhaps you're right and I should be angry at what Coralie wished to do, but we all know we can't stay here forever. The castle belongs to the Monroe family, and we have already outstayed our welcome."

I looked at Grandfather, who was not nearly as moved as I was by this new disappointment. He was staring through the window at the courtyard and seemed to have stopped listening.

CHAPTER THIRTY-ONE

I can't explain what happened next. My grandfather mumbled something about needing time to himself and swiftly marched off in the direction of his apartment.

Wait one moment; I take that back. I can explain what happened, and I just have, but I don't know why he walked away so suddenly, and I can't say for certain what had distracted him at a key moment in our interview.

Whatever caused it, the situation left me at something of a loose end. As far as I could tell, beyond the men out in the fields, the rest of Lord Monroe's many lovers, and a few of the children around the place, there were no more suspects to interview. The Monroe brothers still hadn't returned from their appointment with the nasty inspector, and I couldn't think of anything else to do, so I followed my friends' examples and sat in the kitchen enjoying Annina's handiwork. I found watching her quite enchanting.

Italian cookery seemed a world away from good old British fare – which I do not wish to malign in any way. It was as if she were casting a spell rather than simply preparing a meal, and now that this thought occurred to me, I decided that, with her long, dark locks and Roman nose, she would have made a rather excellent sorceress.

She wouldn't let me get away with just watching and, much like my friends from back home, I was soon following her commands. I prepared stuffed pasta for the families in the castle, carefully cutting small squares from the doughy sheets with lumps of paste-like, dried tomato and meat between them.

The smells of the kitchen were exquisite, and the warmth of the afternoon lulled me into a hazy state of satisfaction. As I worked, I found myself thinking of the girl of my dreams back in Florence. I really was a dunderhead not to have introduced myself. I half considered asking Todd to drive me back there, but what good could it do?

For one thing, she was a tourist in Italy, and I was supposed to be staying in Tuscany for no short length of time. Even if she agreed to talk to me, for all I knew she would be off to another city the following day, and I'd never see her again. The prospect of getting to know her – rather than basing my opinion of her on hair colour and choice of reading material – could only lead to disillusion if we were then immediately parted.

My kitchen dreaming was far more rewarding than reality, and so I pictured myself sitting down opposite her in the conservatory in the Helvetia and Bristol hotel. The waiter would ask us what we wanted to drink, and I would know just the right thing to impress her – something sophisticated like *eau de vie de* raspberry for example. She would laugh at my subtle wit and I would put my hand across the table to tell her that I knew the moment I first saw her on the boat that we were destined to meet again – which, though not quite true (as it had taken me two whole sightings before my heart was hers), it was definitely more romantic than talk of love at second sight.

And then, as our hearts raced, she would…

"What is it, Delilah?" The strange expression on her face broke me from my reverie. Her head was cocked, her muzzle raised, and I realised that she was worried about me. "Thank you very much, but I'm perfectly fine, and I'd ask you to keep your opinions to yourself."

She wasn't the only one who was concerned. After my one-sided conversation with our dog, Todd peered across the room with a similarly apprehensive mien, and even Timothy looked a little concerned.

"'Ere, miniature Lord Edgington, sir. You sound like your grandfather," Dorie commented, which really did alarm me.

"Time for tea!" Signora Acciaioli declared, and her three boys appeared in the kitchen just in time to celebrate.

The youngest ran in a circle around the central table, repeating his mother's words in a sing-song voice. I was thankful for the distraction, as the very idea that I had adopted my grandfather's eccentricities was hard to bear. We each carried a tray of food out to the courtyard – well, Dorie took four in one go and balanced them surprisingly easily on her immense hands and forearms. I was determined to learn my lesson from the night before but equally certain I wouldn't be able to resist the pastries that Annina and Henrietta had prepared.

The band were already in place, and I thought they might play with a little less enthusiasm after Coralie's cruel demise. Perhaps they didn't know how to make such an adjustment as "God Save the King" was just as rousing as ever. We all enjoyed the sandwiches, tea and cakes and I noted no real difference in the atmosphere between that afternoon and the day before. Perhaps it was still a celebration for the people of Montegufoni. Yet another of their foreign overlords had met a sticky end and, at this rate, the invaders would be defeated within days.

Eva Mountstephen was the only person who looked less than joyful. She sat on her own at a far table, and I watched her as my friends gabbed, and Delilah chased the children around the courtyard. Lord Monroe's secretary was rarely a cheery character, but she now looked quite despondent. As I could not bear to see her so blue, I went over to speak to her.

"Miss Mountstephen—" I began before correcting myself. "Eva, if it's not too impertinent a question, are you quite all right?"

A voice in my head said, *That's some question coming from the boy who just had an argument with a dog.*

She smiled ever so sadly and tried to ease my mind. "I will be fine. Thank you, Christopher. I'm merely worried about…" Her words died in her throat, and she smiled in such a cautious manner that I knew she would hold back the truth. "I'm concerned for Dashwood and his brother." The very fact that she hadn't uttered Fletcher's name told me everything.

"Would you mind if I sat down for a moment?"

She looked at her plate, perhaps hoping that she had finished her food and would have an excuse to leave. She hadn't had a single bite.

"No, of course not." She pulled her chair around the table a short distance, as though I needed extra space.

"We don't know one another well," I said to begin the sensitive speech that I'd been preparing since I noticed her there. "And you have every right to tell me to mind my own business, but I have the feeling that…" Now I was the one searching for my words. "I believe that it is Fletcher for whom you are most afraid."

Her eyes darted away and back to me. "Of course I'm worried about him. He is a kind person, and he has lost his father and his sister in the space of a day."

"But if I'm not mistaken, he and his father had stopped talking altogether. Fletcher moved away from Montegufoni some years ago and didn't return until your call yesterday."

She offered no response at all this time. Her eyes were fixed on the round wooden table, and I thought I would have to push her for more, but then a key piece of the information we were missing burst from her. "He wasn't trying to get away from Renwick."

I didn't know how to say anything more without offending her, but Grandfather had long since taught me that, for detectives, this is often inevitable. "Are you saying that you were the one he no longer wished to see?"

For a second, I thought I understood the whole situation. He had loved her, and she had rejected him. It was all so clear... until it wasn't.

"He was sick of me." Her answers were short and bitter, but I got the impression that she wanted – no, needed – to confide in me.

"I don't believe that for one second. I'm sure there was more to it. Would you care to tell me what passed between you?"

This was too direct an approach. She turned away and pulled her arms close to her chest as though I'd been trying to insult her.

"I'm sorry if I've made you feel in any way worse than you already did, but I truly believe that sharing your story with me will alleviate your suffering."

I sounded like a quack doctor trying to sell a patent medicine that had no right to make such claims. Luckily, she didn't seem to notice and, with eyes wide and glistening, she unburdened herself. "I have never understood what happened or why. We had always got on so well and then, in early 1927, I felt that something more had developed. I don't mind admitting that I came to love Fletcher, despite his brother and sister's teasing and his father's eccentricity. I loved him and, for a short time, I believe that he loved me too." Her voice broke and the words barely made it out of her mouth.

"I can only imagine how difficult that must have been," I said both sympathetically and literally. "I know what it's like to have loved and lost." Fine, this was slightly less honest, as I had only loved for a few seconds before losing, but the principle held true. "I know how it feels to have met the person who is a perfect match for you, only to be wrenched apart."

"My goodness, Christopher." She sat up straighter in her chair. "You are so much more experienced than I could have predicted."

I was tempted to disagree with her, but it really wasn't the moment, so I just nodded, as if to say, *Yes, I am both experienced and mature...*

not to mention humble. I'm definitely that, too.

"Did Fletcher ever tell you why he left?"

"He offered no explanation. I know he'd argued with his father a few days earlier, but I doubt that was the reason. What I can say is that he treated me differently after their conversation. Having always shown tender affection towards me, he suddenly turned cold."

"Is it not possible that Lord Monroe warned him off? Isn't it feasible that your employer did not wish for his son to marry you and told him just that? Perhaps he thought he would lose your services as his secretary."

She shook her head quite furiously. "That makes no sense. Renwick always told me that I was like a daughter to him, so why wouldn't he want me as a daughter-in-law?" She gave me a few seconds to respond and, when I couldn't, she looked even sadder. "I appreciate your help, Christopher, but I've considered every explanation, and the simple truth is that Fletcher grew tired of me and decided the only solution was to stay away. It took the death of his father to bring him back here."

"But he looked so happy when he saw you yesterday."

She curled a lock of her hair around one finger and gazed at me through those soulful blue eyes. "I thought the same thing. I really hoped that his return might lead to a reunion between us, but as soon as we were alone together yesterday evening, he was just as he had been before he left. He was so detached. I tried to talk to him in the garden after dinner, and he might just as well have been in his house forty kilometres from here."

It was a sorry tale, and I wished I could say something to make her feel better, but the words evaded me. As I was at a loss, I decided to change the topic and hope she found a way to heal her wounds without my help. Some doctor I turned out to be.

"I am truly sorry for the way he treated you. I must say that I've found Fletcher to be very pleasant, especially given the terrible situation in which he has found himself. His brother, on the other hand, is harder to appreciate. May I ask for your opinion of Dashwood?"

I think that my controlled, unemotional approach helped her maintain her composure, as she soon answered.

"I have some sympathy for him. From what his siblings have told me, he was always the black sheep of the family. I believe that a lot of his problems came from his mother's relatively early death and his father's unusual behaviour. Of course, none of that excuses Dashwood's antagonism. Before he stopped coming to see his father last year, every meeting they had ended in a screaming argument. Renwick was greatly hurt by his son's behaviour. He was a resilient man, but he couldn't hide that."

I was coming to the end of the brief list of points I wished to put to her, and I took my time over the last of them. "I know that it's an impossible question to answer with any certainty, but would you mind telling me whether you think that Dashwood has it in him to murder—"

Before I could finish the sentence, she turned to look at the gatehouse beyond me. She drew a deep breath, as though she were both surprised and relieved at the same time. I turned to see what she had noticed, and there were the two Monroe brothers, standing together under the portico.

CHAPTER THIRTY-TWO

"What happened, Fletcher?" Eva rushed over to ask him, as Dashwood hurried off across the courtyard.

"There's no need to worry. I promise." Fletcher did not look at us. He wore a pained expression as he watched his brooding brother leave.

"Please, Fletcher," she begged, pulling him out of earshot of the locals. "Please tell me what happened."

He had a distant look in his eyes, and I was certain that, for the moment at least, he was more worried about Dashwood than the young woman he had abandoned. "Ispettore Stefani had no evidence upon which to build a case. The man is as corrupt as they come."

"Then how did you get him free?" I asked.

His brother had reached the door to the salon but lingered there for a moment to look back at us.

"I had to pay a bribe. With his sort, it's standard practice. He doesn't care about our dead sister, and he hated Father. Most police officers here are different. If Lombardo had been in charge of the investigation, we wouldn't have had a problem, but Stefani is a monster."

"Fletcher," Dashwood called across to his brother. "I'm sorry, but I'm not in the mood for any of this." He motioned to the jolly scene behind him. "I'll be in my room. You can find me there if you need me."

Fletcher waved across to him but couldn't feign a smile. His eyes stayed fixed on the spot that Dashwood had vacated, and I could see how much he was suffering.

"To be quite honest," he said in a lower voice. "I'd rather be alone."

He began to walk away, but Eva caught hold of his arm. "Talk to me, Fletcher. I'll listen to whatever you have to say. Don't push me away again."

He pulled his arm free and wouldn't look at her. He kept walking, and I was torn between running after him and following his brother. They were surely our most suspicious suspects (of all the people we'd suspected) and yet they were the two people we were yet to interview in any depth.

Dashwood hadn't risen in my estimations just because a corrupt police officer had made use of him, and so I ran to the saloon just in time to see Father Laurence pulling him away towards the chapel. Perhaps he hoped to force a confession from Lord Monroe's tearaway heir.

So that's how I missed my opportunity – and presumably also upset Eva by abandoning her, just like her former sweetheart. I ran back to the courtyard, but they had both disappeared. All the drama and disagreement was at odds with the cheerful scene that was still playing out in the courtyard. The band had reunited and were accompanying Nonna Lombardo, who performed a jaunty romantic song. The old lady swayed as she sang it, and I watched her grandson Guido, who was just as grumpy as when we'd spoken to him that afternoon. He cast a filthy look in my direction, and I tried not to take it personally.

When I didn't know what else to do, I decided to look for my grandfather, who was rarely far from wherever the action was. This couldn't have been closer to the truth as, on the walk to his apartment, I spotted him peering down over the side of the tower. I waved, but he didn't notice, and I wondered what he had gone up there to check.

By the time Grandfather came down to the courtyard, Agente Attilio Lombardo had returned from the task he'd been given.

"Ahh, Lombardo. That's perfect timing. How did you do?"

The young officer looked apprehensive, and I worried for a moment that there was more bad news coming. "All I do is confirm what we know. Three people at his house say Dashwood was in Arezzo yesterday when Eva she call him. There is no way he could push his father from the tower."

"And Fletcher?" I asked, hoping that he had an alibi and wouldn't turn out to be a murderous fiend.

His expression only became more perplexed. "I speak to his housekeeper. He was not home all afternoon. She tells him about his father two hours after the death – plenty time to kill Lord Monroe and return there."

Grandfather did not reveal his feelings on this information but thanked his temporary assistant for his help. "You've done an excellent job. I wonder whether your superior Stefani would have gone to such trouble."

The *agente* winced then, and it was clear that he did not have a high opinion of the inspector. I had to wonder whether he had work of his own he should been doing when Grandfather sent him off on an unofficial mission.

Either way, he bowed to the famous sleuth and hurried back to his affairs. "I tell you more if I know more."

Grandfather returned the gesture and, as Lombardo went to speak to his family, I felt as buoyant as a balloon without air.

"Well?" Grandfather asked as he led me to the tea urn where Todd was already waiting with a fresh cup.

Well, have you solved the case yet, Christopher? I thought he might wish to enquire. Or, *Well, isn't this a lovely afternoon to be outside?*

He sipped his tea, then presumably regretted it as it was still steaming hot. I sensibly, though begrudgingly, resisted any more cakes and sandwiches.

"Well, what have you learnt while we were apart?"

I had to think. So much had happened that day it was hard to put events in order. Had I seen him since having my heart broken? Yes, I believed so. And he'd been there for the interview with Guido. So what did that leave?

"I learnt how Signora Acciaioli makes a simple sauce which she uses as the base for many dishes."

He was not impressed. "How very amusing, Christopher. Now would you please be more serious?"

I hadn't meant to make a joke. I was genuinely impressed by the signora's accomplishments in the kitchen and felt it bore sharing.

Something a little more relevant did eventually come to mind. "The Monroe brothers have returned from the police station. It sounds as if the crooked inspector was mainly interested in how much money he could extort from them."

He gave a dubious, *"Hmmm,"* in reply, and I was about to ask what he'd been doing when I remembered what else I needed to tell him.

"I also spoke to Eva Mountstephen. As I suspected, she's head over heels in love with Fletcher, who once seemed to return those feelings but has since spurned her. It is her belief that this was the reason he cut off contact with his father two years ago – so that he wouldn't have to see her any longer. I tried to convince her she was thinking the worst when—"

"That's actually quite intriguing," he interrupted, but I couldn't say why. "What about Guido and the local cook? Has anything struck you about either of them?"

I shrugged, as it really hadn't. "No, they've both acted in much the same way as before. He is sullen, and she is pacific and kind."

He moved his pursed lips towards one cheek and then the other. "Yes, that is much as I expected." He tried his tea again, and this time it was more to his liking.

"It may be presumptuous to ask, Grandfather," I began as he stood umming and ahhing appreciatively over his favourite beverage, "but what should we do now?"

"I would say that is a simple question to answer, wouldn't you?"

I tried to be polite, I promise I did, but the words, "No, or I wouldn't have asked it," fell from my lips and he had a good old tut.

"It has just gone seven o'clock in the evening, Christopher." He paused, pointing up at the clock that didn't work. Despite this, the bells rang out for the hour, and he had a knowing look in his eyes. If he was hoping that this answered my question, he was mistaken. "It is time—"

"To dress for dinner." I'd realised what he was about to say just before he said it. "I might have known."

CHAPTER THIRTY-THREE

I opted for black evening dress that night – though no one else in the castle seemed worried about such formalities – and then I went to my grandfather's room to wait for him.

I must say that I have always enjoyed watching his preparations for dinner. I remember when I was a very young boy, and I still found him quite terrifying – long before I found out what a softy he is beneath all his huffing and puffing. It was when my grandmother was still alive, so I couldn't have been much more than five. He'd caught me peering into his dressing room, and I was certain he would shout at me to go away, but he called me inside. I sat dwarfed in an armchair as he taught me how to select an appropriate cravat, cufflinks and tie pin to match one's shirt and attire. It wasn't so much what he said as the care with which he said it that made me remember so long after. That may well have been the first time I realised that the Most Honourable Marquess of Edgington – my upright and austere grandfather – was actually human.

"Why are you smiling?" He watched me over his shoulder in the mirror.

"Oh, I don't know." I maintained my sunny disposition.

"We may be coming to the end of this sad episode, and we must retain our focus."

I didn't answer for a short while. I was thinking how lucky I was to have a curmudgeonly, cantankerous genius for a mentor.

"Thank you, Grandfather," I said, aware that such sentimental moments normally come at the end of an investigation, and that this was a touch premature. "Thank you for bringing me here and giving me so many chances to get things wrong so that I can eventually get a few right."

Even he smiled now. "You're very welcome. I'm just sorry that we are once again searching for the lowest type of human being rather than exploring Italian landscapes together or marvelling at the country's great works of art."

I somewhat doubted he regretted having the opportunity to exercise his large brain, but I wasn't in the mood to correct him. I waited until he'd tied his tie and fixed his cuffs, and then we walked down to the shady terrace together to find that there was no one else there.

The table was laid, and Todd soon arrived to offer us wine, but we were the only diners.

"Well, that was anti-climactic," I had to say, and ten minutes later, things hadn't improved.

Grandfather was soon as perturbed as I was. "I admit that, as I changed my clothes, I pictured us all gathered together, as so often happens at the culmination of one of our cases. It will be a lot more difficult to fit the final pieces if there's no one here to answer our questions."

It was rare to see him so disappointed. I thought perhaps he had set himself an objective to finish the investigation within a certain time. I could quite understand him doing this. After all the murders he'd investigated over the years, it would begin to feel easy if he didn't make a challenge out of it.

Todd brought the first course – to which I had been looking forward ever since I saw the cook holding up that large sheet of pasta – but there was still no sign of Eva, Dashwood or Fletcher. I believe that Grandfather was about to give up hope when Eva appeared for the main course.

"I'm sorry to be late," she said, but she offered no explanation.

She was dressed a little more glamorously than normal. She wore a blue dress which made her eyes all the brighter and butterfly wing earrings that caught the light of the setting sun through the trees.

"I'm sorry not to have joined you earlier," Fletcher told us a few moments later, but the pair avoided looking at one another even as he sat down opposite her.

Grandfather was clearly excited that he might get to enjoy his big moment after all, but it would not be easy. The only conversation consisted of requests for condiments to be passed around the table when Todd was elsewhere. It was a real shame to be having dinner in such a beautiful place, only for no one to enjoy it. The food was as good as the night before, the temperature mild, but the atmosphere was frigid.

When Grandfather's attempts to spark conversation failed, I tried myself. "You must have known one another half your lives," I said in as warm a manner as I could muster, but Eva looked down at her plate, and Fletcher just mumbled, "Something like that, yes."

Becoming more desperate, I thought I'd give that old standard "Lovely weather we're having" a try, but even this didn't work, and London's most capable (and manipulative) sleuth could do nothing but look perplexed by our failure.

It was almost a relief when we finished dessert and Eva made an excuse to leave the table. Fletcher waited until she had disappeared up the stairs to the salon before doing the same.

"No, wait!" I demanded, as I could see just how unnerved Grandfather was. "You're not leaving until we talk things through properly."

"I'm afraid I'm not in the mood." Fletcher's voice was terribly flat, and it was sad to witness the change in him.

"Then Todd will make one of his world-famous (in our family at least) cocktails and it will pick your mood up no end." I rose to lead the way. "Come along. We'll have a drink in the Cardinal's Garden."

I didn't wait for him to decide what to do but walked ahead to lure him after me. I was rather relieved that this worked, as I've never considered myself the most magnetic person. We walked along the heavily arboured avenue and up the old stone steps. The sun had hidden itself away beneath the horizon, but the sky was full of colour above the village on the hill. As we reached the courtyard garden beside Grandfather's apartment, the evening was alive with the sound of singing insects that I'm fairly confident have either never made it to Britain or simply don't feel warm enough there to find their voices.

Our clairvoyant retainer was already preparing drinks in one corner, and Delilah was asleep beside him. She was a very loyal dog, though her loyalty stretched to more or less whomsoever she was with at the time. I believe that she considered herself to have at least five different masters, with a few part-time substitutes depending on where we were.

Fletcher sat down at the small, iron table without being asked – which I thought fair enough, seeing as he now owned it. Whether he knew that he owned it was a different matter, as I hadn't heard him mention the amended will, and he had stopped visiting the castle before his father changed the order of inheritance.

"What have you got to say to me?" he asked, and to my surprise, I was the person to whom he directed this question, not my grandfather.

"There's a lot I'd like to say," I began a little combatively as I sat down across from him, and Grandfather did a perfectly good impression of me by hovering about on the periphery. "But first I'd like you to tell me why Ispettore Stefani came here and arrested your brother directly."

Fletcher looked away, already unimpressed by what he'd heard. "Because Dashwood is the only one of us who's clashed with the police in the past – aside from Father, of course. You might even say that my brother took after him."

I could see Grandfather's face beyond Fletcher at this moment, and he didn't look as though he agreed with the comparison.

"For all his faults, your father objected to heavy-handed tyranny," I said with just a touch of pomposity in my phrasing. "Dashwood is a drug user and a debtor. I don't think their situations were ever quite the same."

He shook his head, but at least he took me seriously. "I doubt you know a great deal about my brother's life. He is not a bad man, but his life has never been easy."

"You had the same upbringing, and you seem to have survived well enough," I calmly replied. "You're not sitting here with a heap of white powder before you, so why should you make excuses for him?"

He opened his mouth to do just this but must have failed to summon anything worth saying. "I believe that people deserve second chances."

"After he murdered Coralie?" I wanted to see what impact this accusation would have, even if I couldn't prove it.

"That wasn't Dash. I refuse to accept that he would hurt her." He couldn't look away from me now. His eyes were locked on mine and his voice rose higher.

"Then was it you?"

"No!" This word sounded like a plea or a prayer, and he would need time before he could say anything more. "I loved my sister. I love my whole family. I don't know who killed her – or our father. I would certainly never do such a thing for money, if that's what you're thinking."

"You are the youngest," still standing behind him, Grandfather began. His deep, dramatic voice in Fletcher's ears must have been quite unsettling. "You do realise that, if anything happens to Dashwood, there will only be one suspect that the police consider."

"Perhaps the killer is relying on that very thing," Fletcher was quick to reply. "Perhaps whoever holds a grudge against my family knows that we will take the blame."

"Unless they kill you all," I fired back at him. "If someone wants to get rid of the lot of you, you could be next."

I don't know whether he'd simply never considered this point, or he felt that, as the youngest heir, he was safe from the killer, but he looked suitably shocked.

"I… I don't suppose there's a great deal I can do about that." After a moment, another possibility occurred to him. "Have you considered that my father, who believed himself the benevolent monarch of Montegufoni, and Coralie, who visited regularly, were the only targets? Who's to say that anyone else has to die?"

"You may be right," I conceded. "But it's not a theory I would like to put to the test."

I let this comment linger for a while and was about to speak again when Todd discreetly delivered three brown drinks. Grandfather seemed pleased with his and sat down at the table to enjoy it. He may have felt that this move to hem in Fletcher would help me, too. Our suspect already looked pale and anxious. It wouldn't take much more to break him entirely.

"Can you tell me exactly what you and your brother do for work?" This was a rich question coming from the idle grandson of a wealthy lord.

"I have spent several years preparing for the job, and I am now a full-time solicitor. I always admired our Uncle Andrew and didn't want to be a leech off my father, so I took up a profession."

"And Dashwood?"

He hesitated, running his finger around the rim of the ice-cold tumbler. "Dashwood considers himself a bon-vivant. He believes work to be beneath him."

"Then how does he support himself?" Grandfather asked, his tone soft.

"Father never cut him off entirely, and he is rather skilful at convincing people to lend him money. I have fallen for his charms myself on occasion." He stopped himself from saying anything more on the matter. "You know, you really should be talking to him about all this."

"Don't worry," Grandfather reassured him in a tone that was actually quite menacing, "we will."

I decided to take charge of the interview once more, not because I believed that I would do a better job than my mentor, but because he seemed to be enjoying his role as the disrupter there.

"Where were you when your father was murdered?" I asked, but Grandfather tapped his fingers on the table, and I thought perhaps I was taking us down the wrong avenue.

"I was out driving in my car. I had a lot on my mind, and I like to get on the road to think sometimes."

"Where exactly did you go?"

"I drove north-east for an hour or so and then back to my home in Prato. It was only when I returned that I received the message that Eva left with my housekeeper. I came as soon as I knew something was wrong."

"You have a high opinion of Miss Mountstephen, have you not?" This was my agitator grandfather again, helpfully stirring the pot with his questions.

Fletcher looked at me. I couldn't help, and so he attempted to stutter out an answer. "She has been... Well, she's an excellent secretary for my... my father."

I could see that he wished to avoid talking about her, and so I changed the topic. "You've told us that you loved your sister, but did you actually like her?" It wasn't the sweetest of questions, but he was evidently relieved, nonetheless.

"That goes without saying. We have always been close. Admittedly, I hadn't seen her a great deal over the last couple of years, but we would telephone every once in a while. She was always so busy with her art that I rarely knew where to find her."

"You didn't see her as often because you stayed away from Montegufoni all that time, isn't that right?"

He shuffled in his seat a little and threw his tie over his shoulder, then changed his mind and put it back in place. "It is."

"And why was that exactly? We know all about your brother's fiery temperament, and I can quite imagine he and your father arguing, but from all we've seen of you, it's hard to believe that you fell out with him so badly you would abandon him."

"I didn't abandon him." He was easily vexed, and I kept going.

"So what caused your long hiatus? After all, your house is only an

214

hour's drive from here."

His tongue peeped out from between his lips as he worked on an answer. "I try to be an obliging person." He paused again, and I wondered what he was holding back from us. "I've always wanted to be a good son and brother, but Father wasn't like most people. He loved us in his way, but he never made our lives simple. His idea of a pleasant time was to vex and tease all those around him. He was not so concerned with what we would achieve, over which some fathers obsess, or even how much we loved him. It was all a game for him, and he was more curious about the results of his bizarre schemes than whom they affected."

"So you couldn't take it any more?" I suggested.

"You could say that. There was no big argument when I left – I'm not melodramatic like Dash or even Coralie. I simply exited Father's life, and it turned out that it was forever."

He looked more comfortable again. Grandfather had often told me I had that effect on people, but that wasn't what I wanted. I'd been skirting around a particular issue – getting closer and closer and then pulling away from it again – but there was nowhere else to go now.

"When you arrived here yesterday, you were cheery and blithe even as you learnt of your father's death. You seemed morose shortly after and have been on edge whenever we've seen you since your sister's body was found. Can you explain any of that?"

"I don't understand why you'd ask such a question." He paused to breathe in. "It has been a difficult time for me. Half of my family has been erased in two swift, violent acts. Coralie's death was particularly painful, and I don't doubt I will feel it deeply for a long time."

This was a perfectly reasonable response, but not what I wanted to know.

"And what of the fluctuating emotions you showed coming back here?"

"What can I tell you? My father and I no longer saw eye to eye. Just setting foot in Montegufoni—"

"That doesn't make sense. You're saying that you were so distant from your father that his death barely affected you, but seeing this castle again made you miserable."

This time, Fletcher looked to my grandfather for help, but he had nothing to say. The young man sipped his drink, and I did the same. I hadn't been told what was in it, but it felt like a metal rod being poked down my throat by a particularly maladroit doctor.

"I don't know what you want from me." The young man shook his head and looked confounded. His clear blue eyes that he'd inherited from his father clouded over somewhat in the fading light.

"I believe that there was something else which kept you away – a reason that had little to do with Lord Monroe."

He said nothing, and I realised that it was time to show my hand. Whether this would lead to a grand revelation or a dismissive laugh at my expense, I couldn't say, but I did it all the same.

"I believe you have come to the conclusion that Eva Mountstephen is your father's illegitimate daughter."

He immediately grasped his drink and tipped half of it down his throat. I can only conclude that this had its desired effect as, a moment later, a reply tore from him. "Why would you say such a thing? What has that got to do with the killings?"

I decided to allow him one last digression. "Very well. Who do you think is responsible for their deaths? That's certainly more relevant."

Fletcher looked across the garden to where Todd was packing away bottles into a hamper. He could have finished this task some time ago, but he generally stayed nearby in case we needed him to tackle any fleeing suspects.

"There are so many potential killers that any list I gave you would be redundant. Right at this moment, I'm inclined to believe that the rotten policeman who locked my brother up is to blame." Fletcher looked back at my grandfather. "Do you know that he only let Dashwood go because I paid a bribe?"

Grandfather nodded, but this was my interview, and it was coming to its inevitable conclusion.

"Did you know that your father changed his will a year ago?"

He huffed a deep breath from his lungs. "How could I? We haven't spoken in twice as long."

"Dashwood might have told you," I immediately responded. "And we can't say whether Coralie knew about it."

"Well they didn't mention it to me. And to tell the truth, I have never been the kind of person who obsesses over the legacy I will one day receive, especially as I was the youngest of three and unlikely to

216

inherit as much as my siblings."

"Then why did you go looking for it in your father's office?"

He opened his mouth – no doubt to deny this – then gave up. His eyes fell to the latticework table, or perhaps the ground beneath it. "It wasn't what you think."

I had to laugh at this, as I knew exactly why he'd done it. "I went to see Andrew Longfield in Florence this morning." I leaned closer over the table. "There is something in the will that you may interest you. You see, along with bequests for Father Laurence and Signora Acciaioli, your father made provisions for his illegitimate children."

He still didn't look at me. I believe he was bearing himself for the worst.

"Of the six remaining names, all of them were Italian."

It took him a few moments to realise the importance of what I was saying, but a second later, he was smiling. "Do you mean…? I thought that…" He was so happy he couldn't finish his sentences. He shot up to standing, knocking his chair back into the vines that grew up the wall behind him.

"I think it's very unlikely that Eva Mountstephen is your half-sister," I told him, but he'd worked this much out and was running off through the garden, calling as he went.

"My goodness, Christopher Prentiss, you are a good man. A swine, of course, but a good man nevertheless!"

CHAPTER THIRTY-FOUR

"You'll have to explain what just happened, Chrissy." It wasn't often that Grandfather used my shortened name any more, and I could see how confused he was by the unexpected turn in the discussion we'd just had with Fletcher.

Todd disappeared with his travelling box of libations, and we went to my sitting room to talk before bed. It was true that there were no electric lights about, so I lit a candelabra before taking a seat.

"Well, the first thing you must know is that I still don't think the youngest Monroe is a likely killer. He might have had mixed feelings towards his family, but we've no reason to believe he wished them dead. He also got along with his sister far better than Dashwood did."

He sat down in an armchair beside the open balcony. "I would argue that none of what you've just told me disproves his guilt, but please continue."

Delilah had followed us from the garden and curled up to sleep on my feet. It kept them nice and warm.

"I learnt from Eva that Fletcher came close to proposing two years ago – but then he suddenly grew cold towards her and stopped visiting. I know that he had a discussion with his father just before that, and it made me wonder what caused the sudden change in him."

"And so you decided Eva must be Renwick's daughter? Why?" He sounded no less bemused than he had outside.

"No, I decided that Fletcher believed that to be the case, because that was the first thing I thought when I saw her. She had very similar blue eyes to Lord Monroe's, and you told me that you were both friends with Eva's mother. It would have explained why he brought her here to be his secretary."

"It might have, but I could have told you how unlikely that was. Renwick was as fond of Eva's father as he was of her mother. The three of them used to pal around together in London, and for all his moral ambiguities, you must know that Renwick treated his friends rather well."

"Yes, I got that impression from his solicitor, too. He followed Lord Monroe to Italy and was grateful for his support. But you can't deny that the man who formerly owned this extravagant castle was something of a Lothario. Within a few hundred yards of where we are sitting live three women with whom he sired children."

"Oh, you're quite right there. Renwick had a curious attitude towards fidelity. He even had it in him to scandalise me. But if Fletcher was, or perhaps is, in love with Eva Mountstephen, why didn't he just ask his father whether his suspicion was true?"

"I believe he did." I was far less sure about this part of the story, but I knew enough to piece it together. "Knowing Renwick's penchant for stirring and manipulation, I think he chose not to rule out the possibility entirely, and so Fletcher assumed the worst. He couldn't very well marry his own half-sister, and so he retreated from Montegufoni to avoid the pain of seeing the woman he loved but couldn't have."

"And this theory was in no way influenced by what happened to you in the hotel this morning?"

Was it only this morning? I marvelled, before noticing certain parallels between the two situations (and then ignoring them).

"No, it has nothing to do with the state of perpetual heartache in which I now live." I doubt I convinced him. "I knew there was something between them when I witnessed their reunion yesterday. At first, Fletcher was overjoyed to see her – it was so powerful, in fact, that he was unable to feel the pain of losing his father. And then, if I'm judging things correctly, the reality of the situation settled into his brain once more and he remembered that, although he was ecstatic to see her, and had driven to Montegufoni as soon as she called him, they still couldn't have anything to do with one another."

"Fascinating." He tapped his glass a few times with one extended finger. "But if all that is true, why were you so menacing in your interview? From the way you spoke, I truly believed that you had discovered a damning piece of evidence, and you were about to reveal Fletcher as the killer."

I considered my answer for a short time, as it was hard to put into words. "I suppose because I still had so many doubts. I had to push him as far as I could to see how he would react."

"Good gosh." He said nothing more for almost a minute, but I decided not to interrupt his thinking. "You have done very well indeed. I must admit that I was too concerned about the killings to notice any romantic stirrings. You have excelled where I failed. I've always said you would be a fine detective one day."

It wasn't clear whether he considered this day to have dawned, but I was still pleased with his compliment.

"However," the inevitable caveat soon arrived, "this has not provided us with any great clue as to who was responsible for the two murders."

I believe I grimaced then, as I was very aware of this. "I thought perhaps you had already done that."

"Oh dear." He pronounced these two words with thick layers of resignation and just a touch of disappointment. "Relying on someone else to solve the case is never the best strategy."

"Yes, but I only believed so because, before dinner, you suggested that you were close to finding the solution."

He screwed his lips together so that they bunched up his bright white moustaches. I couldn't tell whether he was about to criticise me or admit a mistake. "I thought I had an inkling of what had happened, but I am no longer certain. And as our suspects have now retired for the night, I don't believe we can tie the last threads together until the morning."

I was a little surprised by the idea that a murder investigation should come to a stop before midnight. It was normally Grandfather's habit to ignore everything else, including sleeping and eating, in order to hunt down the killer – just as Delilah forgets whatever she is doing when she smells one of Cook's pork pies.

"You really were spectacular this evening, Christopher," he told me with great sincerity. "And now I must bid you goodnight."

With a wave, he walked across to the hidden staircase and mounted it to reach his room.

I stayed right where I was for several minutes, just in case it was a trick. I eventually accepted that he hadn't padded back downstairs in his socks to jump out at me and shout, *Ha! You fell for my clever ruse. Now let's stay up until three in the morning, questioning everything we think we know.*

So then I went to sleep.

CHAPTER THIRTY-FIVE

I had the strangest dreams. I was married to my unnamed theoretical fiancée, but it turned out that, like a monster from ancient myth, she had the face of the most beautiful girl in the world but the body of a fish. It was certainly problematic for our day-to-day existence and made romantic walks in the country nearly impossible. In fact, I was just about to push her outside in a bathtub suspended on a handbarrow when I woke up to the sound of someone in agony.

It took me a while to come back to reality. My mouth still tasted of Todd's excessively strong cocktail, which put me in mind of the metal bar I'd found on the floor of the tower. I was sure in that moment that this easily overlooked piece of evidence would turn out to be significant, but before I could harness these ideas and grasp hold of them, that strange, wounded grunting began once more.

"Is somebody out there?" I summoned the composure to call, but there would be no reply.

The noise was coming from the corridor, rather than there in my grotto or the neighbouring room, so I forced myself out of bed and into a dressing gown. The rising sun was breaking through the wooden slats in my apartment, but it barely penetrated the north-facing passage which I now entered.

"Hello?" I asked again, and a noise like someone straining to lift a ton weight came back to me.

I looked along the narrow passageway and, beside a door that led to Grandfather's suite of rooms, there was a figure lying prone on the floor. I ran closer, but the man's head was turned away from me and I couldn't see who it was. My grandfather must have heard something, too, as the door flew open and light from the spacious gallery spilt out to us.

"Christopher, why on earth are…?" He didn't finish this sentence, as I'd crouched down to check on the invalid and he could see what was occupying me. "Is he alive?"

"Yes." I still hear the man breathing and grabbed his shoulder to pull him onto his back. "It's Dashwood, and I think he's very sick."

Grandfather called for Todd, who was already in the Gallery, perhaps to bring his master his morning cup of tea.

"We'll need your help to move him," I told our always ready assistant and, rather than taking him up the stairs to Grandfather's quarters, I thought it made more sense to carry him into my spare room.

"He must have thought we could save him and stumbled down the stairs to find us," Grandfather posited, as Todd and I took an end each – or is that what you say for moving furniture rather than people? We carried the troublesome brother along the corridor and into the Chamber of Aurora. There was a double bed in there, and we soon had him more comfortable.

"What have you consumed, man?" Grandfather demanded before we'd even got him in place. "Was it cocaine? Did you take too much?"

Dashwood smiled up at us, but I could see that whatever was in his body was torturing him. His grin was one of sheer pain, and he gritted his teeth to try to cope with it.

"Can you tell us anything?" I begged. "Please! Whatever has happened, we want to help you."

"Call for a physician, Todd." Grandfather pointed in the direction of the telephone, and his retainer immediately ran off to do as required.

There was sweat on Dashwood's brow. Drops of the stuff stayed fixed in place as though they had been set there with glue, even as he desperately shook and exhaled.

"Not cocaine," he finally managed, but he had to breathe in again and the effort was clearly overwhelming. "Poison. I'm poisoned."

"Then tell us who did it!" Grandfather was beginning to show his distress too now. "We'll do all we can to save you but help us to prevent this from happening to anyone else."

Dashwood actually laughed then, and I couldn't understand why. "Sorry, matey. You've got me all wrong. I'm just not that sort of chap."

I could practically see the sickness running through his veins and around his stricken body. I'd witnessed several intoxications before, but I noticed a number of clear differences this time. There were not the waves of convulsion that I'd seen with strychnine poisoning, but that didn't make what Dashwood was enduring any less excruciating. His eyes were abnormally dilated, his breathing short, and I felt that, if we didn't do something soon, it would be too late to save him.

"Come along, you fool!" Grandfather's voice was wracked with fury, and he seized hold of Dashwood's shoulder to shake some sense into him. "Tell us all you can if you wish to live."

"I had a heavy night of drink and other such delights, but that wasn't what caused it. Something must have ended up in my glass. Something botanical perhaps. I can't tell you anything more than—" He put his hands to his stomach and rolled onto his side. He stayed very still for a moment before turning back to us, and I wondered if it was already too much for him.

Grandfather finally fell into that efficient mode of his that I'd seen so many times. "Christopher, go as quickly as you can and get me mustard, salt – anything that might work as an emetic. But don't dawdle for one moment."

The irony that he could have saved a few precious seconds by being more succinct was not lost on me.

It felt good to run. I shot through open doorway after open doorway towards the Hall of Gonfaloniers and the salon beyond. I thought this the quickest way to the kitchen, but it meant I had to go back on myself through the courtyard.

"Mustard!" I yelled as soon as I found Henrietta preparing breakfast.

"I beg your pardon, young master?"

"I need mustard."

She looked a little reluctant to provide any such thing at so early an hour but answered, "French or English? Powder or paste?"

"You've been Grandfather's cook for decades; you must have prepared an emetic for a dying man before!" This was presumptive on my part but turned out to be quite accurate.

"Right you are." She hurried across to a cupboard which she had already colonised and removed a pot of Colman's English mustard paste. "Start with a few spoons of this in some water. But take these too." She turned to the sideboard to select four large eggs. "They should help neutralise the poison once the mustard has done its job."

"Thank you, Cook!" I put the pot into the pocket of my gown and held two eggs in each hand as I ran back to the courtyard.

"Good luck!" she called after me, and the dear woman's support pushed me forward.

I took the passage around the tower this time and then cut through the Hall of Arms to get there a fraction faster. I crashed into the room to hand over my treasures to the makeshift doctor, who was sitting in an armchair beside the patient.

"We're too late, Christopher," Grandfather whispered. "He's already dead."

CHAPTER THIRTY-SIX

"Why didn't he tell us the name of his own killer?" I sounded like a child and felt guilty for moaning when a man had just drawn his last breath. "Did he say anything more?"

Grandfather swallowed, and I could hear the dryness in his throat. When there was no other response, I had a good look at poor Dashwood. He was staring straight up at the Fresco of the Greek goddess on the ceiling as though anticipating the next plane of existence. I had to hope that he had done enough in life to be on his way to a place full of cherubim and fluffy clouds.

Now that I looked closely, I could see that there were marks on his chest under his open shirt, and bruises on his arms from his journey downstairs. I couldn't bear to think of his suffering as he used the last of his remaining energy to battle his way down to us. If only it had happened earlier in the night, he might have stood a chance.

When Grandfather finally replied, the intensity of his voice startled me. "I did what I could to keep him cool with a glass of water and a wet towel. He told me of his regrets and said that he had been a disappointment even to himself. He said he found it quite astonishing that he had lived into his thirty-fourth year."

He was normally so resilient when it came to the slings and arrows of our outrageous cases but, once in a while, the barbarity of mankind simply crushed him. "No matter how many times I see people die, I will never get used to the emptiness of such moments. It is almost enough to make me give up altogether."

"Not now, Grandfather." I put the eggs on the sideboard beside the water jug and went to stand next to him. "We still have to stop the killer."

"What can I possibly do?"

He looked down at his hands, and I had to conclude that he had taken the guilt for what had happened on himself. In a previous dark moment like this, he had once told me that his fame disproved his brilliance as, if he were any kind of detective, he wouldn't have had so many murders to investigate in the first place. I had argued against this improbable conclusion, and I felt that I had to do it again now.

"This is no one's fault. If Dashwood had come to us last night, then you could have saved him. He was so intoxicated even before the poison did its work that he was presumably unconscious of what was happening. It's more than possible that he didn't even know who was responsible for his death."

He breathed out roughly as he shook his head. "I doubt it, my boy. I got the definite impression that he refused to give us the name out of loyalty."

"Which means there is only one person who could have done it." I didn't want to say these words. In fact, I'd been avoiding them since Fletcher had arrived a day and a half earlier, but there was no sense in denying it any longer.

"You're right; we must face facts. In cases in which a family member is suspected of murder, it is usually for one of two reasons; he either wishes to inherit more quickly, or he doesn't feel he has been granted a large enough share of the estate. I had come very close to the solution last night, but our talk with Fletcher made me question my conclusions. It now looks as though I was right."

I'd fallen into the same old trap and felt like such a fool. Because of my short-sightedness, a third innocent person had been killed. There was little we could have done for Lord Monroe, but Coralie and Dashwood's deaths would remain on my conscience for some time.

"Should we interview Fletcher again immediately?" I asked as Todd appeared from the neighbouring room.

"The doctor won't be able to do anything for him now." Still in silk pyjamas and moccasins, Grandfather climbed wearily to his feet and, for the first time in years, he really did look his age. "Christopher and I have work ahead of us, Todd, but we must change our clothes. In the meantime, I would appreciate it if you could head to the rooms above this one and make sure that Fletcher Monroe doesn't go anywhere. If he tries to leave, suggest that you take breakfast together. I'm sure you'll find a way."

"Yes, m'lord." Todd was more hesitant than normal. He was as experienced at assisting my grandfather with his investigations as I was, but he took a moment to cast his sorrowful gaze over the dead man before hurrying from the room.

Grandfather glanced down at the floor and wouldn't look up again before he left. I felt a little guilty for leaving Dashwood alone, but time was short, and so I raced back to my room to get changed. Most of my clothes from London were heavy and oppressive, but I got dressed in my lightest summer trousers and a crisp white shirt. I resembled a Morris dancer and really only needed bells on my ankles and a couple of handkerchiefs to complete the picture, but at least I wouldn't bake in the sunshine. If it was like this in May, I had to hope I would acclimatise before the warm weather hit in full force.

"Where to first?" I asked, sounding like a police officer friend of ours when I crossed paths with Grandfather in the corridor.

To my absolute lack of amazement, he was wearing his full grey morning suit. I really had to question how hot it would need to be for him to wear anything else. I thought I might suggest a trip to the beach at some point, just to see how long he would stick with his classic outfit.

"We must inspect the victim's bedroom." He would say nothing more but, still just as stern as he'd been when I'd last seen him, he led off towards the centre of the castle on our way to the nearest staircase.

The first-floor landing was high in the building because of the tall rooms below. We stopped there to listen but there was nothing to hear, so we moved along that dark hallway past Fletcher's room to the one where his brother had slept.

"Have you been in here before?" I asked my mentor when he pushed the door open without asking me which it was.

"I have. I looked inside yesterday morning when you were on your way to Florence and the brothers were at the police station." We both glanced around from just beyond the doorway. "It hasn't changed a lot, has it?"

I walked across to the site of the chaos I'd seen there the previous day. There were still bottles on the floor, but I could see that they were not the same ones. The pile of powder on the otherwise empty table had shrunk a good bit, too, and I looked around for other changes but couldn't find anything significant. I remembered seeing a few dirty glasses about the place, so he'd cleaned those away at least, but as he'd spent all evening up there, it ruled out any possibility that he was house proud.

The biggest change, in fact, was around the bed. The covers were thrown back and I don't need to say what evidence there was that Dashwood had been sick for some time, but it was there.

"Do you notice anything else?" Grandfather asked. I couldn't tell whether he was enquiring as to my findings or testing them.

I shrugged. "It seems to fit with what he told us. He got drunk and what have you, which would have made it easier to slip poison into his drink."

Grandfather only offered a short, "*Hmmm,*" in response and turned to leave. As his assistant, one thing that I could definitely still improve is my understanding of such noises. It's a shame he hasn't produced a pamphlet, as I'm certain that the different tones he uses mean different things. For example, there must be one kind of hmmm for sarcasm, another for when he's surprised, yet more for doubt and nonchalance. But in all honesty, I can't tell one hmmm from another.

I drew the conclusion that he was unmoved by our visit to Dashwood's former digs in the house, but what we found back along the corridor in Fletcher's room set both of our brains whirring.

"Two glasses," I said as soon as I stepped inside to examine the scene. "This place was as clean as can be yesterday. Now look at it."

I could see just how excited Grandfather was. He rushed forward to inspect two chairs and a table where the brothers had presumably sat drinking together the night before. "Fingerprints…" He muttered, bending down to examine the glasses in the light. "And we'll be able to send the remains of whatever is inside them to a laboratory to determine whether there are traces of poison."

He had the look of a man who was thoroughly pleased with his work, and while he did that, I put my white cotton gloves on to leaf through some handwritten pages on top of a chest of drawers between two French windows. From what I could tell, it was a business proposal. There was talk of investment and potential returns. What I couldn't see was what kind of enterprise it was or who had written it until I reached the last page and found a scribbled signature that appeared to begin with a D.

I pointed the pages out to Grandfather and continued my search. The bed had clearly been used the night before, and Fletcher's pyjamas were on a chair nearby, but I doubted there was much more to learn by lingering in his bedroom. I was disappointed that I'd clung so desperately to simple ideas of what made a person good, but I was oddly exhilarated to know that we'd finally caught the killer.

I may even have had a smile on my face as I called across to the great detective who had come to the right conclusion, which I had ignored for so long. "I believe it's time to interview our suspect. Don't you agree?"

CHAPTER THIRTY-SEVEN

The courtyard was busy when we made the final trip down there before tying the case together. Todd was sitting with Fletcher at a small table, and the two were engaged in cheery conversation. I could only assume that our man hadn't yet told anyone of the third death in the family in as many days.

In the opposite corner, Guido and Nonna Lombardo were working on… something. Instead of confronting the culprit, when the head mechanic disappeared inside, Grandfather went over to talk to the old lady. I was uncertain whether to follow him or observe our suspect. As I doubted Grandfather's Italian had improved much in the last day, I stayed where I was.

Father Laurence had just appeared from the gloomy passage that led to the hidden-away chapel, and even the chickens were there, picking about the place in the optimistic belief that there was some trace of grain they'd overlooked since their last meal. The only real suspect missing was Eva, and she was about to step out of the ballroom with an enormous smile on her face.

Fletcher spotted her and was up from the table in a shot. He skipped over, full of love, romance, and poetry – or, at least, that's what he wanted us all to think. I had no doubt that his twisted mind was consumed by the question of when we would discover his brother's body.

"It's a beautiful morning," he told Eva, and I could see from across the courtyard that they couldn't take their eyes off one another.

I had to feel sorry for the poor young woman who was about to have her heart broken again.

"Isn't it just?" Eva blushed then and had to look away because she was smiling so much. "The finest in a long time, I would say."

They both blushed, and Grandfather arrived to scare them witless. "Fletcher, would you mind telling me where you went after you left us last night?"

He stared at the eminent detective, who suddenly looked a lot taller than before – and I wasn't even the one he had trapped with his steely grey gaze.

"Last night?" Fletcher responded in a weak voice.

Grandfather never showed such fear and repeated what he wanted to know. "That's right. After you left us in the Cardinal's Garden. Where did you go?"

"I…" I'm surprised he didn't pull at his collar and mop his brow. An interrogation by my grandfather can feel as if you're staring into the sun from just a few feet away. "I looked for Miss Mountstephen…" He turned coy then as he remembered the young woman standing next to him.

She had a flower in her hair, and I must admit that she looked quite lovely. Whatever had passed between them had brought the colour to her usually pale cheeks.

"Yes?" Grandfather had no time for sentimentality.

"And then… we spoke for some time."

"And then?" His words were like pokers that had been left in the fire (only to be taken out and used for poking).

Fletcher grew more nervous by the second, and I considered taking over these early stages of the interview just to make sure that he had the courage to reply.

"And then… And then I went up to my room to go to bed." His tone suggested he was asking whether his answer was right.

"I'm sorry to tell you that our brother died of poisoning this morning." Grandfather can be hard-headed at times, but he was at least a little softer when breaking this bad news.

"What do you—"

"I think you should come with me." Like a soldier on parade, he spun round at a perfect ninety-degree angle and walked off without another word.

"Don't worry," Fletcher tried to reassure his beloved, but he sounded so nervous that it was unlikely to do any good.

As he hurried after my grandfather, Eva Mountstephen started crying.

"I'm sure everything will be fine," I lied, and I wanted to comfort her, but I didn't know how.

"No, it won't," she sobbed, and I put my hands out to hold her as I thought she might faint. "I know it won't."

"Come, come, Eva." I hoped to gee her up a little, but my response sounded insincere. "Neither of us can say what Grandfather has discovered. He might just be putting the fear of God into him."

"That could be true, and you're awfully kind to say it, but…" She took a handkerchief out of her small handbag and dabbed her eyes. "You see, I know that Fletcher is in trouble because he's already told a lie."

This really struck me, and I held her a little tighter. "What do you mean?"

"After he left me last night…" It seemed that she lacked the strength to get the words out, but then she closed her eyes and they flowed once more. "…he told me he had promised to have a drink with his brother."

"Don't give up hope. I'll be back as soon as possible." I waved for Todd, but the old lady who was handy with a spanner came over to help before he arrived. Feeling quite confident that I had left the distressed young lady in good hands, I chased after Fletcher.

I really did pity Eva. If her would-be sweetheart had systematically murdered his family, then he deserved everything he got, but that poor girl would suffer just as much. As someone who had recently gone through a truly traumatic minute-and-a-half-long love affair, I could only sympathise.

There was no sign of Grandfather in the salon, and so I decided they must have turned off to reach the tower – or perhaps towards Signora Acciaioli's apartment, but that would have made an odd spot to conduct the final interview of a very complicated case. Unless she was the killer and— No, no. It was the tower after all. I caught sight of them, and it was clear that Grandfather wanted to finish the story back where it had begun.

"You've already lied," he was saying as I arrived. He pointed at Fletcher on the other side of the small square of concrete and began to lay the charges against him. "Why should we believe a word you say when I know that you were drinking in your room last night with your brother?"

Our suspect looked manic from the start. "Because that's the only untruth I've spoken."

Grandfather snorted in disbelief. "'Untruth!' What a pretty euphemism."

"I promise you, Lord Edgington. I had nothing to do with Dashwood's death."

"So it was just your sister and father you murdered then?"

Fletcher couldn't take the onslaught and turned to look over the side of the tower to the courtyard below.

"This is where your father was in the moments before he fell to his death." Grandfather stood next to him, and his tone was so firm that I thought it might be too much for Fletcher to endure. "This is what led to everything else."

Fletcher put his hand to his forehead, and I could tell he was in no fit state for conversation.

"Only the truth can save you, Fletcher. Tell us what happened after you convinced your brother to have a nightcap."

"My brother never needed persuading to drink," he snapped, and I realised that the fight hadn't quite drained from him after all. "I don't remember whose idea it was, but we agreed to raise a glass in Coralie's honour and—"

Perhaps it was hearing the dead woman's name fall from the culprit's lips, but Grandfather couldn't look at him any more and walked over to look across the gardens. The tower was, inevitably, the highest point of the castle and you could see for miles from up there. Although this was my third visit, I still hadn't had the time to admire the view.

"What do you expect us to believe?" Grandfather demanded without looking back. "That your father's lover found out about the change in his will and decided to murder him? Perhaps Signora Acciaioli believed that the castle was rightly hers as her ancestors built it. If she'd got rid of you Monroes, she would have had a good claim to the property."

"No, I'm not saying that Annina is behind any of this. She's an exceedingly kind person, and we were all very grateful for her putting up with Father."

Grandfather nodded his agreement with this small point at least. "There is also the fact that I asked her to take her children away from here last night for their own protection. They were in Florence when your brother was killed."

I must say, it felt lovely to be able to rule out a suspect conclusively. She might still have had an accomplice, of course, but it was good thinking on the old sleuth's part to send her away. I wonder if he'd done the same with any other obvious suspects.

"Other than yourself, can you suggest one person here in the castle who would benefit from all three deaths?" I asked, as Grandfather had fallen quiet.

Fletcher had rounded his shoulders and hung his head. He was feeling sorry for himself, but it would do him no good.

"Come along, man," Grandfather continued. "At least put up a defence. Choose a name and see where it gets you."

Fletcher looked at him again. There was fear in his eyes. Was it acceptance of what was to come? Did he realise that there was only one place he could now end up?

"Father Laurence then." Grandfather adopted a more helpful attitude and, turning around, he raised one finger as he described another solution. "As a Catholic priest, he certainly disagreed with his former enemy's lifestyle. Your father was a womanising manipulator. He might have believed that he had right on his side as he tricked and punished those who fell afoul of him, but that didn't mean that anyone else agreed." He paused for a moment before delivering a key point. "And don't forget that the good padre has a history of violence."

From the look on Fletcher's face, he hadn't known anything about this.

"Oh, yes. Brian Laurence maintained a respectable façade but, during his time in London, he was a vengeful and aggressive criminal – little more than a thug in a Henry Poole suit. In fact, he was the reason that your father ran away to Italy in the first place."

I don't know whether this came as a surprise to Fletcher, but it beat the stuffing out of me. I'd failed to connect the story Grandfather had told me with what the priest had revealed in the garden.

"I'm sure you know all about Renwick's schemes to impose his concept of justice on the world. Well he chose the wrong person when he went after Brian Laurence. He set out to bankrupt a man who had come to his riches through intimidation and deceit. I don't know the details of his plan, but it backfired, and Laurence threatened to kill him. That's when Renwick came to me for advice, and when I suggested he find a place in the Italian countryside.

"Years later, Laurence found out about the castle and came here to kill him. But he, unlike you, chose salvation instead. He had lost all he owned and would have done whatever your father instructed to have a life again. That is why he changed his ways, and why I never truly

237

believed he was the killer. After all, he didn't have to settle here after he became a priest and, from what I understand, he has shown great kindness to you and your siblings."

"I saw him talking to Dashwood after he returned from the police station last night," I remembered. "The fact that your brother had time for Father Laurence when he shunned everyone else surely shows that he held him in high esteem."

None of this conclusively proved the priest's innocence, but if it was enough for Grandfather, it was fine by me.

"Father Laurence is a dear, dear fellow." Fletcher whispered as the list of suspects continued to shrink. "I'm amazed he has such a chequered past."

"So who does that leave?" There was a gust of warm wind then that seemed to grip hold of Grandfather's words and send them diving over the tower's stone crenelations.

"I don't know." Fletcher was undeniably anxious, but at least he had the courage to look his accuser in the eye.

"Guido Lombardo," I said to move us on. "He clearly didn't like your family. From all that we've seen, he resented your father buying Montegufoni and outright hated him for seducing Signora Acciaioli. Having eaten her pappardelle, I really can't blame him for falling in love with her. Perhaps he was the one up here with your father. Perhaps he decided to continue what he'd started after Coralie made her clumsy announcement to the inhabitants of the castle two nights ago. Dashwood was the easiest of all of you to dislike, so he came next."

Grandfather picked up the thread. "However, as Christopher can surely now tell you, it is not a crime to be surly, and I found another explanation for Guido's reluctance to talk to us. Regardless of that, I very much doubt he would have killed Dashwood."

I'm sure that Fletcher found this assertion just as confusing as I did, but when he said nothing, it fell to me to ask the obvious question. "Why would Dashwood have been the sticking point? Why would Guido have had no trouble killing his employer and poor Coralie but then baulked at dispatching her outrageous brother?"

Grandfather looked a mite pleased with himself, and I realised that I'd fallen into a trap. With all his stratagems, he really wasn't so dissimilar to Lord Monroe. "I didn't say he baulked at the idea, and it certainly wouldn't have been a moral decision. But the police already believed that Dashwood was the killer and, had he been sentenced for the crime, it would have removed any suspicion from Guido."

Fletcher looked so dejected that I moved a little closer to make sure he wouldn't follow his father head first from the tower.

"There is one more person we haven't considered." Grandfather spoke ever so slowly to lend his words more weight. "One person who was close enough to everything that happened to be able to pull strings without drawing our suspicion."

Fletcher saw where the discussion was heading just as I did, and he uttered an insistent, "No."

"Or perhaps… yes?" If I'd said this, Grandfather would have criticised me for being wilful, but he could get away with such things. "Was Eva Mountstephen your accomplice? Or did she kill your family for the sake of the man she still hoped to wed?"

"She wouldn't. She hasn't got it in her."

"And yet, if you think about it, she was the person who really had to put up with your father. As indignant as Coralie was at having to come here once a month, poor Eva spent every single day with him. She can hardly be blamed if she grew tired of his eccentricities. Renwick's peculiar little ways rarely won him any admirers, and I'm glad that I never had to live with him. Perhaps Eva was up here – on whatever mad task he'd assigned her – when she decided that enough was enough. A little push was all it took, and the two of you could be together."

I expected another shouted response to this, but the frightening thing about my grandfather is that he can lay out a case in such a way that you are helpless to ignore it. I felt that I could guess what was going through Fletcher's mind just then. He was thinking the same thing that I was.

"So she killed Renwick because she blamed him for Fletcher leaving?" Perhaps this was too big a jump on my part, but it held a certain logic.

"You never told her why you went away, did you, Fletcher?" Grandfather paused once more to give him time to reflect. "She believed that you loved her, but after a brief disagreement with your father, you just disappeared. It was his death that brought you back here."

"No, it's not possible. I don't believe it…" Fletcher's voice tailed off, and it was easy to see that he was forcing himself to do just this.

"You're right. It's not possible," the wily detective said to put him out of his misery – well, this portion of it at least. "She might have blamed Renwick and wanted him dead, but I doubt that murdering your sister was the most direct route to your heart. And you would have inherited enough with Coralie still alive to live comfortably together.

Grandfather's manner had changed. He was no longer trying to spark a reaction as he raced towards the end of the tale. "The truth is that, from everything we've seen, you are the only person who would benefit from all three deaths. And that is why, when we went to your room just now and saw where you and Dashwood had been drinking – when I smelt a certain pungent sweetness that was notable in one glass but not the other – I knew there was only one explanation."

CHAPTER THIRTY-EIGHT

I had liked Fletcher so much until that day. He was warm, friendly and competent – or in other words: the kind of young man I aspire to be. To think that he would hang for his greed and cruelty was physically painful for me, so I can only imagine how he felt on the matter.

"Tell us how it happened," Grandfather continued in that slow, solemn voice of his. "After you bid Miss Mountstephen goodnight, did you go straight to see your brother?"

He sank to the floor with his back to the wall in the very spot where his father had fallen over the parapet. "Not quite. I changed into my pyjamas and was about to go into Dashwood's room when he came to see me. He was jolly and excited. He'd obviously been drinking, but he chatted away about a project he hoped I would support. He wanted us to establish a business together. He said that I could be involved in the legal side of the enterprise, and he would be the face of it. It was nice to see him so engaged with something other than his own idle pleasure, but the truth was, I couldn't understand what our company was supposed to do."

"We saw the papers on your dresser," Grandfather told him, then he fell quiet to hear more of the story.

"That's right. He'd obviously put a lot of thought into it, so I agreed that we should start the process and see where it would take us. We started drinking to celebrate, and I must say that we both took it too far."

"What did you drink?" I asked to see where *this* would take us.

He put his hands through his hair and tried to remember. "I... It's all rather a blur, but I think there was a bottle of rum knocking about, and then Dashwood went to his room to get some wine."

"How did it end?"

The ghost of a smile haunted his lips for a moment, but it soon vanished. "Dashwood was singing and laughing and making a lot of noise. If I'm perfectly honest, I think he was heavily doped. He was insistent and angry at times, then light and frivolous soon after."

I still hoped it had all been a mistake. I wanted to believe that Dashwood had simply taken too much of his favoured vice and poisoned himself. I looked across at Grandfather and he shook his head to dispel the idea.

"I fell asleep at some point. The last thing I remember…" Fletcher looked up at the bell through the hole in the ceiling. "The last thing I remember was Dashwood rolling about on the floor. I thought he was playing the fool at first, but he clutched his stomach and said he'd eaten too much pasta and should go to bed. I know that he'd gone down to the kitchen to help himself to food while we were outside."

"In which case, that was not how the poison entered his system." Grandfather walked a yard or so across the small terrace but kept his eyes on the suspect. "I believe that the substance that killed him was very bitter and best hidden in a cocktail or strong drink. Did you make sure to ply him with plenty of alcohol before you administered it?"

A short surge of resistance mounted in our culprit, and he shouted his response. "I didn't kill my brother. I didn't kill anyone."

"He was fine when he went to see you. You've just told us that he organised his own supper too, a fact I will confirm with my cook, who was presumably in the kitchen when he was there. By the time Dashwood left your room, he was complaining of abdominal pain because the sickness had begun. He made it through the night and crawled downstairs to seek assistance. However, just minutes after Christopher found him in the corridor, he expired in front of me."

Fletcher stared back defiantly, but he said nothing more.

"Though it may look innocent – much as you do, Fletcher – all parts of the oleander plant are deadly. The pretty flowering tree has been growing in the Cardinal's Garden for decades or longer. Its ancient name in Sanskrit means *horse killer,* and its luscious appearance belies great danger. You could have crushed up some leaves and left them in water to soak or extracted the syrup from the flowers."

"But I didn't."

As Lord Edgington set out the final details of the crime, he placed one foot in front of the other and walked ever so slowly towards the suspect.

"Considering the state that Dashwood was in, I doubt he noticed the taste. Even when he was sick in his bedroom, all those chemicals in his bloodstream would have made it harder for him to wake up and look after himself. If he'd come to us earlier, we might have been able to save his life."

Fletcher couldn't look at his accuser any more. He reminded me of photographs I'd seen of men standing before the gallows, contemplating their imminent fate.

From the tone of his voice, it was hard to imagine that Grandfather would offer him a reprieve. "Your brother was so besotted with drink and drugs that he barely knew which glass was his and which was yours. Just think, he'd gone to all that trouble of cutting flowers when he arrived here. He'd left them soaking in water over night to extract the poison – I know because I saw them in his room. Perhaps he'd needed Dutch courage to go through with it. After all, the two of you got on well enough, but the third of the estate he was supposed to inherit, even after your sister had been removed from the equation, wouldn't have covered his enormous debts."

Fletcher put his head back against the wall. I doubt he could make sense of what he was hearing. I was struggling myself.

"Dashwood must have mixed the drinks in his own room, but he was so far gone that he got the glasses muddled and ended up murdering himself."

There was silence for a moment as neither the killer who wasn't a killer nor I could quite accept what my grandfather was saying.

"What about their father?" I finally responded. "We know that Dashwood was at home in Arezzo when Lord Monroe was killed."

"He was." Grandfather had stopped beside the wooden box that hid the clockwork mechanism we'd previously inspected. "Don't you remember me saying, Christopher, that a stopped clock is right twice a day?"

I did remember this, but it didn't explain how Dashwood Monroe could be in two places at the same time.

"Renwick must have fallen to his death when he came up here to fix the clock. The flat metal spike that you saw was most likely the minute hand. If you lean around the parapet, you can see that it has become rusted and stopped the whole thing from working. I imagine that he was trying to repair it when he got angry and fell from the tower."

"But there was someone here with him!" Now I was the angry one. I really couldn't believe what I was hearing. "I distinctly heard someone running away just after Lord Monroe's body hit the ground."

"That was Guido Lombardo who was in charge of maintaining the castle, though Renwick was never one to leave things to other people. We heard him shouting at Guido. He called him a swine and got upset with him, but that was probably because he considered the man to have used the wrong screwdriver or spoken out of turn. As his grandmother speaks really very good Latin, I was able to confirm that her grandson had been acting so suspiciously because he was afraid that he would be blamed for the first death. In Renwick's apoplexy, the old fool toppled from the tower without a hand being laid upon him."

"But…" This was all Fletcher would manage in terms of a reply. He was breathing more easily, and a look of relief had come across his pleasant features, but that didn't mean he could express himself.

"I'm so sorry to have frightened you like that," Grandfather told him, holding his hand out to help him up. "I had to be certain that it wasn't you."

"How can you be?" Fletcher sounded terribly innocent then. If it had been me, I would have kept my mouth shut in case Grandfather changed his mind.

"Well, for one thing, though you lied about drinking with your brother, you made no attempt to hide the evidence in your room before you came running down to see your little girlfriend this morning. You could easily have washed up the glasses in the sink there, but you left them for anyone to find. Furthermore, while I have known some overly optimistic murderers, I doubt you would be stupid enough to kill the three people standing in your way of inheriting the estate."

"But Dashwood was?" I hastened to ask.

Grandfather was smiling now. It was a sad smile because two innocent people were dead, and another desperate young man had met the fate he may well have deserved. He put his hand on my shoulder and the other on Fletcher's to steer us towards the stone stairs.

"No, no. He was clever in his own way, but he relied too much on his alibi for the first death. He evidently believed that the sheer impossibility of his having killed Renwick gave him free rein to murder his siblings. It seems he was the only one of you who discovered that your father had changed the order of inheritance, so he knew it wasn't enough to murder Coralie if he wanted the castle. As I've already explained, he needed more than a third of the estate, so you were his next target."

244

Fletcher took a large gulp of air. "I don't know whether to laugh or cry or kiss you. I really don't."

"Perhaps don't do any of that." Grandfather stopped walking and allowed us a few seconds to accept that this was the honest solution. There were no more games to be played – no tricks or traps. Dashwood truly was the killer. "From early on in this case, Christopher saw you as a guileless young man, whereas he marked your brother out as a devil. It took me some time to appreciate his way of thinking, but I finally came to see that he was right."

"Are you sure?" I had to ask.

"Quite sure, thank you, Christopher. You see, the reason I immediately questioned whether Dashwood had poisoned himself – more than the flowers in his room, which were there yesterday but gone today – was the lack of effort that had been made to mask Fletcher's guilt."

"Well, that stands to reason," he replied quite honestly. "I didn't make any because I wasn't guilty."

"The papers that Dashwood wanted you to sign were a smokescreen so that he could claim he wouldn't have killed the man who was about to invest in his grand new project. There was no way he could have murdered his father, and he would have argued that he had no reason to kill you. It might have convinced a good police officer, let alone the corrupt and self-interested Ispettore Stefani." We walked down to a small landing where the stairs turned back on themselves, and Grandfather made an important point. "You are a very fortunate man, Fletcher Monroe."

The intended victim bowed his head and breathed out loudly. When he looked back at us, there was an apprehensive smile on his face. "You needn't worry about that, Lord Edgington. I know exactly how lucky I am."

CHAPTER THIRTY-NINE

Fletcher's relief was perhaps even surpassed by Eva Mountstephen's. She was still waiting in the exact same spot in which I'd left her but dashed across the courtyard to see her sweetheart as we exited the salon.

"My darling!" one or both of them shouted, and they wrapped their arms around one another in a tight embrace.

I'm not so sure I would like to fall in love with someone whom I had previously mistaken for a sister, but it was clear that they adored one another. Even grumpy Guido Lombardo looked pleased for them. He was the first person to whom Grandfather spoke whilst everyone else was congratulating the already happy couple. I couldn't blame the man for lying, especially with such a corrupt police officer prowling the area. He must really have believed he would swing for the death of the old lord.

Guido could well have had other reasons for hiding the truth. Perhaps he had a criminal record and was worried that no one would believe it was an accident. Perhaps – as Father Laurence had implied – he'd said terrible things about the family in the past which could have turned a jury against him. Even after his grandmother had admitted what happened, he wasn't particularly forthcoming with the information he gave, though he did admit to returning to the tower to hide the evidence that he'd been up there with Lord Monroe. His grandmother and perhaps even his brother had known all along, and it's a shame sometimes that blood is thicker than water, but even worse when it isn't.

For all his happiness at finally seeing a future for himself with the woman he loved, Fletcher would have to rebuild his life after losing the rest of his family to an accident, a murder and some variety of much-deserved misadventure. The knowledge of Dashwood's cruelty would stay with him for the rest of his life. I did not envy his situation, but I was glad he had someone with whom to share the burden.

"Congratulations to you both," I told them when my turn came.

"Thank you, Christopher," Fletcher replied in that ever so heartfelt tone of his, which I was glad really was sincere. "And I mean that a thousand times. Even if your grandfather was the one to realise what Dashwood had done, it seems you believed in me all the way."

"Well, yes… that's almost true, but even I began to doubt you at the end there."

"Even you?" Eva teased me. "I was standing down here thinking I'd fallen in love with a killer."

"To be quite honest…" Fletcher dropped his voice to show that he was serious. "…up on that tower with your grandfather laying out the evidence against me, I actually began to wonder whether, in my drunken stupor, I really had killed Dashwood."

"Then it is a great comfort all around that you were not the guilty party."

The emotion got too much for them then. Eva seized her almost fiancé by the lapels and pulled him closer to her, and Fletcher did all he could not to cry. I imagine that, when they were next alone together, he lost that fight, but he maintained a perfectly stiff upper lip in public, as we Englishmen are told we must.

"Did you have to be such a bruiser?" I asked my grandfather when he'd finished the final parts of the investigation and Cook and Signora Acciaioli had brought out the necessary ingredients for everyone to enjoy an Italian breakfast *all'aperto* style. I'd never heard this phrase before, but it apparently means *in the open air*. So perhaps I'd been following Italian traditions my whole life; there's nothing I like more than a nice picnic.

"I resent that accusation," he replied ever so curtly. "The conclusion I had formed was too ephemeral for my liking. I wanted to put it to the test by pushing Fletcher as far as I could to make sure he didn't contradict anything that I believed to be true."

"Still," I replied in a dubious tone, "it was unkind, even by your standards."

"Unkind, Christopher? I?" It's truly impressive that he could make this one-letter word last so long. It was practically a song in itself. "We'll see whether you still think me unkind when we go into Florence this afternoon to make the acquaintance of the local ice cream sellers."

The very thought of such a treat made my mouth water, but there was something even more exciting in what he'd said. "So we don't have to run off, then? We can stay for a while before we move on to the next stop on our European tour?"

He tipped his head back in that regal manner of his and looked down at me proudly. "If it is not an imposition on the new owners, I would like to stay here for a few months as we had planned. We will spend time studying the wonders that the Uffizi Gallery holds. I will work on my artistic endeavours, and you can read the books you're always complaining that you don't have time to enjoy."

"Oh, Grandfather. I don't know what to say." I was a little emotional myself now. *Stiff upper lip, Chrissy!* I told myself. *Stiff upper lip.*

"Then say I'm not a bruiser, and all will be forgiven."

I adopted a serious look as I considered this deal. "Sorry, Grandfather, I would be lying if I said you were never a bruiser. But you are a very nice one, nonetheless."

I ran off to see what pastries were on offer before he could clip me around the back of the neck. I ate something called a cornetto, which was essentially a croissant filed with delectable custard. I had a cup of sweet coffee and watched my grandfather from across the courtyard as our staff, the (metaphorically at least) new lord of Montegufoni and a few of the locals came to congratulate him on a job well done.

I didn't mind that he'd solved the case where I had failed. Perhaps I'd pip him next time. The most important thing was that I had been right about Fletcher and Dashwood. While it was true that a black-hearted man had chosen his own solvency over the lives of his brother and sister, Fletcher and Eva really were as nice as they seemed, and that gave me a certain amount of hope for not just my own life but everyone else's, too. It's easy to think sometimes – especially if you know my grandfather – that the world is full of villains. And yet, in our day-to-day existence, that simply isn't true.

There was only one thing missing from this conclusion. Normally when we catch a killer, they are there to hear the charges against them. I felt, in a way, that Dashwood had got off lightly, and so as our old friends and our new ones were having a wonderful time together – and Delilah was scrounging scraps of food from every last one of them – I slipped off to my apartment to speak to Dashwood.

He was in the same position as we'd left him, though someone would soon appear to take him to the nearest mortuary. At the rate that people had been dying, I could only hope that the coroner was given a healthy tip.

I stood over Dashwood's body and looked into his open eyes.

"I came here to say just how evil you are," I began, feeling slightly foolish to be speaking to myself. "You had a family who loved you despite everything. You brought all your misfortune on yourself, and you still felt hard done by."

I stopped then, because I realised that the scratches I'd noticed on his chest weren't from his journey down to see us, but the run-in he had with Coralie. She knew he was too strong to prise his hands away, and so she'd done what she could to hurt him. It was a tragic realisation, and though I'd gone there to tell Dashwood exactly what I thought of him, seeing this made me want to turn away again.

And I would have done just that if someone hadn't come to stand next to me.

"You were cruel and selfish and deceitful," Fletcher told his dead brother. "You are the most abhorrent person I have ever met, but I won't stop loving you because of every good moment we shared."

I stood back then, so that he had pride of place beside the body, but I said no more.

"You were good once. When we were children, we were the best of friends, and it is hard to imagine what changed you, brother." His voice wavered, and he let out a pained breath, but he would not be defeated. "You tried to destroy our family, and you failed. You tried to kill me, and I lived. As you rot in your grave, I plan to be happy with the woman I love. I am going to ask her to marry me this very night. We will have as many children as she wants and not one of them will be called Dashwood Monroe."

CHAPTER FORTY

Later that afternoon, when the celebrations had died down, we drove to Florence full of anticipation. Ostensibly, I wanted to see more of that elegant city, but there was also the hope in my heart that I might cross paths with the young lady I so admired after seeing her for a combined total of around seventeen seconds. There had been a lot to distract me over the previous day, but the image I had of her never left my mind. And perhaps I was a shallow sort of person to become so besmitten with a girl to whom I'd never said a word, but I truly believed that I'd seen something special in her and that our paths were destined to cross once more.

Todd drove us to the city, and I sat in the back with my grandfather. He was clearly pleased with me, despite the fact that I had done very little to solve the case (and called him a bruiser).

"Is there anything you would like to ask about the conclusion of our investigation?" he pondered as we drove into the centre of Florence.

"No, thank you."

"Nothing?" He sounded a touch disgruntled. "There are normally a number of points that have eluded you."

I considered the possibility for a moment or two. "No, I don't think so. A bankrupt narcomaniac took advantage of his father's accidental death to get away with killing his sister so as to inherit a larger share of their family estate before slipping up when he tried to poison his brother and accidentally killing himself. It's all quite straightforward."

"But—"

I cut him off before he could say anything more. "The one thing that evades me is the same thing you have refused to reveal ever since we left home." I waited for him to ask what this was, but he wasn't the type to indulge me. "I still want to know why you brought me to Montegufoni in the first place."

He turned to look at the street along which we were passing but said nothing.

"From what I can tell, you certainly didn't approve of Lord Monroe's behaviour, and I doubt you actually liked him as a person, so why did you bring us here to see him?"

He adopted a tone to suggest that this was of no concern. "I told you, Christopher; I thought it would be good for you. If you're to assume my mantle in a few decades' time when I am gone…" He winked at me then to show that he was (at most) half serious "…you will need to meet a wide range of people. I thought that the mercurial Renwick Monroe would be an interesting enigma for you to study."

I accepted this answer… until I didn't. "No, no. That can't be it. This was supposed to be a holiday. Why would you start us off with such a challenge? And, for that matter, why didn't we stop in France and work our way here? I've known from the beginning that something significant pulled you to Montegufoni."

Grandfather looked straight at me for a few moments, and he evidently realised that lying would do him no good. "Sometimes, Christopher – just occasionally – I miss the naïve young boy you used to be." Even then, he fell quiet again, and I could see the effort he required to produce an answer. "A year after my Katherine— That is to say, a year after your grandmother died, and I had locked myself away from the world like the beast in the French fairytale, I received a postcard from Italy. Upon it was a charcoal sketch of il Castello di Montegufoni. I believe that Renwick himself may have drawn it. There was a handwritten invitation on the back, and I can only say that the sight of that beautiful but distant vista made my solitude all the more painful."

For a moment, I stopped noticing the sound of the Bugatti's engine, or the tyres on the paving stones. All I could hear was my grandfather's ragged breathing as he found the courage to continue.

"Back then, Italy might just as well have been another planet. I saw no hope for myself, and couldn't imagine leaving my estate, let alone the country. You know the next part of the story. Time passed, you came to live with me, your mother bought me a new dog, and I emerged from my self-imposed exile. When I suggested that you and I could travel abroad, I knew that Montegufoni had to be our first destination. There was no other option in my mind, and two days ago, as we walked from the hot, busy bus that left us in the middle of nowhere, and I glimpsed the tower of the castle, I said to myself, *You did it, Edgington. You're finally here.*"

Now I was the one who didn't know what to say. Todd brought the

Bugatti to a stop in the same piazza as the day before, but the three of us just sat there until I found a response. "Well done, Grandfather. I can only imagine how the image of the castle would have pained you back then, and I'm glad to know that has changed. You should be proud that you've made it here." I said something then of which I really hadn't been aware before I uttered the words. "I know it was difficult for you to leave your home and life and so many memories behind, but we're here now."

His smile grew, and the ends of his snow-white moustache looked as though they wished to make one another's acquaintance. "That's right, my boy. Our journey has finally begun."

I put my hand on the door handle and knew that it was my turn to be brave. "If you'll excuse me, I won't be long."

I didn't wait for his reply but climbed from the vehicle to walk under the large archway that led off the square.

"I'll wait here then, shall I?" he called after me, but I wouldn't look back.

I didn't run this time. I walked calmly and quietly, admiring the buildings on either side of me as I travelled along the road towards the Hotel Helvetia & Bristol. There was a commissionaire on duty in the street, and he opened the heavy brass door for me to pass through it.

The same diminutive bald man as when I'd last been there was working in reception, but I had a quick peek into the conservatory in case I didn't need his help.

"What can I do for you, sir?" he asked when my search came to nought.

"Good afternoon." I hurried to remove my hat, as I'd quite forgotten I was wearing one. "Perhaps you remember me lurking here yesterday…" I had to stop to take a deep breath. I was no longer certain why I'd thought it was a good idea to come, but it was too late to change my mind. "I was here yesterday."

"Yes, sir. I remember you." He closed his eyes to recite the details of my visit. "You had a meeting with Signor Longfield. I know him well."

"That's right."

"He is a very nice man," he added unnecessarily, which only threw me further off my stride. "And an excellent tennis player, as it happens. We once enjoyed a game of doubles together with our wives.

Signora Longfield has a fine forehand smash."

"I'm sure she has, but that wasn't what I came to discuss. You see…" I tried to be clear, but the words I needed were in the wrong order in my head and it took me a while to unscramble them. "You see, there was a young lady in the conservatory yesterday with whom I would like to continue the conversation I started." He didn't need to know that it had only taken place in my head. "She had long, brown hair, bright eyes, and she was reading a book."

He looked slightly bemused by this description but then tapped his pen on the polished wooden counter in a joyful manner. "Ah, yes. It was Charles Dickens, was it not?"

His enthusiasm travelled over to me. "That's exactly right!"

"Then you must be referring to the little signorina who is travelling with her father. She is a very nice young lady indeed."

I must admit that I felt rather proud. He was referring to my imaginary fiancée after all. "That's right. Well, I've come here today in the hope of meeting her again. Would you happen to know where she is?"

I walked from the hotel feeling woebegone and defeated. Fifteen minutes, that's how much time had passed since her travelling party had left the hotel. I was fifteen minutes late for my destiny, and even the bright blue Florentine sky could offer no light in the darkness.

"Ah," Grandfather said when he saw me. "So things didn't go to plan?"

I huffed. It's honestly amazing that I had the energy to produce even this limited response. Todd stood beside the driver's door and gave me a sympathetic frown, but it did nothing to improve my mood.

"Whilst you were away, I have been wondering how many balls of ice cream can fit in a single cornet." Grandfather spoke dreamily, as though the real reason he had come to Italy was to discover this very thing. "I think it's time that you and I solved this small mystery."

Even as I wished for the ground to open up and swallow me, he put his hand on my back to guide me to the nearest *gelateria*. Torn between melancholy and excitement, I realised that there are few things in the world that can ease the pain of a broken heart.

Rather expertly, my grandfather had identified one of them.

The End (For Now…)

Get another

LORD EDGINGTON ADVENTURE

absolutely **free**…

Download your free novella at
www.benedictbrown.net

"LORD EDGINGTON INVESTIGATES ABROAD"

The second full-length mystery will be available
late summer 2025.
Follow me on Amazon to find out when it goes on sale.

ABOUT THIS BOOK

I have to start this chapter by saying that I really didn't know where this mystery was going until my then six-year-old daughter, Amelie, came to me with the twist you have just read. She is still very proud of the fact that, when she was five, I read her the first Lord Edgington novella (available free via my website!) and she worked out who the killer was. Ever since then, I believe that some part of her has been plotting to become a great criminal as, when I went downstairs for lunch one day, (**Big spoiler alert! Stop reading now if you haven't finished the book yet!**) she suddenly said, "Daddy, could you write a mystery where the killer tries to kill someone with a poisoned piece of cake, but no one can make sense of it because he accidentally eats the wrong one, and the killer is dead before the investigation begins?" And I said, "Yes!"

Well, the cake didn't make it into my story, but I liked her idea and ran with it. I had such a clear picture of the setting for this book, mainly because I'd spent a week at the real Castello di Montegufoni in summer 2024, but the mystery was a mystery to me until Amelie pointed me in the right direction. So if you liked this book, you have her to thank. And if you hated it, you can blame me.

To explain how the rest of the book came together, let's start with the journey out to Italy. I was sorely tempted to spend ten chapters just getting to the castle. I doubted that would have sat too well with new readers, so I tried to get to the first death as quickly as possible. I also wanted a grand method of transport and, in the previous book, I mentioned the *Golden Arrow* train service, however it didn't launch until May 1929, so I went back and changed the earlier reference before my narrator recorded the audiobook – phew!

The *Golden Arrow* was a daily service that – as Chrissy reveals – connected the English and French capitals in just six hours and thirty-five minutes. When it launched, it was aimed squarely at the uber rich, and only had first-class carriages, to match its similar service on board the connecting steamship, the *TSS* Canterbury. There are wonderful pictures online of the *Golden Arrow*, and even more if you have access to the British Newspaper Archive. The Bystander from 15th May 1929 describes the "all-Pullman" train as "the most comfortable and speedy service between the two capitals that has ever been achieved."

With this in mind, it might have been an idea to start this series in Paris, seeing as we'll be heading back there at some point. But I fell in love with Montegufoni and wanted it on the cover of the first book in the series, so I had to find a connecting train. Luckily, there was a suitably Edgingtonian option available in the shape of the *Rome Express*. In 1929, the train went all the way from Calais to, would you believe it, Rome! And it offered a similar high-level service to the *Flèche D'or*, which was the French leg of the *Golden Arrow*. It offered a sleeper service and was the perfect way to get Chrissy and his grandfather to Montegufoni. What I particularly loved about this is the fact there is a mystery film called *Rome Express* which was made just a couple of years after this book is set. I watched it after finishing the book, and it was a real thrill to be able to experience a realistic depiction of the journey. It's also a very entertaining film.

Moving on to our destination, I first came across the castle when I was researching my book *The Tangled Treasure Trail,* which dealt with the Bright Young Things of 1920s London. Three people who were very much associated with that social group were the Sitwell siblings, Edith, Osbert and Sacheverell, who each became known for their literary endeavours in later life. Their eccentric father bought Montegufoni in 1909, when there were still three hundred Italian peasants residing there. He oversaw its restoration and lived there until just before his death in 1943. During this time, he apparently refused to allow electricity to be installed and only ate roast chicken. He also paid for the instruments of the Philharmonic Society of Montegufoni, but I have no proof that he made them learn the (unofficial) English national anthem.

Although this was what first attracted me to the castle – well, as soon as I saw the fantastic aerial photo of it that would become my cover – Montegufoni has a long and fascinating history. The first construction was built sometime around 1100 AD, but it was destroyed by them pesky Florentines a century or two later. Another hundred years after that, the wealthy merchant Acciaioli family (a name that I doubt I spelt correctly more than once in the whole book!) began to build homes there. Over the following centuries, those separate dwellings were enlarged, adapted and reinforced until they formed one large castle. By the eighteenth century, the owners really wished to show off their wealth and employed artisans to build the incredible gallery, paint frescoes in almost every room, and add details like the elaborate front façade.

That's nine tenths of the book I read on the castle summarised in a few sentences, but it was remarkable to read about the shifting fortunes of the Acciaioli (spelt it wrong again!) family who, by the twentieth century, had lost their fortune and possession of their ancestral home which was close to ruin when Sir George Sitwell was "accidentally" brought to the castle by some locals and immediately decided to buy it. He fell in love with the place and had a massive impact on restoring and preserving it for future generations – literally, as he bought it for his son.

He also paid for an artist called Gino Severini to paint modern frescoes in one of the rooms which would become his sitting room. Severini, who was an important futurist painter, was a friend of Picasso's. In fact, Sir George's children wanted Picasso to do the modern frescoes, but their father did not agree. I think this is the most wonderful turning point in the history of the castle as, surely, had the most famous artist of the century painted the sitting room, it would now be a major tourist attraction, or, more likely, owned by a very rich person and shut to the public. Most visitors to Montegufoni don't get to see the Hall of Masks which now sits empty between two tourist apartments, but I'm cheeky, and asked on my first day at the castle whether I could visit all the most interesting places whenever they were vacated by other guests.

Severini's mural depicts eight life-size figures from the Comedia dell'arte, in their distinctive harlequin's costumes, painted in surroundings matching that of the castle's. Some of the faces are said to resemble the Sitwell children and the artist himself, and the fresco covers all four walls of the small room. It was a real gift to be able to spend time there all on my own to appreciate the work of a great artist.

But Montegufoni played an even more important role in the history of art as, in November 1942, the castle became the temporary home of two hundred and sixty of the most important works from the Uffizi and other Florentine galleries in order to protect them during the war. Most famous of all were three Botticellis, including his painting of *Spring* – which my toddler Osian managed to upstage when we were in the Uffizi by merrily sitting down right in front of the painting, in a semi-circle of thirty snap-happy tourists, and drawing some frenzied camera action of his own.

Sir George had left Italy shortly before the treasures were transported there, and so the empty castle was considered a good place to store them. However, with the uncertainty and destruction of the war, over six hundred homeless people moved into Montegufoni. The paintings were protected by a man named Guido Masti, who was the grandfather of the man who wrote the history of the castle that I read.

By 1944, as the Allies made advances across Europe, a troop of German SS soldiers commandeered the castle – sending many of the inhabitants into hiding – and ordered Masti to remove the paintings and burn them in the courtyard. This truly heroic man stood up to the officious general and convinced him to use other rooms and leave the paintings where they were as they "represented a heritage of considerable artistic value and therefore belonged to the whole world". He then came close to manhandling the soldiers from the Gallery, where the paintings were stored, before plying them with Chianti wine. This did not stop them from using a painting of the Adoration of the Magi as a table for dinner that night. I believe the word *barbarians* suits them rather well.

Though the front line would come right up to the steps of the castle, Montegufoni managed to escape destruction, and the allied forces eventually gained control of it. In August 1944, the British field marshal, Harold Alexander, who was then Supreme Allied Commander for the whole Mediterranean region, arrived. He realised how significant the haul of treasures was and formed a division of men to guard the castle. The small group did this for the last nine months of the war and the artworks were then carefully returned to their homes. The painting which had been used as a table had a knife mark and wine stains but was restored and still hangs in the Uffizi. Every other work was accounted for and in perfect condition, thanks in no small part to Guido Mati, who credited this success to a prayer he said each night to Mary and the saints as he patrolled the castle. Considering that

262

hundreds of paintings relocated to other sites in Tuscany went missing, he was certainly doing something right.

Speaking of saints, perhaps I should mention the relics Chrissy finds. I was shown to the chapel by the very helpful receptionist who left my daughter and me to lock up when we'd finished. Amelie took my camera and was enthralled by the bones, skulls, teeth, skin and, yes, full skeletons on display. Interestingly, when the Sitwells bought the castle, it was on the condition that the two hundred and forty-two items in the reliquary remained intact and public access was provided.

I was raised Catholic, but growing up in Britain, I was not used to seeing relics, and so I imagined they would have been a novelty to Chrissy, too. Also, if you bear in mind that, when my grandfather, a born Englishman, died on holiday in Tenerife in 1969, the British consulate told my father they would do nothing to help repatriate him because he was a Catholic, I think it's unlikely that Chrissy would have been raised with a particularly diverse knowledge of other faiths. I should probably mention that such interfaith distrust was a two-way street. My grandfather would have nothing to do with his son's fiancée (my mum) as she wasn't Catholic, so it was probably a good thing he died a couple of months before they were married.

Another doubt I had was how well-known pasta was in Britain in 1929. My uncertainty particularly arose from reading that staple of British cooking, "Delia Smith's Complete Cookery Course" from 1978. It blew me away that, in one recipe, she actually had to explain what pizza was. There is also a section called "What is Pasta?" While it was already quite common in the UK by the late seventies, Delia – a popular TV chef – explains that, during her childhood shortly after the war, her concept of spaghetti was tinned and covered in tomato sauce. Considering Chrissy's relatively sheltered existence, there's a strong possibility he really didn't know what pasta was before his trip abroad, and it was often referred to as paste or vermicelli as his grandfather explains.

As you might already have noticed, I named the characters in this book after real people. You already know where Guido's name came from, and Signora Acciaioli (hurray, I spelt it right this time!) is self-explanatory. For most of the minor Italian characters, I used names from the history of the castle, be they painted on the walls of the Hall of Gonfaloniers – which was where we slept when we visited – or on the family tree at the front of the book. There was one important exception to his. The nice police officer, Attilio Lombardo, was named after possibly the first Italian I ever saw in the flesh.

The real Lombardo was a footballer who played in south London for my team, Crystal Palace. Palace were, and still are, a small team by the standards of the Premier League, and it was something of a novelty to have an Italian player at the time. Lombardo briefly became a player manager for us and stuck with the club through relegation and possible bankruptcy. He is considered one of our all-time greats, even though he only played 49 matches for us. Palace are also known as the Eagles, and as Lombardo had a hairless dome, he was known as "the Bald Eagle". I've never forgotten that, or being in the family enclosure as he came to sign autographs for kids in the crowd each week.

I always write down interesting names when I hear them, and a while back I noticed that Renwick was the middle name of Bob Mortimer, a comedian I really like. After I'd chosen it for the lord in this book, I checked whether it was in use in Britain in the past and discovered the interesting case of one Renwick Williams. Williams was accused of being the "London Monster", a man, or more likely men, who attacked more than fifty women over a period of two years from 1788. The Monster would insult, slash the clothes of, and wound respectable women in the street, but no one is sure whether, after the first few incidents, it was a crime spree or a bunch of copycats. It caused such a panic, or "Monster Mania", that rich women took to wearing copper petticoats under their clothes.

Renwick Williams was an artificial flower maker who was identified as the slasher by one of the later victims. However, he was at work at the time she was attacked and had previously known the victim, who had felt insulted by his romantic advances. Various other victims either agreed he was the assailant – though his appearance did not match their previous descriptions, including one who talked of her assailant's "shabby appearance, much like a hair-dresser" – or were unsure one way or another. By the time he went to trial, the whole of London was against him, and he was sentenced to seven years in prison, of which he served four. He somehow managed to have a child whilst in there and got married to his baby's mother when he was released. So he was all right in the end, but he maintained his innocence throughout, and it seems unlikely he was to blame.

It is very lucky that, considering the number and severity of the attacks, no one was killed, but apparently the crime of wounding women for sadistic pleasure was common at the time, and there was a similar case in France known as the "Hip Stabber", who attacked twenty-three victims in the city of Metz. It is telling that the stabbings in London did not stop even after Williams was arrested.

Speaking of criminals, Eva Mountstephen was the name of a poisoner in India in 1911. She (presumably) poisoned a fellow spiritualist while staying at the Savoy Hotel, Mussoorie in the foothills of the Himalayas. Although she was found innocent of the killing, her doctor was also poisoned a few months after the first death. Rudyard Kipling told Arthur Conan Doyle about the case, who told Agatha Christie, who was inspired to write her first novel, *The Mysterious Affair at Styles*.

One name I'd been meaning to include for a while is Markland Starkie. It sounds like such a made-up moniker that I had to take it out of a previous Marius Quin book but found a place for it here. I often use the names of rock stars in these books – normally fairly well hidden away – and Markland Starkie is a singer I really like, of whom most people will never have heard. He released a few albums under the name Sleeping States about ten years ago and the last one, *In the Gardens of the North* is truly excellent if you like light, melodic indie folk-rock. Sadly, this did not launch him to stardom, and I can see that he only gets 258 listens a month on Spotify, which possibly generates enough income to buy a paper coffee cup, if not the coffee to go in it. I particularly love the song "The Cartographer".

Right, I'm going to finish this chapter with a quick word on fascism. Although I studied Italian unification and the First World War in school, I did not know a great deal about the roots of Italian fascism. In fact, I wrote about a third of this book without giving any thought whatsoever to the reality that Mussolini had already been in power for four years by 1929. I didn't want to focus on this malign and destructive philosophy, but I couldn't ignore it altogether, so I hope the presence of the odious Ispettore Stefani is enough to provide some historical realism, without going too far down that dark road.

In 1929, Italy was still open to international travel, and Italian fascists did not go in for the full-on ethnic cleansing of the Nazis but, on their route to power, they certainly left behind a lot of victims, including murdered and disappeared political rivals. Their secret police, now referred to as the Organization for Vigilance and Repression of Anti-Fascism, had already been established and would go on to be a model for the Nazis' similar force. They spied on anyone they deemed a potential threat, including high-ranking clergy in the Vatican. Nothing was ever written down about their existence, so even their official name is not known for certain.

They came into being partly because of three assassination attempts on Mussolini in 1926. One was by an anarchist whose bomb did little damage, another was blamed on a fifteen-year-old boy who was probably framed to create an excuse to strengthen police power, but the first that year was by a woman called Violet Gibson, who was the daughter of the Irish Lord Chancellor. She had a history of mental health problems, and one day decided to try to shoot *il Duce*. She merely grazed his nose, but the crowd came close to killing her on the spot – as they would the poor scapegoated boy later that year. However, this did not put Mussolini off Irish women. You see – I know this is going to sound like I'm making it up –he gave my dad's aunt a camera.

Yep. The only things I knew about Mussolini when I was growing up was that he was a fascist, he was killed by partisan Italians at the end of the war, and my great-aunt, who died before I was born, used to know him. I checked the details with my mother, and all she remembers is that Dad's aunt was working as a nanny for an aristocratic family in Russia when the revolution occurred. She escaped to Italy and found work with another rich family who were friends with Mussolini and… at some point he gave her his Box Brownie camera which we still have in my family home in London. We have absolutely no way of proving any of this, but Dad was very fond of his jet-setting, Mary-Poppins-esque aunt and talked of it often.

266

I guess this makes me three degrees of separation away from the leader of Fascist Italy. I can think of plenty of people I'd prefer to be connected to, but it's still fascinating. Speaking of which, I hope you enjoy the next chapter in which I find even more disparate topics to connect.

If you loved the story and have the time, please write a review at Amazon. Most books get one review per thousand readers so I would be infinitely appreciative if you could help me out.

THE MOST INTERESTING THINGS I DISCOVERED WHEN RESEARCHING THIS BOOK...

I like to make things difficult for myself, so every historical novel I write comes with a lengthy section on the incredible stuff I discovered when writing and researching.

For once, I think I'll begin with food. That seems like a fair place to start, as the classic Italian cookery writer Marcella Hazan claimed that nothing, including religion, had influenced Italian society so greatly as its cuisine.

All my Lord Edgington books indulge in open-mouthed appreciation of different foods, and this new series gives me the chance to find out far more than I previously knew about the regional cuisine in each setting. I was already something of a fan of Italian food – let's be honest, who isn't? – but I realised when writing this book that there was someone in my phonebook who could be a real help. When we went with my in-laws to Verona a couple of years ago, they hired a local chef to cook for us for my mother-in-law's birthday, and I spent the morning chatting to him as he cooked. I promise I tried not to get in the way, but it was great to watch him prepare pasta, cook the meat dish and even work on an elaborate dessert. It's not always easy to check when foods came into existence, especially as I don't speak Italian, so Andrea was very helpful and pointed me in the right direction on various topics.

Something I've learnt living in Spain is just how strongly even tiny regions of European countries associate with the food they produce. If you ever ask a Spaniard what to do in a certain place, the first thing they will say is what to eat when you go there. In Asturias, you must eat *fabada* (a bean and meat stew). In Cantabria, *sobao* (a slightly lemony sponge cake). In Madrid, calamari sandwiches – which is weird because the capital city is about three hundred miles from the nearest coast.

Italian cuisine is often said to be the most diverse in Europe – people from a certain neighbouring country might disagree, but it's a claim my French wife often repeats. Furthermore, each region is distinct, so I couldn't use my knowledge of tasty Veronese cooking for a book set two hundred and fifty kilometres south in Tuscany. There are even regions within regions, but as Montegufoni is between Florence and Siena, I figured I could use those as my touchstones when choosing what my characters should eat.

While globalisation and improved transportation has meant that we now eat most types of food pretty much everywhere, it's safe to say that cuisine would have been far more local in the 1920s. In fact, when the artist Gino Severini lived at Montegufoni, his Florentine assistant quit because he considered the food of Sir George Sitwell's Neapolitan cook "filthy". Severini liked having his meals prepared whenever possible by Guido Mati's mother, Annina, who cooked traditional Tuscan food and lent her name, of course, to my cook in this book.

A lot of the food in Tuscany can trace its roots back to the pre-Roman indigenous Etruscan people, whose culture began to develop around 900 BC. They were the first to make olive oil and cultivate grapes in the region, possibly including the Sangiovese grape variety, which literally translates as "blood of Jupiter" and is still used to make Chianti wine today. The Etruscans are very interesting as, although they left some inscriptions, their language is still not fully understood and most of our knowledge of them comes from Roman and Greek sources who clearly looked down on them.

Romans also had an impact on Tuscan cuisine, but it wasn't until the all-powerful Medici family rose to prominence during the Renaissance that it really came to resemble the food we know today. The Medicis were so influential that, when Catherine de' Medici married the French King Henry II, she took her Florentine chefs with her to make Italian food, and the French began to copy the habits of their young foreign queen – or perhaps not. Like so much in history, the truth of this is debated.

One thing that is certain is that the Renaissance saw Tuscan cuisine move away from what was considered peasanty food towards richer and more elaborate dishes. Dining itself became an art form with elaborate feasts thrown and, unlike in previous centuries, cutlery now used as standard – astoundingly, it was not until the eighteenth century that forks were widely used across all levels of society in Britain. Before that, they were seen as foreign and not sufficiently masculine. Back in Italy, rich stews like Carabaccia – a sweet and spiced onion soup – and less appealingly cibreo – which… I'll let you look up yourself – would be served at the banquets and travelled with Catherine to the French court. Pecorino cheese is also said to have become more popular – though Pliny the Elder had already mentioned *pecorino Toscano* way back in 77 AD.

Looking at some of the dishes mentioned in this book, the first that jumped out at me in our time in Tuscany was *pane sciocco*. *Sciocco* can mean saltless, but it is also a word for foolish, and it would be mean of me to equate the two, but I can't say that this tasteless creation grew on me. I even asked a hotel employee whether she preferred salted bread, and she misunderstood and told me how difficult it is to get "real bread" in other parts of Italy, so she was clearly a fan. As mentioned in the book, legend says the bread was created after a tax was placed on salted products, forcing bakers simply to do without. It's often eaten with cheese or dried meats which are fairly salty already, but I still prefer my concept of "real bread".

One dish I couldn't get enough of, though, was *Pici* pasta. There are infinite (massive exaggeration) different types of pasta in Italy, and they are often tied to particular regions. *Pici* is from Siena, fifty kilometres south of Montegufoni, but I ate it at the castle and in Florence. It is thought to date back to Etruscan times, and there is even a fresco of a feast in a tomb from the fifth century BC which appears to depict a very similar dish. It comes in the form of skinny, handmade tubes of pasta that are often eaten with *cacio e pepe,* or cheese and black pepper, but I went (both in real life and this book) for the more elaborate sauce with duck, tomato and onion.

My apologies to vegetarian readers for this overly descriptive meat-fest I am about to deliver, but you'll be glad to know I cut some of this information from the book itself. Perhaps the most iconic dish from the area is the *bistecca alla Fiorentina* which Signora Acciaioli prepares for Chrissy when he is – of all things – not hungry. Like *bistec* in Spanish and *bifteck* in French, the name derives from… can you guess? That's right (all my readers are geniuses, so I'm sure you knew), it derives from the English word beefsteak. True *bistecca alla Fiorentina* comes from

Chianina cattle from Val di Chiana, near Siena, which are incredibly lean and absolutely massive.

Weighing around 1600kg and standing up to 2 metres tall, the species holds the record for the heaviest bull ever recorded. They are also one of the oldest breeds and were previously used for agriculture. They are the perfect animal for producing sirloin (or T-bone in the US) steaks. The meat is often served with the wider part of the bone facing down and the meat sticking up in the air. There are two types of meat on the bone, with fillet on one side of the T and sirloin on the other.

My mother argues that the best ice cream in the world is found in the South Wales valleys – easy there, Italians, give her a chance. This is because there was a large Italian diaspora to Wales towards the end of the nineteenth century. By 1911, there were around 20,000 Italians living in the region, and they were known for opening cafés and restaurants, which came to be known locally as "Bracchis" after the family who owned an early chain. As a teenager, my mother worked in a seaside restaurant and cockle stall in the seaside town of Porthcawl. It was owned by the Sidoli family who still own a chain of ice cream parlours today. She says that the two brothers who managed the restaurant were friendly when they weren't working, but real slave drivers who wouldn't close up until every last potential customer had gone home for the night. I can't tell you how many times she has recounted her summer spent selling seafood in the hot and cramped shack on the prom. I think she's glad that she moved away from hospitality into teaching.

And why am I telling you all this? Because of ice cream! I've mentioned before in these chapters that nineteenth century British cookbooks inspired a trend for making ice cream, and that, a hundred years earlier, an Italian doctor wrote a pamphlet recommending chocolate ice cream as a cure-all. Although we all associate ice cream with Italy, and they certainly perfected the recipe for *gelato*, the concept of such a dessert was likely brought to Europe from the east, perhaps by Marco Polo. There is evidence of similar dishes in India, Persia and China before it appeared in Europe. Polo would have eaten something close to sorbet – which comes from the Arabic word for "sweet snow" – but the rich, creamy gelato we all (except my strange wife) love appeared a few centuries later.

Legend states that – her again – Catherine de' Medici introduced ice cream to France, but that is not true, as there was evidence of iced desserts there before she was born. What seems less contentious, however, is that, in the Florentine court, she ran a competition to come up with an original dish and *fior di latte* – a sweet, unflavoured ice cream – was created. Another stage in its development came in 1565 when one of the most important architects in Florence, who worked on the Palazzo Pitti and the neighbouring Boboli Gardens, came up with another recipe which is still made today. Bernardo Buontalenti was a true polymath and worked as a costume designer, engineer, stage designer and artist but is possibly best remembered for his Buontalenti ice cream which features honey, wine, lemon, orange and bergamot. I tried it in the award-winning *La Strega Nocciola* gelateria near the *Duomo* in Florence and I think it was the best ice cream we ate in Italy – and believe me, we tried a lot.

The question of whether it was as good as the ice cream in 'The Dairy' in Penygraig, south Wales, is another matter altogether. My Welsh family have a long-running discussion of which is the best ice cream, with one faction pushing for Joe's in Swansea – another Italian-founded parlour – whereas I favour the one I had every time I went to visit my nana in the Rhondda Valley. The fact it was served in a plastic boat with a chocolate flake, fudge stick, countless toppings and an ice lolly sticking out certainly didn't hurt.

From ice to air. Well, air quotes at least. I wanted Lord Edgington to adopt the patronising gesture, but I wasn't sure if bunny-earing your fingers was a thing back in the 1920s. It turns that out it was… sort of. Although the term was not coined until 1989, Lewis Carroll described "air brackets", and "air question marks" in one of his novels, and there is evidence that the bent-finger gesture was already in use by 1927. By 1937, they had appeared in the film *Breakfast for Two* with Barbara Stanwyck. It looks funny. I might have to watch it.

Something else I previously didn't know the origin of was the term John (or Jane) Doe. As it happens, I didn't have to go looking for this one, as I heard it by chance on a podcast about language called *The Allusionist*. Though the term is now associated with unidentified dead bodies in the USA, it actually originates in English law from the seventeenth century. In an incredibly complicated system I still don't really understand, if a landowner wished to evict someone from their (or rather, *his*) property, it was more or less impossible. That was until some bright spark happened upon the idea of inventing an imaginary evictor (Richard Doe) who had forced an imaginary evictee (John Doe) from the land. When brought to court, the real tenants would have to appear to prove they had done no such thing. If they did not appear, they would be found guilty in absentia, thus enabling the landowner to get his land back.

Cases would occasionally involve so many fictional litigants that a whole host of names would be invented to distinguish between them, but it was good old John Doe, and, of course, his wife, Jane – making her first appearance in the OED a hundred and ten years later in 1703 – who have remained with us.

Sticking with fakes, relics in the early days of the church had a serious authentication problem. It was so common for fake monks to go about the place selling fake bones that Saint Augustine – presumably before he himself was beatified – condemned the practice back in the fifth century. And yet, the counterfeiting of objects of religious worship continued for a thousand years and longer. As a result, the Catholic Church introduced a system of authentication and required each one to have its own sealed reliquary and certificate of authenticity.

Unrelated to my research for this book, I found the most fascinating article in the newspaper over Easter about how new saints are chosen. The same organisation which oversees the authentication of the relics also investigates people put forward for sainthood – and "investigate" is not too strong a term for it. The Dicastery for the Causes of Saints can take decades and sometimes even centuries to decide who deserves canonisation. It usually requires lobbying from influential or at least vocal backers, but one thing I didn't understand until now is how people who have died in the recent past could have miracles ascribed to them – which is a prerequisite for sainthood.

I'm writing this two days after Pope Francis died, but I'd never heard of him performing any miracles, so I assumed that meant he could never become a saint. However, what I learnt from the article is that many miracles are associated with the relics or tomb of an important Catholic rather than something they did during their lives. A good example is Carlo Acutis who will soon become the first Millennial saint. Born in Britain to Italian parents in 1991, he was very interested in the lives of saints and developed websites devoted to cataloguing modern miracles. He predicted at an early age that he would die of a ruptured vein in his head before reaching adulthood, and this is what came to pass when a cerebral haemorrhage killed him aged just fifteen.

Although he considered himself destined to become a saint, and recorded a video saying as much before he became ill, this prediction was not one of his miracles. The investigative panel charged with confirming (or rejecting) his candidacy for sainthood went to great lengths to examine medical evidence that might rule out any purported miracle. However, on the seventh anniversary of Carlo's death, a terminally ill three-year-old boy from Brazil kissed a relic of a piece of his clothing and, hours later, doctors were amazed that his pancreas had apparently healed itself. It would take another seven years for this to be confirmed as a miracle, but in 2022, a similar case occurred with a girl badly wounded in a bicycle accident recovering inexplicably after her mother prayed at Carlo Acutis's tomb. With the two miracles confirmed and the rest of the process completed, he was beatified and, once the new Pope is chosen, he will soon be canonised. People are already calling him the first "gamer saint" for his love of video games.

I should probably point out that I'm not writing about this here in the hope of changing people's way of thinking. I didn't grow up in a very religious household. My mum's family were Anglican, Dad was Catholic, and neither of my brothers has been to Mass for thirty years, but I had a good experience with my church growing up, and the community was very supportive of Dad when he had Alzheimer's, so I've seen a positive side that many people ignore. I do admit, however, that I find all this stuff fascinating. I think that, growing up Catholic in an Anglican country, made the ritual and ceremony of the church seem more intriguing to me, but saints and relics were not part of our everyday lives.

Let's move on to something else that people take as seriously as religion. No, not sport – I've already talked about Crystal Palace's Italian connection. I'm talking about cars. Although some of the most famous

Italian marques – like Ferrari, Lamborghini and Pagani – had not yet been founded in the late twenties, it was already a major car producing nation. In fact, in 1923, Fiat opened Europe's largest car factory at Lingotto, which is a hugely impressive construction in an extremely modern style. Materials were brought in on the ground floor, and the assembly line worked its way up the various levels with finished cars emerging on the roof, where a 1.5km testing track was located. Two years later, eighty-seven per cent of cars sold in Italy were made by Fiat. I'm sure we'll come across more examples of their handiwork as Lord Edgington's journey across the continent continues.

While Fiat concentrated on the mass market, Bugatti was a very different proposition. It was founded by Ettore Bugatti, the son of a famous Art Nouveau furniture and jewellery maker. Just like his father, he took design seriously. Born in Italy, he established his company in Alsace in 1909 and found some success with road car production in the interwar years, but the marque gained particular fame after its racing cars won everything from five consecutive Targa Florios to Le Mans and the first Monaco Grand Prix in 1929.

Surely the ultimate car that the company produced was the one that Lord Edgington made sure to get his hands on in this book. Ettore Bugatti decided to design what he hoped would be the grandest car in the world after he heard a British woman comparing his cars unfavourably to Rolls Royces. The plan was to produce twenty-five and sell them to only the richest clients. The Bugatti 41, or the Royale, as it's known, was one of the longest cars ever made. Complete with all mod cons and made with the most expensive materials (including whale bone). The car was so audacious that only seven of them were ever made for sale. The left-over engines that were produced were used in an electric train that Bugatti built in France, and a few of the unsold cars were bricked up in his house (or hidden in the Paris sewers) to save them from the Nazis during the Second World War.

The first model was supposed to be bought by the king of Spain in 1928, but he never took delivery, was deposed a few years later and, in the meantime, the Great Depression reshaped the world. There suddenly wasn't as much demand for the most expensive car around when millionaires had lost their fortunes and the world's GDP had

276

fallen by fifteen per cent. In the end, only three of the cars were sold. One of those was discovered by a vice president of GM in a New York scrap yard after the war. He paid $75 and spent $10,000 to restore it. As one of the world's rarest cars, it's now worth at least $15m.

From cars to roads now. I admit that I always find it hard to calculate journey times for my books set in the 1920s. While A-roads were beginning to be built – in fact Italy had the world's first motorway that opened in 1924 between Milan and Lake Como – they weren't nearly as widespread or efficient as they are today. Speed limits were much lower, and there would still have been plenty of horses and carts to slow things down further. I often assume that Lord Edgington – with his professed love of speed and speedy cars – drives way over the speed limit, which was still 20mph in Britain in the 1920s, for the simple reason that I don't want the plot slowed down so massively that I have to set aside a whole morning or even a day to get between places. It's interesting therefore that, when the Italian A1 motorway was built in 1964, it reduced the journey time between Naples in the south and Milan in the north from two days to just eight hours.

It's far easier for train journeys as I can consult actual timetables. My depiction of the change between the *Golden Arrow* and *Rome Express* was perhaps a little too easy in this book, but I made sure that the travel time from London to Florence was realistic.

The bus they are unfortunately forced to ride to Montegufoni is based on photographs I found of such vehicles in the late twenties in Italy. Like charabancs, they may more commonly have been used for tourism, but there were definitely some bus services that looked like stretch limousines with the top cut off and ten rows of seats squashed inside.

Sticking with... mechanisms? I had no idea how clockwork clocks were maintained, and so I read up on them. I decided that the clock in the Houses of Parliament's clocktower (you might know it as Big Ben, though it was christened Elizabeth tower in 2012) would be a good example, so that's what I focused on. Although there is now a more modern back-up system, the clock is still powered by a clockwork mechanism. One of the most curious things I discovered about it is the fact that tiny adjustments are made to its timekeeping by adding or removing Victorian penny pieces to balance the weight – with each penny adding 0.4 seconds. It is still known for its accuracy, though it did stop unexpectedly in May 2005, presumably because of the very hot weather. And on New Year's Eve 1962, it was ten minutes late due to the cold!

Big Ben, as I'm sure you know, is the name of the biggest bell in the clock, and it weighs an unbelievable 13.7 tonnes. It is tuned to the note of E and only sounds on the hour. The quarter-hourly bells are tuned to different notes so that Londoners can tell the time just by hearing them. The tower was hit by a German bomb in 1941 but only incurred minor damage. And how is this for a piece of trivia? Big Ben and the Liberty Bell in Philadelphia – let's be honest, the two most famous bells in the world – were both made at the Whitechapel Bell Foundry in London. Both also cracked and were repaired when first struck – with the American symbol of independence from them pesky Brits developing the now famous fault nearly a hundred years later.

Back on the journey, I researched plenty of minor details – many of which didn't make it into the book. In the newspapers from the twenties, the main references to the *Rome Express* train service concerned derailments. On the ninth of September 1924, the train travelling from Genoa collided with another from Rome, and sixteen passengers were hurt. The upside of this was that the English Queen, Mary of Teck, happened to be in the area and went to see the injured. You win some; you lose some.

I really loved looking at the prices of travel back then. I found a clipping from the Daily Mirror in 1929 which offered twenty-nine days of first-class travel across Europe, tips, daytrips and deluxe hotels, for the bargain price of £68. I imagine I'm not alone in daydreaming about travelling back in time with all the knowledge we have now and living like a king. This falls down a little when I realise that I have so little understanding of the advancements that have been made in the last hundred years that they would not enable me to become ridiculously wealthy. I might be able to describe mobile phones, solar panels and supersonic travel, but I'd have no luck recreating them. I think I'd be more likely to be locked up as madman.

Something that I wouldn't have been able to afford back then, and I certainly can't now, are Bvlgari's jewels. The company was started by Sotirios Voulgaris, a Greek silversmith who moved to Rome in the late nineteenth century. He had six children who took over the business, and the current chairman is his grandson. In the twenties, they were well-known for their silverwork and art deco settings, but it was after the war, when an influx of Hollywood stars arrived in Rome, that the fashion house became an international reference. The company's bright designs and use of gemstones are still famous to this day. What I was really interested to discover, though, was that Voulgaris named his first shop in Rome "The Old Curiosity Shop" after the Dickens novel in order to appeal to British and American tourists on the grand tour. Bvlgari's products are beautiful, but if I could afford them, I would honestly rather give the money to charity. And that, dear reader, is why I don't understand rich people and will probably never become one.

Having said all that, I must guiltily and hypocritically confess that I loooooove fancy hotels. Knowing that I would need a location in Florence, I called into the Hotel Helvetia and Bristol while I was there to see if they had any information on the hotel's history. They had a whole book about it, so I stood in their posh lounge, reading the relevant chapters and imagining where Chrissy would meet "the girl". The hotel was established in 1883 by a Swiss called Giacomo Mosca. As far as I can discover, the hotel was probably known as Hotel Helvetia Suisse in the twenties, but I liked the joke Chrissy made, so I allowed myself this small anachronism.

As much of central Florence was bulldozed shortly after Italian unification, sweeping away medieval architecture to make room for its stately modern replacement, whenever work is done on the hotel, they discover ancient remains and, on building the swimming pool in the basement during the last refurbishment, traces of the Roman baths were found. These changes had an impact on this book too. *Piazza della Repubblica*, the square where Todd parks the car, had once been the Roman forum and underwent another dramatic transformation in the 1880s, just after Florence was declared and then undeclared capital of Italy. There had been a market and a Jewish ghetto there for centuries, but that was all done away with to make way for the grand arched square that is still there today. It was lucky I checked as, after the Second World War, the piazza changed its name. In the early draft of this book, I had Chrissy visiting a square that didn't exist until thirty years later.

From the former Italian capital to the current English one. Although Lord Edgington and co. swiftly leave Britain, there are still plenty of references to it. I needed a place where Lord Monroe could host his literary salon, and St George's Square is rather special. Past residents include Bram Stoker – who often appears in these pages – the mystery novelist Dorothy Sayers, and the brilliantly named Walter Clopton Wingfield, who is considered the father of lawn tennis. It is quite an unusual square as it is incredibly long and opens onto the Thames on one side. Oh, and its gardens in the centre were designed by the great-great-great-grandfather of Camilla, the current queen of the UK.

Another London location is Bedford College for Women, which Eva Mountstephen is said to have attended in this book. Founded way back in 1849 by an anti-slavery campaigner, it was the very first dedicated college established for women in the UK. The teachers were so shocked by the low educational standards of the wealthy young women they taught, a neighbouring school for girls was soon established. Thirty years later, as part of the University of London, it became the first institution in the UK to offer degrees to women. It was also the first place in Britain where women were allowed to study life drawing!

And so we'll stick with art. A passing reference to the *Mona Lisa* meant I had to check whether it was commonly known as that or *la Gioconda* in the 1920s. This sent me down a rabbit hole of fascinating newspaper articles from the period. There was particular attention given to the possibility that, having been stolen in 1911, the painting had been replaced with a fake. The first people to be interrogated over the theft were a French poet called Guillaume Apollinaire and his artist friend by the name of Pablo Picasso – it turned out neither was involved. It was actually stolen by a Louvre museum employee who believed that the painting belonged back in its (and his) native Italy. He had hidden in a broom cupboard and sneaked out with his prize at night once the museum was closed. He kept it for two years in his apartment, then tried to sell it to the Uffizi Gallery, who perhaps unsurprisingly phoned the police.

Fifteen years later, in 1926, rumours spread that the stolen painting was actually hidden in an art dealer's cellar in the Place Vendôme in the centre of Paris. This had the newspapers excited, and the painting, which previously hadn't received a great deal of love from the people of France, gained a lot of attention from all of this. However, by 1928, comparatively high-tech tests had been invented to confirm that the painting hanging in the Louvre was the original, and the rumours were put to rest.

Another point of contention in the papers in the twenties was just how many Mona Lisas there were. In 1913, an English art dealer bought a version of the painting from the house of a nobleman where it had hung for a hundred and thirty years. Critics and connoisseurs were soon declaring this newly discovered, though less complete, version to be the work of da Vinci himself. Over the last century, countless experts have come down on either side of this debate. Plenty are willing to admit that, even if they don't believe he painted the *Isleworth Mona Lisa*, the portrait came from the great master's studio. To this day, there is no ultimate consensus on whether da Vinci was responsible or not, and every five years or so, a new scientific study or critical paper is published which claims to establish or rule out its authenticity definitively. Perhaps, one day, we'll get to the bottom of it.

While in many countries the world's most famous painting is known as *La Gioconda* (or the jocund) – which is a pun on the subject's surname and her cheery expression – the name *Mona Lisa* comes from a shortened form of the Italian for *my lady* and the Christian name of the assumed subject of the painting, Lisa del Giocondo, whose husband commissioned a portrait of her. Other possible identities for the model have been put forward, but most accept that it is the rich Florentine's wife.

A painting over which there is no doubt who sat for it is the Florentine artist Filippo Lippi's *Madonna and Child*. Lippi, the master to famous painters like Botticelli, was so highly regarded by the church for his religious works that he became a chaplain and, when he came to admire one young novice nun at a monastery in Prato, he was given permission to paint her. He took things a little bit further than that by smuggling her away to his home and, over the coming years, having two children with her. He clearly took the subject matter of his paintings very seriously.

A serious topic with a lighter side is the Air Battle on Istrana which Chrissy refers to when, what else, watching birds fly around the castle. Perhaps I should have left mentioning it for a Christmas book, as, on Christmas Day 1917, two British planes launched an unauthorised raid on the German-controlled base of Istrana in Northern Italy. They cheekily dropped a large cardboard sign which said, "To the Austrian Flying Corps from the English RFC, wishing you a very Merry Christmas," then shot up the hangars, destroying many aircraft, and killing twelve soldiers.

This surprise attack was avenged the next day when the Central Powers sent forty aircraft to the nearest Allied hangar at Gazzo Padovano. The Brits and Italians saw what was coming and sent all available aircraft up to respond. The end result was seven Allied planes destroyed on the ground but, depending on which statistics you trust, seemingly no Italian or British pilots killed – though six ground personnel died in the raid. This compared to a further eleven enemy aircraft destroyed, eight aircrew killed and five captured. The only damage to the Allied planes that took to the air occurred when one of them came in to land.

Perhaps the reason for the scale of the Allied victory was revealed when one Austro-Hungarian pilot landed at the British base. The soldiers there opened his cockpit to find him not dead or wounded but blind drunk. It is quite possible that the enemy pilots were so unsuccessful because they were a little too full of Christmas spirit (ho ho ho)!

I was planning to describe the interesting things I discovered on the Medicis, Mussolini, and the contemporary British view of Italian fascism, but this chapter is already far too long and will take me forever to record for the audiobook. Instead, I will finish with two brief anecdotes and then, as always, a couple of songs.

The British papers were not impressed in August 1927 when il Duce decided to rename the Italian side of Mont Blanc "Mount Mussolini". In response, a group of French climbers set out to plant a Tricolour flag at the highest point of the mountain in French territory, with one of them saying, "It can fly over Mussolini". Ha, funny.

I love coincidences and I found a rather nice one when reading an article in the London Daily Chronicle from December 1926 on British fears of Italy's imperial ambitions. I realised that the other main headline concerned "Col. Christie and his Missing Wife" – her Christian name is not mentioned at any point in the article, despite the fact that Agatha was the famous one, not him. In the interview, Archie Christie denies that there was any disagreement with his wife before her disappearance (this is at least a white lie as he had announced he was leaving her for another woman).

In a very open discussion of the case, he rules out suicide but suggests that her preoccupation with poison in her books meant that this would be her preferred method to go. Instead, he puts forward the idea that she could have lost her memory. I find this interesting, as it's largely thought to be what really happened to her. I listened to a children's mystery podcast with my daughter this week – Amelie's choice, not mine, I promise! – and it reminded me that the explanation that Agatha suffered amnesia when she disappeared was the official line given by her husband after she was found. The fact that he was already suggesting this a week after she left suggests to me that he made it up to cover his own part in what happened. Perhaps the Queen of Crime really did fall into a fugue state after her car hit the tree near Silent Pool, or perhaps she wanted to make everyone think that her treacherous husband had bumped her off.

Right! To music! I think the thing I spent longest researching this time around was the opera Mefistofele. I was looking for a verse of an Italian song that was suitably ominous and had to assume there was an opera based on the Faust myth. I was right. It turns out there are two in Italian and five in other languages. I found just what I was looking for in the 1868 work by Arrigo Boito, but there was a catch. Boito wrote the libretti for Verdi's two final operas, but Mefistofele was the only complete opera he composed himself. He also conducted it (though he had no previous experience) when it premiered at La Scala in Milan. It was a total disaster. Because of its perceived (un-Italian) Wagnerism, people were so angry that it led to riots and duels and the police had to close it down after just two days.

Boito reworked the opera, and it was well received when performed seven years later. And therein lies my problem. The verse I found evidently belongs to the now lesser-performed version, and I struggled for hours to find a recording of it for George to sing for the audiobook. I downloaded at least five different versions and then tried to work out which part of the opera I was listening to, what the singers were singing and whether I was listening to the lines I needed. I eventually remembered that my friend's dad is an opera singer in San Sebastian in Spain and asked him for help. He sent me a link and now I hopefully have what I need. Phew.

Another nice coincidence arose as the composer had a relationship with Eleonora Duse, who was considered the greatest actress of her day. I was fairly certain I knew her name and, sure enough, she was mentioned in the book in the Hotel Helvetia and Bristol. She had taken rooms at the hotel with another of her lovers, the poet Gabriele D'Annunzio. His name was also very familiar to me, as it had come up pretty much everywhere. Credited with influencing the founding principles of fascism, he was also a playwright and became a hero during World War One for his part in the Flight over Vienna.

 He led a squadron of eleven planes on a 1200km journey to drop hundreds of thousands of leaflets. Half of them were in very poetic Italian that he himself penned, which were deemed untranslatable into German, and the other half held a note to the Viennese explaining that they could have dropped bombs but, unlike their enemies, they were better than that. This slightly mad endeavour enamoured him greatly to the Italian people.

The Italian text, which celebrated their victory in the battle of the Piave and marked the beginning of the end of the Central Powers' defence, gave it the nickname "the Battle of the Solstice" which is how I first came across D'Annunzio, as that is one of the battles in which my character Guido Lombardo served. After the war, D'Annunzio went on to annex a city in the Italian north which had been handed to its neighbour in the peace settlement. He made himself the duke of the newly declared (and seriously short-lived) state, and his actions and policies during this period were a major influence on Mussolini.

However, on writing this, I now realise that this was not the first time I'd heard of D'Annunzio because, as it happens, I'd been to his house. He had an incredible estate you can visit near the gorgeous town of Gardone Riviera where I was on holiday a few years ago. On the hills above Lake Garda, D'Annunzio spent fifteen years planning and building an incredible tribute to himself complete with a Roman-style amphitheatre, the plane he flew to Vienna, a mausoleum, and, most bizarrely, as I really wasn't expecting it when I mounted the hill, the immense bow of a full-size military cruiser, which Mussolini gave him, as you do. Known as "the Shrine of Victories of the Italians", it has been described as a fascist theme park, and it is certainly a curious place to visit.

Right, almost done. Here goes.

The other piece of music that features in this book is "Ta-ra-ra Boom-de-ay!" which, though written by an unidentified American from the Deep South, was made particularly famous by the British music hall singer Lottie Collins. Collins's husband heard the song in a revue in America in 1891 and licensed the rights for his wife to perform it in the UK. Collins came up with the high-kicking cancan style dance for it, and the song soon became her signature act. It was not uncommon for successful music hall acts to race from venue to venue in the same evening, and Lottie Collins would have to perform the song five-times in the same night in everything from pantomimes, variety performances and burlesques to light operettas.

That's your lot. No more. This chapter has taken me about three days to write, and I have another book to finish. I hope you enjoyed it.

ACKNOWLEDGEMENTS

It feels really nice to be starting a new series, even if it is a continuation of the existing story. It has definitely meant I've asked a wider range of people to help me and here are some of them. First up, I have to thank the staff and owners of il Castello di Montegufoni, without whom this book would never have existed. I cannot recommend visiting enough if you're planning a trip to Italy!

I must also thank my Italian advisors. Andreas the chef in Verona, and Fabio, my daughter's classmate Leo's father, for checking my Italian and recording the pronunciation of the terms I used, to ensure we avoid mistakes in the audiobooks.

Thank you, too, to my always kind and generous early readers, Bridget Hogg and the Martins. To Lisa Bjornstad, and Jayne Kirk for arduous close editing. And to my fellow writers who are always there for me, especially Catherine, Suzanne and Lucy.

And, of course, a massive thank you must go to my ARC team… Rebecca Brooks, Ferne Miller, Melinda Kimlinger, Emma James, Mindy Denkin, Namoi Lamont, Katharine Reibig, Linsey Neale, Terri Roller, Margaret Liddle, Lori Willis, Anja Peerdeman, Marion Davis, Sarah Turner, Sandra Hoff, Mary Nickell, Vanessa Rivington, Helena George, Anne Kavcic, Nancy Roberts, Pat Hathaway, Peggy Craddock, Cathleen Brickhouse, Susan Reddington, Sonya Elizabeth Richards, John Presler, Mary Harmon, Karen Quinn, Karen Alexander, Mindy Wygonik, Jacquie Erwin, Janet Rutherford, Ila Patlogan, Randy Hartselle, Carol Vani, June Techtow, M.P. Smith, Michele Kapugi, Helen K, Ed Enstrom and Keryn De Maria.

READ MORE LORD EDGINGTON MYSTERIES TODAY...

- **Murder at the Spring Ball**
- **Death From High Places** (free e-novella available exclusively at benedictbrown.net. Paperback and audiobook are available at Amazon)
- **A Body at a Boarding School**
- **Death on a Summer's Day**
- **The Mystery of Mistletoe Hall**
- **The Tangled Treasure Trail**
- **The Curious Case of the Templeton-Swifts**
- **The Crimes of Clearwell Castle**
- **A Novel Way to Kill** (novella available at Amazon)
- **The Snows of Weston Moor**
- **What the Vicar Saw**
- **Blood on the Banister**
- **A Killer in the Wings**
- **The Christmas Bell Mystery**
- **The Puzzle of Parham House**
- **Death at Silent Pool**
- **Murder in an Italian Castle** (Spring 2025)

Check out the complete Lord Edgington Collection at Amazon

The first fourteen Lord Edgington audiobooks, narrated by the actor George Blagden, are available now on all major audiobook platforms. There will be more coming soon.

THE "MURDER IN AN ITALIAN CASTLE" COCKTAIL

There is a very obvious cocktail that I didn't use in this book, and I imagine some of you might be surprised at that. The negroni, which comes from Florence, does not got a mention because there is nothing to say for certain that it existed in 1929 – though some would disagree with that statement.

Instead, we have the Americano from Milan. Not only can the drink be authoritatively traced back to the 1860s, it is even known exactly which bar it comes from. The bar belonged to Gaspare Campari who, you might already have guessed, invented the bitter aperitif to which he gave his surname. The cocktail is said to have been created when an American came to the bar and ordered a long drink of Campari, which he did not like one bit. He mixed it with soda, but it was still too bitter and so, with Signor Campari's help, sweet vermouth was added, and people are still drinking their creation a hundred and sixty years later. Another little titbit is that, despite James Bond being heavily associated with the martini, the Americano is the first drink he orders in Ian Fleming's first novel, *Casino Royale*.

Some say that the negroni came into being in a bar in Florence in 1919, when a hard-drinking Italian count by the name of Camillo Negroni asked to swap the soda in an Americano for gin. However, there is so much debate over whether this happened, whether the former cowboy was actually a count, and whether he even existed, I played it safe. The first written record of the negroni is from 1949, and so I included the Americano here instead.

And this is how you make it…

35ml Campari

35ml sweet red vermouth

Ice cubes

200ml soda water

A twist of orange - (The word twist didn't exist in the twenties, and also some older recipes recommend a lemon slice instead.)

It's a very simple method. You add the ice to the glass and pour the two spirits over it, then top up with the soda and garnish with the orange. Its relatively low alcohol content is said to make it perfect to drink all day long, but that doesn't mean you should. Cin cin!

You can get our official cocktail expert François Monti's brilliant book "101 Cocktails to Try Before you Die" at Amazon.

WORDS AND REFERENCES YOU MIGHT NOT KNOW

Growler – a horse and carriage taxi known for the sound it made as it growled across the pebbles.

Pullman – one of the words in Italian for bus, but also the company that produced fancy train carriages, of course.

Charabanc – a long bus primarily used for tourism with benches in place of seats.

Aut viam inveniam aut faciam – a Latin phrase attributed to Hannibal, the Carthaginian general, not the cannibal. It translates as "I shall either find a way or make one", and it was apparently what he said when his plan to lead elephants over the Alps was criticised by his men. He succeeded in attacking Italy in this manner, having already laid siege to Roman allies in Spain, so that told them!

Quello che dici non ha censo – (essentially) you're talking nonsense.

Cappello romano – the almost stereotypical black, wide-brimmed hats worn by European Catholic priests when out and about. It looks a bit like an overgrown bowler and has apparently been out of favour for some time. It is also known as a Saturno, as, side-on, the brim looks like the ring of Saturn.

Paletôt jacket – originally a fitted overcoat with a long protruding lower section for men. In its more modern guise for women, it's just beyond waist-length, but still puffs outwards and can look like a nineteenth century military jacket. In fact, it's a pretty vague concept to begin with!

Carabinieri – one of the Italian police forces, and simultaneously a branch of the armed forces.

Tantalus – a small portable holder for decanters and glasses. The man who invented them in the 1880s was poet John Betjeman's grandfather, and original models fetch healthy sums at auction.

Pochette – a clutch handbag shaped a bit like an envelope. The name comes from the French word for pocket. Louis Vuitton still makes them.

Greaser – a nasty, dislikeable person in British slang – not the US insult for a person from Latin America.

Whisky, vermouth and bitters – Chrissy doesn't realise it, but he's referring to a Manhattan.

The eastern tower of the property sank three feet beneath the level of the rest of the house – this is what happened to my wife's family's chateau in the south of France – where I hope to set a book. It was also built on sand, and they ended up selling it to a nearby vineyard because it was too expensive to fix. I'm glad to say the new owners have preserved the structure of the building and, one day, my in-laws hope to build a cabin on their remaining land.

Lipsticked – I wasn't sure, but this really is the adjective for a mouth with lipstick on. It's first recorded in the dictionary in 1928, so it just sneaked under the wire for me to use in this book.

Gubbins – stuff and thingummies.

By your leave – though it might sound rather medieval, it only dates to 1914. *Leave* in this sense means permission – as in parental leave.

Raffishness – disreputableness.

Pussycat – in Golden Age detective fiction, this term is used disrespectfully for older women, and I wanted to find a way to make it almost acceptable. The "tiger of a pussycat" whom Edgington describes deserves the criticism and isn't dismissed just for her age or sex.

Piggy bank – I have a confession to make. Though not anachronistic, this was far more common an expression in the US in the twenties, but if there's one thing I hate to sacrifice it's a joke, so I left it in.

Spit and image – old-fashioned form of "spitting image". This is one of a few different expressions in this list I have used before.

Up sticks – I was surprised to discover that this phrase came from sailing and originally referred to preparing the mast of the boat before leaving a place.

Cod's-head-and-shoulders – a fool!

Parrotry – a word Chrissy made-up in another book to signify the building where a bunch of parrots are kept.

"Non. Non la vedo da ieri sera." – "No. I haven't seen her since last night."

Gonfaloniers – from the French and Italian word for a standard-bearer, it also referred to a high-level magistrate, which is why it was used to refer to the long-dead Acciaioli (nope, spelt it wrong!) noblemen.

Jackstraw – a blackguard!

Iota – the smallest particle of something, a tiny amount. I'm only including it here because I was amused to realise that iota and jot have the same root but, because of non-standard variations in the way that the words were written down, one word became two. Iota was the smallest letter in the Greek alphabet.

Chiffonier – a small cupboard with a side-board top. I didn't know the word, but it was mentioned that a very old one was still in the castle when the author of the book I read lived there. The four-poster bed that is described also matches his recollection.

Lavabo – this is the Spanish word for a sink, so I know it rather well, but it was also previously used in English to mean a small W.C.

The Duke of the Marshalsea – this is not a real person, but something of a metaphor. The Marshalsea was a debtors' prison in Victorian London where Charles Dickens's father ended up for owing £40 to a local baker – he must have really loved bread. This is how twelve-year old Charles ended up working in a factory to pay off the debt and a period which greatly shaped his worldview. Plenty of noblemen ended up in the Marshalsea, and my idea with there being a duke of the place was to suggest that Dashwood compares to the most indebted person in the famous prison. It closed in 1842 but lived on in the public memory and imagination thanks in part to Dickens's work.

What the dickens – I hadn't realised before that this saying pre-dated the novelist and was a euphemism for hell.

Osteria – an inn or restaurant in Italian. The English word hostelry shares the same root.

He-mannish – nothing to do with the 1980s cartoon I watched as a child. It means macho – but that wasn't used until 1949, whereas this is from 1924.

Crock – today I would say "banger" but that's also more modern. An old, beaten-up car.

Odd man – a common job in grand old British houses. An odd-job man. Not a man who is strange.

Blowsabella – an already old-fashioned insult for someone who looks messy.

Death's head upon a mop stick – it doesn't get a mention in the OED but this insult, meaning an emaciated, skinny person, did make it into the Dictionary of the Vulgar Tongue from 1811.

Eau de vie de **raspberry** – a sickly spirit which isn't sophisticated in the slightest, but Chrissy doesn't realise that.

Butterfly wing earrings – common in the Victorian era, they were made with an iridescent blue wing of the morpho butterfly (one of my favourite animals). I bought an antique pair for my wife when we were first together, and they are very beautiful – if a little morbid.

Henry Poole – the oldest tailor on Savile Row and the apparent creators of the first dinner jacket for the then Prince of Wales.

All'aperto – in English, we would say *al fresco,* but apparently that is not the correct Italian phrase after all. *All'aperto* means *in the open air,* and the only common meaning of *al fresco* in modern Italian is used, presumably ironically, to refer to someone in jail.

Besmitten – smitten. This is easy to work out, and I love it when there's another form of a common word that is not in regular use.

ABOUT ME

Writing has always been my passion. It was my favourite half-an-hour a week at primary school, and I started on my first, truly abysmal book as a teenager. So it wasn't a difficult decision to study literature at university which led to a master's in creative writing.

I'm a Welsh-Irish-Englishman originally from **South London** but now living with my French/Spanish wife and our two presumably quite confused young children in **Burgos**, a beautiful mediaeval city in the north of Spain. I write overlooking the Castilian countryside, trying not to be distracted by the vultures, eagles and red kites that fly past my window each day.

When Covid-19 hit in 2020, the language school where I worked as an English teacher closed down, and I became a full-time writer. I have three murder mystery series. My first was **"The Izzy Palmer Mysteries"** which is a more modern, zany take on the genre, and my newest is the 1920s set **"Marius Quin Mysteries"** which features a mystery writer as the main character – I wonder where I got that idea from.

I previously spent years focusing on kids' books and wrote everything from fairy tales to environmental dystopian fantasies, right through to issue-based teen fiction. My book **"The Princess and The Peach"** was long-listed for the Chicken House prize in The Times and an American producer even talked about adapting it into a film.

"Murder in an Italian Castle" is the first novel in the "Lord Edgington Investigates Abroad" series. The next book will be out in late summer 2025. There's a novella from the previous series available free if you sign up to my **readers' club.** Should you wish to tell me what you think about Chrissy and his grandfather, my writing or the world at large, I'd love to hear from you, so feel free to get in touch via...

www.benedictbrown.net

THE IZZY PALMER MYSTERIES

If you're looking for a modern murder mystery series with just as many off-the-wall characters, try **"The Izzy Palmer Mysteries"** for your next whodunit fix.

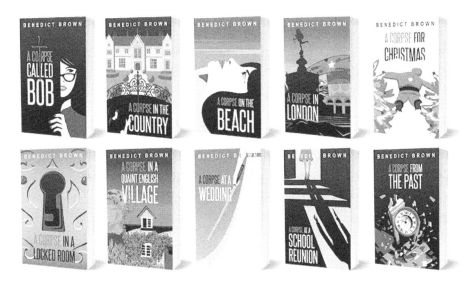

Check out the complete Izzy Palmer Collection in ebook, paperback and Kindle Unlimited at Amazon.

THE MARIUS QUIN MYSTERIES

There's a new detective in town. Marius first appeared in the Lord Edgington novel **"A Killer in the Wings"**, and now he has his own series...

 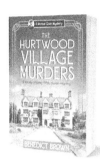  

Check out the complete Marius Quin Collection in ebook, paperback and Kindle Unlimited at Amazon.

CHARACTER LIST

The Travelling Party

Lord Edgington – former superintendent for the Metropolitan Police, nicknamed the Bloodhound of Scotland Yard. After his wife's death he retreated from the limelight for a decade and only returned to his sleuthing aged seventy-five with the help of his grandson assistant…

Christopher Prentiss – the no longer quite so naïve and chubby grandson, whose detective skills have come on a great deal since he left school.

Todd – chauffeur, cocktail mixer, factotum and general nice guy, Lord Edgington and Christopher both rely on him for different reasons.

Henrietta (Cook) – Lord Edgington's favourite person. Back home in Cranley Hall, she was the person to prepare his often unusual meals.

Dorie – formerly a skilful pickpocket whom Lord Edgington arrested, she has gone straight and now faithfully serves the old marquess.

Timothy – the hall boy back home at Cranley Hall. I'll work out something important for him to do one day.

The Montegufoni Locals

Lord Renwick Monroe – a somewhat mysterious acquaintance of Lord Edgington from his days on the force. He owns the castle at Montegufoni near Florence and has invited Chrissy and his grandfather to stay.

Eva Mountstephen – Lord Monroe's young, British secretary.

Coralie Monroe – Lord Monroe's oldest child, an artist who splits her year between three homes.

Dashwood Monroe – her raffish and dissolute middle brother who lives three hours from Montegufoni.

Fletcher – their jolly and civil younger brother who lives on the other side of Florence.

Father Brian Laurence – the local Catholic priest, originally from England.

Signora Acciaioli – the Montegufoni cook.

Agente Attilio Lombardo – the local constable and resident of the castle.

Guido Lombardo – his rather gruff older brother who works as a mechanic and odd job man for Lord Monroe.

Nonna Lombardo – their grandmother who helps Guido out in his work.

Ispettore Stefani – the morally dubious local inspector.

Made in the USA
Coppell, TX
12 July 2025

51783297R00173